WOLF WARRIORS

— THE 4-STORY COLLECTION —

To Drew

Emberlynn Anderson

EMBERLYNN
ANDERSON

ISBN: 978-0-578-61226-3

Printed in the United States of America.

DEDICATION

For my grandma in heaven

THE GREAT PROWLER LEGEND

The world will be as still as stone
The wind will have a perilous tone
But far away, on the run
We will have the Chosen One

This great Prowler that is ordinary
Will become the most extraordinary
They will find the right way
To save the darkness and the day

No Prowler knows when the day will come
But every hope lies upon the stone
Prowlers wait and Prowlers lie
And the One has a chance to try

Upon the world darkness will fall
But the Great Prowler will stand above it all
And no matter what they find
They're the way to saving wolf kind…

THE TRIBES OF WOLF KIND

PROWLER TRIBE This tribe is known for its Great Prowler, who will one day save all wolf kind. The wolves in this tribe are kind and brave and the legend depends on the Prowlers. Each name begins with Prowler.

STALKER TRIBE Consisting of the best fighters and hunters around, the wolves in this tribe are known for their sneakiness, and each name begins with Stalker.

DARKNESS TRIBE All wolves in this group are dark-furred and cold-eyed. Despite their forbidding features they have been known to save other wolves and lurk in the shadows. They tend to be smaller than other tribes.

GRAY TRIBE The Grays always stay in packs. There has never been a Lone Gray. They have habits of sticking together and staying disciplined. The Grays are the most loyal and teamwork-based tribe of the five. Every name begins with Gray.

STORM TRIBE This tribe is the most dangerous of all. Every Stormer has been either cruel or arrogant. They have been known to kill. The Prowlers are told to never speak of this tribe. Every name is deadly and begins with Stormer.

WOLF WARRIORS

BOOK ONE

The

Legend

Begins

PROLOGUE

PROWLER MOON scrabbled desperately to get up the mountainside. Bad wolves were after him. He checked behind his shoulder to see a whole wolf pack storming his way. Their teeth were bared, their ears erect. He turned back around and focused, climbing slowly up, up, up.

Panting and heart beating, Moon turned one way and used his front paws to scramble up the mountain. He was almost up…he was just feet away from getting up there…

Then a terrible thing happened. He slipped. His paws sent chunks of rock tumbling down the mountainside. He gave a sharp yelp and regained his footing. Taking a deep breath, he used his paws for guidance as he scrabbled and slid and crashed. Rocks dug into his paws. His tail clamped to his flank.

He used one last thrust, pulling himself up. He rolled over on the rocky top, huffing and puffing. Looking down below him, Moon watched the pack skid to a stop and give sharp barks up to him. They put their paws on the mountain. They had obviously forgotten his amazing idea for getting up the cliff.

Moon beamed, turning around and gaining his footing on the rocky mountaintop. He was supposed to meet Prowler Sun up here. They seemed connected because of their names, but he hardly knew Sun at all.

"Sun?" he barked out, padding along the rocky cliff and sending showers of rock down the devastating fall. He took a sharp breath and called out again, "Sun? I have the important message!" He was out of breath for a strange reason he couldn't make out.

Prowler Sun came running toward him on the horizon, paws skidding and sliding. "Moon!" she said. "You're here. I didn't think you would be. This canyon takes a little getting used to." The Prowler shuffled her feet. "So you have it, from the Great Prowler itself?"

"Not the Great Prowler," said Moon, "but it has to do with him or her. One day this Great Prowler will come to help our world, but for now let's stand by. I have an important message from Prowler Alpha."

Sun snorted, fur rustling. "Why did he have to call himself Alpha anyway? That's a pack rank, for wolf's sake. And it's actually his name. Ugh." She looked up. "So what did Prowler Alpha say?"

Moon hesitated for a moment, shuffling his paws. He looked up at the ominous sky. It was different on top of this mountain. The sky was a mixture of pinks and reds and oranges and whites. It also was unusually windy. He swallowed.

"Well?" Sun snapped. "You met me up here for this! Don't waste any time!"

Moon sat down. "Well…he sent an important message, that his mate is having pups. She's dying, and she needs our help. Alpha thinks she'll die as soon as she has these pups; they will have to be raised differently because they won't have a mother. And Alpha also thinks one may be the Great Prowler."

Sun snorted again. "I don't think so. Any wolf in the entire world, at least, any Prowler wolf, could be the Great Prowler. It doesn't have to be a pup or anything."

"Well, I know this," Moon said. "No matter what Prowler it is, he or she will save us all. The legend rests upon this Prowler. Once we meet the Great Prowler, his or her past will not be known to any wolf."

"Yes," said Sun, "and like the legend says…"

They said this at the same time: *"And no matter what they find, they're the way to saving wolf kind!"*

And they tilted their heads and howled.

Oh, Great Prowler, Moon thought. *Come save us soon. We need you. The Legend says so.*

And we need you more than ever. Wolves are beginning to die because of this darkness. Come save us. You're the way to saving wolf kind!

CHAPTER 1

THE EARTH rumbled and shook, scattering all prey from every side. It shook hard until trees began to crash and collapse, killing the prey beneath it. Prowler Night stumbled, rolling off to one side, then another. He struggled to regain his balance—his paws felt like heavy stones that slipped whenever he tried. Night set his jaw and tried keeping his paws down on the shaking earth.

The roar rung through his twitching, furry gray ears; his tail cracked like a whip behind him, causing Night to roll swiftly to one side. He staggered and the earth roared some more, like a giant grizzly bear batting the Prowler wolf between its own paws.

Just my luck! I'm about to die because of a stupid earthquake. Run, Night, run! Night's instincts told him. He kept his paws down once more while the earth shook violently. Chunks of rock whacked his face and he had to leap out of the way of a crashing tree. He yelped sharply and swerved as more trees went tumbling down. Dust showered all around him, limiting his vision.

Night rolled over and yelped again, crashing into a tree. Whining, he got to his paws and squeezed his eyes closed while the earth rumbled more. He swerved and shook and yelped. He shook himself. He ran through his mind for ideas, but his mind was blank. He lost focus and the earth gave another violent shake, causing him to crash into a tree on one side of the forest.

Night, you lummox, he scolded himself, staggering again and running and swerving. *Not only are you in the middle of a crashing, violent earthquake, but you are in the Forbidden Forest!*

This was no place for a Prowler, especially a Lone Prowler like himself. Night had heard many tales of this Forest, but hadn't believed them one second. He was destined to find another place to live, so he had had to cross this Forest, forbidden or not.

The earth rumbled before his paws, and Night had no choice but to leap and tumble. Paws sore, he ran in one direction, avoiding crashing trees and showers of rocks, dust, and debris. Night shook his fur, leaped, and swerved repeatedly. The earth got stronger and he tumbled. His panicking instincts told him to run faster.

A black crack began to split through the ground beneath him. He yelped with fear and swerved, crashing into a tree. He ducked and sharply turned as the trees began to crash faster and more strongly than before. The crack opened and he ran as fast as he could.

Checking behind him, Night noticed that the crack was at its full length. The earth stiffened and turned, giving one last rumble before settling down. Did the Forbidden Forest always have earthquakes like this? Night stopped, relieved, and shook the dust and debris off him.

The crack opened down to blackness, one that Night could not see through even when he squinted. It was blackness that led to an endless abyss, something Night had never seen before. Squirrels chattered and held on to the edges, scaring Night. He couldn't believe he was helping the prey, he thought, shoving the fearful squirrels back up with his nose. They scrambled up and chattered, running away.

Night sighed, peering down once more and entranced. He looked behind him. *I need to escape this forest, whether I want to or not. There's plenty of prey here for a lifetime, but earthquakes happen here all the time and it's ... forbidden.*

So he took off through the dense forest, leaping and darting around the settled earth and fallen trees. If any wolf could survive a terrible earthquake in the middle of a Forbidden Forest, he was the lucky one. He called himself a dumb cowardly lummox over and over, muttering to himself as he stepped and climbed.

The Forest stretched far beyond where the eye could see, which meant Night still had a faraway distance to cross before reaching the outskirts and borders. He sighed to himself, stepping his paws carefully over the ground, which had dust remaining everywhere he scrabbled.

Had any wolf besides him traveled through the Forbidden Forest before? Night wondered. Or was he the only one brave enough to cross it with no hesitation? *If I can find another wolf like me, no matter what tribe it is, maybe they can lead me out. That is, if they have been courageous enough to cross this place half a dozen times.*

This made Night's thoughts turn to the five tribes of wolf kind. There was his, the Prowler tribe, where the legend was believed to fall upon. The other four were the Gray tribe, the Stalker tribe, the Darkness tribe…and the Storm tribe. Night shuddered. The Storm tribe held the worst and cruelest wolves of all time. Not only that, but they were the most dangerous wolves in wolf kind. *If I have to meet any wolf, I would not choose one from the Storm tribe.*

The forest felt creepier and creepier while he trod, his paws crunching and turning on the leaves. The wind whispered and made his furry ears twitch. Night sunk lower to where no other animal could see him but he kept up his serious trot. His tongue lolled out of his jaws and he panted rapidly, sensing other creatures of the Forbidden Forest sink.

The rocks ahead led first to crevices, then to rocky cliffs. Night squinted, body still low, and took off into a run. His paws ducked and clomped and stamped. Up the cliffs he went, knowing there would be a high view. *And if it's high enough, I can probably find a way out of this Forest of stupid antics.*

Night realized that he was stomping. Ears pricking, he looked down. He wasn't stomping, he was shaking. Wait, he wasn't shaking! He stopped on the cliff top, looking quickly around and ahead. The view was amazing, but he didn't have much time to stew about it. It wasn't him shaking. It was the earth.

Oh, Stormers, he muttered to himself. *Here comes the earthquake again.* Steadying his paws, planted to the trembling earth, he looked all around the cliff top again. Rocks tumbled and slid around the top, but Night knew he couldn't move. Closing his eyes, he stayed perfectly still with paws planted. *Don't move, Night. Don't move.*

He yelped sharply. His paws had started to slide, because the cliff and the earth were starting to shake again, more violent than ever. *I should never have come here in the first place!* He regained his footing again, only to go sliding to one side, skidding and sending up showers of dirt. He skirted the mountainside, tumbling and slipping.

Rocks bigger than his head began to roll and crash; Night tried to keep his balance on the shaky, roaring cliff, but only slipped again, bumping his head on a huge stone. He yelped again and scrabbled toward the other side while it shook. His paws scrambled and scratched, and he felt a searing pain in his leg.

He yelped again, searching around him for the source of the pain. He found he could not move his hind leg. It was not only throbbing but crushed by a heavier type of rock. He grimaced as the earth began to calm again. *Just my luck! It stops after I'm trapped, and now I can't escape! Oh, Stormers...*

He thrashed and strained desperately, even though he knew he was stuck. His leg would not budge, and neither would the rock. Was he stuck forever? Would he get help? *Please, someone help me. I don't think I've ever been this helpless in my Prowler life. I'm always the tough one. But now—*

He stopped, straining again. No matter how hard he tried, he was stuck. He sighed, leg throbbing, and looked at the calm earth. The dust lingered again, but he ignored that. He looked at the amazing view of the cliff. He'd seen none like it before. The trees of the Forest stretched far and wide, beyond a clear blue lake. The place did not look forbidden at all; in fact, it looked peaceful.

His eyes darted to one side, where prey skittered and chattered as they rushed along other cliff tops. Night's lips drew back and he rumbled a growl, so longingly wanting to chase that prey down. He looked to another side, watching the lake ripple and shine. The wind blew through other trees, and Night swore he saw an opening. *It should only take a day to get out of here. That is, if I can escape this trap.* He thrashed again in agony.

His ears perked and twitched when he heard something strange in the air, something he could not make out, not at all. It sounded like a cross between a growl and a whisper, carried with the wind and breeze. And it rang through Night's ears.

Night... Night...

Night whipped his head from side to side, nose and ears twitching wildly. He ignored his leg, trying to make out what the noise was. It crept into him like a spider. This sounded like it would be heard in the middle of a peculiar, forbidden Forest...

Night... Night...

"Stop yammering and show yourself!" Night barked sharply, looking around again and feeling the earth tremble a bit. But before he could figure out what could be speaking to him, he heard another sound.

Paw-steps, thundering up the cliff toward him...

CHAPTER 2

NIGHT PRICKED his ears further, snapping his head to one side. He saw dust and shadows gathering, enveloping a darker shadow: one with a sleek head, furry ears, and a whipping tail, like him. Another wolf, maybe? Night watched it grow closer; the whispering voice cutting away into the rumbling earth like it was falling into an abyss.

He thrashed, making sure to show that he was stuck. But he stopped when the shadow rolled and ducked as the earth shook harder. He rolled his eyes—another earthquake. He wasn't surprised. But what did surprise him was this: it was a wolf, and it was female.

She slid from one side to another, but her paws gained more traction than his did. She must be from a different tribe than his, because he didn't have the curved kind of claws. The earth shook but the shadow revealed a russet and gray wolf. Her tail lashed out as she planted herself down, a determined look in her brown eyes.

Her eyes fixed on him, and they narrowed as the earth suddenly began to stir a bit and stop. That was the quickest earthquake ever, Night thought as she stared at him. Her lips drew back and she got into a stance. Night saw a white scar on her back leg. "Friend or foe?" she spat. That voice was a bit familiar.

Night trembled from head to claw, but he kept his voice steady and calm. "I am no threat to you. I just need help escaping this rock and the Forbidden Forest. I am a Lone Prowler, Prowler Night." He looked back at her, heart pounding with realization, and returned, "You?"

The wolf stiffened. *Shouldn't she know to introduce herself when meeting other wolves?* Night thought, shocked, but he watched her expression change from fierce to nervous. Her lips returned to normal and she got to her paws. She shuffled.

"Well?" Night snapped.

The wolf swallowed, running her tongue over her chops. She looked down. "You're a Prowler, are you not? Then that means...you have to call me an enemy." She transfixed her eyes sadly upon Night.

The Prowler gasped.

"You can't mean..." he stuttered. He shook his head while the wolf slowly nudged the rock off him, and the others. He stretched out his leg, stunned and gaping at her. "You don't mean...you're part of the *Storm tribe?!*"

The wolf hung her head. Night growled, and she turned over and exposed her belly. She whined and her tail thumped. "Please! I'm not like any of them! I'm not a true Stormer! I just happened to exist in that family." She hung her head, getting to her feet. "I don't *want* to be like the other Stormers. I want to be me." She looked up. "You understand, don't you?"

Leg throbbing, Night shook himself and nodded. "Of course I do. Of course, I've never met a Stormer, but I'm glad you aren't the way Stormers are really. Are you a Lone Wolf too?"

The wolf nodded. "I ran from my Stormer pack, only because I knew I didn't belong. I received this scar from a coyote attack on our Territory." She gestured toward her leg. "And not only that, but I am lost in this Forbidden Forest. I see you are too." Night nodded grimly. She looked ahead. "I was about to escape the Forbidden Forest but I heard yelping and crashing from up here."

Night nodded. He trusted this wolf, despite her being a Stormer. She was nothing like them: not arrogant, not cruel, and not dangerous. At least, not that dangerous... Night locked his golden eyes with her brown ones, showing her he meant his trust. "And what is *your* name, young Stormer?"

The wolf's ears pricked and she stood up taller. As they started down the cliff, ready to start their journey, she looked with erect ears at Night. Narrowing her eyes determinedly, she replied, "Prowler Night, I am Cobra, Stormer Cobra."

*T*HAT'S TRULY a great name, even though it's deadly like every other Stormer name, Night thought to himself at dusk, watching Cobra's shadow slink around the forest. *And she's so smart. I know we'll escape together.* Maybe having at least one other wolf by his side would be useful, especially having a wolf from the Storm tribe. *She knows her way already. She really caught on.* His leg barely throbbed at all as his eyes looked ahead. He rushed to keep up.

"So, did you hear the story of the Great Prowler, or well, the Legend?" he whispered to Cobra, coming up beside her. He was wondering if she believed it or not, or was on his side or not. Cobra's expression remained the same.

"I did. We Stormers all do. Of course they all called it a bunch of wolf-dung, since we are enemies with the Prowlers. I for one was interested. Like I said, I'm no normal Stormer." Cobra closed her eyes as she walked. She looked bothered. "Please, let's not talk about my tribe anymore. It bothers me even if I'm *not* one of them. Okay?"

"Okay. Sure thing, Cobra," Night murmured, tail lashing. He kept his eyes ahead while the moon rose. Instead of talking more, he sat down. Cobra peered behind her, cocking her head. He lifted one paw and closed his eyes. His soft wolf howl cried out to the moon. He did this every night even though he knew no wolf would ever hear. This time Cobra would.

He knew what Prowler howls sounded like: soft and spiritual, but what did a Stormer one sound like? He listened for the cry of Cobra's voice, but the young Stormer was quiet. "Cobra, howl!" he said while still howling.

"I can't." When Cobra said this, Night gaped at her. "I can't because the Storm tribe *forbids* howling. I know that sounds stupid and weird—knowing that there's a kind of wolf that doesn't howl—but I'm a Stormer, so I can't hold back."

"But you aren't one of them anymore!" Night said. "You're free to make your own decisions now, Cobra. You can howl, hunt, fight, and live like you never have before! Just try it!" Night kept an insisting tone in his voice. The Stormer looked up for a moment. Then she opened her jaw and a beautiful sound came out, nothing like Night had ever heard before.

It was a howling kind of note, yet totally different. It had a singing note and a beautiful pitch to it, and Night's eyes went wide. Had the Stormers been hiding this beautiful kind of howl? Cobra finished, wide-eyed, obviously shocked by her own talent; she stared at Night then at the sky then at herself.

"Looks like your forbidden howls were nothing but a whopping secret," Night pointed out. "It's beautiful, Cobra, really it is. Why would you ever hold that back?" Cobra was silent, still dumbfounded and stunned.

The moon was high and Night looked up. This was a perfect time for howling. Cobra had finally seen that, and let out her amazing howling tune. If only wolves everywhere could hear it. It seemed to calm Night's heart, none like he had ever felt before. Could it be that this howl could warm hearts?

He said nothing for a moment as they moved on. Cobra was just as silent as he was, and her paws crunched and turned. It would only be a little while until they escaped the Forest. Night peered at her scarred leg and then at the back of her head, watching her ears swivel; he almost wanted to shout, "Howl again, Cobra, howl again!" but he stayed quiet.

Night did not feel tired at all, even though it was late. He felt energized and ready to move through the forest. "Cobra," he whispered. "I just feel this feeling that tells me I want to run. If we run, we'll get out faster. We can rest when we get out." Cobra looked at him for a second and then broke into a run. Night followed, tongue lolling with joy.

He slid and swerved and darted. The trees dashed past like whizzing elk, and the hard ground beneath his paws felt like nothing but air. He loved the feeling he got when he was running, and he spent most of his exploration time as a Lone Prowler roaming and running like the wind.

He thought of the wind, then the whisper he had heard back at the cliff. It had spoken sharply but whisperingly, growling and insisting in his ear. It sounded luring, but all it had said was "Night... Night..." He set his jaw. What was that stupid noise all about? Was he hallucinating, except through sound? *That's nonsense. I can't hear voices, even in a Forbidden Forest.*

His paw-steps rapidly approached a small clearing, with Cobra just at his heels. Prowlers tended to be faster than other wolves, the Darkness tribe sneakier, the Grays more loyal. The good sensation he felt strengthened when scents caught his nose. Cobra seemed bothered too, sniffing and swiveling her ears; Night sniffed and turned his nose. These scents smelled dangerous and strong, yet luring.

"Should we check it out, or take another route out of the Forest? We've already gone this far," Cobra said. "I have a bad feeling in my stomach." They skidded to abrupt halts, ears swiveling and noses twitching. "They may be enemies. Night, sniff harder; Prowlers have better senses of smell than any wolves, and they can tell what tribe the wolf scents are most likely in."

Night sniffed. He inhaled. More scents lingered, but they were stronger. He ran through the details in his head. Then he opened his eyes and looked to Cobra. "They smell like Prowlers, at least, most of them must be. I think I sense a Darkness wolf in the mix too. Should we go?" He hesitated, which he hardly ever did. He had entered this forest with no hesitation whatsoever.

"I think we should. But...would they accept me, a Stormer? But you shouldn't go alone... What do we do?" Cobra threw herself down and thrust her paws over her head. "I hate being a Stormer," she muttered. Night ran through solutions in his head but none seemed good enough.

"What about I approach them first? We have to go, since there's really no other route. This is the way out and I'm not turning back. I'll approach them, and if needed, you jump out behind me as backup. We'll go from there." Night sounded confident. "Maybe they'll have an idea on how to escape."

"I can't let you go alone," Cobra protested.

"I'll be fine," insisted Night.

Cobra licked her chops, getting to her paws. "If you're really sure, then let's do it. Let's follow your plan. I will wait here." She looked at him. "Be careful, Night."

"I will." Night nodded sincerely. Looking ahead, he padded forward in his lowered-body position. Sniffing and letting the scents drift, he crept and padded. The scents lingered and mingled and got closer. One of the scents was indeed *guaranteed* to be a Prowler wolf. It smelled fierce and brave. Night felt a new interest grow inside him. *This wolf may be the key.*

He broke into a run, still low. He heard slinking between bushes, and knew Cobra was searching for a place to hide. The clearing got wider and he knew he was going the right way. The way out was this way. They'd have escaped in no time...as long as they got past these wolves... Night slunk and skittered quietly, and he finally heard growling among the bushes.

The voices were faint and they started to grow farther. The clearing opened up to a fenced area, one that engaged Night's urgent sense of curiosity. He sniffed. The wire smelled weird but he kept sniffing it and following it to the heart of the space. It was green and short and...

A sharp bark split the air and Night snapped his head up. Fierce wolves shot out from every side, ripping teeth showing and ears up and torn slightly—it must be some kind of mark, Night thought. He was too startled to move as several wolves emerged and moved into fierce stances. The bark rang again and they surrounded him in the wired-in space. Night's jaw hung and he stared around at them, speechless.

They drew closer, and one of them, the largest, crept toward Night, making him draw backward into a few others. His tail tucked and he felt afraid. The wolf's eyes were cold and narrowed; her gaze was fierce. She took an authoritative step closer and barked sharply again. "Don't let him escape!" she ordered.

Some of the wolves held heavy chains in their jaws. Some pawed the hard ground. One wolf darker than the others was glaring back at Night. He was a bit smaller than the others and considering he was thin and dark, looked to be part of the Darkness tribe.

Night didn't even have to bark summons. Cobra leaped out from the bushes and pounced upon the leader wolf, snarling and drawing her lips back.

The leader growled, shoving her off. "A Stormer?!" she bellowed fiercely. She snapped her head to stare at the dark wolf. "Honor, wrap her in chains and make sure that Stormer doesn't escape! Stormers can never be trusted!"

So that was the dark wolf's name: Honor. The dark wolf bowed his head and yanked chains from another wolf's jaws, looming over the larger wolf, Cobra. Honor wrapped them tightly around her with his teeth, pinning her and leaving her wriggling and struggling while the other wolves held her tight. She also had a sad look in her eyes, which probably meant, *why can't a Stormer change?*

Night growled, baring his teeth. "Leave her alone," he hissed. "We are Lone Wolves trying to escape this forest. We had nothing to do with you." He glanced at Honor then at a wriggling Cobra.

The leader growled back. "Oh, we'll escape it for you, and bring you to our camp. As captives." Her eyes flickered. "You might be happier there in this case. And maybe that Stormer may learn to leave us Prowlers alone!" Night's jaw hung and she growled again. "Yes, I am a Prowler, Prowler Scarr. The rest of my pack is Prowlers, except Honor, our Best Wolf." She looked to the dark wolf and he bowed his head. She turned back. "Wolves, chain him too!"

Night snapped the air as wolves began to close in tighter. One wrapped chains around his legs and around his neck, pulling in tight. He yelped, his voice choky as the wolves started to trot ahead. "Let us go!" he choked out.

Honor tightened the chain. "You better keep your jaw shut," he growled in Night's ear, "and don't struggle. You might as well move along. It's no use. I was a captive once." His eyes flickered and he returned to his formation.

Scarr really did resemble her name. Her eyes were cold and dark, her paws stable. She had two scars along her muzzle and one through her back paw. A healing wound that would make another scar ran along her back—it looked like a bad scratch from a past fight.

Her pack members kept their formations tight, and Night was a bit impressed. To avoid being choked by the chain, he moved slowly and kept his head low, and he watched Cobra wriggle and thrash. *Oh, well,* he thought. *Maybe we will escape eventually.*

CHAPTER 3

*H*OW COULD wolves *do this?* Night thought, pacing around the prison cell he was in—at least it looked like a prison cell. Chains were bound around his back paws and lower body, confining him into the space. He could barely trot around the back part of the room.

It was like a cave, yet different. The walls were made of sparkling stone with a small carved space in the wall where moonlight shone in around him. Night noticed another carved space on the right side of the wall, where he could see Stormer Cobra wriggling and thrashing violently, teeth bared in her prison-cell cave. He flinched. *I guess she can be dangerous and vicious when she wants to be.*

Night reared back, ready to thrust himself toward the entrance. His chains doubled back and he peered at the way out. It was barely blocked but had a small layer of stone on its ground, so a wolf would have to leap over to get in or out. Hopefully he would not be noticed and would be able to get enough strength to break the chains and rescue Cobra.

Ahead, the entrance's open part could be looked out of, and Night did just that. On the other side of the glade, or maybe a glade, he could see more caves like his, lined up beside each other. This seemed like a prison room. *But why would Scarr capture wolves for no reason at all?* Night wondered. *Even Prowlers like herself?*

Cobra thrashed more but then saw Night's face. "I know what you're going to do, Night," she growled, doubling back and chilling for a moment. "But it won't work. These chains are so strong, *I* can't even break them. And you can barely go anywhere with these stupid things." She thrashed and showed her fangs violently.

"I'm still going to try," said Night. He reared back just a little more and stamped the ground. "If I get out, I'll get you out too, Cobra." Cobra just closed her eyes and nodded.

Night grinned and turned around. Using all his might, Night ran forward like a bolt of lightning, ready to pull when that chain went stiff enough. He had barely run a couple seconds when the chain stopped him, sending him tumbling. It clung to his hind paws tightly and he snarled in frustration, thrashing just like Cobra did.

"I told you," Cobra sighed. "It's no use. We have to find some other plan." Night could tell she was frustrated too. When a few wolves walked by with tongue-lolling smirks on their faces, Cobra barked at them and began thrashing again.

Now Night sighed. He lay down with the chains winding around his front paws, lying in the light of the moon, which was beginning to set. He could see other sad wolf prisoners in a few other cave cells. Some looked like Stalkers, some like Grays lost from their packs. But he did not see another Stormer like Cobra. Maybe the Stormers always avoided the Prowlers.

Cobra barked and pulled and struggled wildly. *Hush up, Cobra!* Night thought sharply. *You're going to make a scene, or worse, get yourself killed!* He thrust his paws over his ears the best he could, trying to show he wasn't a part of this.

He closed his eyes but heard paw-steps getting closer. A shadow formed outside the cave as Night opened one eye. He opened the other and stifled a gasp. It was Honor the Best Wolf padding over, delicate paws clicking. Did a Best Wolf always visit the prison?

Honor narrowed his eyes at Cobra when he rested at her cave cell. "You!" he snarled. "You are keeping every other prisoner awake! And my Alpha, Scarr, will not tolerate this behavior. I always knew Stormers were stupid, always thought." Night tried not to growl. Honor looked thoughtful, and then turned to Cobra, who stopped wriggling. "Maybe I should join you two in one cell," he said, gesturing to Night. "Maybe you'll behave better with your filthy comrade."

Night didn't like the way Honor spat those words. He could tell the Best Wolf didn't like him. But Night was relieved at the thought of having Cobra in his cave cell. Maybe they could think up a plan together. Honor barked to the other wolves, which were lingering at the prison entrance. "Wolves, remove the Stormer!" The wolves bowed their heads. That must be the sign of respect.

Cobra finally stayed still and did not struggle as the wolves took off her chains and escorted her to Night's cell. Instead she kept her head low and allowed them to chain her to another side of the cave, but still near Night.

The dark wolf Honor nodded and padded off, giving Night one last dirty look. *What had he meant by 'being a captive once,' anyway? He's a Best Wolf, for Stormers sake!* Night watched Honor and the other wolves leave the prison, his mind filled with curiosity.

Cobra caught his attention. "We need to escape. I can't take this anymore. Why would Scarr ever capture victims, even Prowlers, for no reason at all?" It was as if she had just read Night's mind. "What in the world does she ever do with them anyway?"

"Maybe she tries to get them to side with her," Night suggested. "Or maybe…" He gulped, not sure if he wanted to tell the rest. "What if she makes the wolves kill one another?" He had said it. He closed his eyes and Cobra gasped.

"You're right. What if she makes us kill other prisoners? Then that would make every wolf think I'm just a dangerous Stormer that loves killing!" Cobra bellowed. "I am *not* one of them, not! Do you hear me?" She looked to all the wolves in the prison, but some were shrunk back against their cells. Others had their paws over their heads. She sighed. "But I may really be meant to be savage…"

"You're not!" Night insisted. "Okay, let's just focus on getting out. How can we get out of our cells and the camp with these chains being so strong? We need to think." He thought for a moment, but he had no ideas.

"What we need to do," Cobra said sincerely, "is question Honor."

"What?" Night's eyes widened. "Why would we do that? He's cruel and you know he hates me! He hates you for being a Stormer as well. We need to get out and make sure we are never seen again by Scarr."

Cobra shook her head. "No. We have to question him...because I have a plan."

I T WAS daybreak, just as the sun rose. More light streamed in to the cave cell, and Cobra and Night were fast asleep. When Night awoke, his stomach grumbled viciously. Did Scarr ever mind giving her prisoners food, at least? Night did not like that wolf, even if she was a fellow Prowler.

What if...she's the Great *Prowler?* Night thought in horror. He doubted it but there was a chance. If any Prowler could be the Great Prowler, it shouldn't be Scarr, he thought.

Suddenly, two squiggling, slimy things were flung into the cave cell, hitting Night in the face. "Ugh!" he said as he retched. Cobra wrinkled her nose in disgust.

"Fish," she spat. "That's my least favorite food. But at least they gave us something." She took her piece and closed her eyes tightly before chewing a bite. She licked her chops. "This kind of fish is good, Night. Try it."

Night hesitated but chewed off a piece of the squiggling thing between his paws. It fell limp while he chewed its deliciousness. "It *is* good," he said. "It's nothing I've ever tasted before. I wonder where they got it."

Cobra gave a doggy shrug but her ears pricked. "Honor," she growled. "He's coming. It's time to question him."

Night had barely agreed the day before. But he said nothing while the shadow of the Darkness wolf came to the entrance. His face was cold. "I see the Stormer is doing better. I won't have to hear her yapping and crashing from all the way across camp." He turned to glare at Night. "And our Prowler...quiet as can be. Not a surprise." Night swallowed, glaring back.

But Cobra spoke up, sounding gentle with her head bowed. "Best Wolf Honor," she said, "I would like to ask you some things, and so would my friend, Prowler Night."

Honor widened his eyes, still looking cold. "Never call a Prowler your friend!" he snarled. "Stormers and Prowlers are common enemies! Don't you know?"

Cobra set her jaw. "Well, I'm no ordinary Stormer, Best Wolf. All I want is to ask you questions."

Who knew, maybe the same questions in Night's head were in Cobra's head too. Night jumped in immediately, before Cobra or Honor could speak another word. "Honor, what do you mean by 'I was a captive once'?" He didn't bother calling him Best Wolf. "If you were a captive, how did you get to this rank?" His eyes flickered as if he were angry, but in reality he was in awe and full of wonder.

Honor put his raised paw down, narrowing his eyes. "I do not talk about my story with a bunch of filthy prisoners!" Night was about to blurt "But you were a prisoner!" when Honor spoke in again. "My story is only known by Scarr, my Alpha wolf! No others speak of it. But Scarr says that I was an orphan pup and she took me in."

Night thought about this. "So...if she took you in, why were you held captive?" he questioned. Honor snarled sharply.

"Because I was a scared little pup and tried to escape, brainless!" he bellowed. "What a stupid Prowler!" Honor stepped back and growled at them both. "Now if I hear another noise about *me* or *my* story or *my* business, I will rip you both to pieces! Is this understood?" The rage in his eyes subdued Night, and he shrank back and bowed his head.

Cobra ran her tongue over her chops and lowered hers too, and both were silent. Then they heard the pattering paw-steps of the Darkness wolf trotting away. Honor was muttering, "Those stupid not-wolves."

When Night picked his head back up, he was wide-eyed and silent. He took in what he had been told but couldn't figure it out. Darkness wolves were said to save other wolves, and be sneaky as well as kind and passionate. But he knew this:

Honor was not the wolf he was supposed to be.

CHAPTER 4

"WE NEVER got to ask him what *happens* to the prisoners," Cobra sighed, running her paws over loose rock and sending it tumbling in another direction. She kicked it again, frustrated. "We'll *never* get out now!"

"Yes, we will," Night insisted, "as long as we have a plan. This one may not have worked out, but we need to have another plan."

"I suppose *you* have a plan?" Cobra snorted. "I hope it doesn't involve breaking chains or peeing on the guards' heads or anything..."

"What?" Night was dumbfounded. "I never considered that one!" Then he laughed. "Okay, anyway—" Something interrupted him: another wolf. It was male, coming up to the entrance of their prison cell and hopping over the rocky canvas. He looked nervous as he walked up to them.

Night's ears twitched. This one was indeed a Prowler, gray-and-white and with anxious eyes. He chewed and pulled on the chains binding their legs and they immediately became undone. "How did you...? How did you do that?" Night stammered, stretching his legs gladly. Cobra lolled her tongue.

"Don't ask," said the wolf. "I'm already breaking enough pack rules without telling our prisoners the secret chain-unlocking technique." He stood up. "Please don't tell Best Wolf Honor that I was here." He looked them in the eyes. "Please? I'll get in big trouble…"

"Of course we won't," Night cut in. "You helped us, so we owe it to you. What's your name? I am Prowler Night, and this is Stormer Cobra." He gestured to his fellow wolf.

"What?" The other wolf was taken aback. He leaped backward, trembling a bit. "She's a…Stormer? She's in the Storm tribe? Then this is the first Stormer we've ever caught! Stormers are enemies!" He looked at Night with an "I-can't-believe-it" look. "Why on wolf earth would you have friends with a *Stormer*?!"

Night scratched himself. "I can't explain right now, but to make this short, she isn't any ordinary Stormer. Cobra!" he said fiercely. It was all part of his plan to prove Cobra's loyalty. Cobra cocked her head but he gnashed his teeth and pulled back his lips, getting into a fierce stance and gaze. He growled and loomed over her, since he was larger. Cobra whined and rolled over, thumping her gray tail.

The other wolf raised a paw and widened his eyes. "Wow. She's not too dangerous." Night could tell Cobra was trying not to snarl "*I am dangerous, just not in the way you think!*" but the Stormer kept her jaw closed.

"So what's your name?" Night asked as if nothing had happened. Cobra got to her paws and the other wolf shuffled his feet.

"I know my name is like a Stormer name, but I am surely a Prowler. I was trained by Scarr so I am made to tear and rip, which means I'm Best Fighter. I just don't want to." He stopped. "My name is Prowler Pistol. Ask me anything before I sneak out. I'm breaking at least fifty rules."

Cobra's face lit up. "Can you tell us Honor's story?" she asked. Night shook his head rapidly. *No, Cobra! No other wolf knows besides Scarr!* "Do you know how he became Best Wolf?"

"I don't know his *story*, but I do know how he got his rank," Pistol replied. "Like most Darkness wolves, he…saved my life. I could've been killed if it wasn't for him." Night stifled a gasp. So Honor *had* saved a wolf, even if he was cold and cruel right now.

"Scarr didn't want me to die, so she awarded him Best Wolf. She didn't have one until then. Honor has been there ever since, like her second-in-command, basically. And he'd be pretty mad right now if he saw or heard what I am doing and saying to you. Please don't let him know..."

"We won't," repeated Night. "We won't tell anything to any wolf. But...how do we get out of here?" He trod around the cave cell, hesitant but sure.

Pistol set his jaw and leaped right over. "The other prisoners are asleep, so here is our chance. I will lead you through a secret passageway only I know about. That's how I got to you."

"Wait, Pistol!" said Night. "Could you free the others?" He looked at the sad, miserable faces of the sleeping prisoners. "They seem to have been in here for a long time, and I'm no selfish wolf. I care. I'm a Prowler, and so are you. Who knows: one of us could be the Great Prowler, and this is our first step to saving wolf kind."

Pistol was about to answer when Night's eyes lit up. "That's it! This is part of the Great Prowler legend!" He closed his eyes and repeated the third part of the Legend. "*No Prowler knows when this day will come, but every hope lies upon the stone*!" he cried, "Stone passageways, stone cells! They have hope upon these stones! They all do!"

"*Prowlers wait and Prowlers lie and the One has a chance to try*!" Night finished. "One of us may have a chance to try saving wolf kind, one step at a time. These wolves are waiting for this day. What do you say, Pistol?" He looked hopeful.

"You're right!" said Cobra at last. "It all makes sense, even if it isn't in order. Let's go without Honor spotting us!"

Pistol shuffled. "Sure. But I'd be breaking a dozen more rules! And..." He stopped. "You do it. I'm not getting myself killed for this."

Night was taken aback. "But you could be the Great Prowler, and this is your first step! A Great Prowler would never abandon fellow wolves! Don't be so selfish about your puny rank Best Fighter..." He trailed off, seeing that Pistol looked hurt. "Look, the thing is, we need to help. Besides, you're the one that knows how to unlock the chains. We'll cover for you and say we did it. Okay?"

Pistol was hesitant, and then nodded. "Okay." He ran to one cell and unlocked chains. He rapidly rushed around and unlocked every chain in every cell until he was finished. As he was standing there, the prisoners woke up, stretching and yawning, and found that they could walk right out.

They bounded out with joy, barking and exposing their bellies in appreciation before Pistol. Night walked up to the grinning wolf, his tongue lolling from his jaws. "Feels good, doesn't it?" he said, looking upon the happy captives. "Trust me, you won't regret this, Pistol."

"Now lead the way!" Cobra barked cheerfully, and the other captives followed them through a secret passageway in one corner wall, just wide enough for them to go single file.

It led to a clearing outside the prison. Night had not taken time to look around his new surroundings while they had been escorted in as captives. Instead he had stayed silent and walked along with his head bowed, and his ears had been pricked, listening to Cobra wriggle and snarl. But now he took the chance. The place was beautiful, with trees that waved and glistened in the sun. Around them were meadows of flowers and patches of grass.

Night gaped at it all. This place was the home of vicious captive-catching wolves? Pistol was walking ahead, head up high and padding forward. As Best Fighter, Night guessed Pistol was going to protect them no matter what. *Wow. I'm letting another wolf protect me instead of protecting myself. I'm usually the tough one, the Lone one. I guess I'm wandering away from my real self.*

The other captives began to run in different directions, barking thanks to Pistol. When it was silent, Pistol turned. "Well, I got you out. Don't tell a soul. I must go back." He leaped ahead but Night barked, "Wait!"

Pistol turned, ears twitching and swiveling. "Yes?"

"Thank you."

"You're welcome. It's the least I could do."

"Well, we have one more question."

"What?"

"What happens to the prisoners?"

Pistol gulped. "There are no prisoners left so there's no need to tell you."

"Please tell us."

Pistol sighed. "It's bad, and I mean really, really bad," he said, tail tucking. "Scarr sometimes has some become part of her pack, *force-fully*, and sometimes she makes them fight one another. It's either death or victory. And also..." He trailed off, looking at them in turn.

"What?"

"Nothing," Pistol said quickly, "just thinking. Goodbye!" He bounded off before they could say a single word.

"Well, *that* was weird," Cobra pointed out. "He seemed so...nervous the whole time."

"I'd feel the same way if I was a high rank and I let out all the prisoners and broke hundreds of rules," said Night. "We need to make sure no wolf knows about this without being caught again. But how can we?"

Cobra thought and Night shuffled his paws. They stood there, silent, in the clearing, hackles raised just in case danger happened to rush by. Night opened his jaw. He wasn't able to say a word.

Angry barks and snarls sounded from the other side of the clearing, which meant it was over at the prison. "Pistol," said Night worriedly, and dashed ahead and around the prison walls. If Pistol was in trouble, then he'd help.

He could hear Cobra's paw-steps behind him as he dashed to one corner then another. The sounding barks got louder and he gasped when he saw what was ahead. He skidded to a halt, peering around a bush with Cobra just behind him.

There stood every wolf, standing in a warm, sunny clearing in the heart of the camp. Scarr paced around between a glaring Honor and another wolf. The rest of the wolves stayed put, surrounding a trembling Pistol. Night saw Honor clench his jaw while other wolves barked. "Oh, no," Night whispered.

Scarr was talking to a wolf that looked to be a scout. "Are you meaning to tell me the prison is *empty*?" The scout bowed her head and Scarr growled, looking up. "Who did this?"

Pistol ran his tongue over his jaws but stayed still and quiet. Scarr snapped her head toward him. "Pistol," she hissed. "You are my Best Fighter, and this scout says she saw you helping those filthy newcomers free the prisoners!" Her eyes flickered. "Is this true? Tell the truth!"

Pistol bowed his head as well. "I-I did. I was only trying to help because these prisoners are innocent. And one of them, Night, is my friend. I would not let you send him to a fight or make him become one of you!"

Night beamed but said nothing. Pistol went on, "I freed them because they deserve their liberty! Rules or no rules, I'm not that kind of wolf!" He stamped his paw.

Scarr looked angrier than ever. "Is this how you act when I have spent years of my life training you to rip and tear? Is this how you act when I have given you a good rank? Is this what you do in a *pack*, breaking dozens of rules and keeping secrets? We do not let our prisoners go unless I say so! Is this how you act, Pistol? Tell me!"

Night was sure Pistol would say the right thing—*he isn't that stubborn*—but to his horror, Pistol replied determinedly, "Yes, it is."

"WHAT?!" bellowed Scarr. Honor growled threateningly. "You are wrong! And now I must give you the punishment all traitors get in this pack!" First she leapt and ripped at Pistol's left ear. Pistol howled in pain as she tore part of it right off.

Night gasped and Cobra flinched. Scarr really was strong and cruel. *I can't believe she's a Prowler. She could fit in the Storm tribe. No offence, Cobra.* Pistol whined and shrunk back, ear torn and bleeding.

"And now for the final part!" said Scarr, still angrily and stepping back. Honor stepped forward, however, as if on cue.

Scarr said this with real sincerity and surprising calmness: "We'll see just how strong you are when you fight Honor at dawn."

CHAPTER 5

"I CAN'T BELIEVE this," Night growled, pacing back and forth in the clearing behind the prison. "I can't believe this. Why would Scarr ever make a wolf fight *Honor, Best Wolf?* Maybe because she's the stupidest, weirdest, most merciless wolf in the world…" Cobra sounded sad, on the other paw. "And we never stepped in to help," she sighed. "We were not only being cowards, but we also let Pistol down."

"We would've been caught again if we had stepped in!" Night protested. "I didn't even know they'd find out!" He hung his head and his ears drooped. "It's my entire fault. He called me his friend, so I knew he depended on me. But now…"

He thought and then his eyes lit up. "I have a plan. But…we may have to say goodbye, or maybe find each other again."

"What? But—"

"I know." Night filled with sadness. "Yes, Cobra, you are my friend, Stormer or not. This plan could get you hurt or possibly killed for being a Stormer wolf. You must run to somewhere safe. The rest of the plan is up to me. I must sneak in and talk to Pistol about how to save him. Then I will become one of Scarr's wolves."

"What?" Cobra was shocked. "Why?"

"It's the only way. I will get out when I can and possibly find you. But I need to keep you safe, Cobra." The sadness did not leave. "Trust me: I can do this."

"Are you sure?"

"Yes."

Cobra looked just as sad. She ran over and tumbled into him, nuzzling and licking before trotting back, eyes sad. "Bye, Prowler Night."

"Goodbye, Stormer Cobra." Night stepped back, eyes narrowed and ready. "May every spirit of wolves be with you." He watched as Cobra took one last look at him and ran into the trees on one side of the clearing. After the last trace of her tail left, it was silence.

A LL RIGHT, *Night, you can do this*, he thought, making his way around the prison and getting ready to return to the heart of the camp. He saw a brush of gray fur coming from a small open space. It was part of a prison cell, but there couldn't possibly be another wolf in it already. Unless…

Night gasped, running to it and leaping up on his hind paws. He saw a tightly bound Pistol, dried blood on the side of his ear and on his neck. He was chained and bound more tightly and intensely than the other prisoners had been. He really was in deep trouble. Night was just tall enough to put his front paws on the sill. "Pistol!" he barked softly.

Pistol was curled up. But he slowly lifted his head. His eyes narrowed but he looked weak. "What do you want now? I already broke fifty rules for you." He sounded rather sharp.

Night sighed. "Look, I'm sorry, Pistol. We should never have hidden and done nothing like we did. I'm sorry we let you down. I know you depended on me. Please forgive me." Pistol did not answer but groaned and put his head back down.

"Are you sure you can fight Honor?" Night asked, looking at the setting moon. It was almost time. "You could never do that in this condition. Who does Scarr think she is?"

"She's my leader," said Pistol sharply. "And I must obey her and I am loyal to her no matter what. She trained me. She raised me. And I must respect her for that. Of course, I didn't yesterday." He sighed. "Night, you've done all you can do. But now I must accept my punishment, and I have no choice but to kill Honor—"

"No. I have a plan that may not involve any killing."

Pistol lifted his head. "What do you mean?"

Night was serious as he said this, looking ahead at the other cells, which were empty, of course. "I will try to side with Scarr, just for now. I'll do my job and also try to help you. But I can't make promises, in case I let you down again. Just let me try."

"No. You can't. Scarr is very commanding and you probably aren't used to taking orders like that, because you're a Lone Prowler. I'm used to it, so I obey. Our respective sign is bowing our heads when given orders. Scarr would probably give you the mark she always gives new wolves." He spoke all too quickly.

Night gulped. "I'm still up for it," he said. "I'll try my best, okay?"

Pistol sighed and laid his head down. "Okay."

NIGHT SLUNK around the corner, straining his ears and listening for any sound. He was ready. He was determined. He had a plan, a strategy just in case. *Just don't be a stupid lummox and you'll be all right.*

He heard the voice of Scarr just around the corner where he stood. She was pacing around the main cave she rested in. The shiny stone walls glistened and wolf guards were lined up loyally on all sides. They looked disciplined and strong, Night thought, and they made no movement or noise as Scarr paced back and forth, her raggedy tail lashing behind her. Ahead of her stood Honor, still with his head bowed in respect.

He's allowing his leader to get through her worries or plans, because he's loyal and her Best Wolf. And I'm willing to bet he is going to fight Pistol with no hesitation or protest. Night watched them closely, inspecting Scarr's thoughtful expression.

"Honor!" she said suddenly. "My Best Wolf, where do you think I should set you two up to fight: the stadium or the wired space? It's your opinion." *Just what I suspected,* Night thought, *looking to her comrade for ideas. Some leader!*

Honor was thoughtful as well. "Well, I think the stadium. It's the best way for an exciting match, and I just know you'll be entertained." His cold eyes narrowed determinedly at his leader. "However, it's entirely up to you." *He is not the kind of Darkness wolf I expected him to be*, thought Night.

Scarr looked up, closing her eyes. Then she nodded. "Yes, yes, great idea, Honor. I knew I could count on you. Our "stadium" will do just fine. It will look a bit more...official." She looked him in the eyes. "Get the scouts. Tell them that's where we're going."

Without a word, Honor dipped his head and then turned around to find the scout wolves. But to Night's horror, he had stepped in the Prowler's very direction. Night gasped as Honor's gaze snapped toward him. Almost immediately, Honor gave a yelping cry of fierceness and leaped upon him, and Night could not escape. Honor's strong, dark body descended on the Prowler, knocking the air out of Night's lungs. The wolf gave a muffled, breathless yelp.

Honor's eyes flashed and so did his teeth. Night squeezed his eyes closed, ready to feel them shear across his chest and kill him, but instead he heard Scarr's ringing bark. "Honor, let him go! It's the stubborn Prowler."

The Darkness wolf's jaws slavered, but he obeyed and trotted backward, teeth and fangs still clenched. Scarr stepped forward, eyes glinting to go with the white scars across her muzzle. "Well, well, well," she spat as Night sat up slowly, tail tightly in between his legs. "If it isn't the, oh brave Prowler with the Stormer as his mate."

Oh, Stormers, she thinks we're in love, Night thought in dismay, looking darkly up at the other Prowler. "He thinks he can spy on us, eh?" Scarr mused, tail lashing. "If he thinks he can stop our battle, then he's—"

"No! No! I wasn't going to stop you. I just finally realized that my Lone days are...over. So I thought 'Maybe I should help Scarr' and so I came here and overheard and I'm sorry..." Night tried to sound ashamed. "I need to survive, and I cannot without you, Scarr." *Stormers, that was sappy. And pretending to be a weak little runt doesn't help either.*

Scarr had a look of disbelief twisting around her muzzle. "So you finally surrender, huh? Well, let's see if it's complete and total!" Night had no idea what she meant, but he had no time to think as the Prowler smacked his body down, pinning him tight. She showed her teeth and slashed them across Night's ear, grazing it. At first, it did not hurt, but the pain hit three seconds later. Night gave a screaming howl. He had never felt a Prowler's teeth so sharp before.

Scarr loomed over him and did the same to his other ear. Night cried out some more like a little puppy, feeling blood ooze down both sides of his head. This must be the same mark Honor and the other wolves had. Pistol had been right. Night had not considered bracing himself for that even though he had kind of expected it. To be a true member of Scarr's pack, you had to be evaluated, branded.

Night shook himself, splattering drops of blood on the stony ground. Scarr's weight lifted off him and he staggered to his feet, head low and the pain throbbing through his now-ragged ears. A cruel smile split Scarr's muzzle and she ordered, "Honor, escort him to the stadium and make sure he does not escape. He will watch our match. The time has nearly come."

NIGHT'S HEART beat, quick as lightning, as he was chained down over a stone balcony with Scarr lingering ahead of him. The stadium looked nothing like an arena. It was stony like everything else and had some spaces for light to shine through. Logs surrounded a circular space for the fighters and the rest of the stone was for all the wolves watching.

As the wolves bounded in, they murmured or howled or barked to one another, tumbling and sliding in their excitement. Of course, Night could never imagine being excited to watch something like this. But he had no choice but to watch, and he knew it was death or victory. *That means either Pistol or Honor has to die.* Night did not like the feeling that ran through his body.

Honor had not appeared in the fighting circle just yet, but Night knew they would bring in a chained Pistol first. He did not wriggle as a few wolves chained him down good on the far side. He still had a clear view but wished he didn't. Scarr looked just as excited as the crowd of wolves.

Two wolf guards stood on either side of Scarr protectively, and the wolf leader raised her head up high. Night did not like the look on her face. He knew she was amused in watching death matches, which he didn't understand and never would. He sighed and watched wolves continue to file in.

Oh, Pistol. I never meant this for you. I was wrong. I'm the real traitor, because I'm the one that told you to free those prisoners. But those wolves were depending on us, one of us having a chance of becoming the Great Prowler. I don't want to watch you—or Honor, even—die.

There was no stopping this match, so Night just wished Pistol good luck. He watched the wolves howl with excitement when two wolf guards emerged from a side entrance below, with Pistol chained between them. The wolf was drooped over with his head low, as if ashamed. *I honestly can't blame him.*

The wolves howled louder when Honor came from another side with fur up on end and looking more than ready to fight. Honor had braced himself for this. Pistol hadn't. Night gulped. Scarr's cruel smile widened and she howled for silence.

"Attention all Prowlers!" she shouted. "I am happy to announce that this match between Best Wolf and Best Fighter is about to begin! One wolf must kill the other wolf, but I will not tolerate my Best Wolf being killed." *She obviously doesn't care about Pistol anymore,* Night growled under his breath. *Even though she raised and trained Pistol herself!*

"And," Scarr mused with a wicked grin, "this will test my Best Fighter's skills and if he is truly a Best Fighter kind of wolf for me. Enjoy this match, Prowlers!" The wolves all howled in appreciation. Night gulped. Now was the time.

Honor glared straight at Pistol, who had not moved a muscle since the guards had escorted him in. The Darkness wolf had his teeth bared and body low. "When you're ready, runt," Night heard him mutter. He almost wanted to whack that wolf straight in the face.

Night could not read Pistol's expression or guess his thoughts. But Night was sure Pistol was thinking "I hope Night follows his plan" but the Prowler now doubted he could do it now. *I believe Pistol is on his own this time. I wish I could have helped.*

Scarr's ears were pricked in expectance. The wolves were quiet. Nothing happened. Night cocked his head. Was this going to be a silent death match? *Come on, Pistol. Attack him while he's confused,* he urged.

"Argh!" snarled Scarr. "Honor, don't wait for him. Just attack him!"

"As you say, my leader," Honor said confidently, and the moment arrived. He sprang. Night closed his eyes.

He heard ripping and tearing as Honor attacked the motionless Prowler. But then Pistol sprang to action, wounds on all sides of his body as he darted and dove around Honor. The Darkness wolf was surprised, which made Night grin.

Pistol showed his skills while the wolves wrestled and clawed each other. Pistol grazed Honor's neck but it barely affected him. Honor sprang back and ripped off a scrap of Pistol's ear. The Prowler howled in agony. Night couldn't bear to watch.

This was how it went, first Pistol striking Honor and then Honor striking Pistol. *Oh, for wolf's sake, don't take turns like foolish pups!* Night thought desperately. He struggled to believe that Pistol was *Best Fighter*, the rate he was going.

Night almost wanted to leap down, side with Pistol, and kill Honor himself, but he wouldn't be able to even if he tried. Besides, these chains were tightly binding him down.

Pistol was getting weaker by the minute. Red, bleeding wounds ran down all sides of his shaking body. The color had drained from his eyes and he almost looked helpless for a wolf. His tail was drooping and he struggled to dodge lunges from Honor. *Come on, Pistol! Come on!* Night thought.

Honor struck Pistol in the chest and Pistol wheezed as he stumbled backward. Night's hope sunk lower and lower. This could be the end. His plan would've been for nothing...

He tried not to yell "Pistol!" and fought to keep his jaw from opening. Scarr was amused, knowing her comrade was about to win this match.

Did the prisoners really go through this? Was this just as bad as Pistol had described? Honor continuously struck Pistol. *He has no mercy,* Night thought. *He is not an ordinary Darkness wolf. He will not give up. He's a...he's a monster!* Night watched sadly and his hope faded away. *My plan...it won't work...I can't save him...*

The world was getting blurry, but Night kept his eyes open and stared down at the fighting circle. Pistol's eyes were sad and colorless and he had obviously lost hope too. What would Pistol do now? It was either death or victory...

The wolves were howling in agony, waiting for Honor to finish Pistol off, or vice versa. Night was about to close his eyes and let himself pass out, but something horrifying opened his eyes right up, cleared the blur, and made him want to howl as loud as he could.

Honor gave a loud snarling cry and his sharpest claws extended. He drove them right into Pistol's chest, and Night gasped. Pistol's eyes widened, and he looked at Night with a "sorry, Night, there's no hope" look, and his eyes closed before he tumbled onto his side. Silence fell, and even Scarr's eyes were wide with horror.

Prowler Pistol was dead.

CHAPTER 6

NIGHT WANTED to howl. He wanted to cry out. He wanted to whimper his loudest to the sky as dusk arrived. He had no idea what had happened to Pistol's body, because right after that horrifying moment, he had been escorted out of the stadium.

His one friend he could depend on, the wolf that had risked everything to follow through the legend and had helped him and Cobra: dead. He could not bear it one bit. But he knew he could not show sadness in front of the other wolves, or Scarr for that matter.

Honor was wounded badly as well. Pistol's blood streamed along his claws, and his neck was grazed and bleeding. He staggered a bit but nodded gratefully when Scarr ordered him to rest. "You deserve it. You were amazing."

Night did not think the same.

That horrible moment had lasted only a few seconds before wolf guards had rushed out to inspect Pistol's wounded, colorless, and lifeless body. Night tried not to think of the sight too much.

"And you!" snarled Scarr, turning to him. "I could see you were struggling not to jump or howl. What's with you? Pistol was a traitor in my Territory. He needed to be punished. And you seemed to be…

an ally of his. Is this the way you behave when I have taken you under my paw?"

Night bowed his head shamefully, murmuring, "No, Alpha Scarr. It isn't. I won't behave like that again." *At least, I hope I won't.* He wanted to be alone more than anything, but first he had to deal with his angry leader. "May I take a walk?"

Scarr's eyes grew suspicious but she nodded coldly. "Fine... Just don't go past our borders or even *think* of escaping. And make it quick. Soon I'll have a role for you to play in my pack, and you won't be dilly-dallying around."

Night did what every wolf in Scarr's pack always did: bowed his head and then trotted off. He let out his breath in a huge whoosh when he was out of earshot. For the first time, he could relax. *My plan was nothing but wolf-dung. I thought if I pretended to become one of Scarr's wolves I could find a way to escape with Pistol. But I didn't think there would be a death match so soon. Now I'll have to escape for good and find Cobra.*

But had the Stormer gone to a place where she knew Night could find? Night imagined the look on her face when he didn't bring Pistol back and she found out his plan had failed. *Why didn't I follow through? Pistol was desperate and depended on me, and I did nothing!*

Night pulled his lips back and stomped the patchy ground in anger. He trotted in circles for a while, feeling ashamed, sad, and lonely. He needed to form a new plan—*one that would work!*—a plan of escaping the clutches of Prowler Scarr.

For one: I need to find Cobra and we can escape together, run as far away as we can. For two: I have to try fulfilling the Legend like I did before. But this time, I will do it on my own, even though I'm not alone.

Night took another breath and his body allowed him to lie down and doze. He was exhausted and hadn't really gotten the chance to rest and relax. His tail curled around his flank as he turned his circles and lied down. Whining, he watched the world blacken as he drifted into the depths of sleep.

The Prowler kept his body low while wolf guards trod on either side of him. As soon as he had woken up, he had felt fresh. But when the two guards had shown up, he had whirled to action and gone straight with them.

However, he could not follow his plan just yet.

Scarr paced the same way she had before in the main valley. The wolf guards were lined up again and Night was escorted in front of the vicious Prowler. He wondered if she'd make him her new Best Fighter, but he didn't think himself worthy enough for the job. Could he be a scout, or a guard?

The wolf gazed upon him when she stopped pacing. "Prowler Night, Lone Prowler no more, I have finally found a rank for you to play in my pack. I gave up the possibility of another Best Fighter. I don't want any more...*traitors*. I have enough scouts and guards..."

Night got very curious. Those were the only ranks he knew of here. Was there another one? Scarr looked thoughtful. "Yes. Yes, yes. You would do as a...prison-keeper! We have never considered it before, but you'd do very well." She glared at him. "And if I tell you the secret chain-unlocking technique, don't use it for *treachery* like Pistol did." She spat the name "Pistol" like it was a hunk of garbage.

He used it to save us! Night thought with rage, but he closed his jaw and avoided taking it out on Scarr for what she had said. *It's your fault he's dead.*

"A prison-keeper watches over the prisoners. They must bring leftover scraps of meals and keep the prisoners *in order*. No prisoner is to be freed without my permission. I hope I don't regret trusting you for this job."

Night bowed his head but said nothing. Honor looked strong again despite his wounds as he trod out and dragged a chain behind him. Scarr showed him how to pick the lock with his claws and bite down, although Night wasn't sure how it helped. Scarr also demonstrated how to lock the chains on the prisoners.

"But...we don't have any prisoners," said Night.

Scarr growled. "We will soon," she hissed. "The scouts report intruders and other wolves and we send guards. For now you will *clean* the prison."

"Like how?" retorted Night, exasperated and angry. He was still upset about Pistol's death, but there was nothing to be done.

Honor bared his teeth and fangs. "Do *not* disrespect Scarr, stupid Prowler. You must dust it out with your paws and fling it outside. And then you line chains inside each cell."

"Sure, *Best Wolf*!" Night jeered, "Also known as the wolf-that-killed-a n-innocent-Prowler-that-could-have-been-the-Great-Prowler!"

Honor growled louder and Scarr stepped in front, nipping Night's ear. "I said not to side with Pistol, you *brute*!" she snarled. "Now get to work! You have a lot to do, runt."

Night tried not to snarl back and bite her neck. He did the respectful bow of his head and walked off to the prison. He really was alone this time. He scraped dust and particles out of cells, wondering how they got there in the first place. He pushed a pile of scraps into one corner; and lined and unlocked chains in every space.

The sooner I get out of here and find Cobra, the better. This is stupid.

Night still thought about Honor while he worked. The Darkness wolf had been trained and raised since he was a pup by Scarr, like Pistol, but he meant much more to Scarr. Darkness wolves weren't supposed to kill. They weren't vicious. They were known to *save* wolves, not to *kill* them. Scarr was vicious, so she had passed her personality down to the orphan wolf.

I don't know how that is possible, but I know that's not how Honor is meant to be. He's more like a Stormer now than a Darkness wolf. If he had been raised in a Darkness pack, none of this would be happening. And I don't think I can change him back, Night thought sadly.

His ears perked up when he finished his work. *But maybe I can convince him to come with me and Cobra! It would be hard, but it's worth a shot. But he doesn't like Stormers, just like any other wolf... and I must find Cobra...*

He heard clamoring and banging and barking. Three unfamiliar wolves, wrapped in chains, were escorted inside. For the first time, Night felt respected as the scouts and a few guards bowed their heads at him and walked out of the prison cave.

The wolves struggled but one stopped when he saw Night. "It's a Prowler," he breathed, gesturing toward Night. The other two stopped as well and spun their heads around. They looked to be triplet wolves, because they were identical. Yet Night couldn't even tell by their look what tribe they came from.

They continued to stare at him and didn't struggle as Night bound chains around their back legs and lower bodies, like the wolf guards had done with him and Cobra. He locked them tight and did not glance at them. They were all plain gray, like no wolves he had seen before.

The remaining guards nodded their heads and trotted out as well. Night flung scraps into each of their side-by-side cells. "Thanks!" one yelped, and dug in.

"It's nice to meet you. Are you a prison-keeper?" the one that had spotted him first asked, licking his scraps but not actually eating.

Night looked up. "Yes. I just got the job." He didn't know what else to say. "I am Prowler Night. I only sided with Scarr so I could help this one wolf that was my friend. It was a lost cause so I'm escaping soon."

"So Scarr is her name? It fits," murmured the first one. "I'm Stalker Broken, and these are my triplet brothers Stalker Star and Stalker *Hungry*." Hungry, the one that had first eaten glared and Broken shrugged. "That's what they named you," he said. "Doesn't it have a nice ring to it, Night?"

Night nodded. "And yes, I promise I will try to free you like me and my friend did the other prisoners. I'm just playing along." He thought about the three wolves for a moment. No wonder he couldn't tell who they were. They were Stalkers! He had never met one before, because they were extremely sneaky. "Broken, can you tell me how you three got separated from your pack? I thought Stalkers were sneaky and powerful."

Broken shuffled his front paws. "Well, yes. But Scarr likes to take in prisoners to side with her, right? Especially young ones like us... We were on a hunt until she came along and took us away."

"Yeah!" yelped Hungry, who had finished eating. The three looked to be nearly adult, but Hungry still sounded and acted like a small pup. "And she has that angry Darkness wolf too! Do you think she'll have a Gray, or...a Stormer?"

The other two yelped and flinched. Night did the same but said, "Shh! Keep it down! They'll know I'm talking to you! I had a friend who was a Stormer—" the Stalkers stared "—but to use my plan she had to leave. She is no ordinary Stormer."

Star changed the subject quickly. "How did your other friend die?" he asked, his eyes saddening.

"Ergh, there he goes again." Hungry shook his head. "He gets too emotional."

"Well, that's a good reason," said Night firmly. "Now keep it down. They knew about the wolf—Prowler Pistol's—treachery, and they had him fight the Darkness wolf, Honor, their Best Wolf, in the stadium. Honor killed Pistol. And I miss him so, especially because I caused him to die."

"No, you didn't!" said Broken. "Honor did!"

Night sighed. He explained the story and the Legend. Star nodded. "We've heard that legend," he said.

"Ooh! Ooh! Maybe he's the Great Prowler!" Hungry shouted.

Night flinched.

Broken nipped at his brother through the open space in his cell; Hungry shrank back. "Hush up already, Hungry! You're going to get *Night* killed!"

Night shushed until all was quiet. "I know I shouldn't be sharing my business with you, but it made me feel better to talk it out. Thank you." The Stalkers beamed. "For now you will have to be held captive here. I will come up with a plan for all of us to escape eventually. I will take good care of you."

"Thank you!" yelped Hungry.

Night just hoped he could keep his promise this time.

CHAPTER 7

NIGHT SPENT his days cleaning the cells and feeding the triplet Stalkers. He had conversations with them when the wolf guards were not around. Every now and then Scarr would call meetings of wolves and called him to attend. However, he did not see what the use was.

He spent time during his work thinking of a plan to get out of there and help the Stalkers escape. And if any other prisoners were held, he would free them all, no matter the risk. *I won't risk it on another wolf like I did Pistol.*

He thought hard the next few days, and the Stalkers were quiet and solemn, even though the chains were not tight and they had plenty of scraps to themselves. It gave Night a chance to think in peace and quiet.

Suddenly, Honor rushed in, lips drawn back. He wrapped chains around Night to the Prowler's horror and drew them tight. Night gave a muffled whine. The chains tightened just near his neck and around his muzzle. What was going on? The triplets howled with terror and Broken snapped forward but couldn't reach Honor.

"What's going on, Honor?" choked Night. Honor shook his head.

"Scarr sends for you immediately. She has a strong wolf that she has just finished training. She wants to test his skills against you. Which means…" said Honor, eyes narrowing, "…we're going to the stadium."

Night stifled a gasp and the prisoners barked louder. *I have to fight now? I could get myself killed, for all I know! How will I escape now?*

Broken spoke up above the others, quieting them: "If he's going, then we're going to watch. Best Wolf, bring us to the stadium now." He spoke with great authority, as if *he* were the Best Wolf.

Honor narrowed his eyes further. He barked summons to the guards outside the prison. "Chain these three up on the balcony! It's time for the match!" As he and a drooping Night walked along the stony ground, Honor snorted, "There. Now you have your little buddies with you," and then quietly in Night's ear, "You are so helpless sometimes."

Night tried not to snarl. His new friends had wanted to come with him. He hadn't said for them to *come* watch him. They had decided it themselves. *For wolf's sake, quit bullying me, Honor. You know it won't work.*

Scarr perched on top of the stone balcony-shaped space. Night saw Stalkers Broken, Star, and Hungry chained there like he had been during the last match. Night gulped. Now *he* was in the match. And he had to kill the other wolf or *he'd* be killed too.

But I don't want to kill anybody! And what will Scarr's reaction be if I kill her newly trained wolf?

Night's chains were removed and he stood there, frozen to the spot like Pistol had been. He knew how the other Prowler had felt when he descended upon the stadium. Wolves howled once more as the other wolf made his way in. He was large and sleek and looking ready.

"Now I announce that the match between Prowler Night," Scarr barked, "and my newly trained wolf, Prowler Strength, will begin! One wolf must kill the other. Let's see if Night is as strong as he says he is!"

The wolves howled. Night growled, getting into a fierce stance before Strength. The other wolf looked fiercer than he did, considering he had been trained by Scarr. Night leaped first and clawed Strength's back. Strength growled and threw him off like he was a little speck of dirt.

Night was a lot smaller, so he could dart and weave between the other Prowler's legs. He bit and tore at one paw and Strength yowled in pain. The Prowler spun around and grazed Night's chest with his fangs.

The pain seared through Night's body but he kept going. Strength bit and scratched him several times, wounding Night on all sides. Night staggered and fought to keep going.

Strength gave a roaring howl and leaped. He slashed Night with his claws, creating a terrible gash in Night's neck. Night thrashed uncontrollably and fell on his side, blood pouring down his front. The pain was terrible and he began to feel woozy.

"Kill him! Kill him! Kill him!" the wolves chanted together, watching Strength creep closer.

Night fought to get up but instead he thrashed and bled and choked the words, "I'm not finished!"

"Oh, yes you are." This was the first time Strength had spoken. Night growled and thrashed some more. Then words from the Legend ran through his head like visions.

This Great Prowler that is ordinary will become the most extraordinary. They will find the right way to save the darkness and the day.

"I will find the right way," said Night to his mind. He thrashed himself upward and got to his feet. With a confident leap, he tore as savagely as he could into the other Prowler's neck.

Strength stared at him in shock, yelping and tearing away quickly. He gnashed his fangs and stood his ground, despite the wounds Night had dealt him. Setting his jaw, the larger wolf sprang, and Night dodged.

Night squeezed his eyes closed and ignored the raging pain in his neck. Instead, he concentrated on his conscience, and the legend. *Find the right way. Find the right way without killing him.*

He snapped his eyes open, and suddenly new hope and strength surged through his body. He dodged another blow and locked eyes with his opponent. Strength stared back, and the two faced one another for a moment, silent.

"What are you waiting for?" roared Scarr. "Fight, Strength, fight!"

Her trained wolf did not respond. He just stared intently at Night.

Night made sure to narrow his eyes sharply. Then he moved his gaze and slipped his haunches underneath him, sitting and unmoving. Silence fell over the stadium.

Then Strength nodded, expression all at once softening, and he sat too.

The triplets stopped, jaws hanging and staring at him.

Scarr came to her senses. "Our prison-keeper *and* my trained wolf are just sitting there! How dare they?! Chain the Prowler runt up!" she roared. "My own prison-keeper can get a taste of prison again! Go! Now! Go!"

First, the Stalker triplets were escorted out of the stadium. Wolf guards poured out from every side of the fighting circle, angry expressions on their faces. Some nodded to Strength, as if not angry at all with him. Others ran straight toward Night and wrapped chains all around him. Night submitted despite his wounds, staying still with his head down while they chained him.

Everything isn't going how I planned it, even if I did find a way to not kill Strength. And you're welcome, Scarr! Be thankful!

As they began to shove him out of the fighting circle, a shadow crept, body low, out of one side opening. It was Honor. The other wolves bowed their heads. Honor growled, snapping his gaze to Night. He looked sharper and colder than ever.

"I killed Pistol," he hissed, "so you're next."

CHAPTER 8

HONOR HATES *me. He wants to kill me. He'll do whatever he can to do it.*

Dreading realization lingered in Night's gut as he thought this through. He didn't even think of a plan to get out of the cell a second time. He just stayed near the back of the cell, chains wrapped everywhere on him. He was bound tighter than ever, like Pistol had been before. He stayed as still as possible so he wasn't choked.

A face appeared in the open space on the side of the cell. It was Stalker Star, looking upset. "I'm so sorry, Night," he whined. "You didn't deserve any of this. You just fought for your life, which was the rule! And you even spared that wolf! That stupid Prowler only wanted *her* wolf to win, and—"

"Honor hates me."

"Huh?" said Hungry.

"Honor hates me. He wants to kill me. He'll do whatever he can to do it." Night repeated his earlier thought. "You three and I must get out of here ASAP. Honor has it in for me. I know it."

"Aren't Darkness wolves supposed to *save* wolves?" Broken inquired, looking confused. "All *that* Darkness wolf wants to do is kill, kill, and kill wolves, not save them or help them! Why is Honor like that?"

"Because it wasn't *him* that got him that way," said Night.

"What?"

Night cleared his throat. "It wasn't him. He was probably a whole different wolf as an orphan pup. Scarr took him in and raised him as her own, so she was able to train him and make him vicious and cruel like herself. Honor's just an image of his Alpha, that's all." There was a hint of anger in his voice. "And I'm thinking we need to change him back, once we find Cobra."

"Cobra?" said Broken. "Who's that?"

"The Stormer I was with before Pistol came along," Night answered solemnly. "Now she's out there, in the wild, by herself and maybe even in danger. She's skilled as a Stormer but she may still need a wolf by her side. I will bring you back to your fellow Stalkers and find Cobra!"

"And?" said Hungry, as if expecting more.

Night sighed. "Yes, there's something else. I need Honor to come with me. I just don't know how I can convince him."

"Are you *crazy*?!" shrieked Hungry. "You can't ask *him* to come with us! He'll kill us all! He's too cruel and arrogant."

Just like a Stormer. Night gulped. "Yes, I know. But I am unwilling to give up."

L ATER, GUARDS filed in and unchained Night. "What's happening now? Another match?" snorted Night, following them. "Or some kind of *council* meeting on whether or not a tree needs to be marked with two lines or not?" He kept a sneering tone in his voice. One guard snapped at his muzzle and Night ducked, laughing.

Honor stood at the entrance to the main cave. "Stay out," he ordered the guards. "Scarr needs time alone to discuss things with her trained wolf." The guards bowed their heads and backed up. This seemed to be unexpected.

Night laughed uncontrollably. "What a pup! She wants to discuss something with a trained wolf that couldn't even beat me?" He continued laughing until pain seared through his neck where the gash was. He gave a wheezing gasp.

Honor was outraged. He crept closer, body low. "What did Scarr say about behavior?" he growled in an almost hiss. Night shrank back, gash searing and bleeding. "That's right! So *hush up!*"

The Darkness wolf turned around and slunk back into the main cave. Night struggled in the chains but they seemed all too loose. He broke out immediately and spun around to bite each guard in the neck. Some guards fell back, surprised and yelping, then groaning.

Night beamed and dashed over to the entrance. He cocked an ear and peered inside. He heard muffled conversations between Honor and Scarr. "We need to get rid of that Night as soon as possible," Scarr said with misery. "If he wants to behave like this, he will be killed."

Night growled. They *did* want to kill him. So he needed to escape more than ever, if he wanted to live.

"I understand," said Honor. "We can either kill him ourselves or let him flee and be killed by a Stormer, either of the two." A cruel smirk split his muzzle. "Which do you think, my Alpha and my mate?"

What in the name of Stormers?! Night gasped under his breath. *They're mates too?!*

Honor nuzzled Scarr in comfort and stepped back. Scarr said, "Whichever comes up. Go."

Honor bowed his head again. He slunk out of the entrance but went the opposite direction from where Night had been. Night sighed with relief and took one last glance at the wounded guards. He ran straight to the prison and used the secret chain-unlocking technique to undo the triplets' chains.

"Thanks so much, Night!" said Broken.

"How did you escape?" asked Hungry.

"I'll explain later," said Night. "Follow me."

The Stalkers slipped after him as he ran across the cave and to the secret way out that Pistol had shown him. He squeezed right through, tail wagging, knowing that they'd make their escape. The Stalkers came up behind him and they ran as fast as they could into the wired area and into the end of the forest.

They were finally out of the Forbidden Forest and Scarr's camp. Night had never been prouder.

CHAPTER 9

THEY TRAVELED a long way through an unfamiliar valley of hills and cliffs. Night could not track Cobra's scent or any sign of Stalkers, but he had a good feeling they were going the right way.

"Did the guards bring you from this way?" he asked the triplets. "I just want to be sure."

Broken stepped up next to him; his eyes shone and his head was up. "As leader of us triplets"—the other two protested at this—"I will try to remember." He thought. "Yes, I think it was this way! As long as we follow my and Night's noses, we'll be able to escape!"

"And ours!" the other two triplets protested. "Don't count us out, Broken!" Hungry shouted.

"Shh!" Night's voice was sharp. "Be quiet, and follow me. I have wandered the wild *all my life*, so you better not try to contradict me." He kept his nose in the air as they broke into a run across the valley. If they could reach the end, they might be able to find a Stalker pack's Territory. Hints of the wolf guards' scent still hung, which was extremely distracting.

"Is this place familiar?" asked Night after an hour of trotting and silence. They had reached the end of the valley by running and trotting.

Not too shabby. Broken nodded and Night felt a new hope rise in his gut, and lifted his nose and sniffed. "Then let's keep going."

They traveled across an open glade that looked like an abandoned Territory. No wolf was there, and Broken said they needed to go much farther. They ran and trotted and walked until dusk arrived.

They flopped down near a tree and fell asleep immediately. Night looked at all the tired faces of the wolves, and he curled up too, next to Broken. The Stalker's tail was thumping gradually. The others were still and quiet.

Broken really was a serious adult. Night thought Broken would make a great leader, a great Alpha wolf one day.

W HEN THEY awoke, Night used his hunting skills to catch a few squirrels. Each wolf got one whole squirrel to eat. "Make sure you chow down before we go!" Broken used an authoritative voice; Night could tell Broken wanted to be leader-like.

"Can you stop *demanding*?" Hungry protested, digging in. Star shook his head in annoyance.

Broken growled but Night put a paw on him and he stopped. "Let's go now," said Night calmly. They hurried on until they reached another valley. The triplets got more and more excited as they went. It seemed more and more familiar.

Many Stalker scents lingered in this valley. They were getting close to a Territory of Stalkers, Night was sure of it this time. He and the triplets were happy to be free and in the wild again. Night did not think of his Lone Prowler times again until now. It felt great.

They crossed a few more glades. Hours went by. When they stopped to rest, they slept for a few hours. During the afternoon while they ran, Broken halted from up front. "We're here," he said, a little worriedly.

"Why so worried?" asked Star.

"It looks like something bad happened here." Broken was solemn. "Follow me." His brothers didn't even protest this time as they trod to the center of the Territory. Broken had been right; Night smelled the fear in the air with the other scents.

"Pack, it's us! It's us! We're alive! It's us, Stalkers Broken, Hungry, and Star!" called Broken. "You can come out! We won't hurt you! We have a Prowler with us!"

Immediately, wolves hopped out from every side. But there weren't enough to make a pack. They stopped, gaping at Night. "It's the Great Prowler!" gasped a male wolf. "The time has finally come!"

The wolves howled with joy and tumbled about. Night barked sharply and they stopped, sinking down as if in respect. "We respect you, O Great Prowler," murmured the male.

Night was taken aback. "No, no, no! I am *not* the Great Prowler. No one knows who it is yet! I'm only here to bring these Stalkers back to you." The wolves gasped but welcomed the triplets with joy.

"I was a captive too," said Night, "in Prowler Scarr's Territory. She is merciless and cruel, not like a Prowler at all. Your triplets were captured but I brought them back. No worries."

The wolves were still shocked.

"So...what happened to your pack? There aren't nearly enough of you," said Night.

A wolf sighed. "Well...there was a horrible darkness spreading over our territory. Explain a little more about the darkness, even if it's just to say, "We don't know what it is." It has passed through, but it killed our new pups, our Alpha wolf, and many others. Now it's just us." The triplets—at least Star and Hungry—looked terrified. The wolf said hastily, "But we'll still keep you three safe."

Night shook his body. But before he could say anything, a Stalker barked, "Stay, Prowler, stay! You're the most powerful! Be our new Alpha wolf!"

Night was shocked. "I-I can't," he stammered. "I mean, I'd like to, um, but, I am a Prowler, not a Stalker, first of all. And, um, I'm not that good of a leader, and, um, well...I am a Lone Prowler."

"What?!" cried the same wolf. "You have to lead us! We won't be safe!"

Night turned his expression and voice to sharp. "What is *wrong* with you, Stalkers? Stalkers are the best hunters and fighters around! So why are you acting so *scared* and *helpless*?"

The Stalkers were surprised. They looked at one another. "You're right, Prowler," said the wolf, ashamed. "The darkness is just so overwhelming, it's changing us. Well, just this pack, but, um…"

"Don't worry," Night interrupted. "The world is changing every wolf forever. But when the Legend is followed through, things will be normal again. One day, our Great Prowler will complete our legend and save wolf kind. We just need to wait."

The Stalkers howled cheers in response. Night looked upon them all. *They're depending on me. They're depending on every Prowler, Great or not. They love us. I've never been loved before.* He loved the feeling inside him as the Stalkers howled their thanks.

"So, triplets, are you ready for me to leave?" Night joked. "I have to anyway."

"Please stay with us!" a wolf pleaded.

"Sorry. I would love to, but you all can survive on your own. I am a Lone Prowler, and I have to go somewhere where I'll be safe as well. And as for your new Alpha—" Night grinned and looked to Broken "—pick him."

The wolves turned their heads to look at Broken. Broken hung his jaw, his gaze unbelieving. "Thanks so much, Night!"

The wolves howled.

"Congrats, Broken," said Night. "Lead well and stay safe."

The wolves barked goodbyes as Night turned and left, treading across the nearest valley. Leaving the Stalkers behind, Night hoped they'd stay safe against the darkness.

I must find Cobra. I need to help any wolf that needs me.

It's time to fulfill the legend.

CHAPTER 10

NIGHT RUSHED like never before across cliffs, hills, valleys, and glades. Surely Cobra had used her smarts to escape the Forbidden Forest to safe land? His paws tread and turned and he barely felt rocks dig into his pads.

He was determined, even if his wounds throbbed terribly and he was getting tired. The faster he got away from the unfamiliar surroundings and toward the Stormer's probable path, the better. *Please be safe, Stormer Cobra. Please be safe.*

Now that he was away from Stalker Territory, he could focus on finding Cobra's scent. Had she taken a safe, not forbidden path? Night came to a forked turn, with a right path and a left path. Which had Cobra gone down?

He crept across the left path and sniffed everything around it. There was a faint scent of a female Stormer, but it wasn't very strong. Perhaps she had gone down the path on the right, but her scent had lingered on the left one as well. He turned to the other one and sniffed deeply. There was a much stronger scent here, and almost immediately afterward he bounded straight down the path.

Maybe I'm not so stupid after all. Honor was wrong. I found the right path, the one Cobra went down. Once I find her I will surely believe I'm not a "stupid Prowler." Night ran full speed, eager and anxious to see the Stormer again. He was also ready for a rest. His wounds throbbed painfully.

"Cobra!" he called, just in case she could hear him. It was a possibility even if she had most likely traveled a long distance. He kept calling her name as he ran down the path, hours passing by. He barked again, "COBRA!"

Nightfall arrived, and Night was exhausted. However, he kept running like the wind, following the path around twists and turns. The trees and glades went on, as far as he could see on the horizon. Squirrels and voles skittered by like Night wasn't even there.

The Prowler's eyes drooped sadly. Cobra's scent was strong but within hours he still hadn't found her. His hope lowered as he took a rest under a shady tree. It was the dead of night, and stars glimmered above. The glade was silent and Night looked up to the moon. It was full today, and he hadn't had a good howl for a while.

Night gathered all his breath and sat down, gazing up at the full moon. He lifted his muzzle and his cry, his howl, rang out through the stillness and silence of night. It made him feel much better, hearing his howl echo and fade as it went on.

Still a little hopeful, Night lay down and continued to gaze tiredly into the night. And before he could fall asleep with hope still in his guts, he heard a beautiful sound.

He swore he heard the beautiful singing of a Stormer's cry.

NIGHT STRETCHED and followed along the path like he had before. The hope in his gut rose and fell while he ran, catching Cobra's scent with the wind making it fade every now and then. He was getting closer and closer—he could feel it.

And no wolf can stop me from finding my... What was it? *My friend? My fellow wolf? My...love?* Night felt weird for a second. No way. What he had just thought was the weirdest thing. That was exactly what Scarr had thought about them. Night did feel affection for Cobra, but whoever heard of a Prowler with a Stormer as its mate?

He didn't even feel hungry, or thirsty. He ran quickly and shook the weird feeling out of him. *I need to focus on finding Cobra first.* The scent continued to get strong. Maybe Cobra had settled somewhere to wait for Night, rather than going even farther.

"Cobra!" he howled. "I'm back! And alive! Where are you?"

He heard a bark up ahead. "Night, Night! Night! I'm here!"

"Cobra," he breathed. He saw her russet and gray shape, standing there with her eyes saying *I knew he'd find me.* He tumbled into her, and the two of them nuzzled one another. They came to their senses and stood up.

"So what happened?" said Cobra. "Did you save Pistol? Tell me *everything*, Night, no matter how long it takes! How did it go?"

Night was silent. He did not want to tell any of it. Instead he explained *almost* everything. He looked down at his paws and twisted his face to look innocent, as if he *had* told everything.

"That explains why you look like this," Cobra observed, inspecting his wounded and bleeding body. "And what happened to Pistol?" This was the moment Night had been dreading.

"Well...he, uh...I tried to help and I watched the match...and encouraged him...but, uh, Honor was too strong..." Night's eyes grew sad, and he didn't even have to continue before the realization hit Cobra like wildfire. Her eyes were sad too and she muttered, "Oh, poor Pistol."

It was a moment of sadness and misery. Night murmured, "He was a great wolf. He really was. He would've done as the Great Prowler."

"You do too," insisted Cobra. "The Legend could fall upon you, who knows? Only you can follow the Legend now, if no other Prowler will." Her words were gentle and wise, and Night felt comforted.

He nudged her playfully. "Since when were you such an oldie?"

Cobra snorted, "It runs in Stormers."

They were silent for a moment. "What happened to Honor?" Cobra asked next. "Has he changed, like, at all?"

"No, he hasn't. I was going to convince him to come along, but that would never work. So I just ran when I got a chance and led the Stalker triplets back to their pack. I just hope they're okay since that darkness spread over their Territory. But I know Broken will lead them well."

Cobra nodded. "He will, I can tell, even if I haven't met him."

This reminded Night of something he wanted to ask Cobra for a while, but had never had the courage to bring up. "Cobra…do you remember your family? I don't remember any fellow Prowler of mine. I don't even know my own past."

This silenced Cobra. "Umm… I thought we weren't going to talk about my tribe anymore," she said almost nervously. "And anyway, Prowlers are forbidden to speak of it."

"I'm a Lone Prowler. Who's going to forbid me, the moon?" snorted Night. "Just tell me. I won't speak of it anymore after this unless you want to, I promise. In fact, I swear." His face was sincere and he tried not to grimace at the throbbing pain from his wounds.

Cobra shuffled her paws like Night had seen Pistol do. He tried not to think of the dead Prowler. "Well…I don't remember them much either, only that I had a brother named Stormer Terror. He was the most vicious in the tribe, and I never saw him again after he ran away to start his own new life. He was called Terror because he had overgrown fangs like no other wolf. I don't remember the name of any other Stormer." She squeezed her eyes shut tight and cringed. "I don't like talking about it. Let's stop, for real."

"Of course," said Night. "Besides, it's all in the past. You're *different* now, Cobra, and you know it. You aren't like them. And I think you'll be a good wolf too." His eyes glimmered and he finally collapsed to take a rest. "Goodnight, Cobra."

"Good*night?*" laughed Cobra. "Come on, Night, it's daytime. You're just sleepy. Go ahead, get some rest. I'll catch prey."

Night groaned contentedly. "Thanks."

That was his last word before he drifted off.

"**N**IGHT, NIGHT!" Night felt himself being licked frantically. He stirred and groaned as he opened his eyes. Cobra was bent over him, licking as fast as she could over his muzzle. Night wriggled away and shook himself.

"What?" he panted. "What's wrong, Cobra?" What was so important that he needed to be woken up?

"I smell something. And I think it's a wolf. What tribe is it? Smell, Night, smell!" urged Cobra, nudging him until he was fully awake. He snapped to action and sniffed deeply. The smell made his heart pound.

"Darkness," he whispered. Cobra gasped.

Bushes rustled creepily, and wind blew through the trees as the sun shone overhead. The wolf was close, and getting closer. Night was sure, absolutely sure, that he knew who this Darkness wolf was...

Panting and whining like Night had never heard before from him, Honor leaped out of the bushes, coming to a halt and cringing from wounds all along his sides. They looked fresh, with dark blood trickling out onto his already dark fur. His head was bent low, huffing and wheezing. Cobra growled and backed up.

"Honor," hissed Night. "What are *you* doing here? I thought you were *Best Wolf.*" He spat the last part.

"I was," wheezed the Darkness wolf, "but I'm not anymore."

"What happened?" Cobra demanded, taking a menacing pace forward. Honor huffed and wheezed and gurgled, barfing on one side of the clearing. When he regained his breath, he began speaking, sinking down painfully.

"It was Scarr," he choked. "She was originally going to be my mate—we weren't planning on it yet—but when I found several guards wounded, I reported back to her. She punished me for letting you injure her guards and escape, even though we were most likely going to let you do so rather than...kill you." Night glared but Honor went on. "She wounded me worse than I wounded Pistol. So I ran as far as I could."

Night stepped closer. Honor sounded like a whole other wolf right now. "We were about to start our journey away from the Forbidden Forest, until you came along," he snapped.

Night growled. "It's your fault. It's your fault Scarr punished you. You could've been *paying attention* to the wolf eavesdropping outside the cave."

Now Honor growled, standing up and acting like the wolf Night had once known. "You want to *test* me? I killed the Best Fighter, you know. And did I mention that *you're next?*" Honor warned. His eyes flickered coldly.

Cobra jumped in, however. "I think we should keep Honor with us, to interrogate just in case," she suggested. "He will walk between us and we'll see if we want to let him go."

"Good idea," decided Night. "Come on, *Best Wolf.*" They walked along and Honor surprisingly obeyed. The leaves and wind rustled along the wolves' path. Honor kept his head low but also kept his teeth bared.

The path stretched out and the coast was clear of enemies and prey. They would get as far as they could from the Forbidden Forest and the worst of the dangers. They could find a place where they would be safe and Night could continue trying to fulfill the Legend.

And for the first time, Night knew they were on a path to destiny.

CHAPTER 11

"YOU KNOW I can still *kill you both* while standing here, right?" Honor hissed at them during their journey. "You can't just take me *prisoner* like Scarr did!"

Night nipped at Honor's neck for quiet. "I need to concentrate," he growled. He sniffed the air and found more unusual scents. They were well away from the Forbidden Forest, but Night knew they had much more to do than escape. They needed to fulfill the Legend and save every wolf.

"There may be problems in every tribe this very minute," Night said, "just like in that one Stalker pack. Let's find the next tribe pack and help them with whatever troubles them. Then we fulfill the parts of the Legend we think can help. At least, that's my plan. Do you have any plans, Cobra?"

"I have one." Honor twisted his muzzle into a smirk and shoved his way from between their bodies. "Why don't you two surrender to me, complete and total, and I can *kill you both*?"

Night growled. "Stop it, Honor."

"Oh, so I'm *Honor* now? No more Best Wolf for the two of you?" Honor's eyes flickered madly.

Cobra stepped in. "I for one think—"

Honor gave a crying snarl and threw himself on top of the Stormer. Her gasp was muffled and choked. "I don't care what you think, Stormer!" Honor bellowed. "All I know is that you don't deserve to be alive!" And he raked his claws down Cobra's chest. Cobra screamed a howl.

Night was horrified. Despite his own wounds, he leaped and knocked Honor off Cobra. "Leave her alone!" he howled. He tackled a stunned Honor and bit into him even more. Honor howled madly and shoved Night away.

The Prowler did not stop attacking the former Best Wolf. He would *kill* Honor if he had to. "Stay away from her!" Night snarled as he kicked and bit and scratched.

Honor swayed when Night stopped, panting. His eyes drooped. He had wounded Honor enough to make him collapse. Blood poured out on every side of the Darkness wolf's body. Night felt a little sorry for attacking this much, but he would protect Cobra no matter what.

"Night, you didn't have to do this," a voice said behind him. It was Cobra. "I know he wounded me, but I'm a Stormer. I could've fought him."

Night turned just as Honor collapsed on the ground, shaking and whining. Never had Honor sounded so helpless. "Well, I did it anyway," he returned in a kind voice, helping Cobra stagger to her feet. Dark red blood trickled down her front. Night flinched but helped her lie down, and licked her wounds.

"He'll never hurt you on my watch," Night growled. "Or any wolf, for that matter. I will always protect you." This was when the same weird feeling in his gut deepened. He shook it away again and watched Honor stir and shake.

Cobra closed her eyes slowly, saying, "Thank you, Night. Thank you…"

WHEN SHE and Honor awoke, Cobra was able to stand but still staggered from her wound. Night's wounds felt much better. He watched Honor get to his feet, blood dried on his body. His wounds still looked horrible, but his eyes had lost their coldness.

"W-Where am I?" he choked, barfing again. "W-What happened to me?"

"That's my question," said Night. "I don't know." Honor sounded a little....less vicious. He had no coldness or darkness in his eyes. What had made him look and sound so different? Then a sound Night had heard before struck him like it had in the Forbidden Forest.

Night...Night...you have done it...
You have changed a wolf....forever...
You have done it...

This time, Night knew where the voice was coming from. It wasn't from the Forbidden Forest. It wasn't from the wind or another wolf. It was from his heart. His heart had told him to help wolf kind, and change one wolf—Honor—forever.

Night staggered but he snapped his gaze up. "I think I know, Honor," he said confidently. And he explained everything.

"Your *heart*?" said Cobra. "I never knew you were that sappy, Night."

"Come on, you're sappier," returned Night. "Anyway, that whisper...it needed me to help a wolf, which means...there's a possibility that my road ahead has many fates and destinies." Honor just nodded, his wounds looking like they were throbbing.

"Still sappy," snorted Cobra.

They continued on the road ahead, this time Honor letting them keep him between him, since he was swaying painfully and couldn't walk without help. Night silently apologized to Honor because he couldn't bring himself to say it aloud. *But he had had to protect Cobra.* Honor kept stealing glances at the Stormer, looking cautious. Night wanted to bite his ear off like Scarr had Pistol's.

Pistol... *Night, don't think about him. Please. Don't think about him. He's passed and gone, and there's nothing you can do.* Sadness bubbled up inside the Prowler but he shook it back as he had done with the weird feeling. What did all these feelings mean? Next he needed to find out what all *that* meant.

"Where are we going, anyway?" said Cobra. "I thought you had a plan, Night!"

"I do." Night sniffed, and halted. "Wait. There's...there's something coming."

"Don't tell me," Cobra rolled her eyes, "another Darkness wolf."

Honor looked hurt.

"No. It smells like…" Night began, but a shape gathered on the horizon, growing closer by the second. It was a gray wolf, and its shape made way through the trees. "Broken!" he gasped.

"What's he doing here?" Cobra asked. "I thought he was Alpha of his pack."

"I don't know," Night breathed. "But do this." He sank down on his hindquarters, bowing his head. Honor hesitated but did the same, and Night knew Cobra was doing it too. Stalker Broken skidded to a halt just in front of them.

"What are you doing?" he gasped. They all bowed their heads lower. "I have *no pack* left to lead!" His eyes were wide with grief and surprise.

Night got up. "What?!" he howled. "How do you have no pack left? We left you just a few days ago!"

Broken hung his head; his ears were drooped and he looked clueless for the first time. "I tried to stop it, really, I did. It was the darkness. It spread over the Territory again and it killed every one of them."

"Every one of them?'" gasped Cobra, "Even Star and Hungry, your *brothers*?"

Broken flattened his ears, his head lower. "I tried. I ordered them to hide but they couldn't make it in time. The darkness was too fast for them. I'm the only one that survived." His eyes flickered with sadness and he looked up at them. "Can you forgive me? I tried, and now I'm not safe. Neither are any of you. Neither is any wolf!"

Night remembered the last quote of the Great Prowler Legend. "*Upon the world darkness will fall, but the Great Prowler will stand above it all. And no matter what they find, they're the way to saving wolf kind.*" He thought. "You're right. We forgive you, of course we do. The Legend says 'darkness will fall' but not just some rush of dark air. It must be more than that, something that will endanger every wolf until the Great Prowler comes."

"Don't you understand?" said Broken. "*You're* the Great Prowler, Prowler Night! You haven't thought that all this time? Don't doubt it; don't be that way. You know it's true. You've depended on every other

Prowler to be great. Yet, it was you that lives this destiny. Think about it. Think it's you. It is."

Night hung his jaw. "B-But, I can't be," he stammered. "I'm too ordinary. I could never do anything like it says I would."

"This Great Prowler that is ordinary will become the most extraordinary," Broken quoted. "It says so in the Legend. The Legend chooses a most ordinary wolf for this destiny. You must take this path and make it your fate. And as an Alpha wolf, I order you."

Cobra joked, "Maybe he's an oldie, not me." She laughed.

Night bowed his head. "I will try, Alpha Broken. No matter what it takes, I will choose this path as my own. I could be the Great Prowler. There is a chance." He looked up.

"And I will do everything I can to fulfill this prophecy."

CHAPTER 12

THE FOUR wolves ran once more, still not completely sure where to go. Night insisted they keep going straight, because his instincts told him so. If he really was the Great Prowler, he needed to be cautious and smart with whatever he heard or saw.

Honor staggered along but did not act vicious even one time while they ran. Maybe Night really had changed a wolf...and it was something he could believe. Honor showed no signs of desperateness to get back to Scarr. *Maybe he won't be how he was before, because he doesn't have a menace influencing him anymore.*

"Soooooo," said Cobra slowly, "were you *really* an orphan pup?"

"I'm sure of it. Scarr raised me since I was young. She would never tell me anything made up." Honor's eyes twisted to look at the road ahead, and Night could tell he was trying not to look surprised that Cobra knew this much.

Yeah, right. Like she wouldn't! Scarr's a merciless menace, for wolf's sake! Never trust a wolf like her. Night shook away his thoughts and stepped ahead of them, making sure they were single file behind them. He felt just like a leader. "I can smell it: we're almost in Gray Territory! I've never met a Gray before!" He felt a rush of excitement.

"Then that will be a good experience," said Broken casually, as if he didn't care much. "Lead the way, Great Prowler."

It actually felt good to be called by that, so Night enjoyed it while he could. He treaded his paws along the path, sniffing the strong, loyal, milky scents of Gray wolves.

Maybe they'll have an idea on what to do...but what happens if I bring Cobra in?

He glanced to the Stormer, who looked ahead with her eyes narrowed in determination, despite her dried, bloody wound on her chest. She looked back at Night and cocked her head. The weirdness flooded Night again. The Prowler shook his head and paced on.

They ran until dusk arrived once more. When they curled up to rest under the moonlight, Night got into a tight ball but couldn't sleep. For a while he just laid there, eyes gazing upward. He whined, and he did not know why. The others were fast asleep already, but Night knew he'd never fall asleep, so he got up and paced a bit into the forest.

He whined more, and he realized the reason. He was thinking of his friend, Pistol, another Prowler that may have had a destiny too...but he had died.

The moonlight shone down like radio waves of heat on Night's perch. He hung his head and whined softly. He sat there sadly, feeling as if he'd been clawed in the stomach. Light blazed in front of him, catching his eye. He gasped when the light, a white-yellow color, formed into a shape of a wolf he loved.

"Night," it said.

"Pistol?" breathed Night. "B-But...you're dead. Honor killed you."

Pistol nodded, eyes gleaming in his shape of light. "I am now a spirit, Night, and I will be your spirit. I know you're sorry and that you made me risk everything, but I would've done it anyway. I think the Legend falls upon you now. Don't feel sad. Your destiny lies ahead and you must fulfill it, and it was meant for you, not for me."

Night felt sadness grow inside of him. "But it's all on me. I caused your death. You risked...everything for me. I owe you but now I can't repay you for risking your life for Cobra and me, because you're dead. I tried to help you..."

"Don't worry, Night. I am thankful for your bravery. But now I have passed. It's up to you, Night, and I know you can do it!" Pistol's eyes narrowed. "Go."

Owls swirled around the moon in a circle and sang their hooting song to the darkness as if this were a ritual. Pistol's shape started to fade away and Night gasped, doubling backward. One owl looked down at him and its eyes twitched.

The Prowler was amazed at what he had seen.

N THE morning he didn't dare tell the others about last night. Instead they continued on, getting closer and closer to Gray tribe Territory. "We're nearly there!" he exclaimed. "This will be great!"

The scents were stronger than ever to the point that even the others, not Prowlers, could tell they were smells of Grays. "Night, slow down!" called Cobra. "You're getting overexcited!"

"What do you mean?" Night called back. "I'm the Great Prowler— maybe—who's excited to help wolf kind!" He ran faster and saw markings along trees and scents of Grays nearby. "Here we are!"

The Territory looked just like any other. Wolves were gathered in a group on the far side, and as Night, Honor, Cobra, and Broken approached, they yelped sharply and scattered, getting in a formation as if they had planned it already. One wolf took a pace forward from the middle. "What brings outsiders?" he growled.

Night halted, the others doubling back. He sank down and bowed his head hastily. "We mean no harm. We are just here to help wolf kind—"

"The Great Prowler is here!" howled the Gray pack, bushy tails lashing from side to side.

"The day we've all been waiting for!" one yelped.

Night was overwhelmed. "Okay, stop a minute! I am Prowler Night—" the wolves howled cheers as he spoke "—and these are my friends Darkness wolf Honor, Stalker Broken, and..." He squeezed his eyes shut. "Stormer Cobra."

"Aahhhhhh!" howled the wolves, sounding as if they were screaming.

"Why are you friends with a Stormer?!" the first wolf bellowed.

"Because she is no ordinary Stormer," Night growled. "Don't judge or contradict her. It is my command as probable Great Prowler. She is my friend, and you can't take her away!"

This silenced the wolves. "O-Of course, Great Prowler," stuttered the first wolf. "Of course we'd have respect. Welcome to the Gray Territory." The other wolves were left speechless.

Night let out a whooshing breath and gave the others an "all clear'" gesture. They hopped beside him and he kept his gaze fierce as the Grays showed them around. They were as teamwork-based and loyal to one another as Night had expected. Broken looked as if he had something on his mind, but he did not say.

However, Cobra stayed behind, tail tucked and ears drooped sadly. Her head hung and Night hurried over. "What is it, Cobra?"

"I wish I wasn't a *Stormer*," Cobra growled. "Then wolves would actually treat me *right* the way I *deserve*." She kicked the grass with her hind leg and snorted dirt, running off to the other side of the Territory. Night was sorry for her but kept going with the Grays.

"I must speak to you," said Night suddenly, to the first wolf that had spoken when they came to a stop. "Are you the Alpha, the leader?"

"Well...nnnooooo," the first wolf said slowly. "I just help the pack make decisions. They kind of look up to me—we don't have a leader yet. We're trying to decide, but...none of us seem cut out for the job. I'm Gray Magnus." He gave a curt bow with his forequarters.

The Stalker's face lit up. He looked thoughtful and jumped in front of them. "I am Stalker Broken, as you know. I used to lead my fellow Stalkers...but they were all killed. They depended on me." He got straight to the point. "So maybe—I know I'm a Stalker, not a Gray—*I* could lead you?"

Night grinned and stepped back, out of this conversation. He had planned to start this before, considering Broken had that gleaming look. It was left between Broken and the Grays. Magnus looked all around and nodded. "You are a Stalker, but that doesn't matter. You can lead us. I think you'll do well," said Magnus.

Broken looked like he was trying not to burst; he went and licked Magnus's face and stepped backward, head held high.

Night spoke up, "*This* is what you're meant to do. Every wolf has a place in the world. You will be happy here as the Grays' Alpha, Broken. Good luck."

"You're right," said a beaming Broken. "It's my destiny."

CHAPTER 13

"**W**HOEVER HEARD** of a Stalker leading a Gray pack?" said Cobra, not as sad and angry as before. "I mean, that's great and all…"

Night shook his head; he was deep in thought. He, the probable Great Prowler, had helped yet another group of wolves—he had helped the Grays find a good leader, a good Alpha. And Broken, the only Stalker that had survived out of his pack during a horrible darkness, was perfect for that job. Night was sad about Hungry's and Star's death, but was glad the darkness hadn't spread over the entire wolf world.

That means I may be needed more desperately than ever.

Night picked up his pace, ignoring the yammering of Cobra behind him. Honor limped a bit but kept up surprisingly well. He still looked stunned at how he wasn't vicious anymore.

Suddenly, instincts and images rushed and piled through Night's head. Some were telling him to run faster, so he did, but not even Cobra's stunned shouting behind him was clear. They piled up and piled up like voices inside him, like the whisper back at the Forbidden Forest, except clearer through his mind.

"Run, Night, run!"

"The darkness is coming!"

"You, the Great Prowler, have to stop this!"
"Wolves need your help!"
"There are coyotes coming!"
"Run!"

Night panted harder than he had before and ran even faster. Honor and Cobra shouted, "Night!" behind him, but the Prowler's mind was flooded with voices, screams, shouts, instincts...

"Stop, Night!" Honor roared a warning.

Night skidded but his mind kept telling him to run. However, he saw several menacing coyotes standing in front of him. He shuffled his paws and fought the urge to run. His instincts were telling him something, and he always followed his instincts.

"Attack!" cried Cobra. She leaped and savagely tore at one coyote, which snarled and kicked.

"You filthy not-wolves!" snarled Honor, knocking several into oak trees. One nipped his neck and he snapped at its flank. Coyotes were the peskiest creatures Night had ever met, but his mind was so flooded that he stood there, staggering and thrashing as if he had been pinned by a bear.

Honor knocked another aside but when one coyote crunched on his front paw, he screamed a yelp. Coyote teeth were amazingly strong, so Night knew, even with flooded thoughts, that Honor's paw would be hurt for a while, even if his other wounds closed up.

Night tried to run but found he could not move. He couldn't fight. He couldn't run. He couldn't do *anything.* "Help!" he managed to choke out. He saw coyotes jump on him and nip at him like pesky flies.

Cobra saw him and leaped to the rescue, fighting away coyotes rapidly and savagely. However, Night kept croaking, "Help, help!" The thoughts crowded up again.

"Run, Night, run!"
"Why are you standing there, O Great Prowler?"
"Don't be a helpless wimp! Do something!"
"Fight, Night, fight!"

Night couldn't take the flood anymore. His paws thrashed and he choked before collapsing into a world full of darkness.

He woke up to Cobra's voice. The coyote raid was over, and he was lying face down in a cold, quiet cave. He guessed Honor and Cobra had managed to push him here after he had passed out. The flood had washed out of his mind, so he was able to lift his head and inspect his surroundings.

Honor was growling and wincing whenever he put down his crunched paw. The rest of his wounds were scabby, so the only burden now was his paw. Night sat up and gazed into the eyes of Cobra. "Stormer Cobra," he choked.

"Prowler Night," she said back calmly.

"What happened?" Night asked, coming to his senses. "How could I fall unconscious when I am needed in a situation? My mind…it seemed to be flooded with thoughts and instincts and…I heard screaming." He shuddered, remembering the high-pitched shrieks. "What does it all mean?"

Honor was thoughtful. "Well, if you're the Great Prowler, by chance, maybe that's what happens to them when they have a world to save. You must be overwhelmed so much that this was what happened. Just a guess," he said. Then he looked down as if ashamed.

Night thought this over. Yes. That sounded accurate. Maybe he really was the Great Prowler, the Chosen One, to save wolf kind. He had had flashing images of terrorized wolves. He had heard the screams of battle. He could feel the feelings of many wolves in need.

Maybe he had been overwhelmed by all these things, knowing he had many wolves to save. "I may be," he said. "I have lots of wolves that need me. Even being the Great Prowler, I can't do it alone." He grinned to the others and their jaws hung.

"B-But I was an assassin!" Honor cried. "I-I tried to kill you!"

"I'm a *Stormer*, enemy of Prowlers!" Cobra shook her head. "Why would you choose me or Honor to help you? We're…we're nothing."

"You are not!" Night insisted. "You mean more to me than anything, Cobra. And Honor, it was Scarr's fault that you were killing off wolves, not yours." He felt the weird sensation after saying the first line, but felt kindness rush through him in the second.

Honor hung his head. Cobra nodded. "Thanks, Night. That means a lot," she said. "We will help you, no matter what. Now that you say it, it doesn't seem so bad. We can help you with your worries and over-whelming thoughts." She brushed her body against his and licked his muzzle.

Night tried not to collapse with shock. Here, right here, Cobra had licked him straight to the muzzle. He nuzzled her back. *Maybe she really is my love, but not in the way Scarr thinks.*

"Are you ready to move on, Night?" Cobra grinned, nudging him forward.

"Yes. Come on, Honor."

"I can't go." Honor shook his head.

"What?!" gasped Cobra and Night together.

Honor turned. "I was cruel. I nearly had you killed. I killed Pistol. And you changed me forever. I saw such bravery in you, and I became ashamed at all I had done. I know it's Scarr's fault, but I'll never forgive myself for being influenced by that menace!" Honor spat the last word and lashed his tail. "Sorry. I have to go."

"No, you don't! Honor, you're different in a good way now. You were an orphan pup and you were raised by her! That *made* you the way you weren't meant to be. But now you're okay. You will forgive yourself someday," said Night.

Honor seemed to take time for these words to sink in. "Okay." He nodded. "I will. Thank you, O Great Prowler."

Night flinched. Even that worshiped name, which he'd always wanted, was actually too much. "Please, Prowler Night," he insisted. "You two are helping me. You don't have to call me the Great Prowler. And besides, what if it's really another wolf?"

"Oh, no, it's you," Cobra said matter-of-factly. "We'll just see if we're right or wrong. Let's go. Lead the way, Night!"

Night barked a laugh as they trotted along. And feeling the weird tickle inside him once more, he knew at last, Stormer or no Stormer, that he had found a wolf to love.

CHAPTER 14

NIGHT GULPED. The only two tribes left to visit were the Darkness tribe...and the Storm tribe, at least in his world. Right now he didn't want to be bombarded by other Prowlers. "Should we see...the Stormers?" he asked, already knowing the answer.

"No way!" Cobra howled. "Leave them out. I swore to myself I'd never come back, which means I won't. Anyway, they hate Prowlers. In fact, they hate every wolf besides themselves!" She gritted her fangs. "I pass."

Night nodded. "What about the Darkness wolves? Honor, you could finally fit in with your own kind. I know you aren't a Lone Wolf like I am."

Honor shook his head hastily. "Not right now," he said nervously. "I want to wait until I'm ready. Let's see the Prowlers, and maybe we can figure out if you're really the Great Prowler." Night knew he had to help all wolves, so he nodded.

They trekked across a large glade that would do for a Territory but looked natural. Their paws crunched, turned, and thundered, and even Honor, who limped, went very fast. Night used his instincts—now they weren't overcrowding his mind—to find his way, and knew soon he'd be in a Prowler Territory.

Pistol was the only wolf I knew who was a Prowler. I don't remember any Prowlers in my past, not even my parents or wolf sisters or brothers. A pang of sadness reminded Night of Pistol's death. He'd rather not bring up to the others how sad he felt as to not make Honor feel worse about killing him.

However, he still remembered the horrifying moment—the moment Honor had driven his claw, the final move—and the "there's no hope" look on Pistol's face before he died. He remembered the beat-up body of the Prowler. Pistol had known that Night had tried.

Night stole a look back at Honor, whose face was twisted with pain from his paw. But Night also saw a look of shame on the Darkness wolf's face. *He's sorry. He's changed. He's not cruel anymore. I don't have to be cautious. He'll forgive himself soon, just like we did.*

His pace quickened and he caught Prowler scents. Over the course of a few hours they had already reached their destination. "We're here! Don't worry, Cobra! I will explain!" he called over his shoulder.

The marked trees up ahead caught his attention. These Prowlers must live in the forest. He ran faster and saw gray bodies of wolves and their pups. The wolf pups bounded all around, wrestling and licking each other. The leader wolf sat licking her paw. Other wolves lay around and talked.

Night took deep breaths. Here he was, about to meet Prowlers just like him. "Ready?" he mouthed to Cobra and Honor. They nodded. He kept his body low and non-threatening and made his way through the borders.

"Who goes there?" Several wolves leaped up and rushed over, ears erect and fur on end. One sniffed and cried, "It's another Prowler, and a Darkness wolf!"

Wolves looked ahead and the Alpha stepped up.

"What brings intruders?" she growled. "What's your name, Prowler?"

"I'm Prowler Night," said Night. "These are my partners Honor, a Darkness wolf, and...Stormer Cobra." The Prowlers gasped, the Alpha growled, and they all backed away to let the Stormer walk in and sit. Night explained about Cobra.

The Alpha growled again. "I see. Well, we cannot let her out of our sight. Guard wolves, keep your eyes on this Stormer. Welcome, Prowler Night."

"This isn't the whole pack, is it?" Honor cocked his head.

The Alpha shook her head. "The rest are on patrol, but apparently they didn't see you coming."

"We are here to know if Night here is actually the Great Prowler," explained Honor. "He changed me; I used to be cruel. And he has helped many wolves so far. Could you help us?"

The Alpha wolf's eyes widened as quickly as they had narrowed. One wolf cried, "It's the Great Prowler!"

Night got in a rush. "No, no! We don't know yet. It's probable, but not definite, that I'm the Great Prowler. We just want to be sure. Do you have a way to help? I'm not, you know, selfish or anything…"

"Of course we'll help," said the leader, hiding her surprise. "Prowler Rookie, watch the Stormer…*carefully*." Her eyes flickered with distrust as they gazed upon Cobra. The Stormer was setting her jaw, trying not to explode before their eyes.

"I *said*—" defended Night, but he did not get to finish. A young-looking Prowler was guarding Cobra just as thundering paws grew louder and louder. Night widened his eyes, flinching back. It must be the wolf guards that were on patrol. One, with colors just like Night's pelt, was oddly familiar.

Night's eyes widened more when images flashed through his mind like during the coyote raid. This time, they showed this same wolf, looming over him with kind eyes, whispering, "You could be the Great Prowler. You are as beautiful as the night."

No, no, not again. Don't let them overwhelm you… Night couldn't help but think about that voice. *It's just like my name*, he realized. The wolves murmured and reported to their Alpha wolf, but the one stopped abruptly in front of Night. His eyes went from the Prowler to Honor to Cobra.

"These are our guests. Don't worry. The Stormer will be kept under close eye vision. Prowler Night could possibly be the Great Prowler." The Alpha looked sincere about it this time and Night didn't even take time to argue.

The wolf looked thunderstruck. "D-Did you just say...Prowler *Night?*" he gasped. "H-He's back? After he ran away? How is this possible?"

The Alpha was struck with realization too. "Prowler Alpha, you are right! Your runaway son is back!"

Night didn't even think why in wolf's sake that a wolf's *name* could be Alpha. Instead, his face twisted with realization and shock. It was Prowler Alpha in his mind, the wolf that was whispering those things. He was standing—face to face—with his own father.

CHAPTER 15

NIGHT COULDN'T speak. He couldn't move. All his memories of his family came rushing out as if they had been lost all these years. He was a runaway? How could he have forgotten? He had spent all his life thinking that he'd always lived in the wild. Now realization hit him like he had never known.

"I remember the day," breathed Prowler Alpha. "I remember when you, Night, were the only one that wanted to live as a Lone Prowler. I let you go but it was hard. It was hard enough losing your mother, who died shortly after she had you pups. All your siblings stayed behind, and grew up. Rookie is a brother of yours." He gestured to Rookie, who was staring, aghast, at Night.

"I missed you so much, Night. I named you all—my sons and one daughter—something other than my own. And you, Night, I named the best. I used to say—"

"'You are as beautiful as the night?'" said Night. Everything made sense now. He had seen all the visions, heard all the voices, felt all the thoughts. And now his own family rested here, welcoming him with open paws. But he felt a pang of sadness. *If I really am the Great Prowler, I won't be able to stay...*

"Yes. You were the most beautiful son I had. So I named you Prowler Night. It fits, doesn't it? I never thought I'd see my wonderful and beautiful son again. I haven't seen you for at least five years."

Night felt sadness grow bigger in his gut. He was happy to see his father again, but he couldn't help but think he most likely would have to run off again, to help wolf kind. His father wolf was already happy, so there was no use in bringing it up right now. He looked up. "Father," he breathed. And he ran until he tumbled into Prowler Alpha affectionately. He felt cold licks from his happy father wolf and they rolled around for forever, which felt good to Night.

This is my family. This is my pack. This is where I belong.

But what if I can't belong here, being the Great Prowler?

"I remember those fur-heads Prowler Sun and Prowler Moon. They never thought one of my pups could be the Great Prowler. But now I have a chance to prove them wrong." Prowler Alpha grinned as he gave Night another lick. "They hate me for my name," he joked.

Night couldn't help but laugh. He felt a slight twinge of happiness and decided to let his worries go for a while. For now he wanted to be with his father. And he could get to know his brothers and sisters too.

"Night, Night!" another wolf guard howled, bounding toward him. "It's me, your older brother! It's me, Prowler Titan!" He gave Night a lick like their father had and knocked his brother down. Night felt the wind knocked out of him but he choked out a laugh. He had never felt the joy of siblings until now.

"Titan, give your brother some space!" snarled Prowler Alpha. The leader glared at Titan as well and Night's big brother backed up meekly. He murmured, "Sorry."

A female wolf lay chewing a stick. She stopped and looked Night in the eyes. She lolled her tongue shyly. "I'm Prowler Ember, your only sister. I've missed you in a way that I've never missed a wolf before." Night grinned and licked her muzzle in response.

"You have one more sibling," said Prowler Alpha. "You have Prowlers Ember, Titan, Rookie, and...our most vicious, Prowler Axe. His name is like a Stormer's, but I named him that for a reason." He gave a doggy shrug and a sharp bark. A fierce-looking wolf with scars all over one leg bounded right up.

"Is that...Prowler Night?!" he cried, lashing his tail back and forth. "Oh, Night, I've missed you!" He ran up and licked Night all over just like the others had. Maybe Axe could be a little vicious, but Night could already tell he had a good heart inside.

He saw Cobra glance at the beat-up leg on Prowler Axe. *Don't start musing, Cobra. Remember: your leg is scarred too!* Night shook his body, looking around at *his* pack, his family. How could he just leave them like this?

"I have bad news," he managed to choke. The sadness inside him could not stay in any longer. He howled. "I would love to be with you all but if I am the Great Prowler—like you thought I'd be, Father—I would have to make a journey and help all wolves. This time, it wouldn't be a runaway. It would be a mission, a mission to save you all." He made sure to sound sincere, not desperate.

"Father, Ember, Axe, Rookie, and Titan, you're my family and I would never desert you. The rest of you, you're my pack. I couldn't leave you. But I have a feeling, deep down inside my heart that tells me *my* destiny. Every wolf has a path, a destiny. And mine is to save every wolf forever. So pack, Father, every wolf, that's my destiny. I must leave to fulfill the Legend that every wolf depends on me with."

Silence fell. Night clenched his jaw and closed his eyes, waiting to hear howls of protest or cries of sadness. Instead, he opened his eyes and saw his father nod sadly. "I have the feeling too, Night. It's your destiny. Nothing can stop that. And if you have to leave to help all wolves, we will let you. The Great Prowler is selfless and is willing to help wolves besides their self. And you, Night, match that perfectly." Prowler Alpha grinned. "Who agrees? My son is destined for it, and I will allow him to find *his* place in the world."

Night listened. His siblings were solemn but wore looks that said "He's right." The leader nodded quietly. Cobra and Honor, of course, said nothing. Night patted the ground with his paw. Nothing else was said.

"Thank you, Father. Thank you, everyone... I know this was a hard choice, and that you don't want to lose me again. I know how that feels. I missed you all too. But it's my job to save the wild, to save all wolves.

My father believes that, and I know you do too." Night's tongue lolled and he felt like crying out in sadness.

"Yes," said the leader finally. "I believe that, Night. You may begin your quest. At least, I'm okay with it."

His siblings nodded and grinned. "I want my brother to help wolves," Ember murmured, kicking dirt with her paw. Titan ran up and licked Night again. Night knew all the signs were yeses. He stood up straight and tall and tilted his head. Now that he knew wolves could hear it, he cried out his howl to the sky.

It didn't matter if it was day or night. The wolves all joined in to his howling and the cries cheered through the whole sky. Night turned his howl into a quote, repeating the whole Legend in his howling cry. As he did so, he heard Cobra's beautiful cry as well.

"The earth will be as still as stone. The wind will have a perilous tone. But far away, on the run, we will have the Chosen One," Night howled.

Cobra repeated the next line immediately. *"This Great Prowler that is ordinary will become the most extraordinary. They will find the right way to save the darkness and the day."*

"No Prowler knows when this day will come, but every hope lies upon the stone. Prowlers wait and Prowlers lie, and the One has a chance to try," Honor joined in. His Darkness howl went perfectly with all the others.

Finally, Prowler Alpha howled the rest. *"Upon the world darkness will fall. But the Great Prowler will stand above it all. And no matter what they find, they're the way to saving wolf kind!"*

The wolves continued their howl. Night felt a smile spread over his face while his howl brought out all his thoughts and emotions.

The song faded, and Night felt like he really was the way. He could do it, no matter what it took. These wolves were by his side. And he would change the world forever.

Watch out, darkness, he thought happily. *The Great Prowler is coming.*

EPILOGUE

"**A**FTER ALL I did for him, my Best Wolf had to betray me," Scarr hissed to herself, pacing back and forth. "Maybe I'll have a *better* Best Wolf over time. And Honor will pay someday. So will that pathetic Prowler Night and his Stormer soul-mate."

"What will you do after you find Honor?" a guard wolf asked. "He'll find out everything if we don't stop him! He'll find out you lied and everything!"

"Shhhh!" snarled Scarr. "I will *kill him* if I have to, as long as he doesn't know the *true* story of where he came from." She grinned wickedly. "Too bad he fell for that orphan-pup story. We will stop him before he gets back to the Darkness wolves."

The guard nodded grimly. "I will discuss your plan with the others," he growled. "Unless you have some other things to tell me."

"Ergh!" bellowed Scarr. "Of course I do, stupid! I have something to say!" She stepped forward and grinned before crunching her fangs down on the guard's neck. He collapsed, wounded. She snorted and walked away toward the meeting cave. "Honor will pay," she hissed, "and soon."

She turned a corner and saw her remaining guards, the ones that hadn't been badly wounded by Prowler Night—those had died soon after—staggering to their feet with bleeding wounds. "Let's go," she snapped. "We have a plan to discuss, one that will stop Honor and Prowler Night." She grinned in a wicked way.

Once they had gathered, wolves licking wounds, Scarr caught every wolf's attention. "My plan is to leave this place and find a new Territory, closer to where those pathetic wolves may be. We will track down my former Best Wolf and Prowler Night, and make sure they don't try to stop us, or fulfill that stupid Legend of theirs." She rolled her eyes.

"Yes, Alpha Scarr," said one respectively. "But may I ask: how *do* we do that?"

Scarr gritted her teeth. "We will hold them captive—leave out the Stormer; she's no use—and we will make them pay for what they have done. We will stop them from following the Legend and talk some stupid sense into Honor. He must know that he is *nothing* special like the Darkness wolves say he is."

"We will do so," said the one. "I understand completely now, Scarr. This plan of yours will work out better than I imagined, now that I think of it."

"Of course!" snarled Scarr. "My plans always work. Maybe not the one before, but this one will not be stopped. Those wolves will see that they cannot test Prowler Scarr!" Her eyes flickered. "And Honor will realize that it was better for me to take him under my paw anyway. He'll turn away from his destiny and come back here, the way he's really meant to be."

"If that's your plan, we will do it. We will never test you. And those wolves won't either." The one grinned. "You're Prowler Scarr. You're invincible. You're powerful."

This made Scarr smirk with satisfaction. "Prowler Stinger, I think you should take over as my Best Wolf. Honor will never serve that position again because of what he's done."

Stinger beamed and bowed his head.

Scarr spoke again. "Does every wolf agree? Whoever doesn't will be thrown in the dungeon," Scarr threatened. Every wolf nodded hastily and licked their wounds.

"Once we've all healed up, we will start. And every wolf will work hard because I have to stop Honor!" Scarr announced.

Get ready to realize you are nothing, Darkness wolf.

WOLF WARRIORS

BOOK TWO

FOREVER

HEIR

PROLOGUE

LOYALTY HELD her head up high, scraping her claws down the coyote's back. It yowled as she sunk her teeth into its flesh and she knew it was dead after it went limp. This was the last coyote in the coyote raid. She looked proudly to her mother wolf, who was nodding in approval. "Yes, Loyalty," the black wolf said. "This will be great to show your long-lost brother when he returns someday."

Loyalty gritted her teeth. That's all her mother ever talked about, was her "long lost brother." *I know we lost him during that phenomenon a long time ago, when I was just a small pup, but maybe he just might not return! I'm tired of hearing you talk about it!* She shoved the coyote into the river in her anger.

The black-and-gray female walked to the other side of the smooth stone where her mother, Pebble, lay. She climbed up and looked into her mother's eyes. Even though she was angry, Loyalty still saw sadness in her mother wolf's eyes. She knew Pebble missed her son more than anything. And the sadder thing was: he had had no name before he was snatched by a cruel Prowler. She never thought Prowlers could be so mean.

Pebble had wanted to name her wolf children names far beyond her own, ones that resembled their nobleness and loyalty, like Loyalty's resembled. But she had never gotten the chance to name her brother. Loyalty had some names in mind—*Noble, Justice*—but she never mentioned them to her mother. Pebble was sad enough as it was.

Loyalty gave her a lick before treading off the rock and into the woods, where her half-brother was chasing toads near the creek. His name was not like hers, but she wasn't annoyed at that. She was annoyed at the fact that Razor always chased toads, no matter if it was day or night, rain or shine. "Razor, stop chasing puny frogs for once and do something useful!" she spat, wrinkling her muzzle in disgust. "Besides, it's gross."

"Why should I?" Razor snapped, watching the toad leap away and glaring at his half-sister. His muzzle was streaked with mud and so were his legs, but it didn't do much to his already dark body. "And FYI, they're toads, not frogs. Chasing them is my favorite thing to do when I'm bored."

"Then in this case, you're *always* bored!" Loyalty returned with a tongue-lolling smirk. She shuffled away from the mud puddles, fixing her eyes on Razor. "Your father should have named you Boredom instead!"

Razor flung choppy mud at her face. "Go away!"

Loyalty took off laughing, away from her half-brother and to her mother's stone. She grew serious again when her mother asked, "Are you getting up to any mischief?"

Loyalty shook her head with an "Of course not, I'm too old for that, Mother," as the rest of the pack started filing into the Territory.

"I have a question," said Loyalty. "Could my brother—not Razor, he's my *half-brother*—my long-lost brother, be the Great Prowler?" She knew this question was stupid, because they were in the Darkness tribe, not the Prowler tribe, but the question still got her thinking.

Pebble laughed. "No. But that would be great if he was, because he'd be out there saving wolf kind. But no…only a Prowler can follow this legend. And someday, it will happen. For now we must stay safe and wait for our long-lost heir."

I wouldn't exactly call him an "heir," Loyalty thought to herself. *But he must be important, because he's Mother's first-born.*

"Is there something important about my missing brother?" she asked Pebble.

Pebble looked thoughtful. "Well, yes, but not because he's first-born." She started to look excited. "The Darkness tribe is said to have a new King Wolf someday, one that has a special feature no other wolf in the tribe has and can lead us well." Her eyes gleamed. "And your brother has that feature: a special spike-blade on the tip of his tail. He is the heir to our next King Wolf, which our first one was a thousand years ago. I never told him, because he was too young. But someday, when he returns, he'll discover his destiny, his fate."

Loyalty was stunned. Her own brother, destined to be a King Wolf? She grew a bit jealous but amazed as well. "Wow. That's amazing. I'll have to tell Razor. I never knew about that till now. Thanks, Mother." She ran off toward her half-brother, ready to tell him, not to annoy him this time.

"Razor, Razor!" she called. She told her still-glaring half-brother everything. He looked just as stunned and amazed as she.

He gasped and said, "Wow, we need to tell that to the pack!" and forgot all about chasing toads.

The pack filed in more, shuffling and murmuring. They didn't look as excited as the two young wolves were. "If he really is the heir destined to be King Wolf," Loyalty grinned, "then we need to be ready for him."

CHAPTER 1

"**H**OW IS your paw, Honor?" Prowler Night asked the Darkness wolf the day before they would leave for Night's Great Prowler journey.

"It's okay, I guess. I mean, I can put weight on it," Honor replied, placing his recently injured paw on the hard ground. "We can leave soon, whenever you're ready, really. You've taken a few hard weeks to stay here already. I know I'm ready, and so is Cobra." He felt a twinge when he said the Stormer's name. He tried not to show so to Night.

Night nodded sadly. "It *is* almost time to go. I don't want to leave my family, my pack, but I have to in order to complete my quest for saving wolf kind. And I'm thinking of where we should go next, other than the Stormers…"

"The Darkness wolves!" cried Honor. "I'm ready to see them. After seeing your reaction to your family, I want to see *my* reaction to my own kind. Can we go?" He realized how changed he really sounded, and now believed that Night really had changed him forever, which made him feel happy.

"Of course we'll visit them!" Night replied. "I will visit every wolf I can and help them! I just don't know what we'll do with Cobra…every tribe hates the Stormers."

Honor gulped. "Well, let's worry about that when we get there," he said excitedly. "I want to meet my kind! Maybe they'll know my parents before they died."

The leader of Night's former pack had overheard. She padded over. "We met the Darkness wolves a long time ago, and they said they had a long-lost son as well as we did, and they say that son is the heir of King Aghast."

"King what?!" cried Honor. "What's all this about?"

The leader looked sincere. "A thousand years ago, a young Darkness wolf named Aghast found out he was the first heir to become King Wolf of the Darkness wolves, and so he ruled over them with great force instead of what the tale of the King Wolf called for. He was said to have caused the Legend to come alive. For a thousand years there hasn't been another heir—a Darkness wolf with a kind heart and a secret blade on his tail. However, greed, power, and pride overtook Aghast, and his heart changed. That may happen to every heir if they aren't careful.

"So these wolves thought they saw something small and sharp on their pup's tail and got excited. They thought he could be, finally, the next heir to King Wolf. Maybe you, Night, and the Stormer can help them find their heir-to-be."

"Do we know for sure?" asked Honor.

"They are definitely sure of themselves," the leader laughed. "You can be on your way whenever you're ready. This is another chance to help wolves." Other members of the pack trotted over, agreeing.

Night looked a little sad but nodded. The pack gathered round. "Thank you so much for letting us in. I would never leave you for the world, but this world *needs* me. And I have to help the Darkness wolves find their heir. Thank you, my Alpha. Thank you, my siblings. Thank you, my father. I'm thankful to all of you. But now we must be on our way."

Prowler Alpha, Night's father, nodded sadly, licking his son. "Goodbye, Night," he whined. Night looked like he was trying not to howl. Honor heard Prowler Alpha whisper something in Night's ear: "Remember, you are as beautiful as the night."

After Honor, Night, and Cobra had crossed three hills and one valley, Honor felt exhausted. "Should we rest? Tomorrow I think we'll have found Darkness wolves. I smell the clear scents."

"Sure." Night nodded, and they curled up almost immediately. They had eaten only an hour earlier, so they were just tired, not hungry. Honor's eyelids closed slowly and he drifted into sleep.

He awoke and found that Night had brought scraps for them to eat. Stormer Cobra was a lot quieter than usual. She spoke up at last. "What will they think of me?" she asked softly. "Will they think I'm there to kill them?"

The word "kill" rang through Honor's dark ears and his heart sped up. *I killed plenty of wolves…and I'm not even a Stormer. I feel terrible now for killing Prowler Pistol. They don't understand that I can't forgive myself…ever.* He whined and laid his head on his paws.

"What is it, Honor?" asked Night.

"I-I just feel so bad for killing Pistol. I know you two forgive me and it's all in the past, and that I'm different now, but I still think about it every day, and how cruel I was. I could've been a Stormer. No offence, Cobra." Honor hung his head.

"Oh, Honor," whispered Cobra. "Forget it; it's in the past. I bet if Pistol was standing before us, he would forgive you too. And besides, Scarr made you that way. Night has said that many times, and it's true."

Honor felt a little better. "Thanks, Cobra. I'm glad you said that."

They started up another valley, Darkness scents becoming clearer and clearer to Honor. He could tell Night smelled them too; Prowlers had the best senses of smell of any wolf. He felt a rush of excitement when they had crossed the same valley an hour later. This made him start running, with Night and Cobra trailing behind him.

I get to meet my own kind! Now I know how Night felt when he was getting "overexcited." I could get overexcited just about now. I'm about to meet Darkness wolves that may have known my parents, and help them find an heir!

The scents got stronger and Honor grew more and more excited. "They're this way! Up here! I know it!" he howled. His tail wagged like never in his life—it had never wagged under the clutches of Scarr.

Night looked excited too. He looked ready to help wolves like the Great Prowler Legend said.

Honor had grown up with Prowlers and being the only Darkness wolf, was ready to meet some wolves like him. He knew Darkness wolves had dark pelts and were the smallest wolves out of the tribes. They were known to save wolves and use shadows to get past enemies. He had never seen a black or dark gray pelt in his life.

A glade surrounded by oak trees came into view. This must be the Darkness Territory they had smelled. Honor's heart pounded incredulously. "Let's go!" he howled.

This apparently caught the wolves' attention. Dark-colored wolves sprang from the shadows of the glade, all in elite formation. The leader was a female, curled up on a stone with two young wolves: one female and one male.

The other wolves growled at Cobra and, knowing what to do, they cautiously guided her as if they knew she wasn't too much of a threat. Maybe a patrol wolf from Night's pack had told them, since the packs knew each other.

Night stepped ahead. "I am Prowler Night, and I believe I may be the Great Prowler. Stormer Cobra here isn't a threat. And this is our friend Honor, a Darkness wolf like all of you. He was raised and trained by Prowler Scarr so he was extremely cruel and killed many wolves." Honor flinched and Night went on. "But I believe that his heart is changed forever, and that's how I believe I'm the Great Prowler. We are here to find your lost heir."

The wolves were speechless, and the leader gasped. "D-Did you say Prowler *Scarr*? S-She took our heir when he was just a little pup and raised him as her own."

Honor tried to take these words in just as a voice howled "That's right!" and immediately Prowler Scarr and her wolves leaped out from the undergrowth, as if on cue. Had they been...searching for him? Honor growled at Scarr and the leader gasped again.

"That's her!" shouted the leader. "Her pack raided our Territory and took our honorary pup for herself, knowing he was the heir!" Her jaw was hanging.

Honor knew the obvious answer now. Every wolf's head turned to look at him.

"Honor," breathed Night, "*you're* the heir."

CHAPTER 2

HONOR COULD not believe any of this. He had been an *orphan pup*, hadn't he? He was the heir to King Aghast? Was he somehow related to the first-ever King Wolf a thousand years ago?

"That means...you lied to me!" he roared to Scarr, rage pouring out of him. "You liked about everything! You just wanted the heir for yourself! I was never an orphan pup! I had a *family*! I'm the *heir*!"

Scarr wore a wicked grin. "I had to come up with something. Too bad you fell for it. How helpless can you get, *King Wolf?*" Then Scarr looked angry. "You were all mine, the way I wanted you, until *Prowler Night* had to ruin everything! You had a perfectly good life."

"No, I didn't." Honor stepped up, head held high. "You made me do your bidding. You used me to kill other wolves. You made up my story and my destiny for me, when I have a *real* destiny ahead of me. And now you will pay for all you have done." Without hesitation, he leaped and gave the final merciless kill he would ever give.

He lunged and crunched down on Scarr's neck. A loud whining sound came and Honor knew Scarr was dead. Scarr's wolves gasped, and they hurriedly pulled Scarr's body away with them into the forest, crying "Our leader is dead!" Honor raised his head as wolves applauded with howls. "That's the end of her," he muttered to himself. *He had killed Scarr.*

A minute later, it was quiet. "Honor… At least she named you something proper," said the leader. "Honor, I am your mother, Pebble. This is your sister, Loyalty." She gestured down at the female wolf. "And this is your half-brother, Razor." The other dark wolf had splotches of mud on his body, and his tail thumped.

Honor's tongue lolled from his jaws. He had spent five years of his life believing the stupid orphan-pup story. Now he knew he had a family of his own, and it made him happy. He leaped into his mother's paws, feeling like a pup again, and enjoyed the warmth of her body.

"Do we know for sure that he's the heir?" Night asked at last.

"I'm sure of it. Honor, hold up your tail, my son. I need to see if you really have that blade," said Pebble. Honor obediently held up his dark tail and was surprised to see that something sharp gleamed the slightest bit even though it had blended in with the dark colors.

The wolves breathed in agony. One cried, "He *is* the heir!" A still-surprised Honor grinned. He would be King Wolf, and he wanted to find out how that had felt to King Aghast.

Pebble nodded her head. "Honor, my son, you must be extremely careful being King Wolf. Like King Aghast, you may have power and pride and greed taking you over. Don't let it happen."

Honor bowed his head but said nothing. *I just hope it doesn't happen. What if I can't control it, like they said King Aghast couldn't?* He swallowed back a whine and turned to address the pack, hiding his blade like he could.

"As the heir to King Wolf, I *command* you to treat Stormer Cobra as a friend, not a foe. She and Night have showed me so much even under the terrible clutches of Scarr. So I say no guarding her or even growling at her!" Honor raised his voice to a snarl. His sister looked astonished, and his half-brother licked his chops.

The wolves looked upon each other. "W-We will, Prince Honor. Of course! But we've never done that before. Every wolf hates the Stormers," said a wolf, shuffling her paws. "The Stormers even hate each other!"

Wolves murmured in agreement. Cobra's jaw hung and Honor

howled. "I know that!" he snapped. "But she is our friend and is no ordinary Stormer! I will soon be your King Wolf, and Prowler Night agrees about this with me. So do what I asked!" He hadn't meant to get so angry, especially when he was just meeting his own kind, but couldn't they understand?

The wolves were dumbstruck and looked at each other. "Alpha?" one murmured to Pebble. Pebble nodded.

"My son, long-lost heir for four years, has finally returned. He has the same stubborn streak I knew he'd have, but he's still changed. You wouldn't want him the way he was with Scarr. So listen to his instructions as well as mine. After all, he will be King Wolf someday."

The wolves seemed subdued to this. They nodded and bowed their heads before Honor. Honor felt the feeling that the wolves were loyal to him, but for good measure, he kept glaring with his dark paw raised. "Thank you," he hissed, exasperated.

Night had been silent this whole time. "So, do you mind showing us around?" he asked in a respectful tone. "I mean, this must only be part of the Territory."

"Sure thing, Great Prowler," said Pebble. "Every wolf let the Stormer go and do your own thing. Loyalty, and Razor, and I will show these newcomers around." She leaped off her rock with Honor's siblings following.

Cobra was no longer guarded. She shook herself and her face was full of relief. She gave both Honor and Night a "thanks-so-much" look. *No problem, Cobra. You know we don't hate you,* Honor thought. *I definitely don't think Night hates you.* Very recently he'd seen odd behavior from Night when he was around Cobra. Honor knew what that meant.

"Follow me," called Pebble from six paw-steps ahead. Honor bounded up to her side, right next to Loyalty.

"Um," said Loyalty, "hi." She had her tail slightly between her legs but she gazed right up at her brother. "We've been waiting for your return. Mother was really sad before you came, and I had gotten tired of her talking about you so much, to be honest." She squeezed her eyes shut.

"Oh." Honor cocked his head. "Well, what happened? Like, when I was taken?" He had wanted to ask this question ever since arriving at the Territory.

Loyalty opened her eyes. "I didn't remember, since I had been a small pup. But then Mother showed me."

"What? Showed you? What does that—?" began Honor, but Pebble had already started speaking.

"Here is where we eat and rest. pack meetings take place in wherever a wolf can get to the quickest. During emergencies we have a special drill that I will show you soon, Honor."

Honor nodded hastily, but Loyalty's words rang through this head. *But then Mother showed me. But then Mother showed me.* What did she mean by that? It was all in the past so how did Pebble *show* Loyalty anything?

The heir had no time to ask more questions, because he was right to work on the drill while Razor and Loyalty watched. He assumed Night and Cobra had gone elsewhere. *Probably to build their secret relationship*, he thought with a grin.

The drill wasn't too hard. He was told that every wolf would run to the center of Territory and always get in the same formation together. They would either run far from the Territory till the danger passed or fight the danger if it was, say, foxes.

Honor listened carefully but when he finished his lesson he was still going over Loyalty's words. He followed Pebble back to her stone since Loyalty had run off for hunting. He needed to ask his mother.

"Mother?" he whispered. "I mean, Alpha Pebble. I'm too old for 'Mother,' aren't I?" Pebble did not answer but looked him in the eyes as if waiting for him to go on. "I asked Loyalty about how I was taken. She said she hadn't remembered. But then you 'showed' her. How?" he asked.

Pebble lolled a smile. "Go to sleep tonight and you will find out," she said.

Go to sleep?

THE MOON was just rising overhead as the pack gathered around Pebble's rock. The dark-furred wolf shook her body to address the pack. "Now we must howl, for there is a full moon tonight," she said. "And then we may sleep in peace, which means the Stormer too."

Loyalty's eyes gleamed, and Honor knew she must have a love for howling. Razor leaped and darted around the crowd of wolves, chasing a toad like Loyalty had said he always did. She said he was immature, despite being barely older than Honor.

Pebble's eyes had a twinkle in them too. "This will be a very special howl because my long-lost son has returned. We will celebrate by letting loose our cries." She brought her head to the sky and opened her jaws. A low and deep *CAROOOOO* escaped them. That must be a Darkness howl.

Honor had never howled with joy before, but he released his own special Darkness cry. He heard Prowler Night's from behind him and saw Cobra hesitate. *I know. Your tribe forbids—*

Then a most beautiful sound was let loose. Honor whipped his head around, but he felt his heart swell. Who was doing this howling? He turned and saw Stormer Cobra with her muzzle to the sky. *Whoa! That's a Stormer howl?*

Other wolves had stopped to stare, their eyes gentle. Prowler Night just grinned. He seemed to know about this howl. Why would Stormers ever hold back that calming, beautiful sound? It seemed to put every wolf in a heart-calming trance.

Pebble's tongue was lolling as her eyes moved toward Cobra even while she was howling. Honor joined back in with more joy than ever, and when the howls died down, so did the most beautiful sound. It was luring, and it made Honor want her to do it forever.

Every wolf was still staring at Cobra and the Stormer shrunk back. "What?" she whispered in an almost growl. Her tail began to tuck.

The wolves grinned and shook their heads. Cobra smiled as well, and Honor swore he saw Night nuzzle her. *She's really no ordinary Stormer. Night loves her so, and that has never happened before.*

When he curled up for the night, despite the confusing words still in his mind, he drifted right off feeling like the joy he felt would never leave him.

CHAPTER 3

*H*E EMERGED *into the Territory, bounding along like there was no tomorrow. He had never felt such joy, and he barked greetings to the other wolves he passed. They didn't answer.*

Why? Honor thought. He came to the stone and found his mother was not there. "Mother?" he called. There was no answer.

He felt fur brush up against his shoulder. He turned and found Pebble was standing in front of him. "Mother, what's going on?" His voice seemed to echo.

Pebble just closed her eyes and nodded. "I meant to tell you, but I am a mother of an heir. What wolf says I can't come into dreams? It's all a mystery, but right now I'm taking you through time..."

"What?" Honor echoed. "Why?"

"You know how Loyalty said I showed her something, and I told you you'd find out what it meant when you slept?" Pebble asked, giving Honor a sidelong look. "Well, here's your answer. No wolf can see, feel, or hear us, so you'll get to see just what happened to you when Scarr came."

Honor said nothing while they ran through the undergrowth, a light shrouding behind and around them. Into the Territory he went, but it looked a little different.

It was sunny, and beautiful, and there were flowers and shiny undergrowth everywhere. The wolves walked in pairs or alone, their dark pelts glistening in the sun. He looked and saw Pebble, a lot younger than she was now.

"This is four years ago, when you were a small pup. Everything is perfectly fine until Scarr shows up," whispered Pebble in his ears, the real Pebble. He nodded.

He saw past Pebble's jaw moving, as if she was talking. Yes, she was talking. She was bent over three small Darkness pups, and they were the most adorable things Honor had ever seen. And one of them had been him. He looked for the blade, just a tiny glimpse, but the pup that was him was too far away, and he knew it was only a small sharp sliver.

He finally caught some of past Pebble's words. "I'm sorry, my pup. I still don't have a good name for you yet." Her eyes looked sincere when she stared down at the pup of Honor.

Honor felt a whine rise in his throat. He wondered how he had felt right then, as a small pup, his siblings having names but his mother not finding one for him. He watched him stretch to his small paws and wag his tail after a moment's silence.

He saw puppy Loyalty yip and follow him into the beautiful trees. "Don't go far!" past Pebble called. Honor thought, Things were perfectly fine until Scarr came along. Every wolf was happy. Everything was beautiful. Now it's not the same even though I came back.

He shook away the second whine and watched intently. He waited for so much as a howl, a whimper, a yelp, a yip. But he heard nothing. Did Pebble really know what she was doing? What if this was a false past before their eyes, not exactly what it was supposed to be?

He saw more wolves pass by, and once a couple wolves stepped right through them. Honor shuddered. Stormers, that's creepy. I hope this will be over soon.

Then a terrible sound filled the sky and the beautiful Territory. It was the sound of a crying pup. Honor perked an ear and before Pebble could say anything, he leaped ahead and began to run.

A horrible, cruel wolf laugh split the air as well and other wolves ran too, as if they had seen Honor do this. They darted past the beautiful undergrowth and past Pebble leaped off her stone.

"Loyalty, Razor, and my pup!" past Pebble howled. Her Darkness howl saddened Honor's heart. Here it is. I'm about to see when I am taken away from my destiny, for all these years... He watched the pups, huddled together under the shade of an oak tree. Several vicious wolves surrounded them, looking just a bit younger than Honor remembered them.

He recognized Scarr immediately, four years younger. She looked almost no different: she still had several scars along her body and her teeth were gnashed. Her fur was up and she had the same cruel look in her eyes. Well, I killed her. There's no more Scarr for me, thought Honor grimly.

"You're mine, pup!" she barked. "I heard you're the heir and I want that power for myself!" The pup of Honor looked extremely confused and terrified. Honor gritted his teeth. I didn't know anything about this. But now I really know she lied.

Past Pebble stepped protectively in front of her pups. "I won't let you take any of them!" she growled. "Find a mate and have your own pups!"

Scarr laughed. "Ah ha, ha, but then none would be the heir. So hand over that one!" She pointed her nose toward the unnamed pup. Past Pebble growled. "Or I'll make you."

Honor held his breath. Scarr looked into past Pebble's eyes. Past Pebble looked into Scarr's. Scarr gave a shrill howl and jumped, raking her claws down past Pebble's back. Past Pebble cried out and doubled backwards. Pup Loyalty and pup Razor ran off and huddled on top of past Pebble's rock.

However, the unnamed pup did not move. Pup Honor seemed glued to the spot, shaking all over. "Mean Prowler!" he squeaked. "Mean Prowler!"

Honor's heart saddened again. This was the moment. The other wolves around him looked as if they did not know what to do. Scarr had a wicked grin across her muzzle. "Come with me, pup, and I'll name you. I'll make you powerful! I'll make you the best Darkness wolf in the wild!"

Honor clenched his teeth. Liar! Pup Honor still trembled, and Scarr gave a growl of frustration and grabbed him by his scruff. Pup Honor thrashed and gave puppy howls, and past Pebble got to her paws shakily and howled, "NO!"

Her howl echoed as well, and Honor's own body began to shake. Scarr and the other wolves had run off with the other Darkness wolves howling shrilly. Honor could not stop the shaking, and he whined. "I never want to see this again," he said shakily.

HONOR'S EYES opened and his breathing came back. He was no longer shaking. But he was still scared. Had this all really happened to him and he just hadn't remembered? Tucking his tail, he followed the other Darkness wolves to the center, where Pebble had just woken up too. She shared a special look with him.

Honor ducked, scrambling onto her rock and huddling against her, feeling like a scared little pup again, like he'd been when Scarr had taken him. Loyalty and Razor seemed to know what was going on—apparently they had both been shown—and licked him with understanding.

"All wolves, I have shown my sons and daughter what really happened four years ago. Just last night I showed Honor what happened. His reaction was just how I thought it'd be. I understand, Honor—but I know you wanted to know."

Honor just nodded. He searched the group for Night and Cobra, and saw them in the middle, giving him sympathetic looks. "Thank you for your understanding, pack. And Night and Cobra, I'll tell you all about it later."

Pebble sat on her haunches, head rose. "But first, Honor, I've wondered what it was like when you were raised by Scarr. Would you care to tell us some things?"

Honor gulped. Why would he ever share the fact that he had killed Prowler Pistol, mistreated Prowler Night, and all the other vicious things he'd done? *I wasn't a good Darkness wolf then. They'll understand. Scarr is cruel, and that I couldn't help it. And it's all in the past...right?*

And he opened his jaws to begin.

CHAPTER 4

"IT WAS terrible," he started. "I mean, not when I was made Best Wolf. It happened when I saved Prowler Pistol's life; I was around no one but Prowlers when I grew up. Scarr was pleased to not lose her Best Fighter she had raised as an orphan." He gritted his teeth.

"I was so cruel. Scarr made me like her, like a Stormer. No offence, Cobra. And I killed off several wolves and mistreated even my own pack members under her command. I grew up believing her stupid orphan pup lie. And she made me fight and kill her 'useless wolves' in her stadium. Soon I had to kill Prowler Pistol, who had been a traitor in the pack."

He heard wolves gasping so he closed his eyes. "But when Prowler Night came along, I started to see something in him I'd never known or seen before. When Scarr punished me—even though I had been her temporary mate—thinking I'd let him escape, I ran off and found him and Cobra. Night changed me forever. No wolf knows how, but he did." Night beamed and Honor looked around at every wolf.

"At first, I was anxious to meet my own kind. I thought, 'What would they think of me?' But then we heard about your long-lost heir from Night's pup pack. I knew the time had come for me to meet you.

And finding out I was the heir—that was even better." Honor grinned. "And I will make sure nothing overtakes me and only use my blade and power to protect you all."

The other wolves gave meek smiles. *I know. It's hard to believe I was that way, and the way Scarr was. It's hard, and I understand.* Honor sneaked a glance at Loyalty, who shuffled backwards as if she were shy.

For the first time, he was loved. Scarr had never shown any love to him, even when they had planned to be mates. Honor still could not fathom why he had wanted to be her mate in the first place.

Honor raised his head high. "Now that the morning meeting is over, we can go hunting and all that." He sounded lame. "Pebble, Mother, should I call them?" he asked. His mother nodded.

"I think we should go in groups," he announced, "or pairs. Then each pair can bring back the prey they got. Like...Prowler Night and Stormer Cobra could go together." He gestured toward them.

"Loyalty and Razor could, too," he said. "And—"

"Is every wolf going to hunt?" Night asked, but not rudely.

Honor sighed. "No. I want the wolves I've chosen to come off to the right and when I finish the not-chosen wolves will do whatever Alpha asks." He looked around the group and found different wolves that would fit together. There was one more to choose...for himself.

Pebble spoke up. "I think your partner should be Midnight," she suggested, pointing her nose at a black female wolf. "She's a lot like you." Honor looked at Midnight and Midnight looked back.

"Okay," said Honor, "I'll take her. Every other wolf, you know what to do." He bounded from the rock toward Midnight, who was extremely surprised. "Ready to go?" he said. "I'm Prince Honor."

Midnight nodded. "Yes. I knew that. I'm ready." She looked just as desperate as Honor to get hunting. Honor knew that much because it had been so long since he had hunted—ever since leaving Scarr's, he hadn't had to.

They watched the other pairs of wolves run off in different directions. Honor gestured silently toward one angle of the forest and they started there, prowling low and turning their noses. "I smell something," said Midnight, "and it's strong. I think the prey just came through here."

Honor agreed. "We have to catch that prey. If it thinks it can sneak around then it is *wrong*! We'll find it and maybe follow it to its den and catch ten of its kind if we have to!" His voice belted with excitement.

Midnight laughed. "You are *stubborn*," she said, "but that's the way I want you to be. I think you'd make a good King Wolf."

Honor stiffened. He froze. Had she just said that? *Maybe she doesn't care about the vicious self I had been. Maybe she's letting it go and accepting me for who I am. I like that.* He licked her silently in thanks and sniffed the air again.

The trail was still fresh, thank the wolf spirits. However, it seemed to go in odd directions. The prey most likely had tried to confuse them by twisting and turning and darting between trees and logs.

"Let's follow the trail wherever we need to," he said. Midnight nodded. She had obviously found the odd-going trail as well. Honor kept his body low and carefully put each paw down. Turning around a tree, he found the scent again.

He felt Midnight's fur brush against him so he knew she was behind him. He stalked around another tree and over a log. The scent grew the slightest bit stronger so they were headed in the right direction.

There had to be more than one of this prey. If they brought back enough then the pack would actually trust him as the heir, even if Darkness wolves couldn't trust Aghast one thousand years ago.

Midnight leaped ahead of him so he trailed her now. He felt a little awkward around her now that he thought of it. Did she actually...like him? He shuddered. *No. She just respects me.*

The trail got clearer and clearer so now up ahead they saw the small den inside an oak tree. They slowed down and got into their low, prowling position. "If we want to catch this prey, we have to stay low," said Honor.

Circling around the den, Honor pushed his ear against the trunk and listened: chattering. He sniffed. Squirrels! He looked around at Midnight's face and she looked back in realization. "There are a whole lot in there, at least eight," he whispered. "We *have* to catch them."

So they continued to prowl until the chattering stopped. Midnight motioned with a cocked ear and Honor sprang, digging his muzzle into the den. Midnight circled him, ready to catch any escaped squirrels.

Honor emerged with two dead squirrels in his powerful jaws while two more skittered out for Midnight to catch. She crunched on them and Honor dug his muzzle back in. The other four squirrels were huddled against the back of the den, far out of reach.

The Darkness wolf snarled in frustration. Midnight had piled up the bodies of squirrels. "What do we do now?" she whispered. "That's not nearly enough to feed the pack."

"I know." Honor sighed. "But the others must have caught things too." He and Midnight turned to pick up the bodies and head back when a bolt of realization struck Honor. "Wait," he said. "I have an idea."

He crouched and peered into the den. The squirrels were in the same position. Giving Midnight a sidelong look, he unleashed his blade. Midnight gasped, realizing it too. In one quick motion, Honor slashed his tail into the den and heard cries. He looked back and saw the four other dead squirrels. He hid the blade again and used it to pull the bodies toward him.

Honor and Midnight, grins across their muzzles, carried the squirrels back toward where the pack was already gathering again. Pebble was curled up on her stone but perked her ears and saw them. She stood up.

Night and Cobra had already returned, and near them were two rabbits. They had ashamed faces as if to say "this was all we could catch." Some others had returned as well. Loyalty and Razor hadn't yet though.

When the pack had heard about Honor and Midnight's hunt, they all had shocked faces. "You used your blade? That was such a smart solution," Pebble said thoughtfully.

"That's amazing!"

"Way to hunt, Prince Honor!"

Night and Cobra looked astounded and Honor smiled at them then back at the pack. He bowed his head at the praise. "Thank you, pack. I appreciate it. But let's also praise every other wolf's hunting."

"Like ours?" The voice had a slight sneer in it, and Loyalty stepped out with a quiet Razor by her side. "Although Razor chased toads almost the whole time!" she said, and glared at her half-brother. "But when we did the actual hunting, he…helped."

They moved to reveal two dead does. Gasps ran through the pack. "H-How did you do that? All on your own?" breathed Pebble, jumping down for a closer look. The pack separated to let her through. "This plus everyone else's prey will last for two nights instead of one!"

Honor was speechless. That was *way* more than what he and Midnight had caught. It was more than *any* of the wolves had caught. And it had just been his sister and brother. He didn't like the look Loyalty gave him, as if to say "in your face."

At dinner, Honor could not eat. First, it hadn't been how dinner was in Scarr's pack. Second, he was still shocked. *How? Why? Were they trying to hunt as if this was a competition? It's about feeding the pack!*

And I swear I saw Loyalty look at me like that. Loyalty isn't like that. Why now? What's going on with her? I better ask her after dinner.

He finished a doe leg, however, and trotted to his sister's side. "Loyalty…nice catches today," he stammered. "I mean, I'd never be able to catch that much with just me and another wolf. But—"

"But how did we do it?" Loyalty said, in the slight sneering tone again. "It was easy. First, we followed the scent. Then we—I, found a strategy for us and we hunted them down. Then we—"

This time Honor interrupted her. "No. Why did you…? Never mind. I'm just…tired. I'll see you tomorrow. Again, good catches." He turned and thought, *awkward,* as he walked off. He also realized something.

Loyalty is jealous of me.

CHAPTER 5

"**W**HEN WILL I be King Wolf?" Honor asked Pebble that morning. He had always wondered when the time would come for every heir to become King Wolf.

"The year Aghast turned five was when he became King Wolf. I'm assuming it's the same for you, too," replied Pebble, looking to the beautiful sky. "But Aghast was not the best King Wolf. The Darkness wolves have always worried for the next heir. I can tell the pack and every wolf that hears will be worried."

"But I *won't* be like King Aghast!" protested Honor. "I'm nothing like him! They may have doubted *him* but they don't have to doubt me!"

Pebble shook her head. "That isn't what I said, is it, Prince Honor? No, you will be a great King Wolf, just as Prowler Night has the potential for the Great Prowler."

Honor thought about this as Pebble asked, "Is there anything else on your mind?" He shook his head. He did not really want to tell her about what Loyalty was doing.

"What do you dearly want, straight from your heart?" he asked suddenly. He had always wanted to be home, with real Darkness wolves just like himself. But what did his Alpha, his mother want?

Pebble stopped to think. "What I dearly want, what I have wanted for many years," she said, "is for things to be beautiful again."

Honor let these words sink in. He looked around the Territory. It definitely did not look as beautiful as in his dream four years ago. The undergrowth had no flowers or shiny, dewy leaves. Instead, it was dark and frayed. The ground was also dark and the trees had grown tall and shady. The sunlight barely streamed in.

Looking at all of it saddened the Darkness wolf. Pebble was right. Things could be more beautiful again. But how could he help do it? It seemed like the forest had gotten gloomy since he had been stolen.

Spirits of wolves: please make the forest happy again. Or allow the Darkness wolves to get a new Territory. I want them to be happy just as Night was in his pack. And I want Loyalty to stop being jealous and be happy too.

HONOR DID not even go with the hunting. He didn't care about it right now. Without saying anything to Pebble, he crossed the undergrowth and peered around it. Every bit of it he could see was frayed and dark, like before. How could he change it?

Perhaps there were many problems in his pack, or in the Territory. Perhaps the forest hadn't realized he had come back. Honor thought hard, studying the landscapes and the nearly hidden sky.

Maybe there was a way. He was the heir, and he had to make all Darkness wolves happy. Whenever he became King Wolf, he would make sure of that. He could help out as just the heir first, though.

How can I help...?

He looked around him again and saw his sister stride up to him. "You're lucky to be the heir," she hissed, glancing at his bladed tail. "I would love to be one, but apparently *you're* too *special.*" Honor did not like the voice she was using.

Loyalty looked straight at him. He looked back, narrowing his eyes. She turned and strode back the way she had come, her tail lashing. Honor just stood there, blinking. What was wrong with Loyalty? This wasn't like his sister at all.

Honor returned to the undergrowth, but right now he was focused on Loyalty. *This is really not like her. I know she's a kind, brave wolf inside. She could do as a Prowler, maybe even the Great Prowler.* He stood there for a moment, thinking.

Then he heard something: a howl, then more howls. The Darkness howls split the air like lightning and Honor was forced to run back into the Territory. He heard other Darkness wolves' quick paws across the ground. Night and Cobra reached him first. "Did you howl?" Cobra rasped.

Honor shook his head worriedly. More Darkness wolves arrived, followed by Pebble. "What is going on?" Pebble shouted above the other Darkness wolves' clamoring.

The last of the pack came with thundering paws. Honor was horrified when he saw Razor. He was streaked with blood, all over his chest and muzzle. "I howled!" he choked. "There...there's..."

"Razor?" said Loyalty. "Say it!"

Razor huffed for breath and managed to say "Bear!" and fall over, blood seeping onto the ground. Honor growled. He had saved Prowler Pistol's life by fighting a bear. He could do it again. "Come on! In formation!" he called, and Pebble began to call out commands as well.

The pack obeyed while Razor staggered to his paws. Honor licked him as he passed and ran to the front of the pack. "I faced a bear before it killed Prowler Pistol! That's how I became Best Wolf! I can lead the formation!"

"Of course, Prince Honor," Pebble said, nodding. "Everyone, do what the heir tells you!" As soon as she said this, Honor snuck a glance at Loyalty. The Darkness wolf's jaw was set and her eyes were flashing with anger and jealousy.

At first, Honor was clueless on what to tell the pack. He got his mind off Loyalty and called, "Fight!" He jumped outward just as a large brown grizzly thundered and crashed through the undergrowth. Its thundering steps shook the earth.

Things wouldn't be beautiful with the bear around, Honor realized. He narrowed his eyes. *Let's do this. I'll do it because I'm the heir and I will protect my pack and make things better again.* He made the first move while the pack ran forward.

He sliced his claws across the bear's leg and the bear yelped before thundering toward him. Honor took the right time to dodge and the other wolves, together, barreled into the brown bear. The bear was knocked off its feet and Honor gave a joyous laugh.

He saw Loyalty attack from behind and just barely dodge the bear's claw. *She's trying to prove that she's powerful too*, Honor thought as his claws went down the bear's other leg.

Pebble was barking orders. Stormer Cobra was tearing into the bear viciously with her curved claws. Razor was staggering and another wolf was telling him to stay back and rest. Other wolves were snapping and bleeding.

Honor tore back into the bear and sliced with his claws again. He watched some other wolves fall backward, tired or wounded. They were running out of power and the bear was still standing. Now it was only him, Night, Cobra, Pebble, Midnight, Loyalty, and few others.

He dodged while suffering a painful scratch down his backside. Loyalty, living up to her name, kept attacking from behind and on the sides. She barked and snapped, and Honor flinched when he saw a small scratch on her muzzle.

Honor hung back, panting for breath, and was about to sit down when, to his horror, the bear spun around and sliced a claw through Loyalty's hind leg.

An ear-piercing wolf scream from his sister made him leap into action, not even realizing what he was doing.

"Never hurt my sister again!" he bellowed into a howl. He unleashed his blade. A howling Loyalty widened her eyes. Pebble gaped. Honor slashed right across the bear's stomach and the bear cried out and thundered into the ground.

There was silence, but Loyalty had brought her howl down to a sheer whine. She fell over on her side, wheezing and whining. The pack trotted over and Pebble leaped right over. Honor still had his teeth clenched, he realized, and let go.

"No," said Pebble, widening her eyes. "Its claws…it cut way, way deep into that leg. Loyalty…"

Honor couldn't help the whine that rose from his throat. He held back a howl and watched his sister, whose eyes were wide with horror and pain. She kept thrashing and wheezing. Razor even staggered over, not nearly as wounded as she was, and gave a loud whine. "I really care about you, my sister," he cried, licking her.

Every wolf hung his or her head. Honor widened his own eyes. Were they just...giving up? Was Loyalty going to die? He watched the blood the seeped onto the ground or soaked into Loyalty's leg fur. She wheezed and looked at every wolf in surprise. "You're going to let me die?" she rasped.

"No," Pebble said, "but you are badly wounded. We'll have to look after you. You would have died if your brother had not been there for you." She looked gratefully at Honor.

Honor saw Loyalty strain her head as if in anger, teeth clenched, and eyes closed. Then she screamed, "Stop obsessing over my brother!" Every wolf went silent and Loyalty began wheezing out these words.

"Every wolf cares so much about *him* that I feel like no wolf cares about anyone else! It's *all you care about*, Mother, and I'm sick of it!" Loyalty managed to sit up. "It's always 'Yay, Prince Honor!' or 'We depend on you because you're the heir!' or 'You're so special that we don't even show others that they are too!'"

The wolves were still silent. Pebble opened her jaw to speak, eyes wide, but Loyalty gave a wheezing howl. "I'm done with all of you! Obviously all you care about is your *stupid heir*!" And with that, Honor's sister got to her feet, yelping on her bleeding leg, and ran, limping, into the forest.

T HINGS HAD been gloomy since Loyalty had run away, even when they had gotten to feast on the bear they had killed. Pebble had said gloomily that the bear would last for several dinners.

Honor was sadder than any wolf. Was that really how his sister felt about it? Why couldn't she have said so at the start? *She's kind of right. They do pay more attention to me than anything, and she feels like she and other wolves are forgotten.*

He watched the wolves, their wounds no longer bleeding, eat the bear meat as slowly as he was. There was nothing they could do now that Loyalty was gone. But her leg would only get worse if she kept running on it and didn't get any rest.

And besides, where was Loyalty going to go as a Lone Darkness wolf? She could run into all sorts of dangers: Stormers, more bears, coyotes, storms, or lack of prey. There could be anything out there that would get her killed.

But maybe she'd come back. Maybe she'd change her mind and things could actually be *better*. The place would be spacey and beautiful again, just like Pebble wanted. And it was something Honor wanted too.

He decided something right then and there, something he felt like he *needed* to do, for he would be King Wolf someday.

I have to find Loyalty.

CHAPTER 6

"YOU WANT to find Loyalty?" breathed Night. "But it's dangerous, and not only will Loyalty be dying out there, you could be too! There could be more bears! There—"

Honor clasped a paw over Night's jaw and the Prowler looked at him with wide eyes and a muffled growl. He shook himself away and Honor spoke. "I know. But that's my own *sister* out there, and she could be killed." He looked upon the crowd of wolves. "I have to do it. And when I bring her back, things will be beautiful and peaceful again."

Pebble took a paw-step forward. "My son is right. We have to find my daughter, his sister. I will send out a search party every night, and—"

"No," said Honor, "*I* will find her. My return caused all this. I'm the one you're obsessing over. I started this, so I will find her and make things right. Loyalty will feel that she's special too and come back to us."

"Are you sure?" Pebble asked nervously. "I don't want you killed. And I certainly don't want more than one wolf to be missing. Please, Prince Honor—"

"It will soon be *King* Honor, so that should tell you that it's up to me to help my tribe, and every wolf in it," Honor interjected. "Let me go, Mother. Visit my dreams if possible and I'll tell you everything."

Pebble sighed. "Very well," she whispered. "Be careful, Honor. And most importantly, find your sister. Good luck." The other wolves nodded and Honor saw Night's face fall.

"Stop worrying, wolves! Geez, when I become King Wolf I'm going to stop you all from being such worrywarts!" Honor grinned, raising his head high. "I promise I will return. I have to find Loyalty, right? She and I will both be all right."

And his eyes narrowed. "And remember...treat the Stormer like one of you!" The wolves' faces gradually grew more surprised. Honor laughed. "Your faces," he chuckled. "Alright, I'll return soon, and things will be okay again!"

"I promise!" he called over his shoulder as he dashed for the forest.

A FTER HOURS of running, Honor was ready to rest. His tail thumping the hard ground, he slept inside a den he took half an hour to dig. His chest rose and fell, and before he knew it, he was asleep.

He stretched and yawned at early light. If he wanted to get a good head start on finding Loyalty, he needed to make a quick catch of prey and move on. Turning his body in circles, he took time to sniff all the mingling scents of the airy forest.

Remember, Honor. You need to talk to Loyalty as soon as you find her. You need to tell her you aren't that special, and that she's just as special. Honor felt a twinge. All his life he had thought he was useless, except for working for Scarr. But now he felt loved and respected. Maybe it had pulled him so close that now other wolves were being forgotten.

The way it really should be was that wolves needed to be treated equally. He needed to make sure that everything became beautiful, and that every wolf was a part of this when he became King Wolf. He promised himself that things *would* get better, no matter how much he doubted it.

As he stalked down a squirrel and crunched it between his jaws, he began running again and thinking hard. *I can't doubt it. Things will be fine back at the Territory, and Loyalty will live...right?*

The valleys and hills he passed were not familiar, which meant he had been careless and gone in a direction from the Territory that he, Night, and Cobra had never passed. *You're so stupid for being the heir, Honor. Maybe Scarr's stupidity rubbed off on me.*

Before he knew it, sunset had arrived again. As the sun was nearly disappeared beyond the horizon, Honor looked up and saw pinks and yellows and blues in several shades together under a rising moon. The sky had never looked so beautiful before, and no clouds streaked it like usual.

The night sky is beautiful, and so is the coming dawn. But I've never seen this before. Things will be better...in both the pack and the wild. The Great Prowler may come someday, and that will be Night. He will help save the wild. And I, who will soon be King Wolf, can take part in that and help Darkness wolves as well. I know everything will be okay, down in the bottom of my heart. My heart could never be changed, not even by Scarr.

He felt his tail wag like it seldom did. He felt a rush of joy through his body and he picked up speed while watching the beautiful colors of the sunset and moonrise. He also knew in his heart that he'd find a surviving Loyalty, wounded but alive.

Later, he didn't realize how tired he was. He also hadn't thought of Loyalty getting *this* far away from the pack. *Even on a wounded leg! I'm impressed, Loyalty. I'm also annoyed.* Honor yawned, and he knew his white teeth were glistening in the moonlight. *Oh, well. I'll have to find her tomorrow.* He turned his sleeping circles and curled up, tail close to his flank in warmth.

Please find a way to come in my dream again, Mother, he prayed before dozing off.

S*HE DID. At least, he thought she did. Honor squinted and saw paw-steps growing nearer. Here came Pebble, but was she real? Was she from the real world? He tried swiping a paw at her but found he could not move. He tried to howl but it made him choke. He squinted again, suddenly having to rasp for breath, and saw that this wolf was not Pebble.*

119

It was Scarr.

Honor gasped but it came out as a choking croak. He rasped some more and he watched her stop, a wicked grin splitting her muzzle. "If it isn't the Darkness wolf, the heir to the useless King Wolf throne," she spat, tail lashing madly. "Honor, you are nothing. Face it. Over time your power will overtake you."

"Hush up!" Honor gave a choking howl. "You're dead. I killed you. Why are you talking?"

"Oh, I'm not dead," laughed Scarr, narrowing her eyes. "My body may be dead, but I'm still alive in your soul, your mind. Just face it, Darkness wolf. You have no purpose. You have no powers. You're just nothing."

Honor became dizzy, his vision blurring. He tried to turn and run but his body still would not move. He choked another howl as Scarr laughed wickedly and lunged toward him, slashing her claws and tearing into him...

HONOR SNAPPED awake, still rasping like in his dream. His tail was gradually tucking and his heart was racing faster than he could ever fathom. What did that dream mean? Was it just a nightmare or was it a vision?

Please be a pup nightmare, he prayed, closing his eyes. *Scarr is gone. And I don't want any more killing happening. I've already killed so many wolves as an assassin.*

Honor took deep breaths before walking on through the still forest. The white moon still hung overhead and he knew it would be hours until morning. *Should I go back to sleep, or keep walking until dawn?* He knew that he did *not* want to have another nightmare like that one.

He walked for a while, debating and taking breaths—his heart was still racing from waking up. He was scared and alone. Why had he left in the first place? Then he became firm with himself. *You said you'd find Loyalty. You're loyal and you will do anything you can to find your sister, won't you?*

He told himself again that he'd find Loyalty and bring her back, and not to doubt it. He decided then and there that he needed sleep before getting on the move again. It didn't matter if Loyalty got farther away—her scents may still linger at dawn. He turned his circles again and sighed. *Please don't have another nightmare. And Mother, please find a way into my dream.*

And he fell asleep once more.

CHAPTER 7

*T*HIS TIME, *he was sure this wasn't a nightmare. There was bright sunlight all around him and he saw Loyalty, alive and well. She looked like a pup, bounding and leaping in circles with excited wolf yips. Things seemed...perfect here. He saw other Darkness wolves too, having friendly conversations or bathing in the sun.*

He saw a warp in front of him, creating the mass of a Darkness wolf he knew. Pebble stepped toward him and he felt her fur brush his. "Don't worry: it's me, in the real world. I found a way in. How has the search been? Did you find Loyalty?"

Honor didn't want to disappoint his mother, but he shook his head sadly. "But I have a feeling I'm almost there. She can't have gone far with the injury she has. I'll find her and bring her back as fast as possible. Make that faster than possible."

Pebble laughed even though her eyes were full of disappointment. "You have the same stubborn streak I wanted you to have," she repeated. She nuzzled him and he enjoyed her warm fur against his. "Don't worry, my son. Things will be okay back at the pack. But the Prowler has been pacing around muttering words of worry."

Honor laughed too. "I hope things are okay. I mean, things are okay with me too. Even being gone for a day or two is sad for me. I only just arrived to the Territory, and I feel like I belong. Some empty space inside me was filled up when I got to meet you all, to know I really had family, and a purpose."

Pebble smiled. "And it's a good one," she said. "Every wolf believes you've changed, and respects you. You were always special, Honor, and always will be. Neither your sister nor that menace Scarr can contradict that."

Honor took a moment to enjoy the silence and nuzzled closer to his mother. "But...what will I say when I find Loyalty?" he whispered, cutting the silence. "What will she say?"

"Those words I cannot make up for you. The words you say should come straight from your heart. Show her that you love her, and that she's special too, no matter what. Show her you're nothing like King Aghast."

Honor breathed in those words and stood up straight, nodding. "Thanks, Mother. Nothing will happen to me with Darkness wolves on my side! I will never become like Aghast. I will return soon, Mother!"

He felt like he was being pulled away from his mother, and knew he was waking up from the depths of dreaming. He let it happen.

H ONOR OPENED his eyes. He gave a sharp yelp when bright sunlight caught them. He scrambled to his paws and felt calmer than he had the night before. He stretched and yawned, padding over to a stream to lap water.

Jerking his head upright, he realized what he'd forgotten to ask his mother: *did she think the dream meant anything, like in the future or something in the past?* He began to think about this as he managed to grab two sloppy fish from the stream.

He crunched up the fish. Even though it didn't taste the best and he wrinkled his muzzle in disgust, it was the only thing he had to eat. He licked the remains off his chops and lapped some more before beginning to run across the sunlit glade.

Maybe our pack does find a new Territory after all. Or maybe it was a dream that gets wolves' hopes up and ends up disappointing them and totally crushing their hearts! Honor growled with frustration through clenched teeth. Not only had he not found Loyalty yet but he also was confused by everything that had happened.

No, Honor. Think about the important things for now. You have to find Loyalty. That's top priority.

He shook himself so he'd snap to his senses and sniffed the ground and around him. The smells of Loyalty weren't faint here so he knew he was getting much closer than when he'd left the Territory.

"Loyalty!" he howled to the sun. "Where are you, my sister? I'm so sorry about what happened! I didn't mean for it to happen! It's all my fault and I came to find you and bring you back! You're special too! No heir obsession could change that!" He thought all this yelling would cause him to lose his voice, but he managed to repeat these words in case Loyalty could hear.

He heard something faint in the distance and got into his prowling position. He took deep whooshing breaths and picked up his pace a little. If it really was Loyalty he heard, he'd make sure not to make a random appearance and scare her out of her fur.

"Come on," he muttered hopefully.

He heard the sounds again, but he could not make out what they were. Again he quickened his pace. If his sister was in danger, he didn't know what he'd do.

Then he knew what he was hearing: yips and howls. And they weren't from wolves. They were from coyotes. He had heard that coyotes—for some super strange reason—were always stalking wherever they could find Darkness wolves. Loyalty had told him on his first day with the pack about this and how she could easily take one of those "not-wolves" down.

If they're stalking her, it shouldn't be a problem, if she's that strong. But that may only be when she isn't wounded... They could kill her! Before he could think any more, Honor ran so fast that his paws barely hit the ground.

He swerved around a tree and didn't notice when rocks cut into his paw pads. "Loyalty!" he howled again, ears erect. He heard the coyotes much more clearly now, and he was guaranteed that was what they were.

He saw a flash of fur and a blur of a tail. He heard more yipping and yelping. And he saw two small coyotes leap out at him, snapping their vicious teeth. Without even thinking, he whipped around and slashed his blade at them, causing them to cry out. They fell over, not dead but wounded, and he ran right past them.

"Loyalty!" he panted. "I'm coming!"

He knocked aside two more coyotes with his muscular shoulders and gnashed his teeth at others. He saw more flashes of fur ahead and kept going. Immediately he saw a Darkness wolf pelt and knew it was his sister. "Loyalty!" he said.

He saw the wolf's head turn around and gasp. "Honor!" she rasped. Her voice was almost a wheezing whisper and she yelped even though the coyote in front of her had barely nipped her shoulder. *She must be in such pain from her leg that even the slightest attack hurts.* Honor flinched.

"I'm going to help! Just stay there!" he called. Loyalty looked back at him with eyes that said "I heard your howls, and I'm so sorry" and he knew that was what she was trying to tell him. She painfully sat on her haunches and winced.

Honor ran rapidly toward the coyote attacking Loyalty and quickly slashed across its front. It yowled and he saw it fall back, only to go sliding down the hill and crashing into the glistening lake. More were running toward him, yipping, and he closed his teeth around one scruff and flung it toward the lake. Others he knocked aside to send them tumbling.

Loyalty was watching in awe, as if she hadn't expected Honor to be this fierce and strong. *What do you expect?* Honor thought with surprise. *I was raised and trained by a mad killer wolf. Of course I can fight.*

He flung other small coyotes in quick motions. There had to be at least twenty coyotes. However, Honor felt everlasting strength as he flung, bit, tackled, and slashed each not-wolf. Some crashed into the lake and drowned, and some lay, groaning, on the ground with wounds on their sides. Others had died immediately after being attacked.

Once it was all over Loyalty was speechless, and Honor stood there, tongue lolling and panting rapidly. Blood from a cut on his ear was seeping down the side of his muzzle, and his claws were stained with fur and blood. He turned to his sister. "Are you all right?" he huffed.

"I-I think so," wheezed Loyalty at last, but then she whined and collapsed on her side. Honor nosed her worriedly and she whispered, "I don't think I'm fine."

Honor pulled himself up. "Don't worry. I'm here, so you'll be protected. I'll help you when we find our way back."

Loyalty ducked her head, and Honor knew she was ashamed. "I'm so sorry," she whispered, and Honor could swear he saw wolf tears gather in her eyes and one drip to the ground below them. "I didn't mean all those things I said. And I shouldn't have acted like a foolish pup, acting all jealous just because you were here. I was actually the one that wanted the wolves to welcome you with open paws."

Honor stayed quiet, because he knew there'd be more.

"I was so excited to know that my own brother had such an amazing destiny, that I made sure we were ready for your return someday. And return you did, but I never knew I'd act this way when I was so excited before. I'm so, so sorry, my brother." Her head did not come up, and her eyes did not meet Honor's.

Honor stood there for a moment, and he realized he was clueless on what to say, just like in his dream. Pebble's words to him ran through his head: *Those words I cannot make up for you. The words you say should come straight from your heart. Show her that you love her, and that she's special too, no matter what. Show her you're nothing like King Aghast.*

Straight from my heart, Honor thought, and right then and there he knew just what to say. "I know what you mean, my sister. And no matter what, I'll always love you. Heir or not, you're still a good and special wolf to me. You're the best sister I could ever ask for, and you have a kind heart. I love you, and always will, no matter what you say or do." He didn't care how sappy he sounded; he had meant everything he said.

Loyalty lifted her head, and the wolf tears stopped coming. She looked at him with something Honor loved to see on another wolf: happiness.

And he had made it happen. He knew now that he was forever changed.

CHAPTER 8

"**H**OW EXACTLY will we get back at camp?" Loyalty asked as the wheezing tone escaped her jaws. She winced and Honor realized that it hurt her just to speak.

"I'm strong. I can help you walk. I don't care how long it takes if we walk. I just want you to be all right," said Honor, inspecting her leg closely. He shook his head slowly. "Loyalty, it really was a bad idea to run away. And not just because of your stubbornness, but because you've damaged that leg a whole lot on your way."

Loyalty winced again. "You think? It's kind of obvious." He heard the small whine from her throat. It must hurt a lot, he thought.

"On a scale of one to ten, what's the pain?" he inquired, hoping it wasn't too bad.

Loyalty flinched, her neck bristling. "Ten," she said. "I'm sorry, but I'm not sure I'll be able to walk even with your help. You said it's damaged and I believe you, but I think it might be *too* damaged for me to move anywhere."

"Don't worry. On the way, we'll find some wolves to help you first," Honor promised. "Then we'll take the rest of the way home. We'll find a wolf that knows what he is doing and knows a thing or two about your injury."

His tail lashed and he looked sincerely into Loyalty's eyes to show he truly promised. But instead of looking back, Loyalty gasped and threw her front paws over her head. "Your tail," she whispered.

"What?" At first, Honor thought this was some sort of joke. But then he turned and saw the blade on his tail. Had it grown *bigger*? "What happened?" he stuttered, heart beginning to pound. This must be bad news.

"I don't know," whispered Loyalty, uncovering her face. "We really need to get back, more than ever, so that we find out what's going on." She began to stagger to her feet, wincing, but Honor tried not to flinch when she let out a sharp yelp, collapsing back on her side.

"It *is* way too damaged," he said worriedly. "It's still bleeding badly, which means you lost a lot of blood. The slash is deep and I think your leg has lost its feeling. Oh, oh, what do I do?" This time he covered his own head with his paws, feeling lost like he never had.

Loyalty winced. "I think I can walk a bit as long as you help me, though. Wasn't that your plan?" She looked at him and he opened his eyes to look back. He nodded.

"I can't lose hope," he said aloud, getting to his paws. He walked over, grinning, to help Loyalty to her own feet, her wounded leg hanging in the air and limp. "Let's go."

The rate they were going, it would take several weeks to get home, a journey that had only taken about three days for Honor. However, he was patient and helped Loyalty along as they passed several trees and found faint wolf scents.

If they could find a nearby pack, that would be great, thought Honor. Loyalty needed care and he was almost exhausted from the coyote fight. He told himself that it was worth it because he had not lost his sister and they could return safely back in Darkness Territory.

Oh, and don't forget the blade mystery. Did this happen with King Aghast? What will happen to me this way? How did my blade grow? So many questions unanswered!

"Are you okay, Loyalty?" he would ask every few moments and she would wince or nod. He sighed with relief and felt a new hope that his sister would live even if she was losing a lot of blood. Help would come soon as long as they kept going.

Honor thought he might die of thirst and fatigue when they stopped an hour later. Lolling his tongue tiredly, he panted, "I'll catch some food for us and we'll both get a drink. Let's sleep then and get back on our way."

Loyalty winced. "Do you think I won't be dead by then?" There was a slight smile across her muzzle and Honor shoved her playfully. She laughed.

Hang in there, little sister. I'll make sure you don't die. Your leg will be okay. Just hang in there. I'll help you. Honor ran off to find prey and managed to catch a couple squirrels for them. Loyalty crunched hers and it looked like it took effort.

Then she lay on her side and gave a shrill whine. "I'm too weak, and it hurts to do anything. Just go without me, Honor, and become King Wolf, then get me."

"No!" Honor cried. "I'm not going to leave you here. I'm going to get you back because that's who I am. I'm not the vicious and cruel Honor I once was." And this time, he believed it himself. "Now I'm about to be King Wolf, and help many wolves. I changed. And I would never leave my little sister to die, who has done so much to prepare for my return." He helped her to her feet and she whispered a "thank you."

Honor smiled as they hurried toward the creek for water, feeling his own heart swell up at his words. *I think I knew just what to say all along. Loyalty forgives me. I forgive her. And every word I said came from my heart.*

Loyalty collapsed after their drink, whining and licking her bloodied leg. Honor grew more worried, and erasing his thoughts, he examined the wound. The gash sure was deep in that leg. He didn't even want to know how it'd feel, or what Loyalty's reaction would be if he touched it. He shook himself and began licking it, Loyalty still whining.

"Don't worry, little sister," he whispered in Loyalty's ear. "Just hang in there. We should be there in a couple days. I'll be able to show that I can survive out here, and so can you."

Loyalty licked him back and he felt the warmth of her tongue on his muzzle. He lay down right next to her and felt her body was shivering.

So he curled up close without hurting her and her body began to calm down.

He kept licking her until she fell asleep, her tail thumping the ground. For a moment he lied there, watching the steady rising and falling of her chest and her tail. Then he laid his head on his paws and fell asleep.

"**W**HERE IS *Loyalty?" A voice cut the air and Honor squinted ahead. Sure enough, it was Pebble, who had found a way into his dream again.*

"I found her. She's sorry, and I forgave her. I'm sorry, and she forgave me. It's all okay, except she's lost a lot of blood and will need extra care. We'll try to find a pack to assist and then move on. And Mother...my blade...it got bigger. What does that mean?"

Pebble stopped dead. "Bigger?"

Honor nodded, all his worries rushing back into his head.

"Then you'll have to be careful. Even I, a Darkness wolf, don't understand why. I know it happened to Aghast, but I have no idea what it means."

Aghast, *Honor thought with horror.* No. I can't be becoming like King Aghast. I *can't* be. No. No. No... *He saw Pebble fade away with a confused howl and he felt himself being pulled back again. Instead of letting it take him back to the real world, he panicked and thrashed against it, thinking* Aghast, Aghast, Aghast...

Honor was still thrashing when he opened his eyes. The forest was quiet, and it was still daylight. He didn't feel tired anymore, which was the upside, but he definitely didn't want to go back to sleep.

Loyalty was still sleeping peacefully and he decided to let her. He went to hunt and brought back a measly rabbit for them to share. As he was lapping at the creek, he was deep in worried thought.

I'm nothing like King Aghast. Yet the same thing that happened to him is happening to me. I don't want to be like him! I don't want more darkness to come because of me. I can't let my heart change yet again, back to the old times.

He thought he would howl as he finished his drink and was padding back toward Loyalty. She was already eating part of the rabbit, thumping her tail. She looked at him and gave a wolf shrug. He laughed and they finished the rabbit.

He helped Loyalty get her own drink and they both sat there for a moment, licking their dripping chops. Loyalty opened her jaw but then Honor stiffened. "Do you smell that?" he growled, his nostrils flaring.

The smell was familiar, one he hated. It wasn't coyotes, it wasn't an earthquake. It smelled like Scarr's former pack. And it was coming this way.

"Hide!" he cried, but found he was too loud. He saw vicious wolves creep out from the shadows, surrounding him and Loyalty. He shrank back.

"Well, if it isn't the Best Wolf," sneered a voice. Honor saw another wolf step out through the middle. Had they chosen a new leader? "Oh, the traitor, that's all. The one who killed our leader!" he barked. The other wolves howled in agreement.

Honor tried not to show his fear. "Yes, I killed her, only because she was trying to kill my *destiny*. I ran away and was changed. It's as simple as that." His muzzle twisted with fierceness. "And my sister is wounded. I'm trying to get her home. We'll go right by."

"Oh, I don't think so, Darkness wolf. As the new leader of our pack by the name of Prowler Stinger, I order that you two should be held captive again. Prepare for a repeat of your puppyhood, traitor." The leader gave a wicked grin and the wolves closed in.

"My sister is wounded!" shouted Honor with rage. "I have to get her home!"

"Oh, we'll treat her," Stinger said, the grin not leaving his muzzle. "And we'll decide what to do with you after you killed my one sibling." Honor's eyes widened. *Scarr was his sister. He must have been her next Best Wolf and so he took her place when she died. He's her brother!*

With a dismissive flick of his tail, Stinger turned and strode off with two wolves by his sides. The other wolves wrapped chains around Honor and Loyalty, escorting Loyalty rather gently. Honor growled through clenched teeth.

Apparently this will be our stop.

CHAPTER 9

HONOR FINALLY found the courage to open his eyes and look around him. Sure enough, the same landscape he'd always known was there. *Great! I'm back right where I started. Thanks, spirits of wolves,* he thought grimly.

They were in the same cavern where he'd met Scarr for meetings or personal conversations, especially when they had been *almost* mates. Honor shuddered, and still did not know why he'd wanted to be that menace's mate.

Prowler Stinger stepped up from a high stone. "Welcome to the Main Cavern," he said, raising his head high. Honor growled. Around them were the same wolves that had escorted them there, in line like they usually were. They didn't look like the same howling wolves in the Territory.

Honor looked next to him and saw Loyalty, collapsed and writhing in pain. He swore he saw her bloodied leg thrashing while the rest of the body was barely moving. *The wound got worse. I have to get her help or else she might not make it...*

He didn't have time to deal with these stupid wolves that he'd thought was his pack all his life until now. He gnashed his teeth and shouted, "Don't you see this?!" He pointed to Loyalty with his nose and Stinger snorted, making Honor want to bite his neck.

"Yes, I see it," the new leader said almost impatiently. "And she'll get help. But first, I have to deal with this...*traitor. Which would be you*," he growled.

Honor growled back. "I had to. She was trying to ruin my destiny. She was ruining my *life*. I had reason to—"

"Not listening!" howled Stinger. "Hush up because I'm not listening!" Honor muttered "Smart aleck" under his breath and lashed his tail.

Loyalty had not spoken, only writhed. Now she opened her jaw. "Leave him alone," she growled. "Scarr was trying to use him—the *heir*—for herself. Honor killed her for a reason, and if you say *anything* else to him, *anything*, I will kill *you*!"

"Ha, try," snorted Stinger. "See what it does to you. Because I'm Scarr's *brother*! And you are about to die!"

"She will *not* die!" Honor snarled, and lunged for the Prowler's throat. Instead, strong force that pulled him back by his neck. He hacked and choked and found it was a chain they'd bound his neck with.

He looked over and saw Loyalty with her neck bound too, and saw that both their chains were tethered to the same post. He tried to run to break the chains but instead he felt the choking force again and staggered.

"There's no escaping," said Stinger with another wicked grin. "I'll see what I'll do with you two." He began to walk out of the cavern, with several wolves following.

"Hey! I thought you were going to help Loyalty!" Honor shouted with rage. Stinger turned, his muzzle innocently twisted.

"Oh, that. Well, we'll see," he called, trotting away. "Prowlers Bolt and Echinoderm, stay and guard the prisoners. Meanwhile, I'll go get a good sleep." The two wolves left behind bowed their heads and each came to rest near Honor and Loyalty. The Darkness wolves exchanged glances that said "there really is no escaping."

Honor just lay there with the chain around his neck that would surely strangle him if he kept moving. *Loyalty looks extremely pained. That Second Scarr is a big filthy liar! For Prowlers, these wolves aren't very kind or caring...* He was lost in thought and kept glancing over to a whining Loyalty. *She needs help, and we may not escape. She could die right here.*

He was so worried about his sister that he couldn't stand it. Why were these Prowlers so cruel, especially to him, who used to be their Best Wolf? *I'm no traitor. That's just their definition of me. I'm changed, and for a good reason.*

I am not the Honor I once was, and I'm proud of that.

Honor stood up slowly so that the guards wouldn't hear him. He glanced at Loyalty, then back at the guards. He narrowed his eyes. *I think I know what to do.*

He turned slowly around, raising his tail and unleashing his blade. With a quick, deadly motion, he slashed and heard the chains break with a chink. The guards turned around with a "What in the—" but before they could make their move, Honor made his, slashing across their muzzles.

Their wolf screams reverberated through the cavern as Honor quickly slashed Loyalty's chain open. She gave him a grateful look and they edged away while the guards shook their muzzles and yowled.

As fast as they could when they had exited the cavern, Loyalty and Honor raced across tunnels and other caves Honor had only been through once or twice. Loyalty had amazing speed even while her injured leg dangled in the air like a leaf swinging on a branch. They rushed past other surprised guards and found another tunnel to dart through.

"Stinger!" cried one wolf. "The prisoners are escaping!" shouted another.

Honor's heart raced just as his body did. "Hang in there, Loyalty. I know this place like the back of my paw. We're almost out." He hoped he was telling the truth, because he was slightly clueless.

They scrambled into one last tunnel before they found open air and open sky around them. The grass was nice and cool but Honor did not take any time to enjoy it. Soon word would get around that they had escaped and wolf patrols would quickly find them and capture them again.

"Follow me!" he called to Loyalty, and ducked around a corner, running as fast as his paws could carry him. He didn't care how his paws ached, or how deep rocks would cut into them, or how hard he was panting and rasping. He needed to escape and get help for his sister.

He emerged into the wired-in area, the place he knew the most. It had flat grassy terrain like no other place in the wild, with wire strung across the rectangular area. He stopped for a moment to pant and huff, finding Loyalty stopping and writhing again.

"Don't worry, little sister," he said, licking her affectionately as she collapsed again, whining.

Then he heard thundering paw-steps and knew he had no time to rest. "Loyalty, we have to move again!" he cried, but it was too late. Wolves sprang out like their encounter with Prowler Night and surrounded them, growling and snapping.

"Where do you think *you're* going?" a voice snarled. Stinger emerged from them, straight in the middle. "I know this much: you aren't escaping, either one of you." He glared at each of them.

Honor growled through clenched teeth, shrinking back. "Well *I* know *this much*: you won't hurt me or Loyalty, or take us back, for that matter. We had nothing to do with you."

Stinger laughed like what Honor had said was a joke. "Well, we have *everything* to do with you, Darkness wolf! Just realize you are nothing, and say it, and we'll let you go. Scarr didn't want you to find out the truth, and you are nothing."

"Oh, I did find out," Honor growled, "and I will never say such a thing. Besides, Scarr is *dead,* you fool. She won't be able to make me say or realize anything. So good luck."

At first, Honor thought he'd gotten Stinger good. But the new-found pack leader wrinkled his muzzle. "You're more of a traitor than I thought," he hissed. "And I will make sure you don't escape, and pay for what you've done."

Honor gnashed his teeth but the wolves closed in again, so fast he didn't have time to react, and one knocked into him so hard his world went dark.

HE SLOWLY opened his eyes but everything was blurry. His paws were stretched out in front of him as if he had just been in a sleeping position. His tail was tucked underneath him and he found he could not move. And it wasn't because of his dizziness.

There was a wolf on top of him.

He thrashed but whichever wolf that was pinning him had amazing strength. When the feeling came back to his body, he realized that his paws were splayed out quite uncomfortably, making them ache. He clenched his teeth in pain.

He could see again, too. He slowly turned his head and saw he was in another cavern that he'd never been in before. "The trial room," a voice called out, answering his never-question. "You've never been here before, have you, traitor?"

It was Stinger. He loomed not far away from Honor. The Darkness wolf looked around the cavern and saw the two wolf guards he'd slashed jumping in place, shaking their muzzles.

"My face!" cried Echinoderm.

Honor's eyes moved and gazed in another direction, where the area that had to be the entrance was covered with rocks and wolves lined up in front. *How would they escape now?* Honor thought sadly.

Finally, he saw Loyalty, sprawled out and writhing still in the middle of the trial room. Stinger had been looming straight over her, examining the wound on her leg as if it was something special he'd never seen before. Honor began to believe a little that the pack leader would help his sister.

Wolves were gathered round, murmuring or whining to each other. Stinger barked to silence them all. "Welcome to the trial room, wolves. The reason most of you have never been here before is because Scarr never really cared for this cavern. Of course, I did, and came to see it and clear it of dust and particles every day."

Honor's ears pricked and his eyes looked up as far as they could go to see a very serious wolf on top of him. Honor didn't struggle: it would take too much effort to escape this strong wolf pinning him down. Instead, he let loose a sigh and listened.

"But I'm here to see if this Darkness wolf will even survive this wound. It's very doubtful as I see but her *brother* will never shut himself up about it until something is done." Stinger looked straight at Honor then back at Loyalty. "So this is what I'm doing. Then I'll...decide."

Decide what? Honor snapped in his thoughts. He hoped this wouldn't involve anything bad. Maybe Stinger would help Loyalty and they could also find a way to escape.

Honor opened his jaws but for some reason he could not speak. Was he still stunned or still slightly dizzy from being knocked out like that? He got himself used to the uncomfortable ache of his splayed paws and the painful weight of the wolf on top of him. Then he didn't flinch anymore.

His teeth remained clenched as he watched Stinger circle Loyalty and mutter to himself. What was he saying? Could Loyalty hear? He saw that Loyalty's eyes were closed and her muzzle was still twisted with absolute pain. She'd waited so long, yet Honor couldn't do anything for her.

Some heir he was, he thought. Now Loyalty would have to sacrifice more pain before he could help her. Honor's eyes got misty and he tried shaking it away.

Stinger finally finished his examination. "Hmm... I see it's very doubtful that she'll live. The wound may be too deep and she seems so very pained. She won't live."

Honor was finally able to speak. "She *will* live, you filthy, insolent—"

"There's no point in calling me names," said Stinger casually. "Just call *her* dead."

And to Honor's horror, the Prowler lunged straight for Loyalty.

CHAPTER 10

HONOR SCREAMED and un-tucked his tail, slashing the wolf on top of him; the wolf howled and doubled backward. Honor leaped up but felt a bite on his tail and yelped. Trying to spin around, he felt two shoulders ram against his sides to keep him there. He strained and yelled, "Loyalty—you can't kill her!"

Stinger stopped short until he was straight over a cowering Loyalty, his ripping claw raised. Honor strained and the growl rumbling in his throat reverberated through the trial room. "Why not?" Stinger asked in an innocent voice. "She was going to die anyway. There's no way she would have survived."

"She *will*, you filthy hothead!" bellowed Honor, immediately knocking the two wolves away and yanking his tail out of the jaw that had bitten it. Stinger shrugged.

Honor got even angrier. "What's with you all? Why are you *Prowlers,* anyway? You aren't meant to be Prowlers as I see. You're cruel, arrogant, and uncaring, so why couldn't you all have been Stormers?!"

Stinger looked back at Loyalty. "Because destiny made us this way," he whispered. He grinned and Honor could take no more.

The Darkness wolf lunged and swung his tail toward Stinger's front.

He heard an ear-piercing howl and he stood over Loyalty, teeth bared and ready. "Don't come near her," he growled in a low tone as Stinger was staggering back toward him.

Blood seeped down Stinger's chest and he gave a summoning howl. More wolves around the room bounded toward him with ripping teeth and claws poised. Before they could act, Honor slashed them as well, hearing screams and howls that made his ears ring.

"I will *always* protect wolves," he growled. "I won't let you wolves stop me. I'm the heir, and I have power. And that power will not take me over." The horrified looks on the wolves' faces made him think they were especially scared. But instead Stinger stuttered painfully.

"Y-Your tail," he whispered.

"T-The blade; it g-got bigger!" every wolf stuttered.

Honor believed them, turning around and his jaw sagging open. His blade was unbelievably shiny and long. Right then and there he knew exactly what was happening to him. *The more I use it, the bigger it gets. I have a feeling Aghast used it a lot, and it grew bigger along with his pride. But I'm using it to protect, to serve, and to save wolves. So I don't think I'll be like Aghast at all.*

He promised himself that he'd tell this theory to the pack when they returned. He kept knocking away and cutting into wolves with his blade, until every wolf lay, groaning or wounded. Honor gave one last growl as Loyalty stood up behind him, staggering.

"Thank you so much for not giving up on me, Honor," she wheezed. "I know no matter how greedy, selfish, prideful, or powerful you get, you'd never let Stinger kill me."

Honor smiled right back at her and they both ran for the rock-covered entrance.

"Wait! Don't leave us here!" Stinger howled as the rocks came tumbling down after Honor rammed into them. "We'll die if you don't help us!"

Honor gave him a look. "Easy for you to say," he returned, and he and Loyalty hopped across the remaining stones. Leaving the yowling wolves behind, he helped Loyalty as they dashed back toward the wired area.

"Come this way and follow as quickly as you can," Honor said. He darted past some trees and Loyalty followed, leg dangling once more.

He felt Loyalty's fur brush against his shoulder and found that she was keeping up very well. He opened his jaw to say something but immediately Loyalty said, "I lost all feeling in that leg. It's so numb that I can run." Her eyes still had lost their color and she still had that terrible wheezing sound in her voice.

Honor became even more worried. Maybe Stinger was right. Maybe she wouldn't survive. He tried telling himself to keep believing in his little sister, but he couldn't bring himself to complete confidence again.

They zipped past more trees, treading and turning their paws. "Scale of one to ten?" asked a worried Honor. Loyalty winced while closing her eyes. Her pace slowed a bit. "Nine…"

It had gotten worse, just as Stinger had proclaimed. She could die right this very minute, or possibly lose more blood. Her leg was still soaked with dried blood, even though the other small scratches she had had already scabbed. The strength looked as if it was already seeping out of her body completely. "You'll be okay," Honor whispered.

T WAS silent for the next hour, and Honor and Loyalty had not stopped running. The Darkness heir was surprised that Loyalty had come this far and hadn't collapsed right on the forest floor. She whispered after a moment, "I think I know what's going on with your tail."

"Me too," said Honor. "I think we know what the other is thinking. Just don't talk. I know it hurts to act or say anything, Loyalty, so you don't have to stop the silence."

"I know," wheezed his sister, and he flinched when he heard it.

He saw Loyalty's ears perk forward. "I smell wolves," she rasped, "and they aren't the same or Stormers. They're Grays, I think, although we don't have the same awesome sense of smell the Prowlers have. I just know by the milky smell."

Honor's nostrils flared and his nose turned. He nodded and their pace slowed a bit to a trot. "I smell it now, Loyalty. Maybe this pack of Grays can help us." He so desperately wanted to be right, and he couldn't stand another minute with Loyalty in so much pain.

I swear to the spirits of wolves that if this does not work out, I will never forgive myself! Honor's mind shouted. On the scale of one to ten of desperation, he knew it was a ten. He watched Loyalty's pained expression and her colorless eyes as she continued her sniffing.

She's just as desperate as I am, or maybe even more desperate.

Honor quickened his pace again and Loyalty followed as quickly as she could. The sun was setting over the vast horizon, making the sky overhead shades of pinks, oranges, yellows, and light blues. He saw the moon on the other side of the darkening sky, getting ready to jump awake and start the night.

The Gray scent was getting a bit stronger, trailing around and around the trees. Just as Honor knew already, the scents stayed close by one another because Gray wolves were almost never alone. Maybe, thought Honor, they could really help them.

The land got flatter, the scents stronger, and the grass began to soften as they trotted hastily. The crickets began their chirping song and Honor, hoping the Gray pack could hear him, gave his own Darkness howl and song.

He heard Loyalty's come after his, but this howl sounded more like a rasping whine. He nudged her and looked into her eyes as if to say "you don't have to" and again quickened his pace.

Then he heard something that rose over the crickets' song and the owls' hoots. Gray howls—the louder, stronger type. Honor's ears perked up and he knew the Grays would expect them now.

He glanced on all sides of him and sniffed. First, he could see markings on trees where wolves had claimed Territory, and second, he could smell the scents the strongest they could be. They were in Gray Territory.

"Hello? We come in peace," he barked, his words reverberating. He heard the slight rustling of bushes and low whines. Slowly wolves began to trot out of the depths of the forest and stand in front of them. They all looked at him, then at Loyalty, then back at him.

"We come in peace," repeated Honor, bowing his head. Loyalty sat on her haunches painfully and did the same. He hoped he was making a good impression. He tried not to show his blade so he wouldn't scare the wolves into thinking he was dangerous.

The wolves simply nodded under the moonlight. "Follow us," one whispered, and they turned, still in formation. Honor had met Grays once before so he knew he could trust them. He motioned to Loyalty and they began to pad after the pack.

Their leader was the largest, with a string of leaves circling his neck, obviously to show his authority. His eyes were kind and they moved to the two Darkness wolves when they came to his mossy rest place. He stood up. "Outsiders?" he said.

"Yes," Honor said with a bow of his haunches. "We're sorry to interrupt whatever you Grays are doing, but my sister really needs help. She was attacked by a bear and her leg…it's lost a lot of blood and the wound is deep. She says she lost feeling… Could it be dislocated?"

The leader sniffed and his eyes became fearful. "We'll check," he said very anxiously. "I am Gray Minx, the Alpha of this pack. Just call me Minx for now, outsiders. We'll do what we can to help your sister. Where are you from and what is your name?"

"This is my sister, Loyalty," Honor said calmly as wolves began to help her to the center to check her wound. "I'm Honor…Prince Honor." He showed his tail and he heard stifled gasps from the wolves.

"You're the *heir*," Minx breathed in disbelief. "You've finally come. I hope you haven't hurt any wolves!"

"I haven't—only when I had to save my sister! I promise I am nothing like King Aghast!" Honor protested. "Although this blade is getting longer, I have a theory. The more I use it, the more it grows. But I'm using it for good things, I promise."

Minx was still speechless. "I…believe you," he said, regaining his senses. "Just…take some scraps from leftover dinner, and get some sleep if you please. We'll see what we can do for your sister." He glanced toward Loyalty and back at Honor.

Honor mouthed a silent "thank you" and as he picked a rabbit hide from the small pile of scraps nearby, he realized just how hungry and tired he was. He lay there under the moonlight, chewing and yawning. He watched some wolves circle Loyalty and murmur among themselves, Loyalty looking more pained than ever.

"Please live, Loyalty," he whispered, even though no wolf could hear him. Laying his head down, he watched them and his sadness rose up again. He shook it away, thinking *no, I have to pull myself together. She will live; just believe it in your heart, Prince Honor.*

He moved his gaze up to the sky, which was now dark with the moon hanging overhead. Stars littered the darkness, making it look beautiful. Honor hoped inside his heart that the Darkness Territory would look just as beautiful again.

His eyelids closed and his tail tapped the ground with anxiety. Despite all his worries for Loyalty, he gradually fell into the depths of sleep.

CHAPTER 11

AGAIN HE found Pebble, and didn't doubt for a moment that she was real. He knew already.

"How is Loyalty?" said Pebble worriedly, her tail lashing from side to side. "Are you hurt? Will you be back soon?"

Honor swallowed, running a tongue over his chops. His neck fur bristling, he told Pebble everything. "I'll tell the pack," said a worried Pebble. "Do they know for sure what's wrong with Loyalty, I mean the Grays?"

"I believe so. Their leader is worried too, so I know they'll find out sooner or later. I just hope it's nothing too serious. She said she had lost feeling in her leg and it felt numb, and it does flail out sideways when she runs. I'm not sure it will ever be the same even if it does get healed."

"I'm not sure either," Pebble sighed. "If only some wolf had sensed the bear coming we would not have gotten such a surprise. And if only the whole pack had taken down the bear."

"How are my friends?" Honor blurted. "Like, Cobra and Night?" He was dying to know what they were doing and whether or not they were worried about him. He knew Night was sometimes a worrywart so of course he was, but what about any other wolf?

Of course, he thought, they were worried. Why wouldn't they be? Pebble replied hastily, "They're doing fine. However, that Prowler is doing a lot of pacing and muttering."

Honor laughed. "I know. He's full of worries sometimes. It's like his brain is a giant worry. I'm glad to hear things are okay." Then he paused, thinking of something else. "Mother, can you take me in time again if possible, to see who my father was?"

Pebble looked a little sad. "That I cannot show you, because it's not even me that takes you through time. Dreams take you through time, if the wolf that dreams it is pure of heart. It's all hard to explain, Prince Honor, and I'd love to show you. But all I'll tell you is that your father's name was Soldier, and Razor's father's name was Toil. They were my two loyal mates."

Honor was sad inside as well. "Okay," he sighed. "Well, I'll soon let you know what's wrong with Loyalty, and if she may live. I'm trying to believe in my heart that she will, but... Never mind. I just believe she dislocated something."

"I see," Pebble said with anxiety. "Well, I hope you return soon, my son."

"Me too," were Honor's last words before the air pulled him back.

H E OPENED his eyes and saw the sun shine brightly down on the Gray Territory. This place was nothing like where the Darkness wolves lived, with beautiful flowers and undergrowth everywhere he looked. *This is how it used to be in Darkness Territory, but when I was stolen...*

He shook his dark pelt and greeted Gray Minx, who was stretching and yawning with anxiety flashing through his gaze. "Go check on your sister," he said with a bow of his head. Honor bowed his head back and made his way toward the cluster of wolves around Loyalty.

"Is she okay?" He nosed through several Grays until he came to the middle. There lay his sister, still wheezing and rasping, but looking not as pained. Rest had obviously helped a bit, and he saw that the Gray wolves had cleaned the wound the night before. He gave them all grateful looks and they nodded.

Loyalty did not say a word, but looked into Honor's eyes with a "there's-still-hope" look. Her tail thumped slowly and Honor's tail began to wag too; even if the blade was showing, he wanted to show her how relieved and happy he was.

Minx shouldered his way in and talked to another wolf. "Gray Maxx, could you tell me anything about the injury?"

The wolf he had addressed nodded. "Yes, I can, Alpha," he said rather calmly. "There is a dislocation because of how much she's put weight on it. If we can fix it, as long as she rests for a while afterwards, she should be fine, even if the leg still acts strange."

Honor looked and saw that Loyalty's tail was thumping faster and she looked at him with happy eyes. The Darkness wolf asked, "What will you do?" and perked his ears. Maxx began speaking.

"We'll try to shove at her leg and see what happens. It may sound a bit horrifying, but I believe it will work." Maxx nodded firmly and turned to the wound. "This may hurt for a moment," he warned. Loyalty nodded and closed her eyes. Then Maxx lowered his head and rammed straight into one part of her leg.

She screamed a howl and began to thrash for a second, then she stopped, her rasping turning to slight wheezing. Then she lay there, tongue lolling and panting. "I think you did it," she said weakly but with a relieved tone. "Thank you wolves *so* much. I wish I could repay you."

Minx shook his head. "You don't have to. We Grays are just like this. It's also another way to help the Great Prowler fulfill the Legend, isn't it? It's no problem, really."

Honor swore he saw Loyalty smile. He felt like smiling himself and he turned to Minx. "I wanted to say thank you, too. I wanted to help you in return, no excuses. What would you want me to do?"

Minx actually looked thoughtful. "I suppose maybe you could. Umm…what about you bring us some prey back? We could really use the help. And that blade of yours will be especially useful." He nodded toward Honor's tail.

Honor nodded as well. "Of course; anything," he said with gratitude. "I'll bring back some tasty squirrels or something!" He bounded off immediately, his head and tail up high as he sniffed.

Following the trail he found just at that moment, Honor's thoughts returned to his previous hunt with his pack. He hadn't realized how much he liked Midnight, and how good a help she'd been on their hunt together. Had he found a wolf to love, just as Night was obviously in love with Cobra?

These thoughts left his head as he looked ahead and saw at least five squirrels ahead of him, all bounding in different directions around the trees. That explained why the smells kept looping around and around to confuse the Darkness wolf.

"I'll take down those squirrels quicker than you could say 'King Aghast,'" he said aloud in a stubborn tone. Then he ran forward at full speed, lashing his bladed tail toward two squirrels that clustered in one corner. They made no noise but he knew they were dead.

He doubled around to take off after the only scampering squirrels, who chattered their heads off. He slashed and got them too. There was one more, and it darted swiftly around logs and trees and he knew he was getting far from Gray Territory.

In his frustration, Honor swung his tail hard and watched the squirrel get knocked into a tree trunk and onto the ground. He picked it up in his jaws and went to gather the other squirrels. This hunt had been successful, he had to say.

And after Loyalty rests for a while, we can move on and get home, to my true home. It will only have taken a week and we'll be alive and well. No wolf will ever doubt or test me again.

He ran back to Gray Territory and found that Loyalty was fast asleep. "I caught your prey," he reported, dropping the squirrels in front of Minx.

Minx studied the prey. "Impressive," he said with certainty. "Thank you so greatly, Prince Honor, for catching this prey for us. You didn't have to do this."

"I did have to," Honor insisted. "You helped my sister when she could've died. I owed way more than this to you." He could not resist against the great happiness that flowed through his body, his veins.

Loyalty's chest rose and fell with each breath as Honor padded over to check on her. Her leg twitched slightly and Honor could see where the dislocation had been. The wound was no longer bleeding but red surrounded the outside and the inside. Honor shuddered and his gaze went back to his sister's face. Her tongue gradually ran over her chops as she slept, and he saw her face was full of relief.

He gave her muzzle a lick and whispered, "Thank you for hanging in there, little sister. You'll be all right. You'll live." He didn't doubt that one bit now, because the Grays were such kind and loyal wolves to the wild. *Thank you, spirits of wolves.*

Another day or two should do it, Honor thought, and soon they'd be on their way. He remembered Stalker Broken, who was currently leading the Gray pack he'd once met, with Gray Magnus as their "kind of leader." He knew this pack was just as kind and disciplined.

Maxx sidled up to him. "What's it like...being the heir?" he asked rather curiously. "I mean, I'm nothing special, so I've never known how it feels."

Honor shook his head. "You *are* special," he said. "You just don't know it. Every wolf is special in their own way, and has something unique about them. Being the heir is still shocking, but I know I can take part in my friend Night's—who may be the Great Prowler—journey to help wolves by helping my own tribe."

"T-The Great Prowler?" shrieked Maxx with an excited tone. "You really think he is?!" His tongue lolled and his tail wagged into a blur.

He had caught other wolves' attention, and all the Grays were gathering with ears pricked. "Um, yes," Honor stammered. "I mean, he could be. There's a possibility for every Prowler, right? I used to be vicious and cruel, not like a Darkness wolf should be." He'd told this tale so many times already, he thought. "But I was changed forever by my friend, Prowler Night. That's the reason *I* believe he's the Great Prowler."

Maxx's eyes widened and his tail picked up speed. "So touching!" he said. "That is amazing. This Prowler Night sounds like a great wolf. And if the Great Prowler is coming, then soon everything will be okay." He tilted his muzzle and howled a Gray howl.

The other wolves joined in and even Minx's blended in with a tone of happiness. Honor smiled to himself and found that Loyalty was waking up. The howling must have been a little *too* loud.

She lifted her head with ears erect, and whipped her head around. She grinned when she saw and heard the wolves howling. She gave her own Darkness howl and Honor could not help but join in as well.

The Darkness howls seemed to give the Gray ones some flare and spirit. Honor howled joyfully to the sky and hoped that over in Darkness Territory the wolves would hear their cries and know they were alive and okay.

Thanks again, spirits of wolves. Thanks again, Heir Destiny. Now I know where I'm meant to be and how I'm meant to live. And that is what I've always wanted.

CHAPTER 12

"**T**HANK YOU, Alpha Minx," said Honor again, bowing his head. He and Loyalty were both near the borders of the Territory, ready to take the last trip back to Darkness Territory.

They had had some prey to eat and lapped a good many times from the river. Now it was time to finally return to their pack. Honor could never be more grateful to the Grays for saving Loyalty. Pebble would be just as grateful when they returned and told about everything.

"It was the least we could do, Prince Honor and Loyalty," Minx returned with a smile. "Maybe we'll see you again, or visit your Territory when you become King Wolf. We all wish you good luck, Honor, and hope you become a great leader for your tribe. Ah-roo!" he barked, as if it was a farewell sound.

"Ah-roo!" the other Grays howled, following along. Honor and Loyalty bowed with their haunches and turned with last goodbyes. Honor felt the same happiness as they began to run as fast as they could to follow the Darkness scents.

"How's that leg?" Honor asked after a moment, glancing at Loyalty while following the trail.

"It's actually fine," Loyalty said, no longer wheezing. She was clearly getting better and the Grays had been a great help to her. "I'm so grateful." She winced. "But I'm still at a two for pain, sorry."

Honor chuckled and shouldered her playfully. Loyalty laughed as Honor's nostrils flared. Yes, they were going in the right direction, back around to Darkness Territory. This Gray pack did not live too far from Honor's pack.

"But what will I say?" asked Loyalty anxiously. "I...I ran away and I was angry. Will *they* be angry at *me*?" Honor knew she was worried, so he answered her.

"The words you say should come straight from your heart," was all he said.

A**FTER A** little while, the Darkness scents lingered among the trees and Honor felt a rush of excitement. They were *home*. And this was his true home, not with Scarr or Stinger. He belonged here. He was changed.

He heard clamoring up ahead and he signaled with a sharp bark. The wolves he finally caught sight of were barking and howling with excitement when they saw him. Pebble gave a shrill yelp and ran straight to Loyalty, nuzzling her and crying, "Loyalty, thank goodness you're all right!"

He saw Prowler Night shoulder his way through the group and run into him, and the two went sprawling and licking. "I was so worried!" Night yelped. Honor simply laughed.

"You two are okay!" Razor howled with joy as he stopped chasing a toad to dance like a pup.

"You should see what happened to the Territory while you were gone," said Stormer Cobra with a smile. At first, Honor didn't know what she was talking about. But he pushed through some attractive undergrowth into a sunny clearing, open and wide, into a glade.

The sun shone down brightly and the new undergrowth was dewy and green, making the outline of the new Territory. Honor's jaw was wide open. "H-How?" he stuttered with newfound joy. "How did this happen?"

"No one knows," Pebble said happily, "but it did. And I love it. Everything is beautiful again, like you promised, Honor. Things will be okay."

"Yes," agreed Honor as the wolves spread out, lying in the grass or scratching themselves. "I love it too. And darkness will fall but the great Prowler will stand above it all." He smiled at Night, who ducked his head.

Loyalty looked bothered, limping into the center of the sunlit, open Territory. "I have something to say," she said, catching the wolves' attention. "I'm terribly sorry for everything I said and for running away. But I meant what I said and I wish you'd stop obsessing over my brother!"

The wolves murmured and Pebble nodded. "In a way you're right," she said solemnly. "And I say, indeed. I know along the way my son realized that he was special, but I want to say that every other wolf is special too, in their own way." She grinned at Honor and he wondered how she had possibly known.

Oh, well, he thought, and allowed Pebble to speak. "I want every wolf to respect Prince Honor the way he deserves, but also each other like you would him. A few wolves may have felt like they were forgotten—" she glanced at Loyalty "—and I want every other wolf to feel special too, because they are."

Loyalty smiled and the other wolves bowed their heads in respect and slight shame. Night nodded sheepishly and Cobra ducked her head. The Darkness wolf still looked slightly pained from her leg but was also looking much better.

"I'm glad everything worked out," said a grinning Honor, lashing his bladed tail. "And by the way, I think you already heard from Mother about my blade theory." He looked upon the pack, *his* pack. "I used this tail of mine to protect, serve, and show loyalty. There is nothing better than that to say that I am *nothing* like Aghast was."

The wolves agreed silently and Honor's grin spread. "And now I *think* it's time to tell about our…adventures," he said, glancing at Loyalty. His sister smiled and he opened his mouth to begin, telling tales of his search with more confidence than anxiety.

When he finished, the wolves were bounding with joy around the Territory as if they hadn't discovered their new home already. The glade and open sunlight looked just as it did in Honor's dream. *I knew my dream had meant something,* he thought with extreme happiness.

He padded to where Night lay, gazing with gleaming eyes up at the sky. "Night, how were things in the Territory while I was gone?" he asked the Prowler, already knowing some of the answers. Night snapped his gaze at Honor's grin and chuckled.

Cobra lay next to him, her gaze transfixed to the sky as well. Her eyes held a wondrous curiosity in them, and Honor had no idea what it meant. Maybe she was considering meeting her own kind, the Stormers, whether she wanted to or not. Or maybe there was something else…

Honor lowered his haunches, tail wagging, to listen to Night's stories about what had happened in the pack. "I'll tell you, I did a lot of pacing and Cobra did a lot of 'Night, stop worrying.' And things were normal as well. Razor chased toads and the hunting wolves were lucky by the spirits of wolves. Things were fine even with you and Loyalty gone."

"Did Mother worry too much?" asked Honor. He wasn't sure that Pebble had been completely honest with him during the dream visiting.

"Well…a lot," Night confessed. "Maybe my pacing didn't help."

Honor laughed, picking himself up.

"Hey, Honor," said Night slowly. "You know you're special, right? You're an heir. You really have a family. You're changed. And I'm glad to have you on my Great Prowler journey."

Honor smiled but didn't say anything, making sure his sharp blade was hidden. He nodded and looked up to the sky, his mind getting into the same trance Cobra was clearly in. He *was* special, and so was every wolf. All his life he'd thought he was nothing. But here he was, saving his sister and serving his pack, knowing for sure that he had changed.

And as the wolves surrounded him and praised him for saving Loyalty, Honor knew that this—*this* was where he was meant to be.

CHAPTER 13

"**H**OW IS your leg?" Honor asked Loyalty again the next day. Things were bright and cheery in Darkness Territory for the first time in four years. The sun shone down and the wolves were happy and Loyalty was okay.

His sister was lying contentedly beside an oak tree, where warm sunlight streamed onto her dark pelt. Her tail was thumping and her injury looked much better than before. The red was turning to pink and the dislocation was back in place and healing. "It's great," she returned with a smile.

Honor turned, watching the peaceful Territory unfold before his eyes. Wolves sat in pairs, talking or lying in the sunlight, just as Loyalty was. Pebble was on her shiny stone and Honor caught sight of Night and Cobra, having a peaceful sleep in the streaming sun.

But what could *he* do? Honor wondered, looking around him. He was a bit lost. Wasn't there something he could do to serve his pack too? Then his eyes brightened as a black wolf he knew well was bounding up to him.

"Honor!" she cried.

"Midnight," he breathed. The two crashed into each other with yelps of joy, rolling all around and licking each other playfully. "I was most worried about you," her voice said through Honor's fur. He continued his wrestle with her and felt more joy slither through his body.

He had never felt such joy in his life. Not once under the clutches of Scarr had he been truly happy. His tail seldom wagged but now it did in one black blur with a sliver of silver at the end. Midnight trusted and liked him so much, and he could say the same for her.

"Oh, Midnight," he said happily. "I-I wanted to say this for a while, ever since I met you." His words made the other Darkness wolf's eyes gleam and her face twist in happiness.

"What?" she said, and Honor had a feeling she knew what he'd say.

"I…love you, Midnight. I mean love, love you. As in like you, a lot. And—"

"I get it," said she. "I love you too, Honor." Her eyes shone as she looked into his. He knew his were shining too, and he put his paws on her shoulders, licking her straight in the muzzle. He had not been afraid to tell her this, and he knew she loved him back.

The two wolves wrestled again, neither one of them saying a word but looking happily into the other's eyes. Honor's heart beat at a steady, joyful pace as he rolled and got dirt all over his fur. He heard a voice behind them that stopped them short.

"Are you two done with your love ritual?"

Honor looked up. Razor had stopped chasing a toad to look at them with his muzzle wrinkled in disgust. The toad leaped away, happy to get away from its death chaser. Honor felt the slightest bit embarrassed, especially in front of his half-brother—who was barely older than he was. He rolled back over and they both stood up.

"Yes," he growled. "Why don't you stop being a nosy-fur?" His tail lashed from side to side and he trotted away before Razor could answer, and he felt Midnight's fur brush against his side. "Love ritual," he snorted. "Over time he'll understand."

He heard Midnight's soft laugh behind him, and he felt another wave of happiness. *Geez, I'm getting so happy that I might blow up.*

The moon was shining overhead later. Stars dotted the sky and the night was beautiful, just like the Territory. The wolves were all gathered together, faces shining with joy and peace. Honor spotted Cobra and Night in the mix, with his mother and sister padding up behind them.

"We gather here tonight," Pebble announced, "to celebrate not only my son's return once more but also because of how things are returning to peaceful right now. It could never be better." She smiled, and immediately after her cry filled the night.

Honor joined in with no hesitation, his Darkness howl blending in with the other howls that soon came. Then he heard Night's Prowler howl, and the beautiful howl of a Stormer. It warmed his heart just as it always did, and he hoped someday to learn more about the Stormer howl.

The howls resounded and echoed in the night, filling the sky with more cheer than it already had. Honor felt as if he could howl forever—that was how much overwhelming joy was inside him. His life was better now, and he knew he wasn't a lost cause.

I never was, and never will be.

HONOR STRETCHED and yawned in the morning sunlight. He had slept well the night before, and he could tell every other wolf in his pack had too.

The wolves gathered together around Pebble's stone, clamoring and wagging their tails. Loyalty was curled up on the stone as well, with her leg sprawled in front of her. "It may not be the same," she was telling Trekker, Honor's uncle and Pebble's brother.

"I see," said Trekker, eyeing it curiously. "Where was the dislocation, exactly?"

"I think near the joint. The bear must have gotten that part the most," Loyalty replied, gazing down at the injury and wincing a little. "It still hurts but I'll be fine."

Honor swung his head to another part of the crowd of wolves. Midnight's parent wolves, Twister and Rose, were deep in conversation with Night and Cobra. Honor sighed with contentment and pushed through the wolves.

"Mother," he said, climbing onto the stone. "May I come up here? I *am* your son, and the heir," he added.

Pebble nodded and he sat next to her, feeling respected once more as a few wolves bowed on their haunches and another wolf gazed into his eyes with loyalty shining in them. *These wolves...they trust me. They respect me. They depend on me. They believe in me. That's all I could have asked for.*

He gathered himself up and shook his body, feeling slightly bothered by something. "Everyone," he called out. The wolves faced him. "There's something I need to say." He took a deep breath.

"I know you depend on me and I just returned after four years, but I still need to help Prowler Night on his journey. He says he cannot do it without wolves by his sides. He's wandering farther and farther away from his Lone Wolf personality and he says it's a good thing. And I think so too. But I need to help him with *his* destiny as well as mine."

This silenced his pack for a moment and he thought they would protest: "Please don't, Prince Honor!" "We need you! Without you we'll all die!" "The darkness hasn't fallen but it will soon, and what if you aren't here?"

Honor swallowed. Pebble said finally, "I understand, Honor, but what about becoming King Wolf?"

"Mmm, I think I'll wait until I'm five and have helped Night more than I have already," said Honor with a decisive flick of his tail. "If...if that's okay with you," he added sheepishly

Loyalty thumped her tail. "I for one don't object."

"Neither do I." Night stepped forward and Cobra did the same. "I could use the help, Honor, but you really didn't have to... I don't object anyway." Honor smiled.

Other wolves agreed and Pebble nodded sadly. Honor knew how she felt but he also felt he needed to do this. "I will return again, alive and well," he promised, and he knew he could keep his promise. "I will help the Darkness tribe no matter what."

The pack's silence and nodding decided the rest. Honor held his head high. "Thank you," he said. "My destiny will come someday, but for now another wolf needs me more."

EPILOGUE

"**I** THOUGHT TERROR was going to report," Stormer Anaconda growled through gritted fangs. "Some promise-keeper he is."

Pinscher hissed. "At least he finally agreed to do the assassin work for us," she mused. "Maybe he isn't so bad a Stormer after all. I'm telling you: he's got the guts for killing wolves, even if it means every wolf that hurts us. He's our shield, our protection."

"Yes, and those overgrown fangs will help too," agreed Shearer with absolute certainty. "Every wolf will stay cautious around him. He's extremely unique and no wolf will stand in his way—even his pathetic sister won't try to stop him."

"His pathetic sister!" snorted Pinscher in a laugh. "Good old Cobra. I remember when she ran away six years ago, and no wolf knows the story behind the tale. Maybe she's already been killed by an enemy."

"Or by the Great Prowler," said Shearer. "That would be awesome."

Anaconda snapped at his ear. "That wasn't funny."

"Yeah, the Legend is nothing but nonsense," Pinscher said in a rather stern tone. "We Stormers never speak of that wolf-dung anyway, so why even joke about it?"

Shearer shrugged, his tongue lolling in a way that said "just being humorous." Pinscher rolled her eyes.

"Anyway," she said to Anaconda, "I'm sure he'll have a report in soon. I hear they have it in for us Stormers—they're tired of us. Now that Terror is going to spy on those plotting wolves, we'll know exactly what will happen."

"If he doesn't get killed first," growled Anaconda. "You know Terror. He'd get himself into any trouble, really, may it be a strong current in the river or peeing on someone else's tree."

The other Stormers stifled laughs. Anaconda gave a shrill growl and turned to stalk off.

"Wait!" said Pinscher. "I never gave you the real report!"

Anaconda gave her a sidelong look. "What report? Terror hasn't reported yet, *remember?"* he asked impatiently.

"No, this is something else," Shearer said, sidling close to Pinscher, who tried to shoulder him away but failed. "Just listen to her for once, Anaconda, and maybe you'll do more good for yourself."

"I'm not interested unless my son comes back with an assassin report!" Anaconda yelled, tail lashing furiously. "No other report will be useful!"

"This one will," Pinscher insisted. "I heard that pathetic sister of Terror's, Cobra, has sided with a Prowler." She hissed like a rattlesnake and seemed furious just with the mentioning of this news.

Anaconda was surprised. "She has?" he growled in disbelief. "How would she? Prowlers are enemies!"

Shearer shrugged. "She really isn't an ordinary Stormer," he pointed out.

"Too not ordinary," Anaconda hissed, looking to the moonlit sky. "We have to do something about this. There's no way I'm letting any Stormer *ever* get in *contact* with a Prowler. That isn't how our tribe works. Once she finds out I'm her secret father, I'll make sure she becomes a *true* Stormer and become a traitor to that...*friend* of hers."

Pinscher growled in agreement and Shearer said nothing. They both knew Anaconda was right.

"And I'll try to do something about this *Great Prowler Legend* the other tribes speak of," Anaconda announced, moving his eyes on his two comrades. "Things can run the Stormer way if we try."

This was it. He had made his decision. It was time to change Cobra into a comrade the Stormers could really trust, and once Terror reported back, his plan would begin.

And there was no turning back from it.

WOLF WARRIORS

BOOK THREE

SHATTERED

TRIBE

PROLOGUE

NEPTUNE THOUGHT himself weak. He never thought he was true. He rushed to the council meeting with other Darkness wolves, but with some Stalkers as well. *This meeting may change everything.*

Blizzard took a pace forward from where he stood as well. Blizzard was not named well, because his pelt was dark, like a normal wolf in the Darkness tribe. *His parents must have been mad.* Neptune sat down with the other murmuring wolves; every wolf could have an opinion here, except the complaints of other wolves about his opinions ran through his head.

Neptune, why do you think of everything as downfall?

Neptune, don't share opinions unless they're acceptable!

Neptune...Neptune...blah, blah, blah!

More wolves filed in until Neptune was snapped out of his thoughts. "Today is the day, wolves, that we conquer this tribe!" Blizzard announced as if he was in charge. Every wolf got to speak. But it was a democratic meeting, not a dictatorship!

"But how will we do it?" asked Bluetooth, who always had worries about how they would do things. "There are several of them around with powerful wolves as guards."

"I know how," Force cut in. "We fight them, of course, with our own power! And if the Great Prowler finally comes…" She always got excited about the Legend being fulfilled, and Neptune was ready for it himself.

"Those are all good suggestions. But we need more than that! Does any wolf have anything?" Blizzard shouted.

Neptune wanted to rip that big jaw off his face; *this isn't about dictatorship, you fool!*

"We need to be more than basic," observed Stalker Venom, who was missing a leg from an attack from that tribe. "I'll show them a piece of my mind once we find out a plan." She had always wanted to get vengeance, but Neptune had never sought it before, no matter what happened to him.

Stalker Observer complained, "Hey, that's my job!"

"Who has something besides basic?!" roared Blizzard. "Any wolf know? Any wolf?" He was obviously fed up with all this chit-chat about simple things.

Neptune wanted to cover his ears with his paws, but instead barked sharply. "We have our main idea," he said calmly, "but we don't have the actual plan."

"Then what kind of plan do you have, smarty-pants?" sneered Blizzard. "What plan besides basic would a wolf as stupid as you have?"

Neptune gritted his teeth; he hated when the wolves teased him. "We could start patrols that could go down and along the sides, checking for enemies. Then they could report back. Soon we could encounter them face to face, when we're strong enough—"

"We are strong enough, useless!" Blizzard bellowed.

Neptune flinched. He was done with this. "Then I won't be a part of this. All I get is grief from all of you. Goodbye. Good luck taking them down without me." He growled and turned to run.

Behind him, he heard Blizzard and the other wolves' voices, as if he hadn't just lost his temper at them.

"Let's end all Stormers!"

CHAPTER 1

T WAS a beautiful day as the three wolves were turning their paws over the forest ground. No, this wasn't the Forbidden Forest. But Cobra knew this forest was creepy enough by looking at the spider webs in the trees and the acorns that fell onto the ground.

"Don't you just love the air out here?" Night asked, inhaling through his flaring nostrils. "It's so extremely fresh and amazing, right, Cobra?"

The Stormer came to her senses and nodded. She still did not feel completely comfortable with wolves she was supposed to call enemies. Of course, she wasn't the ordinary type of Stormer. All she wanted was to live a life of her own, where she wasn't hated or guarded all the time.

You're different, she told herself, *and at least some wolves believe that. And don't ever consider visiting your tribe, on the Great Prowler journey or not on it.* Cobra moved her eyes from the ground to up and Night was looking straight into them.

"What's wrong, Cobra?" he asked her with anxiety of his own flickering in his eyes. "You can always tell me. I know you. And soon other wolves will see you in the same way I do."

Cobra doubted that. "Night, you have to understand," she said. "I'm a Stormer. And Stormers are wicked and cruel, and merciless. I may not be that way but you're the only one who really understands and loves me."

This silenced Night for a moment, and she knew he was taking in her words. "You know it's true," she said, looking to both Honor and Night. She sighed inwardly. "Every other wolf hates me."

"Hey, I made my Pack trust you," Honor said, "with real force. I am the heir, after all." He was right. Not long ago he *had* found out he was the Darkness heir to King Wolf, following King Aghast.

Night had also found out that he might be the Great Prowler. Cobra, well, she hadn't found out anything that was special about *her*. Before they'd left the Darkness Pack to continue on Night's Great Prowler journey, she'd said to Honor, "Your outstanding speech was moving, but maybe I'm really *not* special."

No Stormer seemed special to *her*. There was nothing extraordinary about Cobra, easy as that. She thought it best to think she was a normal, boring, everyday wolf. She gave another sigh, and she knew in her heart that she was depressed.

Trying not to show this to her fellow wolves, she forced her tail to wag. "Why don't we howl tonight?" she asked with a smile. She knew her tribe forbid howling but she'd only just discovered that her howl was extraordinary, a calming song.

Night nodded quickly, tongue lolling excitedly. "You know I love hearing you, Cobra," he replied, his tail wagging as well. Cobra ducked her head. She knew Night loved her, and always would.

The forest was still as usual, the sun bounding across the sky and blinding their eyes. The sun always loved to play with wolves during the day and so did the moon at night. The spirits of wolves would keep them safe from any danger—most of the time. Cobra had much belief in them as any wolf. She even believed the Great Prowler Legend—even if her tribe called it a pile of wolf-dung.

As the three wolves kept up their trotting and bounding throughout the shining day, Cobra was deep in thought. She barely remembered running away from her tribe as a small pup, only just surviving the wild. She had lived her life as a Lone Stormer.

She also hardly remembered her tribe. The wolves there were cruel and powerful, with curved claws and deadly fangs. Cobra had hardly ever needed to use those claws and fangs except for defense. The only other Stormer she still remembered…was Terror.

He sure was terrifying. She remembered him separating from his tribe temporarily to gain something he needed. She had no idea what and wondered if he was back in the tribe yet. What could he be working on? She shook her body, telling herself not to worry about it and that Stormer Terror was a mere memory.

"And if any wolf says anything or contradict you, I'll just slash them in the face," Honor was saying later. "You know I will, Cobra. I have a blade and I'm the heir." Cobra couldn't help but smile at him, feeling grateful as can be.

"Where will we go next? I mean which wolf tribe?" asked Night at last when the moon had begun to rise. "We've met a Stalker Pack, Gray Pack, my Pack the Prowler Pack, and your own Darkness Pack, Honor. But…we still have the Stormers left—"

"Don't even bring it up, Night!" said Cobra sharply. She took a breath and tried to calm down. "Please, Night… You know what I said. I said *no Stormers, ever*! I don't care if they're in need of the O Great Prowler or not! They hate all wolves and won't treat you as friends, anyway. Please!"

"Okay, okay!" said Night hurriedly, tail lashing as they stopped for a rest. "Okay. But don't blame me if we just happen to run into Stormers."

"Ergh!" snarled Cobra with uncontrollable frustration. Night looked away and his tail tapped his flank with discomfort. Cobra took another breath and curled up head to flank. Her tail rested peacefully beside her body and she felt Night and Honor's bodies on either side of her. Were they trying to protect her or something? Cobra decided to let them do their thing. Tomorrow they would catch prey and move on, to who knew where.

But the question was where would they go, if they wouldn't go to the Stormers? Cobra thought with a twinge before drifting to sleep.

HONOR HAD already brought back tons of mice he had "whipped up" with his tail. Cobra crunched and chewed with slight exhaustion and yawned, showing her glinting teeth and fangs.

"Ready?" said Night, stretching and making his tail lash. Cobra nodded and they began to cross the valley into the unknown, somewhere where Cobra had never been. The wild was a huge place full of many dangers and paths.

They were getting out of the creepy forest every second, which relieved the Stormer. As the wolves ran Night nearly tripped but Cobra's curved claws gained more traction and she ran like the wind. "Where are we headed if not the Stormers?" Honor shouted over the rushing breeze and kicking of their paws.

Was the heir able to read minds? Cobra laughed inwardly and watched Night's expression. "I don't know," he confessed. "We're just, um, exploring until we find wolves that need us, I guess." Cobra could tell he was embarrassed for being clueless and she sidled closer while her legs still flew across the grass.

Cobra glanced over while running and swore she saw something slinking between the trees. It was black and in a shape of a wolf, and it snuck carefully in the shadows. She squinted and knew she wasn't imagining it. Was a wolf stalking them, or was it a wolf they knew? Or what if it was Prowler Stinger, the new leader of Scarr's Pack?

It could be any wolf. Her pace did not slow and she hoped they got as far away from that shadow as possible. Maybe she was just seeing things because she was still tired. She shook herself and blinked her eyes, turning them back to the road ahead.

Assuming Night and Honor had not noticed the shadow, Cobra decided to say nothing. Now maybe she really was seeing things. The breeze drifted and their pace gradually slowed instead of quickened. Cobra wondered if there was something wrong.

Night's nostrils were flaring hastily and his ears sprang erect. They stopped and he stiffened. "Do you smell that?" he hissed, ears beginning to swivel.

Cobra sniffed. She smelled it too. It was a strong, sneaky, sort of *evil* smell. Was it the shadow? She glanced around her and noticed that the shadow was gone. Her heart beat wildly and she realized with a jolt that the thing she'd seen was real.

Honor was stiff too, bladed tail lashing alertly. Cobra was about to tell them about the shadow when suddenly a flash of fur emerged and Prowler Night was tackled. Cobra jumped back and so did Honor, and Night gasped a yelp, turning over to face his opponent.

Cobra gaped. The wolf was, indeed, a Stormer, and his curved claws dug into Night's fur. He was the same color of fur as she, and his eyes flickered with strong hatred. The overgrown white fangs draping over his strong jaws were familiar…all *too* familiar.

"Who are you?" she choked anyway.

The wolf's eyes struck hers, still glinting. "Stormer Terror," he hissed. "Your brother."

CHAPTER 2

COBRA WAS stunned, and could not move. "T-Terror?" she stuttered. "Look at my sister, cowering before me like I knew she would!" Terror laughed. "I found your scent and thought I would stalk you, and I knew it was my runaway sister!"

Cobra pulled back her lips and growled. "Terror, I'm not coming back," she hissed. "I have a better life than any Stormer. Maybe all Stormers should be this way!"

"No way," said Terror, his muzzle twisted with anger. "Stormers live the Stormer way, not with a *Prowler* or Darkness wolf!" He looked especially terrifying now that his mouth was open in a snarl and the top fangs hung over the rest.

Cobra's tail began to lash. "Don't tell me how to live my life!" she snarled sharply. Night was still struggling and yelped when Terror's claws dug deeper into his body. Honor had his bladed tail up and ready.

Just then the Darkness wolf growled and began to slash. Cobra leaped in front of him and he reared back in a panic. "Don't kill my brother!" she pleaded. "I know he's terrible, but he's the only family I have!"

"How nice of you to spare my life," Terror's voice said behind them in an almost sneer. "I thought you hated your tribe. I could hear you saying that. And yet you stopped your own comrade from killing me. He could've made me die right here. But you were especially kind, sister."

Cobra spun around. "Shut up and be glad I was," she growled.

Night was thrashing still and would not stop. Terror jumped off him, flexing his curved claws. "Come with me," Terror ordered in a calm voice, spinning on his haunches to move forward.

"Where are we going?" Honor snarled. His tail looked as if it was ready to strike again at any moment. "Tell me or I *will* kill you." Terror chuckled up ahead, turning his head around. Cobra hated seeing her brother's...*ugly* face.

"Stormer Territory," he said with a wicked grin slicing his muzzle.

"No!" Cobra howled. "I'm not going back, I said, Terror! Don't make me! Don't take away me or any of my friends!" She stepped protectively in front of Night and Honor. Her fangs showed as she growled.

"Sorry, but it is assassin duty to take in captives," Terror said casually, flicking his tail back and forth. "Hate to break it to you but you *are* coming. Cobra...you could be respected. You could live a better life if you just come back to the tribe. I promise!"

"You do not!" snapped Cobra. "If you're an assassin wouldn't you just *kill* us?"

"There's more to it than that," chuckled Terror. His face twisted. "Now follow me or I kill you."

"No, I'm not submitting to my 'terrifying' brother! You aren't so terrifying to me, Terror! You're not even—" She was cut off.

"I'm merciless, like you said all Stormers are. And merciless means I will kill you with no mercy!" Terror's howl reverberated through the valley.

Night sniffed. "Terror, you're right," he confessed. "Without realizing it we got extremely close to Stormer Territory!" This made Cobra's heart pound.

"We're not going!" she snarled. "I'm helping Prowler Night on his Great Prowler journey!" When Terror's muzzle contorted up with rage she went on. "Yes, I believe the Great Prowler Legend, Stormer or not. And I howl! Our howl is so beautiful!"

"Really?" jeered Terror with a look of shock on his face. "I didn't know my sister would be brave enough to break all Stormer rules!

You're coming with me, no matter what. I can spin around and kill you all quick before you can say my name if you don't follow."

Cobra trusted what her brother had said. She stood there for a moment, hesitating, but nodded with anger flickering in her eyes. "Don't expect me to submit all the time," she growled. Night and Honor had looks of horror but she gave them her own look. They hung their heads.

Terror turned with a wicked grin and began to stalk across the edge of the valley, followed by the three wolves. *Now I'm finally meeting my tribe, after all these years,* thought Cobra with a twinge. *And whether I want to or not.*

Her brother's tail lashed back and forth and she could tell he was grinning all the way. *You're lucky, brother.*

She straightened herself and kept her eyes on her brother whom she had one memory of, five or six years ago when he ran off when he was young. He must have been strong and brave because he had survived all this time.

"You're good at stalking, Cobra, like me," Terror said from in front of her later when the moon was just rising. "You'd be amazed how similar we are even though you ran away."

"We're nothing alike!" she snapped, curling her claws. She so badly wanted to slash her brother across the jaw for saying that. She was nothing like any of the Stormers in her tribe. She was different, and glad to be different.

"What's Stormer Territory like?" Night whined fearfully. "Is it like Prowler Scarr's Territory?" Terror just laughed.

"No way," he said. "It's only three times worse with taverns and halls and streams. It's pretty awesome and I think you'd like the pee-covered prison!" Night wrinkled his muzzle and sneezed at the thought.

Cobra hated hearing Terror sound so casual all the time. Was this how an assassin worked? If it was worse than Scarr's. Territory, then what would it really be like? She tried to imagine what Terror had described. How could any wolf find a Territory like that?

"So…if it's that big and amazing…the whole tribe lives there?" she asked, although she hated to be having conversations with her brother.

"You bet," Terror said. "It's amazing, I have to say, sister. You'll like it, I promise. Maybe you'll fit in and become one of us."

"I will not!" Cobra snapped and she leapt to nip at his tail but it seemed like he'd expected her to. His tail flicked right out of the way.

"Just wait and see," Terror said. They were out of the valley and Cobra could squint and see movement up ahead, which meant the Territory was right up there. She saw stone walls and a big clearing.

Setting her jaw and hoping for the best, Cobra and the other wolves trudged up the hill and into the middle clearing. Wolves like her with curved claws and deadly fangs were up ahead. *My tribe,* she realized with a pang.

"Who is in charge of the tribe?" she asked. "I mean, if the whole tribe lives here?" She wondered who could possibly lead an entire tribe besides the King Wolf of Darkness wolves.

"You'd be surprised to know," Terror replied. "But you'll find out."

Cobra gritted her fangs as they came to a stop. Terror raised a paw and his head proudly. "Stormers!" he announced, as every wolf's head turned. "I have found my lost sister and her comrades, the heir to King Wolf and a Prowler!"

Uproar sounded from the clearing. The tribe was barking and flexing their claws with hatred as they gaped at Cobra's comrades. One wolf pushed through them all, a bouquet of leaves around his arched neck. "Cobra," he breathed. He was russet and gray like her and had long, silver claws.

Was this wolf the leader of the tribe? "Stormer Cobra," he repeated. "You don't remember me, do you? I am Stormer Anaconda, leader of the tribe." He turned gruffly around to face the wolves. "My daughter is back."

Cobra was stunned. Stormer Anaconda…he was her father.

CHAPTER 3

COBRA COULD say nothing. The Stormers around them had pride and sheer surprise in their eyes. Then uproar sounded again and she flinched back as wolves began to shout.

"Why did she side with a Prowler?"

"Why did she run away from us when she could live a better life?"

"She can't be *too* unordinary; do something, Anaconda!"

Anaconda gave a loud snarl for quiet. "We'll figure this out later," he said gruffly. "First, guards, lock up the Prowler and Darkness wolf! I'll see what I'll do with them." Cobra couldn't even react as her comrades were bound with chains and led to wherever the prison was.

"F-Father," she breathed. "I didn't think I would ever meet you. I only remember Terror. I, uh…"

"Yes, I know. Your brother's a hothead," Anaconda growled, with a roll of his eyes. Terror glared, his eyes flickering to go with his ugly look. "First, this crowd wants to know exactly what's wrong with you, Cobra."

Cobra tried not to sigh. "Well, if I say will you show me around here?" she asked.

Anaconda snarled. "Yes! Now do what I asked! You're a hothead too," he growled.

Cobra turned. "Okay. Well, I thought I'd have a better life by running away, so that's what I did. I don't want to be a real Stormer, if that's what you're wanting. I met Prowler Night and knew the Legend and the other tribes meant something. So yes, I believe that 'wolf-dung' and I know how to howl!"

More uproar followed and Anaconda moved quickly, knocking down his daughter. Cobra gasped with pain and looked into his furious red eyes. "You know *what*?" he hissed.

"I can howl! It's forbidden but I did it! The sound is beautiful, and it seems to calm wolves' hearts. Why did we ever forbid it in the first place?" Cobra thrashed but her father's strength was too much. She let her tongue hang out the side of her jaw. "You can hear it now."

With no hesitation, she lifted her muzzle and closed her eyes. Her cry filled the air and it even calmed her own heart. The sound was strong and reverberated around the large Territory. The Stormers were shaking themselves desperately. "Stop with that horrible sound!" Terror pleaded.

Oh, please, brother. And you said you were an assassin. Cobra stopped her howling and her father wolf's gaze was unreadable. "Get up," he growled, taking his body off her. Cobra leaped to her paws and faced the wolves. All their lips were curled and they all growled at her.

She hung her head and looked away. Her own tribe obviously despised her. They hated her. She knew that. "Follow me and I'll show you around," Anaconda hissed without a second glance as he turned to stalk inside the caverns and stone walls.

Cobra hung back as the wolves scattered, some still staring after her. Other Stormers hung in the halls and glared as she passed. She kept her ears and tail low but still allowed herself to take a look around.

She had to admit this place was nice. The place was clean and fresh with wolves stalking the halls. She wondered where the prison was and if her companions were okay. "Where is the prison?" she asked Anaconda.

"It's a long way away, but your um, *comrades* are already there." Her father snorted. "Now follow me and I'll show you the dens."

Cobra kept alongside him with her brother treading his paws on the other side. "Terror!" barked Anaconda. "I thought you were going to report!"

"I told it to Pinscher already," replied Terror. "So far there are no wolves around stalking us. On the way I found Cobra and the Prowler and Darkness wolf. They had no idea I was even there."

"I saw your shadow!" said Cobra sharply. "Don't think I didn't!"

Anaconda lashed his tail as they walked. "You both need to shut yourselves up," he growled at them. "We're going to the dens and finding a good spot for Cobra to sleep. We'll still provide her with things but we'll make sure you never leave, daughter." His eyes glinted as he looked at her.

Cobra set her jaw. "Soon you won't know why you ever sided with other tribes," Anaconda went on. "I'll make you a *real* Stormer over time, Cobra, whether you want it or not. You weren't born to mate with a Prowler and go on a wolf-dunged Great Prowler journey!" His face contorted into rage.

"No, you weren't," Terror hissed. "And if you try to escape I'll just kill you before you do. After all, I'm an assassin." Their father nipped his ear and he quieted.

"You were born to be like every other Stormer, Cobra. That's a Stormer's destiny, isn't it? Just admit it, it's your destiny as well as every other Stormer's." Anaconda's eyes went straight into Cobra's. The female Stormer looked away.

They had reached a dimly lit cavern full of mossy patches along the sides. Cobra assumed this was where the dens were. She saw through another small tunnel that there were more den rooms. There was just enough room for every wolf and pup in the Storm tribe. This place was downright amazing.

Maybe Terror had been right about one thing…

Cobra shook herself and looked around the cavern. Small Stormer pups lay curled up on one patch of moss. On the other side were a few wounded wolves that looked as if they had just been treated.

Some wolves were sitting, deep in conversation, in the middle as if they were plotting something. Cobra looked to her father and Anaconda gestured and gnashed his fangs dismissively. He and Terror sidled out of the dens and Cobra was left there alone.

She felt extremely nervous as she crept toward the circle of conversation. She pricked her ears and listened in.

"I hear they have it in for us, the other tribes," muttered a Stormer, flexing her claws as if the other tribes were actually there. "Thunderstruck, didn't you hear Alpha Anaconda talking about it with Pinscher and those other wolves?"

"I don't think so, Fang-Tooth," answered a wolf that looked to be older than the others. "But I did hear that news from Terror. You know he discusses with us whenever he's off his so-called 'assassin duty.' I hope the rest of us have a plan."

"I'm absolutely sure they do," insisted Fang-Tooth. "We Stormers are always ready no matter what happens to us. Whether it's an attack, an ambush, an assassin from another tribe…we're always ready."

"Even the prisoners give up hope instead of trying to face us," agreed Thunderstruck. "We *are* the most powerful tribe in the wild, aren't we? There's nothing we can't do."

"I agree," murmured another Stormer with a curl of his lips. "We've got this."

The wolves nodded and scattered, but every Stormer's eyes turned to Cobra and they stopped short. Cobra raised a paw and licked her jaws feebly. "Um, hello," she said nervously, tail beginning to tuck underneath her.

Thunderstruck gasped and pulled back his lips to show his fangs. "You must be Stormer Cobra, the one that doesn't know tribe life!" he snarled. "Stormers *never* greet each other like that! We always suppress a growl—that's it!"

Cobra was embarrassed. "Oh, um…sorry," she murmured, not meeting their eyes. "I'm…new here. I was just brought in here by my father, Anaconda."

"No kidding!" said Fang-Tooth. "You're going to have to learn how Stormers live, because I heard you've been interacting with *other tribes*!"

Cobra tried to think what her life would have been like if she'd stayed with her tribe these six years. She shook it out of her mind. "What are your names?" she asked instead, trying not to show her anger.

"I'm Stormer Thunderstruck," he replied. "And these are Stormers Fang-Tooth, Sniper, and Knife. We all range from one to six years, and I'm assuming you're six because you've been gone five or six years."

Cobra nodded without a word, turning her head to look at each one of them. Thunderstruck looked about her age, and Knife looked to be four. The other two were younger looking, Fang-Tooth looking two or three and Sniper looking about one.

"So, what do the younger wolves do?" she inquired, feeling like these wolves were a lot like her. Thunderstruck snorted.

"You'll hate it," he said, eyes flickering. "They have to train the wolves in the dens for combat, now more than ever, since they have it in for us." Cobra was still horrified to hear this news, but he went on. "So they have us fight each other, and against wolves from other dens. We're allowed outside the dens at certain times but never outside the Stormer base unless an older wolf is with us, and even then, we need to have permission."

So Stormers did protect each other, Cobra thought. *But what could the other tribes possibly be planning? A lot of the wolves we've met have trusted me. But there are* hundreds *of other wolves in the wild that hate Stormers down to their hearts. The question is what do I do? Do I help my tribe defeat the other tribes, even though many have finally begun to trust me? Or do I rebel and show that I'm really not a true Stormer?*

"Umm, earth to Cobra?" a voice called. Cobra shook herself and erased her thoughts. The wolves were staring at her with heads cocked and tongues lolling. "Why do you look like that?"

"Um, sorry," said Cobra. "Just thinking," she added. She looked back at them intently. "Why do you have to fight? I mean, couldn't you train some other way?"

"Stormers are *all about* fighting," said Sniper's young voice. "It doesn't bother us because we're *true* Stormers." Cobra knew Sniper was making fun of her, so she stifled an angry snarl.

"Well...do I have to?" she said.

"If you are six or younger, yes," Sniper barked. Cobra gritted her fangs and nodded grimly. "And I'm very strong for a one year old wolf, untrue Stormer."

So she had been right. Well, Sniper would not beat her if they faced off. "Do they have to kill?" she inquired.

"Of course not!" snarled Thunderstruck. "It's our nature but this is *training*, Cobra. We just fight until they call off the match. But it does cause a world of hurt. We'll toughen you up, untrue Stormer."

Stop calling me that! Cobra's mind snapped. She set her jaw and said nothing. "When do I start?"

"Geez, you have a lot of questions," Fang-Tooth snorted. "Tomorrow at dawn, so you'll have to get some sleep." She turned and flicked her tail as she curled up on a patch of moss. The other wolves nodded and stalked to their mossy beds too. Cobra just stood there, taking in every answer she'd managed to get.

I have to find my friends. But where is the prison, exactly? Anaconda told me...but where exactly do *I go?* Cobra was lost as the other Stormers gradually fell asleep and Knife began to snore. *Oh, spirits of wolves,* she thought over the noise, and crept silently out of the den.

The Stormers stalking the halls had disappeared. These halls were quiet and Cobra sneakily slunk around the walls. She watched a guard wolf in the hall use chains to cover the den entrance so the sleeping wolves couldn't escape. *I got out just in time.*

She felt a little scared as she slunk the quiet, empty stone halls. She knew she was breaking Storm tribe rules and wandering at night, but she *had* to find the prison where her friends were.

She recalled the words her father wolf had snorted about how to get there: *It's a long way away but your* comrades *are already there.* That didn't tell her anything. Instead she sniffed and pricked her ears to try to hear or smell her friends. She heard faint pattering as wolf guards were stationed at the entrance and smelled scents of Stormers everywhere.

She sniffed more and found Night's faint, helpless scent. She wondered what they were doing and if they were all right. Cobra listened to more pattering and sniffed more of Night's scent as she crept closer. The floor sloped down to dark caverns until she'd finally found it.

CHAPTER 4

THE PRISON was musky and hollow, with cavernous stone walls and ledges and chains like in Scarr's prison. Cobra took a moment to look around and leaped away from a puddle in one corner. She knew what that was and she wrinkled her muzzle.

"Night, Honor?" she whispered. "It's me, Cobra. I'm here to rescue you, but I can't do it yet. I have to wait for the perfect time." She didn't know what else to say. But a voice answered hers.

"Cobra," said Night, sounding relieved. "You're all right." Cobra nodded and stepped out of the shadows to see her comrade bound tightly to a rectangular stone inside a cell. His tail managed to thump and he looked weakly into her eyes.

Honor was there too, in the cell next to Night's. Each cell had that rectangular stone where the prisoners were bound. Cobra still couldn't fathom how the Stormers had found a place so great. Honor was tightly bound too, but his eyes flickered with hope when he saw her.

"I can't save you yet," repeated Cobra. "I will soon. Aren't they giving you any food?"

"Yes," rasped Night, "but not much. And it's hard to eat scraps of food when we're chained down like this." He wriggled a moment and gave up, tail thumping with a bit of sadness. "What have you been doing?"

"I met some other Stormers around my age," replied Cobra, keeping her voice low. "They really aren't *all bad* when I got to know them. The bad news is that Stormers six and under have to train in combat fights—not to kill—and I'm one of them. I can tell my father is furious and wants me to be a true Stormer." She sighed.

"It's my fault," said Night lowly. "I brought us into the Stormers' clutches without realizing it. And we never saw Terror coming, either."

Cobra gulped, feeling a twinge. "It's mine, not yours," she murmured. "I saw Terror's shadow but thought I was imagining things. I should have brought it up. I'm sorry."

"I'm sorry, too," replied Night. "I'll listen to you from now on about visiting Stormers. Now I really know how terrible they are."

There was silence. Cobra sighed again. "I have to go," she said hastily. "I'll come back soon but I believe they may send guards in here soon." She turned and Night gave her a farewell rasp of a bark.

She saw more puddles and wondered if she was going the right way. She passed more cells that were identical to each other and found more sleeping wolves chained down.

Then she saw a wolf she hadn't expected. It was female, and it was a Darkness wolf. Her eyes were open but she lay still under her binding chains. "Hello?" said Cobra, stepping closer to the Darkness wolf's cell.

The wolf looked back. Her eyes were weak and she looked as if she hadn't eaten for a while. "Don't hurt me, Stormer," she whispered.

Cobra swallowed. "I'm no ordinary Stormer, and I'm helping my friends Prowler Night and Honor out of here soon enough. I believe the Great Prowler Legend unlike any others, and my friend Prowler Night may be the Great Prowler, because he changed Honor. I'm Stormer Cobra."

"I'm Kaiju. I've been a Lone Wolf for about three years and I just wound up here. The assassin wolf—he threatened to kill me. So I just followed and I haven't gotten to eat for days." Her hungry eyes sparkled weakly as she stared at Cobra.

"I'm so sorry," said Cobra. "I'll help you out too as soon as I can. Maybe I can even sneak some scraps in here for you." She kept her voice low and made sure no other wolf was around. The prison was quiet and still, with its stone walls and shadowy corners.

"That would be great," said Kaiju, perking her ears and twitching her whiskers. "Thanks, Cobra. You really aren't ordinary."

Cobra's tail thumped the floor as she sat on her haunches. "How long have you been here?" she whispered.

"About a week," Kaiju replied, laying her head down. "And it's been gloomy and quiet here. I watched your friends get escorted here and I felt sorry for them. I didn't want them to be treated like I am."

"And that assassin is my brother," snorted Cobra. "He's not really an assassin at this point. Instead of killing us he just led us here. Terror can be a hothead, I admit. I promise to help you out as soon as possible, along with my friends."

"Thank you," repeated Kaiju, and Cobra saw the Darkness wolf's tail wag as it hung from the stone rectangle. "I don't even have the strength to struggle, let alone try to escape this place. I need you."

Cobra bowed her head and took a pace backward. "I'll be back soon," she said. "I have to get back before any wolf notices I'm gone. Goodbye, Kaiju."

"Goodbye," answered the Darkness wolf weakly. Cobra turned and paced out of the prison and down the empty halls. She hoped she could keep these promises and stay out of trouble at the same time.

She just realized how long she'd been gone when the sun began to creep across the horizon, ready to stretch and begin the day. Cobra had gotten no sleep whatsoever and knew she wouldn't do as well in combat training.

Her fellow Stormers were just stretching and yawning inside the dens. The guard wolf unchained the entrance and Cobra slipped in. "Good morning," she murmured, surpassing a yawn herself.

"We do not greet each other good morning, either!" barked Thunderstruck, tail lashing with slight amusement. "We growl, remember?"

"Yes," Cobra sighed, "we growl." She saw the small Stormer pups wriggle awake with vicious squeaks. Even the pups of the Storm tribe could be dangerous.

"Ready for combat?" jeered Sniper. Cobra hated his making fun of her already. "Because you have to learn to be a true Stormer, remember?

Your father said so, and he's the leader of the tribe."

"I know," said Cobra hastily. Just then Terror paced in with his head high.

"Father needs you now, Cobra," he said in his always-casual voice. "Follow me. You four, stay here until Hurricane calls you." Knife, Thunderstruck, Fang-Tooth, and Sniper said nothing as Cobra and Terror made their way out of the dens.

It was silence for a moment, and Cobra felt especially awkward being alone with her brother. "Who's Hurricane?" she asked at last.

"He's in charge of the combat matches," Terror replied. He turned his head and his gaze—intimidating eyes, overgrown fangs and all—flickered into hers. "All wolves six and under must wait for his command."

They walked along and Cobra asked, "Why aren't *you* in there then? And why does Father need me if I have to go with Hurricane?"

Terror gave a laugh. "I'm an assassin, remember? Anyway, you're his daughter, aren't you?" His ugly gaze flickered again. "And you're a special guest and he wants to transform you in time for the war."

"What…what war?" Cobra stuttered, trying to hide the tremor in her voice.

Terror rolled his eyes. "The war between us and the other tribes, of course," he said rather annoyingly. "They have it out for us, remember? We're the most populated tribe in the wild so we're bound to win."

Don't get so cocky, Cobra thought grimly. But of course Stormers were proud and merciless in battle. She thought she had better brace herself for the combat matches in this case.

Stormers lined the halls and they turned a few more corners into a place Cobra had never seen before. It was dimly lit and cavernous, and a large rectangular stone rested in the center. Her father lay draped over it, ears perking when they entered. He stood up. "Well done, Terror," he growled as they arrived at his stone. "Maybe you aren't *too* much of a hothead."

Terror ducked his head but did not move. "What are you waiting for?" snarled Anaconda now. "Get on duty and patrol our borders to see if the tribes have arrived yet!" Terror hurriedly leapt to his paws and galloped out of the cavern.

Cobra just stood there waiting for a command as her father paced across the room. "The war is coming soon," he muttered. "You must lead your tribe into a deathly battle against every other tribe, and who knows which wolf will lead them..."

"Father, are you worried?" said Cobra at last. "I kind of am..."

"Which is why we must toughen you up," growled Anaconda. "I'm just going over battle plans, daughter. Follow me and I will discuss a few things with you."

Cobra got to her paws and followed Anaconda out of the cavern and down more halls. The place seemed endless but she hung by her father wolf's side. "So," she said expectantly.

Anaconda shook his fur. "You have to become a true Stormer before the tribe war starts. You must understand that we need as many wolves on our side as possible. No matter what your filthy comrades think or say you must side with us and become a real Stormer. There is no Prowler-loving Stormer, Cobra, and there never will be. I am going to toughen you up and make you realize that your ripping claws and tearing fangs are your destiny."

Cobra let these words sink in, and her heart sunk with them. Her eyes got cloudy and she almost stumbled as she walked. She couldn't believe these words, not even if they were from her father. This was *not* how she was meant to be, and she hoped that stubborn streak would remind her of that.

They turned one last corner and emerged into a small stone arena where Cobra assumed the combat fights took place. On the sides of the arena were several lined-up wolves, from younger than one to nearly seven. Anaconda nosed her forward and she padded solemnly next to Thunderstruck.

A sleek and glossy black-and-tan Stormer stepped out into the arena. He must be Hurricane, Cobra thought. None of the Stormers she'd seen in the halls had had these fur colors before. She wondered if he was a hybrid. *No! Stormers never mate with other tribes, remember? Maybe he has another tribe in his ancestry instead.*

Hurricane silently addressed Thunderstruck and a two-year-old wolf from another one of the dens. The two wolves stood in the center growling at each other before beginning to strike with curved claws. Cobra hated watching blows being dealt and scratches being slashed, but she had to get ideas from the other wolves.

After many wolves had faced each other in combat and come back with bleeding scratches or pants from exertion, Cobra snapped to attention and realized that only she and another wolf remained.

She turned her head to see who it was and listened to Hurricane address them. This wolf looked…young, too young for a six-year-old like her to face. "How old are you?" she whispered, hoping not to sound rude.

"I am Stormer Blade-Edge," said the extremely young voice. "I am ten moons old."

CHAPTER 5

COBRA STOOD stock still. How could she possibly face a wolf this young? Why would any wolf put a not even one-year-old against a six-year-old? "But do I have to—?" she started.

Anaconda snarled. "You will. Blade-Edge was trained very early as he was orphaned. He was eager to join our war so we trained him. Daughter, don't tell me you're scared when you're more than four years older than him!"

A few Stormers snickered and Cobra wanted to bite all their necks. "I will," she decided. "Bring it on, young one." Blade-Edge's muzzle twisted with fury.

"Don't call me that!" he snapped in his young voice. "I'm stronger than you think!" Cobra recalled once more that Stormers were arrogant wolves. She set her jaw and nodded.

The two wolves faced each other, and Cobra looked especially large compared to the young Stormer. Blade-Edge was only about three-quarters of her size and had hints of gray with his tan body. His tail was lashing and his fangs were already full grown. Cobra growled through *her* fangs, which had grown a tiny bit longer. Her brother's had definitely gotten long.

Blade-Edge did the same, and before Cobra could spring he did it first. She leaped out of the way and managed to tackle him. She gnashed her fangs in his face but didn't dare bite. She didn't like using her teeth and claws on another wolf, even when she had no choice.

She remembered Anaconda's vicious words as she darted around Blade-Edge and knocked him to one side: *I'm going to make you realize that your ripping claws and tearing fangs are your destiny.*

Cobra's eyes got cloudy once more and she stumbled during a dodge. Blade-Edge managed to scramble to his paws and barrel toward her, sinking his grown fangs into her ear. She yelped sharply and came to her senses, flinging him aside in her anger.

She realized that she could attack when she was angry. She *couldn't* get angry. She needed to control herself and get through this match. She leaped and dug her claws into Blade-Edge's back as she pinned him down. He scrambled and whined, gnashing his teeth at her.

Cobra felt a rush of a feeling she hardly felt: more anger. It overflowed her like Night had once said these voices in his head had done. Her eyes began to fill with imaginary flames and she gave a howling snarl, throwing herself down onto the other Stormer.

Blade-Edge yelped and shouted, "Are you crazy? This is combat *training!*" Cobra didn't hear him. He yowled as her claws slashed into his back, drawing blood immediately. She sunk her fangs into his neck and he cried out more, thrashing and turning.

She wanted to tear and rip into him more, but just then a body knocked into her head and then there was darkness.

C OBRA OPENED her eyes slowly. She heard a moaning Blade-Edge from the next cave over. The small curved cave with dim light she assumed was the healing cave. Was she hurt? She checked herself but she was completely fine except for a little bit of blood dried on her bitten ear.

Wolves were outside the caves, murmuring and lashing their tails. Cobra watched them closely and watched her father and a few others drift in. Her father wolf's gaze was unreadable, but she knew he looked angry. "Cobra," he growled, "you almost killed Blade-Edge. And he's much younger than you. How could you?"

Cobra ran her tongue over her chops, her tail thumping with her lost in thought. *Why did I flip out of control like that? Am I really becoming a true Stormer and becoming a savage like the rest of them? What made me so angry?* Questions were running through her head like a flood.

"I wanted you to be stronger and like a real Stormer," her father went on, "but not to where you nearly kill a tribe mate. That's not even what we do. Terror is an assassin but he never kills wolves from his own tribe!" Anaconda wrinkled his muzzle with fury.

"I-I'm so sorry, Father. I don't know what got into me. I just got so angry and went out of control. Does that happen to Stormers all the time?"

"There is no telling," growled Anaconda. "But I hope to never see that happen again. You used your fangs and claws but not in the right way. If it happens again there will be serious consequences." He turned and stalked off and Cobra's ears drooped with sadness.

She glanced over at the next cave, which she could see a portion of. The wolf she'd nearly killed was yowling with pain as a few Stormers worked to treat his back wound. Cobra flinched and felt immediate shame for what she'd done. The questions she still had were unanswered.

She wanted to apologize but Blade-Edge was hurting right now and wouldn't want to listen. She picked herself up and trotted down the halls, body low and ears pinned. Some wolves which had apparently heard the news glared at her as she passed, making her feel more ashamed.

Quickly, she dashed down the same halls she'd followed before and down to the prison, where she hoped they had not posted guard wolves. "Night, Honor," she whispered again, stepping into the dimly lit place. There was the sound of chains rattling and she came to Night and Honor's cells. Right now they were struggling to eat scraps they had been provided.

"Are you all right, Cobra?" Honor asked with a cock of his head. "It's just…your ears are down and the look on your face…"

"You can tell us," Night insisted when she hesitated.

"You won't like it," Cobra sighed. "I nearly killed a wolf in combat training." Gasps arose. "But I never meant to! I just got angry for some reason and tore into a not even one-year-old and now he's healing in the caves down there. I would never deliberately hurt a wolf like other Stormers would. My father is angry."

"I thought he wanted you to be vicious," said Night with a tone of confusion. "Wouldn't he be pleased with you?"

"No. He said that was too much even on another wolf. They trained him because he was going to help them in the upcoming war between the tribes. I don't want it to happen, but it will, and every one of us has to be ready. I just don't know who to side with—my tribe…or the others, some of whom have begun to trust me."

Night sighed. "That's a hard decision. And I have to side with the other tribes because I'm the probable Great Prowler. And of course Prince Honor has to fight for the Darkness tribe. You're left with the choice, Cobra, and I hope you make it well."

Honor was lost in thought. "How did you get out of control like that?" he wondered aloud. "That's never ever happened to you before. You could have reacted that way because maybe you weren't used to your tribe yet. Or…"

"Or maybe I really am meant to be a savage Stormer, and shouldn't be with you," whispered Cobra, turning her head. "I love you, Night, but the Stormers are pulling me away from you and won't let me love the wolves I want to love." She felt a tear roll to the ground.

"Oh, Cobra," said Night. "Don't be upset. We'll be fine. And you can stand up for what's right because I *know* you, Cobra. You would never kill wolves like that or love another tribe wolf for no reason. You can stand up for it if you have the courage to."

He's right, thought Cobra. *I* can *stand up for what I believe if I am brave enough. I don't want to be like them or tear into creatures like a savage. It's* not *my destiny, no matter what my father says.*

"Thanks, Night," she whispered. The tears stopped rolling. "I'll come back when I can but first I need to visit another prisoner I met named Kaiju. She's been here for a while and has hardly eaten. She needs my help too."

"Kaiju?" said Honor. "So…a Darkness wolf?" he added. Cobra nodded. "My mother Pebble said something about that wolf. I never knew what she meant but I swear I heard the name Kaiju."

"I could ask her a few things for you," Cobra offered.

"Sure," said Honor. He told her a few things to ask and she nodded, turning and saying one last goodbye. She dashed down the corridor toward the Darkness wolf's cell.

"Kaiju, I'm back," she whispered. The wolf's head lifted. "I have a few questions for you, from my friends. First, I forgot to tell you. My friend Honor had these questions and he's the long-lost Darkness heir."

Kaiju was shocked. "He is? I heard all about that heir being taken four years ago. He's back? Do they know?"

"Yes," said Cobra with a smile. "And like I said, I believe that Prowler Night is the Great Prowler. The other two have something special about them. I haven't found anything special about me."

"Are you kidding?" gasped Kaiju. "You're special because you aren't like any Stormer I've ever met. You're kind and brave enough to sneak down here. And you believe things other Stormers don't believe. I wouldn't say you weren't extraordinary, Cobra."

Cobra shrugged, taking in these words. "I guess." She looked around. "Then again, I'll ask questions next time. I hear and smell guards coming. I'll see you soon, Kaiju. Oh, and my father is good about provisions. So if the guards don't give you food this time, shout 'I'm never being fed down here because these guards are secret-keeping stupids!'"

Kaiju laughed. "I will."

Cobra chuckled herself and ran as fast as she could out of the prison, right past the muttering guard wolves. She darted down corridors without a second glance, nearly running into Terror.

"Whoa!" he snarled. "Watch where you're going, sister, I'm trying to head out on patrol. Gee!" Cobra snapped at his ear and ran on by and followed the same path to get to her father's place.

"Father," she said when she entered.

Anaconda was deep in conversation with Hurricane. Cobra wondered if they were talking about her. Anaconda's head snapped up and he gazed at her.

"The war," he breathed into a growl. "It's coming soon."

CHAPTER 6

"I KNOW THAT," Cobra said. "But I was just coming to apologize again and say that I never, ever meant to hurt that wolf. I—"

"I know you didn't."

Cobra looked up. It wasn't her solemn father speaking. It was Hurricane. "You never did. Stormers can get vicious at times."

"But I'm *not* a true Stormer!" Cobra protested. "I just got so *angry* and I'll probably never know why, and I just attacked and…I'm sorry, Father. It won't happen again."

"It better not," growled Anaconda, and there was a stern, commanding tone in his voice. "I'm already worried enough about the upcoming war and I'm a proud Stormer. I don't need my daughter losing her temper on small helpless wolves. Blade-Edge may die because of you, not even living to be a year old. Don't let it happen again. You understand?"

"Yes, Father."

Anaconda straightened up. "Hurricane, you are dismissed. Put extra treatment on all of the trainees, especially Blade-Edge." He flicked his tail and Hurricane bowed his head and turned.

"Wait!" Cobra cried. Then she lowered her voice. "Father, may I go with Hurricane for a bit?" Her tail wagged to show she meant peace in this. Her father nodded gruffly. She tried not to leap as she followed a surprised Hurricane.

When they began to walk the halls, Cobra whispered, "Why did you stand up for me like that? Thanks so much, because my father probably would've done something if you hadn't been there."

"I stood up for what I believed" was his answer. Cobra was stunned, first because she didn't know that Stormers could be this kind to one another. And second, this was the same thing she'd been told to do in the prison. Her tail wagged and she tried not to show it. "So have you always been in charge of the trainees?" she inquired.

"Most of my life, yes," he grunted. "I started out as a trainee myself until I was seven and worked my way up in promotion. Anaconda liked me—your father indeed liked me—and finally put me in charge when the former trainee leader passed away."

It ended up in silence. "I only ran away because I didn't think I'd belong here. And I don't," Cobra sighed. "I believed things in other tribes and befriended other tribes. I'll never be a true Stormer, but my father and everyone else doesn't see that. You understand, don't you?"

Hurricane gave a gruff sigh. "I never will," he whispered, "but I know what you mean. *I'm* not too true either, yet I grew up here from the time I was whelped. I get it; you want to be different. But Stormers don't do changing."

Cobra allowed the awkward silence to fall. She felt as if Hurricane was a good and calm Stormer to talk to, and she felt safe around him. Surely he wouldn't let anything happen to her...and if he liked her, she liked him back.

"What will we do? Like, in the war?" Cobra asked nervously. "I know I'm not ready, after only one training session. And *that one* went quite well." She wrinkled her muzzle.

"We will get together as a tribe and organize groups. At least, that's what I heard from the higher-ranked wolves." Hurricane lashed his tail with shame.

"You eavesdrop on other wolves?" laughed Cobra. "Not what I'd expect from a strong trainee leader!"

Hurricane chuckled, tail still lashing. "I did. I needed to know our battle plans right here and now so I could get the trainees ready, including you now."

They kept walking down the halls until they came close to a small dimly lit cave. This place was like a maze, Cobra thought. "Where is this?"

"The higher-ranked cave, where the wolves meet, where I eavesdrop," said Hurricane with a small grin. They tucked themselves against a small crevice in the wall and Cobra perked an ear.

"Yes, the rest are ready. Terror is still on patrol but he'll come back and let us know otherwise if the tribes are coming. We'll all be in troops by the time they get into the territory," said a female's voice. "How are the mothers and pups doing, Shearer?"

"They're hidden down in our basement, and hidden well, Pinscher," said another voice, probably from Shearer. "The prisoners the tribes won't care about. It's us."

"Of course, it's obvious, hothead!" barked Pinscher sharply. Shearer yelped in protest and the room exploded with barks and snaps from other wolves. Hurricane chuckled again.

"Pretty lively, huh?" he asked with another grin. Cobra nodded with her tongue lolling from her jaws. *So the wolves are ready. My father didn't make it sound that way. How he is still worried when every wolf is prepared, I'll never know.* She shook her head inwardly.

They crept out of the crevice and back down the halls, and Cobra sighed. "Father said I could never leave these walls, but I want some outdoor air," she whispered. "It feels like I've been stuck inside this ghastly place for weeks, even though it's been two days."

"I know," said Hurricane, "which is why I'm sneaking you outdoors. Your father would never figure it out. Just stay with me." He started toward an outer entrance and other Stormers were filing out. Cobra could not see her brother, which meant he was somewhere else on his patrol for now.

She followed Hurricane until they were in the lovely open air, the pleasant breeze and gentle weather filling her lungs. She breathed in and out and leaped about like a pup. "This is nice," she whispered. "Thanks, Hurricane."

The Stormer nodded and turned around. Just then Cobra nearly jumped out of her fur. There stood the five wolves probably from the room they were just eavesdropping in. "Cobra!" barked Pinscher. "What are you doing outdoors?!"

Cobra shrank back, her tail clamping to her flank. "I, uh…Hurricane took me out here because I asked him to. Don't blame him; blame me. I'm sorry." She lowered her head.

Shearer growled. "Sneaking outdoors is not okay," he hissed from in front of her. "You thought we couldn't smell your scents leading to outside?"

"Uh, no," stuttered Cobra. "I never did think that. And I'm so, so sorry. Just please don't tell Father!"

"Oh, we will," snarled Pinscher. "You won't be getting away with this. You—" she glared at Hurricane "—go down with the trainees until Anaconda finds something to do with you." Hurricane tucked his tail and headed in with a low whine. Pinscher turned her head. "Rebellion, go inside and find Stormer Anaconda immediately. Cobra, follow us. We won't hurt you—you're just in trouble."

Cobra nodded meekly and she was surrounded by the higher-ranked Stormers as she was escorted inside and led to Anaconda's cave. He wasn't there but Cobra turned around and found her father standing behind them, growling loudly.

"I thought you could stay out of trouble, daughter," he snarled. "I've been patient with you long enough. It looks like we're taking a trip to the prison. Pinscher, bind her."

"Yes, Alpha Anaconda," Pinscher replied, wrapping chains tightly around Cobra. The female Stormer looked only a little older than her, maybe seven or eight.

Anaconda led the way, and Cobra wondered if she'd ever get freedom again, as when she was on the road with her comrades. What if it never happened again?

L IKE IN Scarr's prison, Cobra could not help but wriggle and snarl viciously. She tried to calm herself but her anger was everlasting. The chains were tight, tighter than those in Scarr's camp. She was bound to her own rock ledge next to Kaiju.

"So, the questions?" said Kaiju. Cobra knew she was curious but also trying to calm her down. She stopped.

"Prince Honor says he heard his mother Pebble mention you once in Darkness Territory. So he wants to know if you were in his pack once before. He's not forcing you to come back. He just wants to know."

"Well...I won't tell you everything but I was in his pack once," said Kaiju. "He was a pup, and soon I found reason to run away. I had to, and I won't tell you why. *I* don't even understand the reason for running myself away. Then, while I was a Lone Wolf, I heard that the heir had been stolen and I decided to search for him. But now...he's been found. And I have been captured by stupid Storm tribe lunatics!"

Cobra flinched. Kaiju muttered a "no offence" and the Stormer shook her head. "I see," she whispered. "Well, you don't have to tell us why. But I do have more questions for you. Who was your family, Kaiju?"

Kaiju looked away. "All I can tell you is that I believe my father's name was Toil." That was all she said. Cobra took in these words and nodded with thanks. She would tell Honor as soon as she could.

"Do you think they'll move me into another cell?" she asked at last. "No, no, never mind. I know. They put me here because they don't want me anywhere near Night or Honor. But I miss them so much, especially Night..."

"Hey, can I ask *you* something?" Kaiju tilted her head. "Is Night... well, is he...?"

"Oh, *no*," said Cobra hastily. "I mean, I like him, but that—*that* is way past the standards. I mean, Prowlers and Stormers *can't* be together. They're enemies in the wild." She didn't meet the Darkness wolf's eyes.

Kaiju gave a whine of sympathy. "For a while, I loved your brother," she admitted with a duck of her head. Cobra gave a reverberating gasp. "Yes, I did. But now that I know he's an assassin and found another wolf he particularly likes, I stopped doing it."

"Another wolf?" said Cobra, "Who?"

Kaiju looked up. "Stormer Pinscher," she said.

"What?" Cobra hung her jaw. "Who would *Terror* love when all he *loves* is to *kill?* I haven't even seen him interact with that wolf!"

"Well, I have," Kaiju said matter-of-factly. "I can tell he likes her and doesn't want to show it. Your brother can be soft sometimes."

"Hush up. He is *not* soft, not even a bit," Cobra said crossly.

Kaiju laughed, rattling her chains. "I'm just giving you a hard time, Cobra," she chuckled.

Cobra snorted and laid her head on her paws. Kaiju continued to laugh as the Stormer became lost in thought.

I have to get out of here, and rescue all these wolves, including Honor, Night, and Kaiju. Also, a war is coming and I have to be ready like every other Stormer to stop it. I have to make my decision about this war and I have other things to worry about too.

Suppose if my father worried about the war, and I'm worrying now, that Stormers are the most worrisome wolves in the wild?

CHAPTER 7

COBRA HAD an idea the next day. It wasn't about the upcoming war or how to escape the place...at least not yet. When the guard wolves began trudging down to the prison she pretended to wriggle. "Guards!" she shouted. "I would like to move my cell because this Darkness wolf is driving me nuts!"

She had already told Kaiju about the plan and of course the female wolf agreed. She had asked all she needed to ask and Kaiju had finally been fed decently. The guards tilted their heads at her, cocking their ears. Then they broke into debating whispers.

"Will she not cause trouble?"

"Is she lying? If she escapes her father will be furious."

"This is her punishment. She deserves to be driven nuts, but on the other paw..."

Cobra waited patiently and gave one defiant wriggle of the chains. She wanted to move so she could be with her comrades. She just had to see them again and update them, even if it meant staying down here.

"Fine," one guard said at last. "But don't even think about getting next to that Prowler and the Darkness wolf, or—"

"Let her."

They spun around on their haunches and Cobra looked ahead. "Commander Pinscher?" a guard stammered. "What is it?"

Pinscher narrowed her eyes. "Move her. To where she wants. I and the other Stormers won't tolerate her *hideous* howling and angry shouts."

The guards nodded and the same one bowed his head. Pinscher turned and began to trot off and Cobra's chains were unlocked. They came close to the higher-ranked wolf as they passed to head to Honor and Night's cells. "Thank you," Cobra whispered to Pinscher. The other Stormer just gave her a glance and began to trot again.

The guard wolves chained Cobra back up and the Stormer didn't struggle. She was next to Honor's cell and she half wished she was next to Night instead…her love. No matter what any wolf said, he was her love. The wolves trotted away, murmuring and glancing back at her.

There was a scrap of fish that smelled like it had been peed on and left out for two weeks. Cobra brought herself to eat it without gagging, as she was hungry. Her comrades were quiet and she suddenly heard ominous conversation just down the hall.

"Have you found the other tribes yet, Terror?" The warning voice of Pinscher sounded from ahead.

"Not yet," said her brother's voice. "I thought I smelled faint scents of them, maybe spies sent to see what we were doing. If I spot one I'll kill it, no doubt. Those hideous other tribes won't even make it past Territory borders with me around."

Oh, come on, arrogant brother. I think I know who's hideous here.

"Terror, if you're going to be an assassin, you need to prove it! The war is coming soon—every wolf senses it. We're all prepared and all you're doing is patrolling around and waiting for the tribes to come in and attack us. Go beyond Territory borders and find them, for wolf's sake!" Pinscher's angry bark reverberated down the hall.

"I will. I'm a real assassin. I was just warming up," said the voice smugly. Cobra knew right then that her ugly-faced brother was grinning with arrogance. As Pinscher's faltering paw-steps left the hall, she heard Terror's distant muttering of "I'll show her that I can kill. I'll kill every wolf from every tribe if I have to. I may even kill my own sister."

Cobra couldn't stifle her growl. It came as a rumble and then a snarling tone of growl. Her body seethed and Honor turned his head to give her a sympathetic look. "I hate you, brother," she muttered into the dimness.

Silence fell and Night broke it. "What did you find out from Kaiju, Cobra? And how did you end up here?" Cobra quickly explained why she was here and the other Darkness wolf's answers.

Honor's jaw sagged open and his tail stopped its rhythmic tap. "Did she actually say her father's name was *Toil?*"

"Well, she said that's what she remembered. She ran from your pack shortly after you were born, remember? What about it?" Night had the same curious look Cobra had.

"Well, Mother—Alpha Pebble—told me she had two mates: Soldier and Toil. My and Loyalty's father was Soldier and Razor's was Toil. That could mean...Kaiju is Razor's sister and my half-sister!"

Night shook his head. "That *can't* be," he said. "Razor would have said something or your mother would have explained. Maybe you heard wrong, Cobra. You are kind of old." He shot her a sarcastic grin and she growled playfully. "Anyway, she could have said 'Turmoil' or 'Turtle.' How could you know for sure?"

"I'm *sure* she said Toil," Cobra insisted.

Night sighed. "We'll go with it for now, Cobra. When you get out of here, don't get into any more trouble, okay? There's a big war and I know you'll be a part of it. Have you made your decision?"

"No," Cobra huffed. "I was busy and it's just too hard. Tribes have already begun to trust me as a 'not ordinary Stormer' so if they see me fighting alongside the Storm tribe, they would think I was lying all along. I don't want that. And if I fight for the other tribes the Stormers would be happy to kill me."

"I understand," said Night.

"You do not!"

Her comrades were stunned silent at her outburst. Like before, Cobra could not control her gathering rage. "You are a Prowler, the *Great Prowler!* Honor, you're a Darkness wolf, heir to King Wolf! I have *nothing* special about me and you don't know or understand how it feels to be an untrustworthy Stormer and you don't understand how it feels to not fit in with anyone! You will *never, never* understand!" She threw her paws over her head and whined into a cry.

"Cobra," Night whispered. "Please. I never meant for it to sound that way. You know I love you, and I know you love me. Everything has been hard on you—everything—and I'm sorry. You're right; we'll never understand what it's like to be a not-trusted wolf and to be feared and forced to be a certain way."

"We want you to know that you are special no matter what," Honor spoke up. "You're special to us, even if you aren't to other wolves. Just think about that, Cobra, and it will help. It may even help you make the right choices. Like we said, stand up for what you believe."

Cobra didn't respond. Her whining cry stopped but she still had her paws over her head and her tail was tapping sullenly. They were sorry and they were good friends—Night was still her love no matter how much she yelled or contradicted him.

Thank you, my comrades. But I still have plenty of decisions to make, mistakes to fix, friends to save, and a war to stop. And I'll stop at nothing until I do these things.

To Cobra's sheer relief, a bit of bird was brought to her and she crunched it up while the guard wolves unlocked her chains and led her down the hall. She assumed her punishment was over, or Anaconda needed her, or both.

Pinscher led the way, shouldered by Rebellion and Shearer. The guards were at their tails and Cobra shuddered when she felt cold fur brush against her backside. The Stormers had obviously spent a lot of time outside in the chilly breeze.

The brighter light outside the prison blinded Cobra for a split second. Stormers, as usual, lined the halls and some shot glares at her, remembering all the trouble she'd caused obviously. The Stormer tried not to make eye contact with them.

"Does…does Father need me?" she asked Pinscher with a lick of her chops. She did not want them to think she was pathetic so she tried to sound curious instead of worried.

Pinscher snapped her head around and growled through her fangs.

"What do you think?" she hissed and Cobra found her quite terrifying. *Like my brother,* she thought grimly. *Now I'm pretty sure they're the perfect match. They're both terrifying…and don't forget the hotheaded part.*

Hurricane was pinned down beneath Anaconda's strong paws when they came over. Cobra wanted to cry "No!" to her father but that would prove Hurricane's guilt. "Don't kill him!" she snarled instead.

Her father's head snapped up. "What did you just say?"

"Don't kill him!" Cobra repeated. "It was my fault! Don't do anything to him, please!" She admitted she really liked that wolf. *But do I choose him or Night? What if he already has a mate?* She shook herself and growled through clenched fangs.

Anaconda didn't loosen his grip. "Don't tell me what to do, daughter," he snarled. "Hurricane was the one that broke rules and brought you out there, Cobra, and you know it. And also, have you forgotten I rule the tribe? There's a war and I don't have time for rule-breaking. Step back and don't interfere." He growled into Hurricane's ear and the male Stormer whined.

"Don't!" Cobra lunged but was shouldered painfully in the ribs and got caught between Pinscher and Rebellion. Rebellion bared his teeth at her and Pinscher lashed her tail with an "I-don't-think-so" look on her face. Cobra lashed out but Anaconda was too far away.

"You have brought this too far, Hurricane. I thought I trusted you with the high-ranked job of taking care of the trainees. Instead you eavesdrop and break rules. Now you will *pay*," Anaconda hissed. His fangs showed and his jaws slavered.

"No!" Cobra snarled in an almost howl. Anaconda let loose a war cry and to her horror he crunched his jaws over Hurricane's neck. She was too stunned to react and her wolf tears came rolling when Hurricane dropped limp.

Her only Stormer friend, dead. The sensation was devastating. Cobra stood stock still as her shoulders were released. *My father is horrible.* Stormers gathered to take away Hurricane and Anaconda's head turned toward her.

"If you do anything else," he growled, "that will soon be your comrades."

CHAPTER 8

THAT NEXT day, Cobra was still lying on her mossy bed. She woke up realizing two things. First, that she had gotten a lot more sleep than she had in a while, and second, the other trainees were deep in brief conversation that she felt she needed to hear.

She stretched her russet and gray body and pricked her ears, sidling over. At the end of the room the entrance was still chain-locked until the guard came for the morning. Every other Stormer that wasn't a sleeping pup was in a circle with everyone else, talking ominously.

"There's been a lot of tension here lately," Thunderstruck said seriously. "Commander Pinscher is much stricter and fiercer now, and did you hear about Alpha Anaconda's rage against Hurricane?"

"He's dead," Fang-Tooth sighed as if she were sad. "I did like him a lot. He didn't seem like the kind of wolf that would break rules like that..."

Cobra sat just on the outside of their circle, scratching at a flea behind her ear. She was sad, too. She liked Hurricane just like Fang-Tooth had, and grieved silently about his death. Her father seemed so worried that he would take his mercilessness out on another wolf that barely did anything wrong.

And now Night and Honor aren't safe either. No one is, with this war coming. I have to make my decision and quick. Something big is coming and we have to face it...but what do I do?

Cobra gave an inward sigh just as Sniper spoke. "I heard Cobra had something to do with it," he growled, turning his head to look suspiciously at Cobra. "She *must* be becoming a real Stormer. But that doesn't mean she gets to get another wolf in trouble!" He gnashed the half-grown fangs in his mouth and Cobra began to shrink back.

The other trainees were all looking at her now. Some had the same suspicious looks and some looked as if they were wondering whether to believe this story. "It's not like that," stuttered Cobra. "I-I didn't beg him or anything. He took me out on his own decision and suffered consequences for it—"

"Likely story," Thunderstruck cut in. "You lie just to cover up for yourself. Now that our leader is gone we won't be ready for the war. And it's all because of you." He flicked his tail. "Gang, let's get some revenge, shall we?"

The others growled in agreement and all began creeping toward her. Cobra gasped with bewilderment and backed up into the corner. She was trapped, with nowhere to go. The trainees were closing in on her and they would almost surely kill her if she didn't do something.

"The world will be as still as stone!" she shouted, blurting out the words of the Great Prowler Legend as quickly as she could. The Stormers flinched back and blinked their eyes in surprise.

"The wind will have a perilous tone. But far away, on the run, we will have the Chosen One!" Cobra shouted to where even wolves outside the dens could hear. *"This Great Prowler, that is ordinary, will become the most extraordinary! They will find the right way to save the darkness and the day!"*

"Stop with that wolf-dung legend!" bellowed Knife over her shouting. "It's hideous! Just stop!" The other Stormers snarled in protest but Cobra went on, bringing herself toward them. They backed up just as she had, ears pinned to their skulls and fangs gnashed.

"No Prowler knows when this day will come, but every hope lies upon the stone! Prowlers wait and Prowlers lie, and the One has a

chance to try!"

She heard thundering paws approaching the den as she backed the other Stormers farther toward the other wall. "Stop!" a voice snarled from behind the chained entrance. Rebellion, Shearer, Pinscher, Anaconda, and many more Stormers were clamoring to get in. Cobra didn't listen.

"Upon the world darkness will fall! But the Great Prowler will stand above it all! And no matter what they find, they're the way to saving wolf kind!" Cobra finished, breathless. She managed to add in a shout, "Don't you want to win the coming war and for the Great Prowler to save you?"

The chains were unlocked and wolves burst in to surround her. Her ears pinned back. "The Great Prowler is a myth," her father spat as he gazed fiercely. "And your Prowler friend surely isn't. And that *King Wolf* couldn't stop us either. Of course we want to stop the war. We're proud Stormers!"

"And *you* will stop yammering and making every wolf's ears ring!" Pinscher snapped at her. "The trainees have a right to be mad at you, for you were the one who wanted to go outside. Hurricane knew you wanted to so he took you. However, it's your fault too."

"But-but—" Cobra faltered as wolves continued to close on her. The trainees growled with triumph and she gnashed her fangs at Pinscher. "That isn't fair! They shouldn't accuse me for Hurricane's death! I would never have let him die like that! I liked him a lot!"

"Humph," grunted Pinscher. "Tell that to the authority wolves." She flicked her tail to the other troops. "Chain her up. Apparently she needs another round of punishment."

"No!" Cobra kicked her way through them and raced down the hall, and she heard thundering paws at her heels. Snarls reverberated through every hall and cavern. Now the whole tribe could hear the phenomenon in the dens. She didn't know where she would go, but she just had to escape.

What about Night and Honor? Cobra's mind screamed at her. She gave a sharp turn and leaped down a ledge to make her way into the dungeons. More thundering paws…

She gave another leap and she was down there. There was pattering and snarling and she darted into a crevice in the wall. Heart beating and head pounding with tension, she stayed as still as she could and heard the wolves emerge nearby.

"Where did she go?" snarled Pinscher's voice. "I swear to the spirits of wolves that I will kill that wolf when I find her!"

"Or have Terror do it," muttered Shearer. Cobra heard Pinscher snap at his ear with a *ca-pok* sound and he yelped. "Just saying," he whined. "He's an assassin!"

Cobra breathed hard and her heart still thundered in her rib cage. She'd stay inside this crevice as long as she needed to. She wasn't far from her comrades' cells and would get to them soon. Maybe they had already heard the commotion even from down here.

"Cobra," Pinscher sneered all of a sudden. "If you don't show yourself I'll kill your Prowler and Darkness wolf friends. You can count on it."

I'm not falling for your wimpy threats! Cobra thought fiercely.

She stayed as still and quiet as possible and hoped for the best. Pinscher snorted from down the hall. "She'll show up soon," she growled, and Cobra heard her paw-steps mix with the others' as they started up the ledges.

Cobra let her breath out in a big whoosh and dislodged herself from the crevice. She stretched with a sigh and pattered quietly down the halls. "Night, Honor," she whispered. "I'm back. I'll explain everything." She heard nothing and went farther. "Night, Honor?" she repeated. Maybe they were asleep. "Wake up! I'm here!"

Nothing... Cobra stood there for a moment in the dim darkness. What could have happened? What if they were already dead? Or what if their cells had been moved by a wolf knowing that she'd been visiting them? What if—?

Then she knew. They were gone.

COBRA DID not leave the prison. She didn't want to risk running into the Stormers again. She knew by now that every wolf in her tribe would be looking for her, so she made sure to slip into the crevice if guard wolves came down.

How long could she stay here? Her eyes were drooping and she had lost strength in her body. Her stomach rumbled with hunger and she knew she'd never survive down here. Not only that, but she couldn't find her friends.

If they were gone, there were only two possibilities: either they had been killed or they had escaped. Cobra hoped for the second. *Please, spirits of wolves, I hope they're safe somewhere, in hiding, away from my hideous tribe.*

"But what about Kaiju?" she said aloud in a whisper. She dashed down the hall, praying that the female Darkness wolf was still here. Her paws thundered quietly and her ears stood erect. Despite her exhaustion she ran rapidly toward the cell.

Yes, she was there. Kaiju lifted her head and perked her ears. "Cobra, what's wrong?" she whined. "I heard everything and I need you to explain."

And Cobra did. She was breathless by the time she finished and Kaiju seemed to be thinking it over. "So you're hiding here," she whispered. "For how long?"

"I don't know," said Cobra with a wolf shrug. She yawned and sat on her haunches. "All I know is that if I face my father now, he'll be furious. He's *been* furious ever since I arrived."

"Your father is horrible," said Kaiju with a shudder. Cobra gave her a sidelong look because she had thought the same thing. Anaconda was a true Stormer, and so was her assassin brother. She didn't want to be.

"I-I have to go," she faltered, stumbling backward dizzily, but stopped to use her fangs and claws to unlock the Darkness wolf's chains. Kaiju shook herself and gave Cobra a thankful look. The Stormer flicked her tail in a gesture for her to leave.

"Thanks for everything, Cobra," Kaiju said with a bow of her head. Cobra bowed back. "I'll escape somehow. Maybe I can dig my way out, although that would take a lot of digging."

Cobra nodded, and felt sudden strength come to her insides. She quickly and courageously fled up the halls and into the bright and open air. She sped past stunned Stormers and her paws thundered, this time loudly.

She caught sight of Pinscher and the others and stifled a frightened gasp. She had to face them, however. She swerved and stopped, gnashing her teeth, in front of them. They growled back and parted as Anaconda stepped in.

"Daughter… I knew you'd show up," he said. "I'm tired of you making trouble and grief for the tribe. I need to fix you up, really, I do. The war is coming. I have no time for this. Use your anger in this battle and it may do you good things." His tail lashed as he turned to trot off. The others did not move.

"He's right, you know. To be a true Stormer, you have to *follow rules* and *act like you can fight,*" snarled Pinscher defiantly. "If not—"

Cobra leaped, anger overtaking her like before. This time she didn't try to stop it. She threw herself into Pinscher and ricocheted into Shearer, knocking him backward. He wheezed for breath and she scratched him across the muzzle with her curved claw. He yelped with shock.

The Stormer gave her beautiful howl and it made every wolf around her pin their ears back and stagger backward. She growled at each of them and lunged at Rebellion, snarls escaping her throat like rapid fire.

Rebellion lashed out with his claws and just barely missed Cobra's flank. The Stormer threw herself toward him and the two ended up in a heap of fur. Other wolves stopped to watch the fight, ears perked. Cobra saw the trainees blink in amazement. Blade-Edge, wrapped in vines in different areas, even looked impressed.

Cobra's anger didn't last long. It seemed to go as soon as it had come. She stopped there, panting and lolling her tongue with exertion. The wolves she'd attacked were sprawled across the floor, wounded or exhausted as well. Pinscher was growling while groaning.

What is wrong with me? Cobra yelled to herself. *What is going on with my anger and my rage? Am I really becoming a true Stormer, or even worse than a real Stormer? I don't want to be that way. I truly don't…*

"I know who's at the top of my killing list," snarled a voice behind her. Cobra whirled around, still panting.

And there stood Stormer Terror.

CHAPTER 9

THE **OTHER** wolves sat up on their haunches. Pinscher cocked her head. "Terror?" she said. "What are you doing here? You're on patrol." She gnashed her fangs into a growl.

Cobra stood her ground in case Terror decided to attack her. "That's exactly why I'm here," her brother said with a raise of his head and flick of his tail. "Their scents are much stronger. They're getting closer, and fast."

Cobra scanned his expression for any sign of fear or worry. But it was her brother's normal unreadable face. She shook her body and lolled her tongue. "Try to kill me," she said, trying to use his casual voice. "See what happens."

Terror growled and his tail continued to flick. "You escaped this one, sister. But I'm an assassin and I'm nearly ready to show it. I won't be the normal casual Terror once I kill wolves. I'll be anything but patient or calm. I'll be the most powerful Stormer the world has ever known." His overgrown fangs glinted as his jaws slavered at the thought.

Cobra could tell he was mostly doing this for the wolf he loved, because his eyes gleamed as they fell on Pinscher. She turned and began to stalk off, shooting looks at each Stormer she passed. Maybe her overwhelming anger had done something good this time, but there was still more to come.

SHE TOSSED and turned inside the dens that night, restless despite her exhaustion. She had been separated from Knife, Thunderstruck, Fang-Tooth, and Sniper, so now she was in the most embarrassing place in the dens: the pup caves.

Everywhere she looked in the soothing dim light there were newly born pups and slightly older pups curled about. There were mossy beds lining up the walls and Cobra was on the largest bed of them all. She was wide awake and with ears perked. First, why would they move her to a place where only pups were permitted? Second, why was she restless?

Is it because my brother finally became terrifying, like he's supposed to? Wait. He must have been merely practicing his assassin tricks when he got casual and hotheaded. It was all part of his plan to kill wolves! Whenever he meets, say, a Lone Wolf and acts like a normal wolf and a Stormer that can be trusted, like me, he could turn around and maul that wolf. But does that mean he'll kill me?

Cobra shuddered. She had finally figured out Terror's antics, though. She got to wondering, in the stillness and quiet of the pup caves, about where the prisoners had gone. She'd checked everywhere around the prison and they were all gone, even the ones she didn't know.

Anaconda had said something about Hurricane breaking a lot of rules. Suppose one of them had been freeing the prisoners? Then again, he had left Kaiju in the prison, and had been killed right afterwards. *This is all so confusing, and there are so many other things I have to worry about right now.*

Maybe Hurricane had forgotten Kaiju. The Darkness wolf might have been asleep and of course her dark pelt could blend in to the eerie darkness of the prison. Cobra nodded to herself, deciding that it made sense. But she couldn't ask Hurricane now, because now he was a spirit in the air.

Cobra positioned herself in a more comfortable position. She rested her head on her paws and stared into space for a while, hoping to fall asleep that way. It was nice and quiet in here, though, so at least she didn't have to hear Stormer Knife's grunting and snoring during the night.

She didn't fall asleep. Instead she got to her paws and sidled to the chained entrance. They normally didn't chain it up since only pups slept here, but they had this time so that she couldn't escape. She snarled aloud with frustration and heard pups shuffling in their sleep at her outburst.

Hothead! Cobra thought to herself. If she was any louder she would wake up the poor pups and Anaconda would be even more furious with her. Her father seemed to be angry all the time. It was probably just his personality. *But I'm nothing like him*, she thought.

Right then, where she stood, she wondered who her mother was, if she had been kinder than her father, if she had helped rule the tribe too—and if Cobra had gotten her personality. She doubted her mother was still alive. But someday, she wanted to know about her.

Maybe part of my father's fierceness is sadness about losing my mother. I would understand that too, but I'd never met her. One day I might ask him who she was and if he's sad. But right now a war is coming on and I have to think quickly.

Cobra came to the entrance and peered through the chains. She saw wolves walking quietly down the stone halls. Were they preparing for the war? She sat down and listened. Pinscher was telling her fellow wolves to get the trainees ready, because the other tribes were arriving soon.

This caused Cobra's heart to race. She had to be ready as well as everyone else. She knew every wolf out there had heard the news and were getting as ready as possible. She knew the 'base' of the Stormers would be secured, and food would be eaten for strength.

The trainees would be nearly ready and the pups would be hidden away with their mothers. But she wondered if Night and Honor had run as far as they could to a safe place. Kaiju must have run away pretty far by now as well.

Cobra thought she'd never sleep. Every other wolf was awake too, so they must be restless for the war like her. She sidled back to her spot and turned her circles before curling up. *Please, spirits of wolves, help us overcome this war*, she thought before drifting off.

S HE WAS right. Cobra stalked the halls, flicking her tail and watching everything around her. Some Stormers were getting outside to make their formations, with Pinscher, Rebellion, and Shearer among them. On her other side wolves were rushing toward the pup caves to hide the tiny Stormers.

Cobra made her way to her father's cave, where he was deep in conversation with some guard wolves. "The preparations are being made as we speak," said a female. "The prisoners are gone so we're bringing the pups down there, to the deepest level. If anything happens we have a secret cavern. The other tribes will assume that we have no prisoners if they spot our escaped prisoners running by."

Anaconda nodded, looking deep in thought. "You may go," he told them. They bowed their heads and their shoulders brushed Cobra's fur as they passed her. Her father looked at her.

"I suppose *you* could be preparing too," he hissed at her like a rattlesnake. "What have you been doing that's so productive?"

"Nothing, Father," Cobra confessed. "But I see everything is taken care of. What should I do?"

Anaconda looked mildly shocked. "What do you *think* you should do?" he said in an unfriendly tone, fixing himself. "Get in the formation with the rest of them. Judging by that anger you have, you'd be good for that. You really are shaping up into a true Stormer, daughter."

Cobra's heart sank. *Am I?*

"Remember what I said," her father reminded her, running a tongue over his fangs. Cobra simply nodded meekly and tucked her tail as she left the cave.

He's right. I'm slowly changing to the wolf he wants me to be. How can I possibly stop it?

CHAPTER 10

COBRA SHIFTED herself on her haunches, feeling restless. Pinscher had ordered her to stay among a few other Stormers, near the front of the formation. They had sat and sat and waited a long time, and Cobra had sat there thinking of where her comrades and Kaiju could possibly have run to.

She had also thought sadly about Hurricane's death. He hadn't deserved what her father had done, even if he had let the prisoners go and taken her outside without permission. It hadn't been his fault at all; and he had suffered anyway.

That's just how Stormers are: cruel, merciless, arrogant, proud, and ferocious—but Hurricane wasn't that way. He was like me...not ordinary and not wanting to pick a fight.

That gave her new feeling and strength to know this fact. She remembered that she could stand up for what she believed in, and what was right. And maybe sometime she'd find her comrades again, just as Night had found her after escaping Prowler Scarr's camp.

She narrowed her eyes and perked her ears, staring ahead and listening closely for any sign of the other tribes crashing through the undergrowth to get to them. However, all she could hear was the muttering, growling, and clamoring of the wolves around her. They must be as worried and fearful as she was to be fighting in a war against the other tribes, despite being proud and strong.

She caught sight of the other trainees a distance behind her line. Even Blade-Edge, who was still recovering from her vicious attack, was there with fangs gnashed and tail lashing slowly. Thunderstruck looked especially proud and ready, head raised and eyes straight ahead. Cobra shifted again and she felt ready too.

Fang-Tooth, on the other paw, was shifting too as if she was nervous. Cobra understood, watching the other Stormer's tail clamp beneath her flank. Knife was snapping at the air as if a wolf was already poised at him. The trainees were ready, but what about everyone else?

She turned her head. Anaconda stood way at the top, over the ledge with his head held high and ears erect like hers. As the leader of the formation, she knew *he* was ready. At the rear also stood Stormer Terror, along with Stormers Pinscher, Rebellion, Shearer, and the others.

Lots of wolves she didn't know were gathered there too. The only ones missing were the severely wounded and mothers with pups, all of which were hidden and safe. The whole tribe looked ready, despite their gazes and tucking of their tails.

Maybe the Stormers aren't too bad, Cobra realized. *The rumors about them hating each other are obviously false.* She returned her gaze to ahead and there lay silence and murmuring. She gulped and tried not to show her nervousness to everyone else.

Pinscher growled from the rear. "Terror, I thought they were coming, you assassin hothead!" she snapped to Cobra's brother.

Terror snorted. "They are," his voice came. "They're trying to be stealthy. That's what we'd expect from stalking tribes, right? And they've had extreme careful planning for this, I can tell. Just wait for it, Commander Pinscher."

Cobra swallowed and ran her tongue over her chops. *Maybe Pinscher is right. What if it's a false alarm and just a scent? What if we're all out here and our hasty preparations were for nothing? Although I do want this to take as long as possible if it means no war…*

It was a mere possibility that the war wouldn't happen. Cobra knew deep down that it would and she needed to be ready. She didn't want the tribes to be at war like this, but maybe just maybe this was part of the Great Prowler Legend.

They think the Legend is wolf-dung, but it isn't. It's true and they'll realize it someday, when the Great Prowler saves us. This could be the darkness that falls and the Great Prowler stands above it! Cobra felt a surge of uncontrollable tremor inside her. If it was, it was good the Great Prowler would come, but it would also be scary.

Every wolf knew the day would come someday, but Cobra decided that she wasn't quite ready for it yet. Instead she prayed to the spirits of wolves that this war would end almost as soon as it began. Maybe the tribes would just decide to leave each other alone.

Cobra perked her ears and her heart raced when she suddenly heard rustling. Was she hearing things? Or was it the wind? Or maybe…it was the other tribes, like Terror said, being stealthy. *Please don't be*, she thought, holding her breath.

She swore she saw shadows in the bushes and heard more rustling. Wolves murmured louder and some looked in the same direction she was. Cobra heard her father growl from the rear, the growl a deep rumbling in his throat. She sniffed but the scents were too faint and were obviously masked.

There was another rustle and it stopped. Cobra let out a whoosh of breath but didn't move from her position. The other wolves were especially quiet, waiting for the slightest movement or sound. They waited a bit.

Then something emerged. Cobra whirled around.

It was a messenger wolf, another Stormer. He was breathless, and had a terrible gash in his side from a very recent fight. "Alpha Anaconda, Commander Pinscher," he rasped, stumbling. Shearer leaped and caught him before he could fall.

"What happened?" Anaconda snarled, shooting a glance at the trees.

"The pups and mothers…they were attacked!" cried the messenger, leaning comfortably across Shearer's back. "All of them! I just managed to save the pups and they ran, but the mothers…they're gone." Cobra swore she saw wolf tears gathering at the corners of his eyes. She didn't know Stormers besides her ever cried or whined. "And one of them was my mate."

Cobra felt overwhelming sadness and sympathy for this wolf, even though she'd never met him or had a mate before. The other tribes must have snuck in for a sneak attack. But why would Prowlers, Stalkers, Darkness wolves, and Grays *ever* attack helpless pups and mothers—when they were the nice tribes of the wild?

They must be super angry with the Storm tribe to be able to do all this. "Was it the other tribes that attacked?" she questioned boldly. Anaconda shot her a look but the messenger nodded and staggered to his paws.

"There was a Stalker...she had a missing leg. There was also a sinister Darkness wolf and a few others, probably first wolves of their formation. They just attacked all of a sudden, from the shadows where I couldn't see them..." The messenger's body shook violently. "The Stalker said she'd take revenge on the Stormers for the loss of her leg, and that was all I heard before I stepped in..."

Wolves murmured among themselves and some gaped at the messenger's wounds. "Take him to where the other wounded wolves are hiding, Shearer," Anaconda ordered, "and I will send down a caretaker wolf." He flicked his tail at a female wolf and she bowed her head before following Stormer Shearer.

Cobra spun around and growled at the air. Why did all these bad things have to happen, especially in the Storm tribe? And why would all these other tribes ever do something like this? She promised herself that she would fight those other tribes to the death if she had to; her rage was filling up in her body and mind and soul.

It's time to end this once and for all.

CHAPTER 11

THEY WAITED a bit longer. Cobra shuffled again and strained to get moving. If the other tribes were planning a sneak attack, then they weren't going to be successful. The Storm tribe knew they were coming. And Cobra needed a wolf to yell at and scratch across the muzzle.

"Terror!" snarled Pinscher. "Are they *coming*?!"

Cobra turned and watched her brother sniff the air. "Yes," he hissed. "Yes, they are." He pondered for a moment, closing his eyes and sniffing the air. "They're coming now!" he called.

The Stormers stiffened and gave howling snarls as wolf upon wolf sprang from the bushes and in their own formation in front of them. There were Darkness wolves, Stalkers, Grays, and Prowlers everywhere. Cobra stood up with the other wolves and they all got into their fighting stances.

Who was leading all these other tribes into war? Cobra wondered. Then, on the other rock ledge, a Darkness wolf stepped on. He was unknown to Cobra but the other wolves seemed to respect him. He gnashed his teeth with a rumbling snarl.

Next to him stood another male Darkness wolf and a female Stalker;

she had to be the same Stalker the messenger had talked about because she only had three legs. She hissed like a snake and looked ready to spring for a Stormer's throat.

Did we really cause the loss of her leg? Cobra wondered, watching her with intent eyes. The other Darkness wolf looked rather nervous. Every Gray, Stalker, Prowler, and Darkness wolf among their formation looked ready.

Cobra perked her ears when she heard the signal: Pinscher's incredulous snarl. She and the other Stormers did not wait. They dashed toward the other tribes, growling and snapping at each others' throats. Cobra leaped toward the nervous Darkness wolf first.

"What are you *waiting for,* Neptune? *Fight her!*" the lead Darkness wolf snapped loudly. The nervous Darkness wolf nodded and leaped at Cobra. His strength was amazingly good while he scratched part of her muzzle and kicked at her underbelly.

Cobra sunk her fangs into his hide and Neptune howled. She threw him to the side, not sure if she wanted to keep fighting him. The sinister Darkness wolf looked her in the eyes and narrowed his. "You," he growled, "the runaway?"

Cobra had no idea how he'd possibly known. But she nodded anyway. "Stormer Cobra," she said. "Who are you and why are you here?"

The Darkness wolf laughed. Like Prowler Scarr, he didn't seem right for a Darkness wolf. Kind of like Honor had been, too. "Me? Blizzard—misnamed for a Darkness wolf, but I like it. The Storm tribe has been horrible to the wild for centuries, even before the time of Python and Aghast."

"Are you trying to *wipe us out?*" Cobra gasped. "You can't! We were on our own, doing nothing to you, and you want to fight us?"

"It's all we can do," Blizzard growled with a wolf shrug. "Try to stop this war now that it's started, runaway." He snorted and shouldered her, only to send her splashing into the river. Cobra surfaced with gasping breaths and shook herself as she came to shore.

The Stormers were bleeding from wounds or attacking viciously. Cobra shivered from the rushing cold to her wet fur. *What will I do? I don't want this war to happen, but I can't stop it,* she thought.

And she was worried enough about her comrades and Kaiju. Now what would happen if she fought to the death? Without thinking, she leaped into battle and found the Stalker, that Blizzard had called Stalker Venom. Revengeful or not revengeful, she needed to be defeated.

"What happened?" Cobra asked her, dodging a vicious blow. "I wasn't here at the time, so how did you lose your leg?" Stalker Venom snorted and flicked her tail as if to brush it away.

"I was two, or three," she growled, still aiming for Cobra's flank. Cobra had to leap while listening. "I came across Storm tribe Territory and they were angry with me. First, they took me prisoner. Then, when I tried to escape, the Alpha wolf tore into me, causing me to lose my leg." She shuddered.

"I'm so sorry," Cobra whispered. "But I know it wasn't my fault and it was probably my father, Anaconda. He's horrible, I agree. But there's no reason to get revenge on him. He won't let it. And you could stay far away and it won't happen again."

Stalker Venom snorted again. "Like I'll take advice from an enemy," she growled, lashing her tail and leaping for Cobra's throat a third time.

Cobra barely dodged this one, tongue lolling. "I'm not the average Stormer, I promise," she protested, lashing out defensively at Stalker Venom's flank. "You can see that from how I'm trying to help you."

"I do," snorted Stalker Venom. "But it's obviously a trick, just like your hotheaded brother assassin is trying to play tricks before he kills."

"I'm not like that!" Cobra cried. "Just stop fighting me and listen!"

Stalker Venom gave a howl and tore into her without a word. Cobra fought back but suffered more bleeding scratches. She wished for a split second that she had the same strange blade on her tail that Honor had. "Stop, please!" she called as she jumped straight over the smaller wolf.

Paws skidding and sliding on the dry, hard ground, Cobra whirled around to face her opponent again. All the sounds she could hear were the sounds of yelping, snarling, growling, snapping, and howling. They were despair to her ears and she knew a war had started between them, the war she had spent the last four days thinking about.

The tribes had reason to wipe out the Storm tribe, but these weren't the good kind of reasons. Couldn't they all just move their Territories away from the Stormers' place? Couldn't they just ignore the Storm tribe and act like they were never a part of the wild?

So many of them trust me; if any of the ones I've met before spot me fighting for my tribe, they'll think I've betrayed them. And if they ignore us, aren't they ignoring ME too?

And my friends...where are they? Where could they have run off to? Will they help us with the war? Is Kaiju with them? Unanswered questions ran through Cobra's head as she darted around other warring wolves to escape Stalker Venom.

"You can't escape me, runaway!" snarled Stalker Venom from behind her. She was still at her heels. Cobra tried zigzagging through the other fighting wolves but found that Stalker Venom could follow her everywhere. She *was* a Stalker, and Stalkers were swift and agile.

Cobra swerved and nearly hit a tree trunk. She whirled around and faced her opponent again. She stood her ground and Stalker Venom sprang and—

Crash!

Her brother threw himself into Stalker Venom, both wolves tumbling and sprawling backward. Was he protecting her, or using his assassin powers? "Terror!" she said. "You seriously don't have to—"

"But I do," he said, eyes flashing as they looked at her. His fangs gleamed and were stained red from wolves he had fought. Cobra shuddered, thinking of the number of wolves he could have already killed. "You'll thank me later, Cobra." He turned and gnashed his overgrown fangs.

"No!" snarled Cobra, and leaped. "She doesn't deserve this!" The three-legged wolf's muzzle twisted with fear and Terror was faster than Cobra. He crunched down. The wolf tears shed from Cobra's eyes.

Cobra stood there, shocked and horrified, wolf tears streaming down her muzzle and plopping to the ground. Stalker Venom was dead, and didn't deserve to be dead. She had been just another part of the wolves that wanted to stop the Stormers, most likely forced to join.

And here she was, dead. Cobra did not move between all the other fighting wolves. Terror gave her a sidelong look and licked his bloodied fangs before running off to tear at another wolf. He really was an assassin, Cobra thought, the tears still rolling.

She saw her father and Blizzard facing off, the Darkness wolf and Stormer growling and in their fighting stances. Cobra prayed that Anaconda would win, even if she didn't like her father. Pinscher and Neptune were on the other side, snapping and bleeding from several wounds. And many other wolves she didn't know were snapping and snarling and fighting to the end.

This war will be devastating, and many wolves' lives will be lost. Yet I can do nothing to stop it. I'm fighting and serving my tribe, but what will the other tribes think? I have to make my decision, right here, and right now. It doesn't matter what other tribes may think of me from now on; I just have to fight and stop this war.

She stood there, far away from the fight, and unnoticed. She was lost in thought about what side she should fight for. She'd be betraying her tribe if she fought for Blizzard. But on the other paw, the wolves from other tribes that had finally trusted her may think she was tricking them if she fought for her tribe. Stalker Venom had been right.

This decision was too hard. What should she choose? She didn't have much time before this war got a whole lot worse…

Then she heard a howl, a howl she knew all too well.

"Stop right there!"

CHAPTER 12

EVERY WOLF stopped to stare in the direction of the trees. There was rustling in the bushes. *"Night?"* breathed Cobra when she saw the wolf she loved step out with Honor close behind. Cobra was relieved and shocked all at once. She even saw Kaiju standing next to Honor.

Prowler Night nodded. "Everyone, I know this is out of control," he said, pacing into the center of the clearing. Anaconda's eyes were wide and Blizzard had his head cocked. "But I and many others believe I am the Great Prowler destined to save the wild. And I don't want this war to happen any more than the rest of you."

Cobra held her breath. *Here are the reactions. Is this it, when the Great Prowler stands above it all?* The wolves around her looked downright confused. The Stormers were snorting and shaking their heads, obviously because they didn't believe in the Legend. *Well, if it comes true tonight, they'll realize they were wrong all along.*

"As you know, we are escaped prisoners. But we are here to help you," continued Night, "and over here is Stormer Cobra, and the two of us can just not be separated. She isn't an ordinary Stormer and she is working hard to make a decision for whose side to fight on." He gestured toward her and every wolf stared at her.

"If she chose you, other tribes then she'd been betraying her own tribe, which, in my opinion, wouldn't be so bad," said Night. Anaconda shot him a look of pure hatred. "If she chose her tribe, then the packs from other tribes that I have pushed to trust her will think she's betraying *them*. Right now she is still thinking even in the midst of battle."

Anaconda shook his head with a rumbling growl. "Outstanding speech, Prowler," he spat, "but *my daughter* is fighting for *us*, not for the likes of *you all*." He shot looks at every wolf from the other tribes. "And *second*, you two *can* be separated if I want you to be. *Prowlers* don't mate with *Stormers*!"

Cobra flinched and a few other Storm tribe wolves snorted. "Prowlers are enemies, and so are the other tribes," Anaconda went on. "Why, Cobra, would you *ever* fall in love with a Prowler?"

Now was the time. Now was the time to stand up for what she believed. "Because I'm not like all of you," she said. Wolves' jaws sagged open. "I don't belong in the Storm tribe like all of you. And I also don't see how any wolf should be enemies with each other. The tribes should be together, united, and kind to each other. Night is one of these and I believe deep down in my heart that he's the Great Prowler and that the Legend is true."

Night smiled at her and she smiled back. "And Night also told me to stand up for what *I* believe, and that's what I'm doing. I believe in the Great Prowler Legend, and the King Wolf tale. I believe in things normal Stormers would never believe in. And I believe I've found a wolf to love, whether you want me to love him or not."

Anaconda was shocked and a bolt of realization hit Cobra like wildfire. *That's what's special about me,* she thought, tail flicking back and forth. *I've finally found it. I may not be an heir to a ruler, or a wolf destined to fulfill a legend, but I am extraordinary. I'm extraordinary for my beliefs.*

Not only had she found what was special about her, but this war could end now that she'd stood up for what she believed. Night opened his jaw.

"So can we stop fighting with each other now?" he asked. "This isn't what we should do. Stormers never really did anything to you, so do nothing to them. The tribes could get far away from each other and be peaceful. That includes *assassins* hanging back, too." He shot a look at Terror and Cobra's brother growled through his gnashed fangs.

"You're not stopping *me* from my *destiny*," Terror snarled at Night. "You're just an insolent 'O Great Prowler' that knows nothing about Stormer life! My destiny is to kill and protect my tribe." He looked around at them all. "I guess it's time for me to leave again," he growled under his breath. His tail flicked from side to side as he turned toward the forest.

"Wait!" Pinscher called. "Come back, Terror!"

The overgrown-fanged Stormer was out of sight shortly after he had gone. Cobra licked her chops and felt the still silence between the tribes. Night looked as if he didn't know what to say. "Could we stop now?" he said again, sounding quite lame. That was one of the things Cobra liked about the Prowler.

Anaconda turned back and gnashed his teeth at him. "*You* just made things *worse*," he snarled. "And now you and these other tribes will pay for this. You lost me my assassin!" He threw himself at Blizzard and the two male leaders snapped and snarled.

Cobra's jaw hung. Now the war was back into place as wolves began to howl and clash once more. Night hadn't *meant* for Terror to run away like that and start the war again. He was only trying to help. She felt a wave of a feeling she'd never experienced before, and it flowed through her veins.

Whatever it was, she felt it for her father. Then she realized exactly what this wave was. She had no idea she'd ever feel it in her life. *It's hatred.* She tried not to get dizzy at this thought. She didn't want to hate her father, or her brother, or her tribe. It was uncontrollable, like the anger that kept overtaking her. She strained herself not to turn on Anaconda and use that anger to attack him.

She looked to Prowler Night and Honor, and they just shook their heads sadly. Kaiju was tucking her tail and backing up into the trees. Cobra just stood there, seething and not knowing why. *No, no. Don't attack your own father. Don't. Don't. Don't!* Her own body was moving toward Anaconda without her controlling it. Her curved claws were extended and her tail was flicking rapidly from side to side. *Don't! Don't! Don't!* She tried to pull back, but the urge was too strong. The hatred rose inside her like a flame.

Night and Honor were yelling, "No!" from behind her. Shockingly, her body did not listen. She threw herself toward her father and knocked him away from Blizzard. The Darkness wolf was mildly shocked and perked his ears.

Cobra looked back for a split second to see Kaiju with a look of horror across her dark muzzle. Her body threw her forward again and Anaconda snarled at her. "What in wolf's sake are you doing?" he bellowed, leaping to his paws and scratching across her muzzle.

"You," said Cobra, "are the most horrible father I could ever have!" She lashed out wildly toward him, overwhelming anger taking her over for a third time. Anaconda leaped over her with shock in his eyes.

"You are my daughter. I can't believe it. You're *nothing* like me. You're not a true Stormer. But it's your destiny. Your ripping claws and tearing fangs *are* your destiny, Cobra," Anaconda growled. "Whether you believe it or not, they are. My favorite part is seeing you *actually act like a Stormer.*"

"You want to know *my* favorite part?" snarled Cobra, lashing out and doubling back. She just had to calm herself down. Her body was still seething and she tried just standing there and facing her father. "My favorite part is when I tear you apart and leave you at the bottom of the river!"

Anaconda gave a laugh, one that sounded especially cruel. "I'd like to see you try, daughter," he snarled. Night and Honor were still shouting behind Cobra, but she didn't listen. This feeling of hatred—she just couldn't control it right now. And this anger was even worse than before.

BOLDLY, BRAVELY, shockingly, Cobra tried tearing into her father. Some wolves stopped mid fight to get a good stare at their fight. Blizzard hung back, clueless on what to do. Pinscher gaped. Kaiju whined a loud howl.

Anaconda bellowed, "Stop. Fighting. Me!" and to Cobra's horror, he slashed his claw out and it tore her shoulder. She screamed in agony and her father shoved her aside. Wolves gasped and stopped completely as her side and bad shoulder hit the rock ledge.

A horrible-sounding *crack* came. And Cobra's whole world around her turned to darkness.

CHAPTER 13

IT WAS sunny and especially warm around Cobra. She inspected everything and thought it was a good place. Her shoulder was not hurting.
In fact, there was no war going on at all. She saw Night and Honor
rolling around in the warm grass like pups, getting small pieces of grass
and dirt in their pelts.

Something appeared in the shape of a wolf. It was indeed Pebble, Honor's Darkness wolf mother. They had learned not long ago
that somehow—and not known how—Pebble could sometimes concentrate and find ways to come into dreams. Wolves thought it was
because she was the mother of an heir.

"Cobra," she said. "I meant to visit you sooner. But I had only found
ways to come into my pups' dreams. Finally, after a week, I've found
you. What has been going on? Is Night and Honor okay?"

Cobra stood there for a moment, awestruck that Pebble had found
her rather than Honor to check if he was okay. Did that mean that Pebble trusted her? "Yes, they're both all right. But ever since we left a lot
has been going on. Oh, I might as well tell you everything." And she
did. It took a while, but once it was all out, she felt better.

"Taken prisoner?" breathed Pebble. "Please tell me they escaped.

Oh, that's right, you did. And there's a war between tribes? I never heard anything about that! And you still have to make a decision for whose side you're on? I understand… And your brother's an assassin? And you attacked your own father? You are such a brave wolf, Stormer Cobra, brave indeed."

Cobra took in these words with a feeling of happiness inside her gut. "Thank you, Alpha Pebble," she said, and she meant it. "Night told me to stand up for what I believed in, and I did. That's what's so extraordinary about me, the thing I never saw until now: my beliefs and them not being like a normal Stormer's."

"Yes, and I trust you. You are truly an extraordinary wolf," Pebble said. "I believe you can stand up for yourself, and you are truly brave."

"It was Night, the wolf I loved, that helped me realize that. And my experience with the Storm tribe did some things, too," Cobra said with absolute happiness. What surprised her was that there was no hatred, no anger or fear inside her…just happiness.

"That Prowler truly is kind and brave," Pebble said. "I wouldn't be surprised if he was the Great Prowler. Many wolves that have met him believe he is, and so do I. Prince Honor is brave as well, but I'm glad he has comrades like you and Night to help him. Night changed him…and you helped him feel better about his past personality. I am truly grateful."

Cobra had never heard such kind words in her life. This was an overwhelming feeling of happiness and kindness rising in her. Everything would be fine if she just stood up for what she believed. "Thank you, Alpha Pebble," she said again.

COBRA OPENED her eyes. There was warmth wherever she was lying, and she heard the murmuring of wolves. Where was she? She stirred her body and found she could move it, but then unbearable pain shot through her body and her injured shoulder. She screamed but it hurt even to make noise.

"Will she be okay?" cried a voice that had to be Night's. She could hear his pacing; the Prowler paced a lot when he was worried. She heard Honor's voice reassuring him and Cobra tried to move again.

Then an unknown voice spoke up. "I am the medicine wolf. I can help her. Just stand back while I check on her." The same female wolf Anaconda had mentioned bent over her and Cobra blinked through the blur and dimness.

"I'm here to help," said the voice. "Your, um, comrades are fine. They're down here, where the pups and other wounded wolves are hidden. Don't move; I'm still treating your wound." Cobra didn't want to move anyway; her shoulder throbbed and occasional pain ran through her body.

She could still hear Night pacing and Honor reassuring. "She's my love," Night was saying, voice breaking. Cobra knew the wolf tears were rolling from his eyes. "I don't want anything happening to her."

Cobra loved him back. She wished she could say so but all she could do was whine. The blurred shape of the medicine wolf loomed over her and Cobra knew she was safe. So she relaxed her body even through the pain. She was hidden where the rest were, and the medicine wolf and her comrades had obviously saved her and brought her here without giving away the location.

She was thankful to them. But she couldn't say that either. She whined and trembled with fear and pain. She tried to keep relaxing her body but worry flashed through her mind. *I probably would've died if they hadn't come. My father would have been glad to kill me. But what will he do now that I've attacked him?*

The Stormer felt water rush over her damp, hurting shoulder. She gave a sharp yelp and nearly jumped out of her fur. Night came over and said comforting things to her that she couldn't quite make out. But the tone of his voice helped her calm down, even though her shoulder was being cleaned and was throbbing and wet.

Then she felt Honor's nose pushing against her shoulder. It was also comforting, and he whined with reassurance as his muzzle rubbed against her wet injury. The medicine wolf paced back over and Honor backed up for her. Cobra blinked but the fuzzy blur did not vanish.

"Night?" she managed to croak. The Prowler's ears pricked and he came to her other side. "You'll be fine," he whispered in her ear.

Honor nodded from beside the medicine wolf. "Your shoulder is torn and fractured, but I think you'll live." Cobra couldn't tell by his voice if he was being sarcastic or serious, but she didn't care, either way. She *would* live, but what about her father?

As if her mind had been read, Anaconda appeared in the dimly lit den. "Cobra," he said calmly, "you were wrong to attack me." His tail lashed fiercely as he looked into her eyes. Night let loose a rumbling growl and stepped back.

"My claws and fangs are *not* my destiny," she said boldly, in more of a whining rasp. "They are." She pointed her nose to Night then Honor.

"Awww," said Honor, but Night shot him a look and he stopped. Cobra looked fiercely into Anaconda's eyes and this time she was brave enough to do so.

Anaconda's eyes narrowed. "You *cannot* get with other tribes!" he roared, and Cobra flinched while Night pulled back his ears and lips. "I don't know how you ever got this way, daughter, but I know now that you are nothing like me. You're nothing like *any Stormer.* You're a *lost cause!*" The wolves all around them gave shocked gasps.

"But Alpha Anaconda, you're her father," murmured the medicine wolf. "Shouldn't you be respecting her like Stormers do each other?" So the rumors *were* false. "Shouldn't you be protecting her and accepting her for who she is? She doesn't have to be the way *you* want her to be, Alpha Anaconda. If I were her mother, I would let her have her own destiny." She smiled at Cobra and Cobra managed to smile back.

Cobra sat up and blinked. It was still blurry and pain shot through her shoulder. She gasped at the pain but watched as her father's body began to writhe with anger. "How dare you?" he snarled at the medicine wolf. "You are *not* her mother, so don't tell *me* how *I* should raise my own daughter!"

"But you didn't raise me," Cobra choked. Anaconda shot her a look of hatred. She shot one back. "I'm glad that I grew up in the wild, away from all of you. I didn't want to be the way all of you are, and I knew I didn't fit in. Fending for myself there made me realize that I can believe what I want to believe and do what I want to do. Mother would have said those things, right?"

Anaconda was silent for a moment. "Your mother was the toughest, most powerful ruler in the tribe," he growled, but there was a hint of sadness in his voice. "Despite her power she was killed in battle…by a Prowler." He snapped his head around to gnash his fangs at Night. "This is the reason *I* hate those insolent Prowlers."

Cobra felt a wave of sympathy. "I'm sorry, Father. But this can't lead to this." A bolt of realization struck her just as another shot of pain ran through her shoulder. She lied back down, jaw sagging open. "Wait a minute!" she snarled. "Are you trying to make *me* the most powerful ruler too, like Mother?!"

She couldn't bear to imagine it. Her, with her curved claws poised and fangs gnashed together while ordering Stormers around and at the same time mauling a Prowler. She shuddered back into reality and blinked, the blur fading slightly.

"Indeed," her father said with a smirk splitting his muzzle. "I didn't think you'd figure it out, Cobra, but you did. You will take the place of your mother, and Terror…well, he's an assassin, so I thought I'd use you instead."

"Use me?" Cobra roared, fighting back bolts of pain as she sat up again. The shouts came out as croaks. "*You* were trying to get me to abandon and betray my friends, weren't you? *You* were trying to make me the way *you* want me! That isn't possible anymore, because it isn't who I am and I grew up in the wild!"

"Calm down, Cobra," said Night desperately. "You'll make your injury worse by getting angry—"

She didn't listen. Cobra brought herself to her paws and the medicine wolf breathed a gasp. Pain shuddered through her body but she stayed upright. Now she knew for sure she could never be a true Stormer. She was proud of that, and proud for good reason. Her anger was for good reason too, to show just that she wasn't meant to be here. All that rage built up inside her weak, pained body and Anaconda cocked his head, cruel grin still across his muzzle.

Cobra got into the fiercest stance possible and told herself, *I have to*, and drew back her lips. She built up all the rage and strength she could possibly muster. Night and Honor took a few paces back and the medicine wolf backed into the corner in fear.

Cobra howled a snarl and lunged. Night gasped with horror. The

Stormer closed her eyes and felt her jaws clasp around her father's neck. At first, for a split second, she hesitated. Then she crunched down as hard as she could, feeling blood enter her mouth.

A high-pitched sound came from her father and she let go, blood streaming down from her mouth and fangs. She licked them just as Stormer Anaconda crumpled to the floor.

CHAPTER 14

THERE WAS silence. Several moments later Night spoke up, stammering. "Cobra," he breathed. "Y-You killed your own father. Why?"
Cobra felt a wave of regret wash through her. She'd *had* to, hadn't she? Yet she hadn't ever killed another wolf in her life...and this was what a real Stormer would do... Her body trembled and her wolf tears came. "I'm so sorry," she said, voice breaking. She sat on her haunches and cried, wolf tears dropping onto the cave. She'd never cried or whined this much before.

Night gave her a sympathetic look and Honor shook his head and paced over. He sat next to her and nuzzled her kindly. "Night," he whispered, and gestured. The Prowler nodded and came to sit by her side. Honor paced backward. What were they doing?

The medicine wolf came to her senses. "What just happened?" she stuttered as Cobra continued to cry. Honor just shook his head. Night sat by her side in place of Honor. Why? He gave her a look. She knew what it meant. With her tongue lolling and the tears stopping, she leaned onto the wolf she loved and he licked her injury fondly.

Honor had a grin across his face and Cobra took the time to lean and lick Night before they came back into the depths of battle. Pinscher must be taking over for Anaconda out there. But how could Cobra possibly fight out there in this condition?

I'm not. So take the time to be with Night, Cobra. He's the one you were meant to have, not another Stormer. It doesn't matter what anyone thinks of a Stormer being with a Prowler. Maybe over time the tribes will know and befriend each other. Cobra sighed and gave a happy whine while Night continued to lick her.

It wasn't long before Cobra took her head off him and staggered without his weight. "What will happen now?" she whispered, glancing at her father's body and back at Night. He shook his head and his tail tucked with shame.

Honor unleashed his tail blade. "I'll take care of this," he said determinedly. Cobra stopped him.

"No," she said, staggering forward. "I think I've got it. It's up to me, isn't it? *I* have to end this."

"But—" Honor stuttered. "But…"

"No," Cobra said seriously, ignoring the pain in her shoulder. "Take me out there. Please." She turned to the medicine wolf. "Everything will be fine for the Storm tribe, and the other tribes, for that matter. I have an idea. Thanks for your care." She was extremely glad the medicine wolf hadn't had to sew her up too.

The other Stormer nodded and Cobra staggered in between Honor and Night as they led her out of the hidden cavern and into the familiar halls. Cobra perked her ears; she could now hear the fighting and howling and barking wolves outside.

"Are you sure about this, Cobra?" Honor said nervously on his side of her. She nodded, the blur coming back to her vision. She hoped she didn't completely lose her strength while making her way to the warring tribes.

Her shoulder throbbed painfully and a wave of pain flashed through her body as she moved. Gritting her fangs and keeping her sides upright between them, they stepped through the entrance and into the depths of battle. The snaps, snarls, and growls were louder and fiercer than ever, and Pinscher snapped her head around after dealing a wound to Blizzard.

"Where is Alpha Anaconda?" she hissed at them. Honor shook his head and gestured to Cobra. Cobra clenched her jaw. *Thanks a lot, Honor. You're making ME tell her I killed him.* She took a deep breath and it caused pain to bolt through her shoulder again. She yelped and gasped at the sensation. Pinscher growled and gave her a look of expectance.

"I…" Cobra tried to stop from breaking into sobs again. "He was ruining my life by trying to change me. So I…I, um…I killed him." Pinscher's gasp was so sharp that Cobra had to stop herself from flinching. Just the motion would send pain shooting through her torn and fractured shoulder.

"I want to know *why you would ever kill your Alpha and father,*" Pinscher snarled. "How could you? First we lost your mother…then your brother…and now your *father?* He was our ruler! And your anger had to ruin everything!" Her muzzle was twisted with rage and her body was seething.

"I'm so sorry," Cobra whined with a lowering of her head. "I never meant it but he was ruining my life. I wanted to be the way *I* wanted to be, and he was trying to transform me into the wolf *he* wanted. Pinscher, the good thing is that you can take over in his Alpha position."

Pinscher snorted. "You're just trying to make me feel better for *your* mistakes," she snarled. "Now we must fight for our tribe and for Anaconda, because of you!" She whirled around. "Attack and don't stop! Our great leader is dead!"

This made Cobra feel even worse about killing Anaconda. Her tail and ears drooped and she couldn't help the wolf tears gathering in her eyes. Night gave her a lick of sympathy. "Do you still want to go out there?" Honor asked worriedly. She gathered her senses and nodded.

They led her reluctantly to a place near the battle, and Cobra couldn't bear to hear the snarls, howls, and yelps any longer. Once she was positioned between her two comrades, she opened her jaws and gathered all the strength she had into this shout:

"Listen to me, every wolf!"

No one listened. The clashing continued. Cobra felt irritation rising in her and she knew what she had to do. She gave her beautiful howl and she knew it had calmed the hearts of the battling wolves. Now would they listen?

They did. They whipped their heads around and stopped once more in the midst of their battle. "What now?" Pinscher snapped, body still seething from the rear. "Are you going to announce to the whole wild that you killed your father and our great ruler?"

Cobra took another breath, ignoring that. "I want every wolf to listen, *every wolf,*" she said defiantly and loud enough for all to hear. "I don't want this war to end this way, with the tribes holding a grudge against each other. I want the tribes just to leave each other alone and be at peace." Pinscher glared at her but Cobra didn't care.

"I thought maybe this could end with each tribe making a certain amount of land in the wild their own. And then they could all stay in their land, many, many, acres of the wild and leave each other alone. All the Packs of that tribe could make different areas of the land their Territories. Does that make sense?"

Some wolves nodded and a few murmured about it to confused wolves, most likely explaining her words. "Every wolf could be peaceful and won't have to worry about each other." *Except Terror,* she thought ruefully. *I wonder where he's at right now.* "Please, wolves. I don't want anyone else to suffer, die, or be made to fight."

Cobra swore she saw some of the other tribes nod in agreement. Even a few Stormers wagged their tails—which was something Stormers almost never did—without hesitation. Pinscher growled and Blizzard stamped a paw.

"We're not stopping our mission!" he snarled, his lips drawing back. "We're so close to killing all the Stormers and we've planned this attack for weeks. You, of all wolves, won't be stopping us." He gave her a hard glare and she tucked her tail.

"I was just trying to help," she stammered, losing her senses altogether and acting just as Night had. "I don't want any of us to die or be forced to fight, like I said. Please, you have to—"

"You don't tell me what to do, filthy Storm wolf!" Blizzard roared with a rumbling growl erupting in his throat. Neptune flinched and Pinscher said nothing but she did glare at Cobra and her comrades.

Night stepped forward, and Cobra was surprised to see how outraged he was. His tail was lashing furiously and his *own* lips were drawn back to reveal gleaming white teeth. His muzzle wrinkled fiercely and he gave a shrill snarling bark. "Don't treat her that way!" he snarled. Cobra just watched him with a look of shock.

Blizzard snapped his gaze to Night. "What did you say, Prowler?" he growled.

"I said *don't treat her that way*!" Night stormed. "Yes, she's a Stormer. And yes, the Storm tribe may have done things to you over the years. But she isn't ordinary like I said! She is *extraordinary*, whether you, the other tribes, or Anaconda ever thought! She's more than a Stormer; she's special and has a purpose to the wild. So I will *rip you apart* if you treat the wolf I love and respect like that again!"

Cobra couldn't hide her smile. She staggered forward and pain shot through her shoulder. Ignoring it, she said loud and clear, "Who is with me?" The wolves were silent, most likely debating or afraid to say yes or no. Blizzard looked baffled at Night's speech and he was right to be. *Night really does seem like the Great Prowler*, Cobra thought to herself.

She *was* extraordinary. And she wouldn't let any wolf take that belief—or any of her beliefs—away. Pinscher's face was softening and looked as if she was seriously considering this idea.

"Fine," she said. "But what will we call the pieces of land?" The other wolves nodded or murmured.

Cobra knew just what to say to that. "We can call the Storm tribe's land 'Storm Land.' Then we can have Darkness Land, Prowler Land, Stalker Land, and Gray Land as well. All we need are some messengers that can spread this news to the whole wild." She grinned at all the tribes. "What do you think? Do you want the wild to be peaceful?"

"But what about the 'darkness will fall' in the Great Prowler Legend?" said a voice behind them. Cobra whirled around, expecting her brother to stand there, sneering at her. But it was just Kaiju, who had silently followed them out of the hidden cavern.

"Well, then you know who to go to," she said, smiling at Night. Night grinned back and the other wolves gave murmurs or barks of cheer. The Stormers were shuffling their paws and Pinscher snorted with a small grin splitting her muzzle too.

"Classic names, but sure," she said with a roll of her eyes. But Cobra knew the Stormer Commander was relieved to have stopped fighting with the other tribes.

Cobra turned to every wolf. "Thank you, everyone," she said, happy wolf tears welling up. "Thank you for listening to me." She had never felt such respect in her life. Maybe other wolves would have an easier time trusting her now.

I ended the war easily. And I didn't even have to make that choice on whose side to join.

"But I recommend *her* for our new Alpha wolf," said Pinscher, pointing at Cobra with her nose. Cobra breathed a gasp, not only from her shock but from the pain flashing through her yet another time. She staggered back and Night and Honor caught her between them.

"*Me?*" Cobra rasped. "But I can't. I—"

"Thank you so much for the offer, good Commander," said Night with a bow of his haunches. Cobra held back her laugh at how goofy he looked. "But first of all, Cobra needs to heal from her injury. Second—" his kind eyes moved to Cobra "—we have some plans happening pretty soon."

Cobra knew what he meant. She nodded, smiling at the tribes. "I believe Pinscher should be Alpha instead. If I had taken the job I would've promoted you anyway. I think you'd do well." Pinscher's jaw sagged and then closed. The former commander nodded with thanks.

The other tribes were murmuring to each other and Blizzard was deep in thought. "Fine," he said stubbornly. "But call this a draw fight, Storm tribe," he added, shooting looks at the Stormers. "Not a win."

Some wolves burst into laughter and Cobra couldn't help but smile again. Now that the tribes all had their own land and peaceful Territories to themselves, things would be great now. And she had found her purpose in the world too: one being helping the Great Prowler on his journey.

Thinking this thought, the happy wolf tears came.

EPILOGUE

I T WAS bright and sunny in the Darkness Territory Kaiju had run away from a long time ago. She was sprawled out with Night, Honor, Honor's close companion Midnight, and of course, Stormer Cobra.

The Darkness Pack was there, too; all doing their own thing. Pebble was lying on her stone talking to her brother, Trekker. Kaiju could not have felt more peaceful as she let the sunlight warm up her dark, glossy fur.

It had been just a few moons since the war between the tribes had ended. Ever since hearing about the Great Prowler Legend, Kaiju had always worried about the darkness that would fall and the perilous-sounding wind. Even if that war *was* over, there was still more danger coming.

And what if Night *wasn't* the Great Prowler, and there was still another wolf that was somewhere in the wild? Kaiju didn't want to doubt that the kind Prowler could fulfill the Legend, but she didn't want to jump to conclusions either.

Cobra was currently lying next to Night, speaking of Prowlers. Night had just become her mate and the two were extremely fond of each other. Cobra obviously didn't care what any wolf thought of hybrid pups, especially of Stormer and Prowler—or if any wolf thought the idea of a Stormer and Prowler together was horrible.

During the war between the tribes Cobra had been severely injured in the shoulder. Night and Honor had guessed that it was fractured and had a bad bleeding tear in it.

Kaiju sighed, getting back to her worries, but the sigh came out too loud.

"What's wrong, Kaiju?" asked Honor, perking his black ears.

Kaiju sighed again. "I don't know," she stammered, her own ears drooping. "I guess I worry too much about things, like the Great Prowler Legend and what will happen. Maybe that's what my father was like, or my mother."

"I heard from Cobra that your father's name was Toil," Honor said, ears perking further. "Is this true?"

"I said I *believe* his name was Toil," Kaiju corrected him. "It's not like I remember him or anything."

"But that's amazing!" replied Honor, fur rustling in the breeze. "Mother said that *Razor's* father was Toil. Could it be that you're my half-sister, and Razor's sister?" His eyes were so wide with curiosity that Kaiju knew she had to reply.

"Maybe," she said with a shrug. "Pebble may have been my mother, but I don't remember *her* much either because I ran away a while ago." She snuck a glance over at Pebble, who was still deep in conversation with Trekker.

"But *why* did you run away?" Night questioned with a tilt of his head. "I mean, *I* was stubborn enough as a pup to run away from *my Pack*, but why did you?"

Kaiju looked away. "I don't know," she confessed.

Cobra looked deep in thought too. "And what do you guys think Terror is doing right now?" she said. "Remember? He ran off during the war. He'll figure out it's over but I doubt he'll want to stop his 'destiny' of being an assassin."

That gave Kaiju another thing to worry about, but it wasn't Cobra's fault. She thought for a moment about what she should do.

"I still feel bad for killing Anaconda," Cobra sighed at last.

"But I'm kind of glad you did," Kaiju said. "He was *horrible.*"

Honor's voice came unexpectedly. "You know what?" he said thoughtfully. "It's been a few moons, and I'm nearly five years old now. I think it might be time to rule my tribe, especially now that we marked each land in a certain way to determine whose land it is now. The whole Darkness tribe will be happy to have part of the wild for themselves. I may rule well."

"I think so too," agreed Night with a smile. Kaiju smiled too but said nothing, since she was still thinking about her already-developing plan. "I'll miss you on my journey, Honor, but you'll be a great King Wolf, nothing like King Aghast."

Honor grinned and unleashed his tail blade. His tail flicked back and forth as he went to tell his mother wolf. Soon enough he'd be King Wolf of the Darkness wolves. Kaiju would be glad to have him as a tribe ruler, but right now she needed to focus on her plan.

I need to find Stormer Terror before he can do anything horrible to the other tribes. I bet he's out there killing wolves right now.

At dawn, I'll tell my friends I'm leaving...again.

WOLF WARRIORS

BOOK FOUR

THE

LOST

STORMER

PROLOGUE

T WAS storming in Gray Territory. This wasn't just any storm. This storm *meant* something.

Thunder cracked beneath the Gray Pack's heads as they hung together under the shelter of their underground base. Ears pointed upward and tails whipped the ground nervously. "Alpha Broken," Gray Magnus told his leader.

Broken had been so lost in thought that he had not heard Magnus the first time. Now his head snapped up and he swiveled his ears around. "Yes? Speak," the newly-made Alpha wolf said.

"I'm not so sure when this storm will end," Magnus said nervously. "I'm afraid it may last all night. If it's that severe, we may not leave this base for a while." He turned his head to look at every Gray around him.

Some of the Grays didn't seem used to having a Stalker like Broken as their leader. Broken had the potential to lead, though. And aside from that, what was his destiny beyond this? He'd lost everything: his home Pack, his brothers, and his friends.

He didn't like to think of his past as depressing. He had had a good life so far except for certain circumstances. He'd hoped it would get a little better. But here he was, in the base, clueless on what to do about this intense thunderstorm.

"I know," he sighed at last. He looked at each of the Pack in turn. "Every wolf must remain calm even through this"—*crack* went the thunder "—storm."

A few wolves nodded and set their jaws. Broken sighed inwardly and sat on his haunches, miserable. He could hear the rumbling thunder quite clearly and the thundering patter of the raindrops hitting the top of the base. Even lightning caused the whole base to flash white.

Broken knew this storm meant something, perhaps a message. But at this point he still hadn't figured it out. "Wolves come together. Hustle!" he ordered. The Grays closed in curiously, their paws clicking on the dirt and ears perking farther than normal.

"I need your help, a little bit," Broken confessed. "I'm trying to figure out what this storm means. I want to hear *every* suggestion possible, from as *many* of you as possible. If we want to get out of here calmly, we must figure this out together, as a Pack. Am I clear, every wolf?"

"Yes, Alpha Broken," they said simultaneously. Broken ignored the loud crack of thunder that sounded and waited expectantly.

Magnus flicked his tail upward and Broken regarded him. "It could mean the Great Prowler Legend is coming true," Magnus growled almost solemnly. "Darkness will fall, it says. Why shouldn't darkness be a storm? This could be the first sign of the Great Prowler Legend being fulfilled."

"Yes, and the Storm wolves will see they're wrong about the Legend!" a young wolf yelped. A couple older wolves shushed her hastily. Broken lit up. Magnus had made an excellent point, that it could be the Legend coming alive.

"Thank you, Magnus. I think we may have already figured it out," Broken said with a forced smile. "If it is the darkness, we all know the Great Prowler is coming."

Come, Prowler Night. We need you. The signs are everywhere now. I know deep down that you ARE the Great Prowler.

The base flashed white repeatedly, as if a wolf was blinking several times quickly. Wolves cowered and Broken growled as thunder sounded once more. There had to be a way to stop it, even before the Great Prowler came.

"Come closer," he whispered to the other wolves through the sound of the rain. "I must tell you something." They did come closer. "Don't be afraid, because the Great Prowler is coming very soon. Come to me when you are upset, but don't worry too much." He looked into their eyes with certainty.

"Soon, this world will be forever changed."

CHAPTER 1

"SO CAN we stop fighting with each other now?" the Prowler was asking. "This isn't what we should do. Stormers never really did anything to you, so do nothing to them. The tribes could get far away from each other and be peaceful. That includes *assassins* hanging back, too." He was glaring at Stormer Terror.

Terror growled loudly, the growl rumbling with violence and hatred. *I won't let a Prowler boss me around*, he thought. "You're not stopping *me* from my *destiny*," he returned with rage. "You're just an insolent 'O Great Prowler' who knows nothing about Stormer life! My destiny is to kill and protect my tribe." He looked intently at every wolf with his eyes narrowed. "I guess it's time to leave again." He spun around, more than ready to dash away.

And he did, as quickly as he could so no wolf would catch him. He heard Pinscher's—the wolf he liked very much—voice behind him, shouting, "Wait! Terror, come back!"

He ran his tongue over his overgrown fangs as he ran faster. *Sorry, Commander Pinscher,* he thought rather sadly. *But it's for the best.* He had no idea what would happen in the war between the tribes while he was away. *Without me, the Storm tribe won't stand a chance, will they?*

His thoughts were rueful but he didn't slow down. *Too bad! My sister ruined it, so they can blame her!*

He had always disliked his only sibling, Stormer Cobra, not only because she never lived like a *normal* Storm tribe wolf, but because she and her comrades were trying to stop him from fulfilling the only destiny he knew.

And it's my true destiny, whether they believe it or not, he thought with a grin. He didn't have a single doubt that this was the right path to take. As a proud Stormer and the only wolf in the tribe that had agreed to be an assassin, he knew it deep down.

And now because of his unhesitant decision, he could actually possibly become the most powerful wolf in wolf kind. *I'll even be stronger than King Aghast or Prince Honor!* he said to himself, gnashing his overgrown fangs arrogantly.

He had not stopped running, and he felt like he could never stop. But he *did* have to get far away from the Storm tribe—even his own father—to start his true assassin work anyway. Now when he perked his ears there was almost no sound to be heard. When he sniffed and flared his nostrils he sensed nothing but faint scents of fear, pain, and anger.

No wolf could stop him now, he thought as he rushed by trees, undergrowth, and streams. He didn't even stop to lap at the fresh-looking water that made his jaws water. He couldn't stop, not even once.

The moon was beginning to crawl back into its daylight sleep, and the sun was rising on the vast horizon in front of him. Daybreak cut into the orange-pink sky but Terror still didn't stop for a break, drink of water, or to hunt. Instead his paws thundered on the ground and his gray-and-tan tail lashed dangerously.

So far he had not caught scents of any wolves nearby or of any other creatures in the wild. Instead there was a creepy, eerie silence as he ran. The only sound he could hear was his own paws.

Twigs snapped from under him. A cowardly wolf would yelp with fear and run for his life, but not Terror. He just growled and continued running. What was this creepy forest and what was it trying to do to him? *Is it trying to make me say "Aah, this forest is creepy and I should run away like a dimwit coward"? If it is, I won't listen.* The Stormer stumbled in place and shook his fur.

Catching his breath, he took a look around him. Patches of moss rustled in the eerie wind, and he perked his ears when he heard random twigs snap without his stepping on them. Nothing else was heard for a moment as he panted and lapped at the stream nearby. A random frog croaked. Terror told himself not to be a coward as he fought the urge to jump.

Instead he clenched his teeth and overgrown fangs and let out a rumbling growl. *Bring it on, forest,* he thought. Then suddenly he knew what this place was. The realization shuddered through his body and flashed rapidly through his mind like riptide.

This is the Forbidden Forest.

He'd heard so much about it but had never actually gone through it before. At first he'd thought it was a scary pup story, but right here, right now, he was standing in it. The eerie stillness and random noises springing up caused Terror to let go of his doubts about it.

He shook himself and came to his senses. *Well, Forbidden Forest. If you think you scare me, you're dead, dead wrong, you got me?* Then he took off running as the sun was fully up and the daylight washed over the Forbidden Forest.

The creepy wind started up again, blowing and vanishing over and over. Twigs snapped under Terror's paws once more and he didn't do as much as let his heart pound. He was no coward, and he was most definitely not weak. He'd done great work as an assassin and hoped to stay that way: tough and merciless.

Do this. Especially for Pinscher, he told himself. He knew the wolf he liked would be sad to see him go, to know that he may never return again. Right now he couldn't decide if he'd be gone forever on his quest, or come back to see Pinscher and the tribe again. Maybe, just maybe the Prowler, Darkness wolf, and his *insolent* sister wouldn't be there once he got back.

And what about the war he'd left behind? What about the plans and power and loyalty he had wanted to show he had just left in his wake? What would Pinscher and his father think of him now? He shook his head so hard it hurt. *Stop thinking for a minute, Terror. You're just as bad as Stormer Shearer.*

It didn't matter what any wolf thought about him, he decided. No matter what, he'd follow his own destiny and path; it didn't matter what any wolf said. No wolf could convince him of anything now.

Again, he did not stop as he crossed the Forbidden Forest, curious and unaware of where he would go. Maybe if he just kept running straight, he'd get right out of the forest as soon as he'd gotten in. As long as he didn't stop, not even for a rest or water break…

He shook the thought away, as it would only make him feel weak and in want. *Keep moving and don't listen to your instincts for once, Terror.* He clenched his overgrown fangs and forced himself to speed up. He ignored the creepy noises and blasts of wind every now and then.

Still he saw no sight of prey or wolves as an hour passed. His stamina had lasted but he did slow down some to conserve energy. Of course, he knew why he couldn't see any signs of life. *Prey: they're probably hiding. Wolves: well, most of them are warring with my tribe, and I'm sure many won't live near or most definitely not in the Forbidden Forest.*

Could he make it for at least another hour? *Yes.* The stubborn streak he'd always carried ran through his body like a tidal wave, and he was thankful for it. He had to keep going if he wanted to escape.

He wasn't sure how long it was before he finally stopped, his breath rasping and wheezing in his throat and body heaving with exertion. He was angry at himself for acting wimpy at this moment. He couldn't be wimpy…*ever.*

The sun was still bright and high. Terror took another look around him and found his surroundings were different. The ground had gotten flatter and the trees less lush. Now he was in a small open clearing with bushes just in front of him, and a space between some of them. It must lead to another clearing or pathway.

He decided to take that path. The ground got drier and flatter and warmer as the sun shone on his back and he trotted down the path. Rocks skittered under his paws and the sounds of the Forbidden Forest were nearly muffled. That meant he was most likely almost out of here.

Wait. What was that? A growl escaped Terror's throat and he gnashed his fangs into the distance. Drawing back his lips and pricking his ears, he got into his battle stance. *Time to show you're an assassin,* he thought fiercely.

Scents drew nearer and his nostrils flared. He was a Stormer, so he didn't have the "amazingly amazing" sense of smell like the Prowlers, but he could still tell that these wolves were Prowlers. And they were arriving quickly.

He stood there, every now and then his eyes darting here and there to see a wired-in area with completely flat terrain and thick bushes. *Wait for it...they're coming.*

Here they came. Wolves crept ferociously out of the bushes and quickly surrounded him. Terror snapped the air near each of them and some flinched back, terrified. *Yes, fear me. I am scary and you know it.*

A couple of the cringing wolves had a horrible, red, scarring slash across their muzzles. For a moment Terror wondered how they'd gotten such nasty wounds. A wolf stepped through the middle and Terror pawed the ground like a bull, gnashing his fangs fiercely.

The wolf had the same slash healing on his muzzle, but his gaze was fierce and his eyes were narrowed mercilessly. Terror thought, *I can be like that too,* and narrowed his own eyes, making sure his fangs were showing.

"Oh, so you're Terror, the assassin wolf they've all been talking about," the wolf sneered, beginning to circle Terror with a vicious look on his face. "I see I finally get to meet you. Prowler Stinger," he added.

"Stormer Terror," growled the assassin, watching Stinger with intent eyes. "I'm guessing you're Alpha of this Pack?"

Stinger's eyes flashed. "Yes," he hissed. "And what are *you* doing so close to *our* Territory?"

"Your Territory?" snorted Terror. "This is the Forbidden Forest. It's the spirits of wolves' Territory."

Stinger barked a laugh as he continued to circle Terror. "Ignorant," he said. "You are somewhat right. But we have a quite nice place to make our home, and it so happens to be just outside of the Forbidden Forest, young Terror."

Terror disliked this wolf already. He growled loudly. "Now that we're done with this stupid conversation," he snarled, "I guess I should be on my way. I will attack you and leave your remains in the Forbidden Forest if you even touch me."

"For wolf's sake, you are *morbid*," Stinger said in a purposefully shocked tone. "Why don't you just come with us and practice your assassin skills in our, um…stadium? We haven't had a good match in ages, not since the scenario with Prowler Night."

Prowler Night! Terror's heart lurched. So the Prowler had been here before, and probably his comrades, too. The place sounded horrible so he decided not to fall for this trick. "No," he snapped. "I'll do just fine without you, thank you."

Stinger grinned wickedly. "I wasn't giving you a choice, was I?" he said, eyes flickering. He gave a cruel laugh and wolves closed in. Terror snapped the air and a few backed up, eyes wide with fear. The two scarring wolves shrank anyway, whining.

"Bolt, Echinoderm!" Stinger commanded. "Don't hang back like stupid cowards. Come chain up this…this *assassin*!" The two wolves looked at each other. Bolt coughed. Echinoderm whined.

"Yes, Alpha Stinger," Bolt sighed. He leaped toward Terror and the Stormer managed to dodge. Stinger barked sharply. Terror ducked a snapping jaw and did not flinch at a nip to the shoulder. Wolves were trapping him, and fast.

Terror gave a wild leap and barely managed to soar over Prowler Bolt's head. Skidding across the hard, dirty ground, he started to dash away. He heard thundering paws.

And his head was slammed so hard that he was enveloped into darkness.

CHAPTER 2

TERROR OPENED his eyes. He was lucky not to be dead. He growled and yawned. Had he been *sleeping?* Or had he been knocked out deliberately? Blinking dizzily, he didn't move but brought his gaze around his landscape.

It was a vast, stony cavern and wolves lined the halls, mostly guard wolves. Terror felt he was pinned down by a strong wolf, but neither Echinoderm nor Bolt nor Stinger. This was a large Prowler he didn't know, and he had a strong grip on the Stormer. Terror decided not to struggle right now.

He heard the pacing of paws and moved his eyes upward. Stinger was the one pacing. He gave a smile that Terror didn't like as soon as he saw it. "You're awake," he said. *"Finally*—for a minute I thought you were dead."

Terror said nothing, but he did grind his overgrown fangs and teeth together. "What is this place?" he snarled at last. "A pacing cave for you?" he added in a sneer.

Stinger gave him a sidelong look. "Umm, the trial cavern," he said slowly. Then he got fast. "And now I'll decide what to do with you! It's as easy as that! That's why this cavern is useful." He smiled at his surroundings, the same ridiculous smile as before.

"If you do anything to me I promise I will bite your hideous butt with these overgrown fangs," Terror snapped at him.

Stinger seemed to ignore him. "This decision will be made by yours truly," he said to every wolf. "And me only. Don't even think about contradiction, protest, or suggestion, because this is *my* decision what will be done about the assassin. Everyone understand?"

"Yes, Alpha Stinger," murmured Bolt, running his tongue over his chops. "How will you make this decision, anyhow?"

Terror snorted inwardly at how wise the Prowler sounded.

Stinger shot a slight glare at Bolt. "You'll see," he growled, beginning to pace again. "Now, this wolf is dangerous. He's perilous. He's an assassin. He's a threat. He's harmful. He's—"

"Do you mind if you stop trying to create synonyms for describing me?" Terror barked at him. "Because I'm seriously considering biting you right about now."

Stinger shot *him* a look now. "Like you could," he snorted. Then he got back to his muttering. Okay. Now *this* was getting boring. Terror craned his neck to try to see the face of the wolf pinning him, but all it did was give him a headache. The grip was still firm and tight and Terror mentally sighed.

Twisting and shuffling, Terror tried dislodging his opponent or just being plain annoying so he could go free. If only he could twist his head and bite that wolf's snout! That would show him not to mess with a Stormer like him.

"Hmm," Stinger was saying. "Yes, I see...putting him in prison would be good too...and yet he'd be too powerful at the stadium, no matter what wolf he goes up against."

Very extremely right, Terror thought with amusement. *I am dangerous and I am powerful.*

There was mostly silence around the cavern as Terror continued to twist and listen intently to Stinger's muttering. He didn't dare speak. He just wriggled and strained desperately even while pinned down. He just had to escape.

Then he felt something sharp crunch on his tail. Probably the wolf trying to keep him still... *How could that help?* Terror thought grimly through the pain, gritting his overgrown fangs in agony.

Stinger's head snapped up. Terror knew the other wolf had an idea and braced himself for it. His tail was not released but he stopped struggling long enough to listen. "I know what to do," Stinger said defiantly. Terror waited.

"I should take you to the Creepy Chamber just below here, underground," continued Stinger. "I've never used it before but now will be my perfect chance!" He looked very pleased with himself and Terror wanted to thwack that look off his face.

And what would happen down there? He didn't dare ask.

"You will be in a world of hurt down there," the Alpha wolf said with a wicked grin. "I will find something to do to you to stop you from killing any more wolves. I may be cruel, but I'd never want wolves to die!"

"Then why use the stadium?" Terror sneered.

Stinger snarled with annoyance. "That was the former Alpha's idea of thrill," he snorted. "My sister, I mean. I only just took over for Prowler Scarr. So keep that jaw shut and follow us." He gestured to the wolf pinning Terror and as soon as the weight lifted, the Stormer began to dash away.

He felt chains being thrown around his neck and tightened. He gasped at the sensation and turned his head. The wolf that had pinned him had one end of the chain tightly in his jaws and had a wicked look in his eyes. Terror knew wolves probably wondered how these wolves could possibly be Prowlers, the kindest tribe ever.

He growled and snarled and bucked wildly, snapping toward the wolf, but his jaws closed on thin air. He was led fiercely out of the cavern and into the open air. Terror didn't take time to enjoy it. Instead he kept ferociously struggling and snapping.

Stinger looked slightly amused as they neared a small round entrance that led downward. He led the wolves down a dim flight of dirt stairs into another cavern that smelled of rotting prey. There wasn't much light, but there was a long stone slab in the middle where wolves began to surround it.

Terror told himself he'd find some way to escape, and deal with whatever "world of hurt" they were going to try to lay on him. He gritted his teeth as he was shoved onto the slab and tied down tightly. Still thrashing, he snapped at thin air again and found he could barely move under the chains that bound him.

Stinger laughed. "Trying to escape, eh, assassin?" he said with amusement. "You won't escape this, I can assure you."

Oh yeah? Terror returned silently.

Bolt and Echinoderm sat on their haunches together on his right and many other wolves on his left. Many of them were grinning with pride and a few others were shuffling in anticipation and impatience.

"Prowlers Sunshine and Orbit," Stinger commanded, "get behind the stone, will you?" A female wolf and a male wolf nodded to each other and climbed up just behind Terror's lashing tail.

What were these insolent wolves doing, anyway?

"I am proud to begin this amusing scenario," Stinger chuckled. "Now we will force Terror to never hurt us again. This may sound stupid, but I don't exactly want an assassin stalking me."

"Ha!" Terror snorted.

Stinger growled at him. "Prepare, or should I say, brace you!" he said. "Begin. Do whatever you want, Prowlers, as long as he doesn't try to hurt us!"

Terror snarled without a word and felt jaws clamp on his tail a second time. He didn't yelp but did begin thrashing furiously. The wolf called Sunshine threw herself on top of him and this time he did whine. *Don't be pathetic*, he thought fiercely.

The other wolf, Orbit, circled the slab and eyed different areas of Terror's body. With a grin, he thrust his jaws forward and crunched down on Terror's hind leg. The bite was not deep but it did hurt; the piercing of the skin was agonizing.

Terror yelped and twisted his head. He could not move his back legs or lower body, so he had no choice but to deal with the pain. Orbit didn't let go and Terror strained to yank his leg out of those slavering jaws. "Let go!" he roared.

"Ha!" Sunshine copied. Terror glared at her and shook his body enough to throw her off. He bit at the chains with, and a few snapped off easily. Twisting and snarling, he dislodged Orbit's grip—at last—and flung off the rest of his bindings.

"Get him!" snarled Stinger, and wolves bolted after Terror. The Stormer knew better. He darted between legs—Prowlers were larger than Stormers—and dashed straight out of the cavern and into warm light.

He swerved, nearly crashing into a tree. His leg was bleeding, but it did not hurt much. Darting into the nearest passageway he could find, he thrust himself through and stopped to lodge rocks into the entrance. Hastily, he ran through the tunnel and into a cavernous place.

There were cells with open spaces for windows and miniature versions of stone slabs lining on each one. Chains dangled from some or held a wolf here and there. There weren't many prisoners here, but at least it was safe. Terror, heart thudding, slipped into the nearest crevice and fought to catch his breath.

That was close, oh what just happened—thank goodness I'm alive—what am I doing here went his mind, twisting direction and thinking like a winding path. His heart pounded with exertion, and Terror allowed himself some deep breaths.

Lowering his body into the prowling position, he heard the thundering of the Prowler Packs' paws outside the prison. "We have to find him!" yelled Bolt. That was all Terror heard before silence came.

He padded quietly down the lines of cells, ears perking and lowering whenever he saw another wolf. Some were Stormers but the majority were Stalkers, all sleeping with drooped, sad ears.

I have to get out of here, Terror thought. Pacing back and forth, he ran over ideas for escape plans, none of which were good. How could he be so horrible at planning?

Then a voice split the silence. "Can you help me?" it called with a slight tremor of weakness. It sounded like it was female. Terror followed the sound until he came to a cell. He lifted a paw in sheer shock.

There was a Stormer in the cell in front of him.

CHAPTER 3

"**W**HO ARE you?" said Terror in an uncontrollable angry snarl. "And why are you here? Stormers aren't overpowered by other tribes! Can't you just break out and go? Straighten up, Storm wolf, because you may need me to help you be like the rest of the—"

"Stop," said the voice weakly but loud enough that Terror could hear. "First, you don't have to be *mean*. Second, I was injured and then captured." She moved to show a horrible-looking hind leg that made even Terror want to flinch. The wound was mostly closed, but the horrible sight was the bone jutting nearly straight out.

"I need your help," she said to him. This time Terror couldn't help but snort.

"Me, help you?" he scoffed. "Why should I?"

"Please, you have to," the other wolf pleaded. "I'm hurt and helpless and may die here. I'm a fellow Stormer and I've been missing for a whole *year*. Didn't you ever notice?"

"Um, no!" said Terror. "There's kind of the whole *tribe* living there, thank you! And I had just returned so *did I* have time to notice a missing wolf, among the *whole tribe?* Spirits of wolves, *no!"* he said sarcastically.

"Gosh. You're really rude," the other wolf said. Her face was set boldly, but Terror could tell she was trying not to scream in agony from her leg. He had a feeling in the back of his mind that told him he should help, but since when did assassins ever help other wolves, even others of their kind?

"First, tell me your name," he demanded. "I'm Stormer Terror, assassin wolf of the Storm tribe." He puffed out his chest proudly but the wolf began talking.

"Pitchfork," she said, "Stormer Pitchfork. I believe I may have heard of you."

"Hmm, never heard about a wolf named Pitchfork," Terror said.

Pitchfork rolled her eyes. "If you had *just returned*, of *course* you wouldn't know me, considering I was gone for a *year* and you must be a runaway, the runaway six years ago."

"That was…my sister," Terror said slowly. "I ran away for good reason, thank you. So…fine; I'll help you. But promise me one thing."

The other Stormer's tail began to lash happily despite her obviously pained leg. "Anything," she said.

"Promise me," said Terror, "that you won't argue with who I kill and when I do it." He hoped he could trust Pitchfork to let him follow his destiny. After all, wasn't she a fellow Storm wolf?

"I…promise. And please, will you help me back to the tribe?" Pitchfork asked. "I know you just left, but this is something I've waited for, for a year, to be exact. I need to come back. I was a good wolf in our fighting formations. I was commander last year." She looked intently at Terror. "Who's commander now?"

Terror swallowed. Did he *have* to tell her? "Umm," he said uncertainly. "It's Stormer Pinscher. She, uh, thought she'd take over since she's strong too, and, uh…I kind of um, like her, and, uh, stuff." Whoa. That sounded extremely lame and stupid for an assassin like him to say.

"What?" Pitchfork's eyes widened a bit and she winced. "Pinscher?" she added with shock.

"Um, yes, I wasn't kidding," Terror returned. "What about her?"

"Um," said Pitchfork. "Well, Pinscher…she's my daughter."

"What?" This time Terror's eyes grew wide. "But she's so—so

ferocious! She's merciless! I like her that way, but to be honest, you're nothing like her." He looked into Pitchfork's brown eyes and studied them for a moment.

Pitchfork chuckled. "You're sort of right," she said, looking down at her own paws. "She isn't even like her father, Stormer Hurricane, if you've heard of him. Anyway, I never thought she would take over for me. I can't help but feel proud."

Realization struck Terror. "Hurricane is...was...in charge of the trainees," Terror said, shuffling his paws. Now he dreaded telling Pitchfork about Hurricane's death. His father, Anaconda, ruler of the tribe, had killed him for breaking many rules.

"Was?" said Pitchfork, cocking her head. Her tail was quickly slowing down. Then her eyes grew sad with realization. "He's dead, isn't he? My Hurricane, dead... I waited to see him again and he was waiting for me. Now..." Terror swore he saw the wolf tears come rolling.

He felt sorry for Pitchfork, but there was nothing to be done. "I'm sorry," he said, which was something he'd never said before to any wolf. "My father...he killed him. He broke a lot of rules and..." He trailed off, knowing Pitchfork assumed the rest. He wondered then if Cobra knew anything about this. She'd been with Hurricane a lot before he died.

"Now...please get me out of here." Pitchfork blinked her sadness away and whipped her head around. Her eyes pricked and lowered and she sniffed. "The wolves are after you, aren't they?"

"Yeah, they are," grumbled Terror. "Come on, follow me." He snapped his overgrown fangs into her chains and they broke immediately. Pitchfork shook herself, relieved, but screamed a yelp in agony when she began to trot forward. She stumbled instead.

"I can't walk," she said breathlessly. "I'm sorry, Terror. I can't go on. Thank you for helping me anyway."

Terror felt a bit weird. A wolf had never thanked him before. He shook it away. "I-I'll help," he stuttered, feeling strange after saying these words. "Come on. Keep that leg up and I'll find a way to help it at some point. When I'm hurt, I hop along, like this." He demonstrated in a circle and Pitchfork nodded.

"I see," she said, imitating what he did. She quickly followed him into the entrance he'd found before. Terror heard prisoners shouting pleas behind him but he ignored it. He could still hear Stinger and the others, but if they ran quickly they'd be able to escape.

Pitchfork moved surprisingly well. Horrible leg dangling and her hopping the way he'd demonstrated, they made their way across the edge of the forest and past the remaining stone walls. As long as they moved fast, they would make it...

Terror hung back a bit so Pitchfork could limply catch up. Circling the side of the stone, the assassin pricked his ears ahead. If he had to, he'd fight Stinger and his Pack, defeating them each one by one... Just the thought of it made him grin and flex his claws as they hit the ground.

The scents and sounds of the Prowler Pack still lingered and the shouts were easy to identify. Terror pricked his ears farther and kept running with Pitchfork at his heels. "Find them!" Stinger shouted from not far away. They were getting closer.

Keep going and don't get killed! Terror's mind screamed at him. He checked behind him to make sure Pitchfork was still there and nodded to himself. This would be the only time he'd help a wolf instead of hurt them. But then again, this was a fellow Stormer.

She's on my side, and I know it. With her to help me, maybe, if her leg doesn't bother her, I might be able to fulfill my destiny more easily. Terror grinned to himself but startled when he heard shouts from up ahead. *Stupid! You just led us straight into Stinger's clutches, again!*

Pitchfork skidded to a halt behind him, panting for breath. Terror snapped the air to make sure the wolves stayed back. Stinger was giving his horrible grin. "Leaving already, are you?" he sneered, "With a prisoner in addition? I thought you were an assassin."

"Don't tell *me* what to do!" Terror snapped at him, lashing his tail furiously. He showed his overgrown fangs and a few Prowlers whined while shrinking back. "Or I'll—"

"Can you stop making threats already?" Stinger snarled. "None are going to stop me from doing anything, you know that? So don't even try to—"

This time he was interrupted. "*Rargh!*" bellowed Terror, jumping and crunching down on Stinger's neck. With the whines of horror from the Prowlers and the scream of agony from the Pack leader, Terror threw him aside like a hunk of prey. "Now try to test me," he hissed. Now was the time to act terrifying.

Some Prowlers backed up as he drew nearer. "That's right, don't do anything stupid," growled Terror, "or you'll know exactly what happens to you." He took one look at Stinger, then Pitchfork, and was about to make a dash for it.

Instead, a messenger wolf zipped in. "Alpha Stinger!" he gasped, both from his horror at the wound in Stinger's neck and whatever else he could be worried about. Stinger lifted his head weakly and regarded him. "There's a-a-a fire!" he shouted.

Whines and cries of dismay arose. Terror muttered "liar" under his breath but the messenger seemed to hear him. "I'm serious!" he rasped. "It's hot and spreading!"

A few wolves snapped to attention and dashed off in search of the fire. Terror promised himself he'd protect Pitchfork from any danger that may arise.

Stinger did not get up. His face was contorted with pain and blood ran from the bite on his neck. Terror hesitated for a moment but remembered his promise and shook it away. He ran with Pitchfork in hot pursuit. "Wait! Don't leave me!" Stinger howled from behind them. His voice died away with the roaring winds and blowing smoke.

The area was getting hazy and full of dust and debris. Terror coughed and Pitchfork rasped for breath. Up ahead, through the foggy smoke, the Stormer could just make out flickering orange and red flames, spreading quickly.

He'd never experienced a fire before, not even in his younger lone days. The air got hotter and he skidded to a halt once he became close enough to the flames. "What do we do?" Pitchfork shouted.

Terror honestly didn't know. He took looks around him but everywhere there was haze, flames, smoke, sparks, flickers… There was nowhere to go. The moon wasn't even visible although the fire lit up the haze the slightest bit. "Follow me," he said uncertainly.

He leaped toward the right and ducked rolling debris and sparks. Pitchfork didn't lose sight of him—she was on his heels the whole time, hopping limply and quickly. Terror passed by terrified Prowlers and the messenger, who was howling with his horror.

Rolling his eyes, Terror swerved and ducked again. He saw Pitchfork still behind him. Then he ran the slightest bit faster along the burning ground. The fire was spreading. He saw more flames make their way across the camp, burning up everything they touched. Soon fire would reach the stone prisons.

"Get the prisoners out, what are you waiting for?" he snarled at Echinoderm, who he passed next. The Prowler just blinked at him and nodded, dashing toward the stone structures. Terror set his jaw and turned another direction.

They were too late. The whole camp was surrounded by flames. Terror stood there thinking *I'm dead, I'm dead,* and *I'm dead.* Pitchfork stopped behind him, whining. "There's no escape," she whispered, her voice carrying with the angry wind.

"There is," Terror reassured her. He wasn't going to die like this. He took a close look around, squinting. Then he gasped with horror. The fire seemed to know they were there, closing in and creating a circle of flames. The Stormers were forced to get shoulder to shoulder and Terror gnashed his fangs in agony.

The wall of flames roared angrily and sparks rose from the tops of the flames. Terror knew what he had to do. It was risky, and it could get one or both of them killed possibly, and Pitchfork was injured…Terror swallowed and hoped for the best. He whirled around.

"Get on my shoulders," he growled. Pitchfork opened her jaw to protest. "Just do it!" She hesitated but then hopped carefully on top of him. Her weight was hard to carry, but this would be quick. "I hope this won't be my fault if you die," he whispered to her, and heaved her up with all his strength.

Now that she was on top, she was just barely higher than the flames around them. "Jump," he shouted. Pitchfork took a deep breath and leaped as high as she could, just barely soaring over the flames.

Terror heard her body thud in the midst of the sounds and howls and roars of the night wind. The fire lit up the area around him, and now it was his turn. "Terror!" he heard her howl from the other side.

"Don't sacrifice yourself! Don't die!"

The Stormer braced himself. "I might have to," he called. Then he backed up just close enough to the back of the fire wall. With all his might and one of the last breaths he might ever take, Terror jumped.

CHAPTER 4

TERROR DIDN'T even know what happened. He was on the other side of the flames, his sides heaving with exertion. Pitchfork looked especially relieved. "Terror, you're okay!" she cried, lashing her tail. Then she peered at him and flinched. "But you're hurt too…"

Sure enough, there were several burns along the sides of Terror's body. He winced at the pain. "I'll be fine," he growled, giving one last look at the flame wall.

"I can't believe we survived. I mean, we're Stormers and we're proud, but this is unbelievable," Pitchfork breathed. "Not many wolves would survive fires like that. Terror, for an assassin hothead, you were pretty smart."

Terror ducked his head and tried not to grin. First of all, he'd never ever gotten a compliment like that before, especially from a tribe mate. Second, he was *always* called a hothead by his father. Sometimes he didn't quite mind the name.

He didn't bother thanking her, at least not yet. More flames were enclosing the camp, and now they might be trapped once again. Ignoring the burning pain, Terror whirled into action. "Follow me!"

He quickly swerved around a chunk of debris and hoped Pitchfork had seen it coming too. Running as fast as he could and nearing the stone prisons and structures, Terror hoped and prayed that the secret entrance wouldn't be enveloped in flames...if it were, every prisoner would be dead.

Of course, sometimes he didn't mind about wolves dying—he was an assassin, after all. But this time he cared. He peered around for the entrance and to his relief found it. He squeezed his body inward and ducked through it, hearing Pitchfork scrabbling beside him. It was hot inside and smelled of smoke, making Terror sneeze and cough. "I'm here to help!" he choked to who he hoped were living wolves.

He had forgotten his promise to himself. He ignored that and found that the messenger was still struggling to unlock every chain, probably because of how terrified he was. Terror snarled at him and snapped the chains open. Wolves gaped at him but he did not care. "Go!" he ordered them.

He then heard Stinger's final cries. "Help!" and there was no sound anymore except crackling and the rapid movement of the ex-prisoners. The messenger may be the only one in the Prowler Pack that would live, Terror thought.

"Quickly!" he roared as they slipped out of the prisons down the main entrance. Was there fire there too? Only one way to find out...

The wolves were quick and stayed together, no matter what tribe they were. A couple of them had relieved looks toward one another, and Pitchfork stumbled as she ran ahead of him. Terror looked back and saw rising flames. "Faster!" he shouted.

They were out. The fires up ahead had stopped spreading but they created nearly unbearable heat. *Don't let us die, spirits of wolves. Make this fire stop soon. The other Prowlers may have died already...*

Running toward the unknown, the prisoners, the messenger, and the two Stormers slipped through the remaining open space between the flames before they closed up.

THEY HAD run for a while, and now the smoke and crackling were long gone. Every wolf was panting and wheezing, and the burns on Terror's body were really beginning to hurt. "Now all of you get back to your Packs," he ordered with a rumbling growl. "You're especially lucky that I helped you considering I'm a Storm tribe assassin. Go."

They all nodded with hasty thanks and scattered with relief. Terror gave a rasping breath and felt that he had gotten weaker. His tail lashed with pain and he stumbled over. "Terror!" cried Pitchfork, leaning over him. "Oh, no, oh, no..."

"I'm fine," said Terror stubbornly, trying to bring himself to his paws. "You have a far worse injury. And I'm a strong assassin, remember?" He huffed as he looked for a direction to go. This place was unfamiliar, beyond the Forbidden Forest. He could even stumble into another tribe's Territory here.

"But we both need help," Pitchfork insisted. "Let's go back to the Storm tribe and get some care. I need to see my daughter. And *you* need to get back to your tribe as much as I do."

"I do not," Terror snapped. "I just left for my destiny and I'm not going back. Especially since there's a war between the other tribes going on right now!" he added with a lash of his tail.

"What?" Pitchfork looked hurt. "You never told me that. Is everyone okay?"

"I don't know," growled Terror, "but all I know is that I'm never going back. Ever! Got it? Those tribes can handle themselves." Pitchfork snarled.

"I thought you promised you would take me back to the Storm tribe!" she said angrily. "I promised I would let you follow your assassin destiny as long as you took me back! You lied!"

"I had to," said Terror, not meeting her eyes. "Look, I don't help wolves. That's not who I am." He heard Pitchfork snort.

"Be that way, Terror," she hissed. "But I'm going back to the tribe no matter what it takes, whether you help me or not." He heard her paws crunching and turning as she padded away in an unknown direction. He then felt a deep feeling of guilt for lying.

Sighing, he turned around slowly and watched Pitchfork get farther and farther away. He swore he heard himself whine. Trying to shake it away, he sat for a moment's rest, heaving and panting without his control.

He was hurt just like Pitchfork, he admitted to himself at last. And maybe he could go back just to see what had happened with the tribes and to get care. *But...I'm strong. Maybe I'll just let them take care of Pitchfork. I'll drop her off without a word and leave immediately after.*

"Wait," he growled, and ran after her. "I'll help. But let's remember both our promises. Okay?"

Pitchfork looked at him with a grateful shine in her eyes and wagged her tail. "Okay. Let's find the Storm tribe."

It ended in silence as Terror's paws crunched down on the leafy ground. The colors of the leaves had changed gradually as weeks passed, in shades of red, orange, yellow, brown, and gold. The sunset happened sooner than normal and now the crying wind was getting colder.

The moon still shone in the night sky, and it showed no sign that there was ever a fire in the first place. The two wolves walked quietly through the valley under that moonlight, Terror taking time to inhale fresh air. He had breathed in a fair amount of smoke back at the camp.

And if that danger hadn't been enough, what about anything else that would come their way? Terror told himself that he'd act like a Stormer and proudly shove away that peril. Pitchfork said nothing as she hopped next to him, horrible leg dangling.

"Did your sister ever come back?" Pitchfork whispered at last.

"Yes." Terror snorted. "But she's pathetic. My father is trying to transform her but now all *she* is worried about is what *side* to choose in the war. Our side should be it, but she's stupid enough to love a Prowler and travel with a Darkness wolf!" Pitchfork's jaw hung. "Yes, I'm serious. It's horrible! And then the Prowler thinks he's the 'O Great Prowler' in charge of the wild and darkness! That stuff is wolf-dung but he just keeps going on and on and trying to stop our war when it's *our* job to end!" He stopped for breath, because all these words had made his throat close up and his burns hurt.

"She's nothing like her family, is she?" Pitchfork asked. "Kind of like

Pinscher is nothing like me or Hurricane." She lashed her tail and said no more.

"Yes," Terror sighed. "Pinscher even got to order Hurricane around when he was her *father*. She was higher-ranked and didn't break rules like he did."

Pitchfork's eyes grew sad again. "That wasn't like him, to break rules," she whispered. "He must have done it for good reasons that no other wolf believed. And now...he's dead."

Terror didn't reply. He just allowed her to mourn and be sad. Right now he had to focus on finding the right path to the Storm tribe. He sniffed and perked his ears to the stillness as they walked. Then he turned his head toward the other Stormer.

"Don't worry," he told her. "I'll make sure no one hurts your daughter or anyone you love again."

CHAPTER 5

THE SUN was high in the sky the next day as the two Storm tribe wolves ran and trod across the Torrential Valley. Terror had never thought they'd actually be crossing it, due to his first journey through the Forbidden Forest. It was almost—nearly—as dangerous.

"Let's follow the path of the, um…" he said slowly, realizing right then that would not work. Pitchfork winced at her injury but shook her head.

"Sorry, hothead. I was gone for a year. There's no way my scent would still be around. And besides, I've never crossed the Torrential Valley before. Are you sure you know where we're going?"

Terror didn't know what to say to that. All these years being gone from his tribe, and never once had he crossed the two dangerous places he knew about. Obviously his instincts wouldn't do him much good on this journey. He snorted at himself, disgusted and angry. *And I'm supposed to be the smart one!*

Pitchfork whined a low, hard sound as she lowered and put her front paws on her head. "Just go without me. You tried to help. If we can't get anywhere, I'll just stay here."

"No!" Terror returned in a rather harsh tone. "I'm not leaving you here! I promised. And I want you to see your daughter and your tribe, if nothing else." His eyes flickered as they looked into Pitchfork's. "Don't give up, Pitchfork. Pinscher never would." He gave her a grin.

Pitchfork's tail thumped slightly, and she nodded while getting carefully to her paws. "I'll do it," she said determinedly. "Let's go." And off they went, carefully and steadily and avoiding loose rocks. Terror sniffed with all his might but could not find good enough scents. Of course, he thought with a scowl, he couldn't. No wolf would ever stalk through here, not even the bravest of them.

He wondered right then, as they walked across the valley, what his sister was doing back at the war. Not that he cared what happened to her *or* her comrades, he thought with a wolf smirk. But how was she getting along in a fight she had never been in? *Pathetic,* he snorted.

Pitchfork had her muzzle risen slightly and nostrils flaring. She was obviously looking for a scent like him. But there was nothing to smell but fear here. Fear was not a word that hung around in Terror's mind. His *name* was fear, and every wolf could use it against him if they liked.

He didn't know how long it took to cross the Torrential Valley, or if he was exhausted or still full of energy. All day they travelled, and the sun was setting and making way for the moon when Terror saw new landscape ahead.

As soon as they stepped into that landscape, scents came rushing to Terror like a flood. First, there were other wolves nearby, most likely ones that were protecting their Territory and ones that did not bother joining the tribe clashing.

Second, it smelled much fresher and all the fear was gone. Scents of prey skittered about as if the prey were actually there, and it was too much for Terror. He nearly sneezed in agony. Pitchfork laughed—something Stormers never did—and Terror shot her a disapproving look.

Their paws made soft crunching noises on the now soft and mossy ground. It was also very green. This land was much better than the Torrential Valley, but it was still unfamiliar. Maybe if they shuffled in another direction and ran for a while, they'd go back on a familiar track.

Terror knew that he did *not* want to come across the other tribes. He could easily get rid of any wolf in his way, but right now he had no time and they needed to keep moving if they wanted to get back to the Storm tribe.

The question was what would the tribe think of their runaway assassin returning a second time, maybe not even for long? When they found out he was merely dropping off a long-lost wolf from their tribe, what would they think then? Terror came up with a few possible responses in his mind and they made him flex his claws with rage.

One, they might laugh and laugh at him, and say, "Look! Our *assassin* rescued wolves from other tribes! He clearly isn't *meant* to be an assassin!" Second, they could shake their heads and say, "What a stubborn, so-called terrifying wolf that doesn't even know left from right. Some killer…"

Terror nearly stomped the ground loudly, but he didn't want to draw attention to anything that may be lurking. He snorted through his nostrils instead, and Pitchfork glanced at him for a second before shaking her head. Without a word, Terror gestured and they began running to a side direction.

Pitchfork did not seem bothered by her leg or tired at all. Maybe the thought of seeing Pinscher and the tribe after a whole year motivated her. Whatever it was, it was a good thing.

Terror got back to thinking, trying to control his rage. On the other paw, the Storm tribe may be overjoyed for the first time to see a lost member. Perhaps Pitchfork had been important to them, despite being a serious commander, and the loss had been devastating. Possibly, they may praise him for bringing her back.

They could say: "Long live Terror, the Storm tribe assassin! He risked his life for one of us, when he was supposed to end other wolves! He may have run away but if he hadn't, we wouldn't have Commander Pitchfork back! He deserves to be moved up in the ranks, and be the Alpha wolf of us all!"

Terror breathed that in. It had always sounded great to think of him, the Alpha wolf, ordering the Storm tribe around. He wanted to be an assassin, but he knew he had the guts for leadership as well, no matter what his father thought. But a feeling of anger crept up into him again as he thought this under the coming moonlight.

Shortly before the preparations of the war and the returning of Stormer Cobra, his father had had a plan. It was a good one, of transforming Cobra little by little into a true Stormer. Anaconda had so dearly wanted to use his daughter and create her into a new version of his long-gone mother. After all, why couldn't Cobra follow in her paw-steps?

But *Terror* had wanted to be in that place. Anaconda had clearly stated that that wasn't the plan. Terror had always wanted that power, that glory in battle, not to be the lowly assassin his father wolf called him to be.

"Besides, I'm the one with the overgrown fangs here! And Cobra barely knows a thing!" he had argued one night shortly before Cobra's return. "I want to be the glorious, everyday assassin! Don't use her, use me!"

"You are not good enough for that destiny," Anaconda had growled at him. "No Stormer has ever taken the job of assassin, as you know. We think *you* can take that job. And I expect you to take it with pride and strength, for it is your real destiny."

From then on, Terror had gradually realized more and more that it was his destiny. But he hadn't forgotten the power and glory he could have had more of. He knew right then that he *could not* spare the lives of other wolves if he wanted to earn that power for himself.

If he could just prove to his father—and to the whole tribe—that he was worthy, maybe he would finally get what he wanted. This was another promise he needed to try to keep, but one he could not tell any other wolf.

Pitchfork was panting with exertion behind him and nodded for rest.

They curled up, not hungry right then, and Pitchfork immediately fell asleep, curled into a tight ball. Under the moonlight, Terror brought his gaze toward the starry night, every little sliver of light something beautiful. The moon shone as it had during the fire, and something about this sky above him put him in a trance.

There wouldn't be any darkness. There wasn't a trace of it out here, in this beautiful night littered with stars. There would be no darkness falling and Great Prowler standing tall. No, there wouldn't.

And soon it will be me that changes the world.

CHAPTER 6

TERROR DIDN'T think they would actually *run into* a wolf on their way. He smelled the scents of another tribe nearby, but was not sure what it was. They had passed all signs of life a while ago, and the area around them was still and quiet.

But something strong caught his nose, and it smelled as if it was coming fast. This made his whiskers and nostrils twitch. He shook his body and lifted his ears. Pitchfork looked as if she was about to say something. "Don't," he said to her. "Yes, there's someone coming." He stalked into a fierce position. "And that someone is about to become scraps left in the forest..."

Pitchfork cringed. Terror didn't know if it was from pain in her wrecked leg or the fact that he'd said something horrible. He fixed himself and took a breath. "Get behind me," he whispered. "I'll take care of them."

"But—"

"If you want to see your daughter and tribe again"—Terror's head snapped around to face her "—you have to listen to me." His tail lashed back and forth for a moment, and Pitchfork took a whooshing breath and nodded.

He turned back around. His ears stayed right up and his gaze snapped ahead. The area was still quiet, but he could just make out muffled rustling of undergrowth. "I know you're in there, stalker," Terror shouted with a snap of his jaws.

Dark pelt…innocent expression…fearfully twitching ears…the wolf sprang out at the last second and Terror was enveloped in dark fur. Snapping and snarling, he rolled over and threw the smaller body off. It was a female Darkness wolf, and one he had seen before.

"You!" he snarled at her. "*You're* the escaped prisoner—Cobra's other Darkness friend!"

From the force of being thrown over, the Darkness wolf staggered to her paws and her legs kicked up dust. "Yes, it's me," she growled softly, twitching her tail and ears in defiance. "And I'm here to stop you."

Terror snorted so loud that it sounded like a laugh. But he did not think it was funny. "That'll always be the stupidest thing any wolf has ever said to me," he returned grimly. "If you think you can stop me, show me. I don't care what happens."

The Darkness wolf looked up, and her eyes ran over the burns along his sides. She pinned her ears back. "You're already hurt," she whined. "I'm not going to—"

"Exactly," said Terror calmly, interrupting her. "That's what I thought. You're too *weak* and *feeble* and *caring* to ever be a good fighter. You fight no matter what you do to another wolf, got it? You'll never make it out here." He shook his head with mock sadness.

"How dare you?" The Darkness wolf leaped again and Terror acted quickly. He swung her to the side and she was sent crashing into a tree trunk. She yelped sharply and Terror couldn't stifle a grin.

"Play with me," he said, grinning still. "Come on, Darkness Prisoner. Don't be shy. Fight me!" He began to circle her, growling with amusement through his fangs.

"It's Kaiju!" the wolf snapped, baring her teeth back at him. "I won't let you hurt any more wolves!"

"Well, I'll hurt *you* if you don't scram!" Terror snarled, throwing his body to the side and slamming into Kaiju. The Darkness wolf gasped in agony and rolled over steadily.

Pitchfork staggered to stop them. "Don't!" she said. "Please!"

"This is for you, Pitchfork," Terror said, bowing low in his fierce position. Then he ran and threw himself on top of the Darkness wolf, pinning her in one quick move. She struggled and gasped and he knew he had to do it.

He bent his muzzle. Kaiju howled for help. Crashing sounds rang throughout the area, and Terror snapped his head upward. Pitchfork stopped short and lifted a paw. *More wolves,* he thought. *Looks like this is going to be my lucky day, huh?*

Kaiju continued her low-pitched howl, and Terror's ears rang in agony. They screamed at him to get off her. Stormers hated howling, and Terror agreed with the idea of forbidden howling. So this—*this* was awful.

"Shut that muzzle up!" he shouted over the howling. "Quit that *hideousness*! Enough!" He slammed his paws down on her chest and she yelped mid howl.

Pitchfork did not move. Her tail was beginning to tuck, and Terror thought, *Pathetic, she needs to toughen up a bit* and lowered his muzzle again. If other wolves were on their way, he needed to finish the job quickly.

"No! Don't!" Kaiju cried, thrashing beneath him. "You can't, Terror, you can't!"

"I most certainly—" Terror was cut short when several dark pelts dashed out of the undergrowth, surrounding them. "Don't worry! We're here to help!" called one male, baring his teeth at Terror.

Pitchfork staggered backward and her flank nudged against Terror's side. The burns flashed with pain, and Terror tried not to gasp. He threw off two Darkness wolves that had leapt toward him and slammed into another.

With tremendous force, he felt himself getting knocked to the ground. The burns stung violently, and he thought through the pain that he'd be dead soon. *Wait, no, don't think that! You're tougher than any wolf! Bite their butts! Get them!*

Not sure where Kaiju had gone after being set free, he swerved around to face another meek wolf. "Fight me!" he snarled at him, and the two began tumbling.

Wolves screamed and howled in agony while he ducked and bit at their flanks. They feared him, just as he wanted them to. He spun around and crunched down on the same wolf's neck. There was no noise, but the wolf crumpled slowly to the hard ground.

Pitchfork was lying flat on the ground with her paws over her eyes. She didn't have to watch this. Terror felt a little sorry for her as he was forced to finish off three other wolves that dared test him. Afterward, he decided he might apologize.

He was about to crunch down on another wolf's flank when a piercing loud howl cut the air, and it wasn't from any of the Darkness wolves around them. It sounded like a Prowler howl. *I swear to the spirits of wolves that if the 'O Great Prowler' was following me too...*

His thoughts were cut off when he caught sight of the wolf. It was not the same Prowler. In fact, this Prowler was smaller and had no wounds along his body, or any scars. In fact, he looked flawless.

"That's quite enough, everyone," said the new Prowler casually. "There's no need for violence here." His voice was young and so were his eyes. But that voice...it was so calm and fearless.

A wolf cocked her head and a bleeding scratch dripped from her ear. "Who are you?" she asked. "Are you the Great Prowler?"

"I don't think so. But I hope to be," said the Prowler. "Prowler Fathomer, everyone," he added without a hint of tremor in his voice. "I don't want any wolf to be hurt."

"Oh, yeah?" challenged Terror, sidling up to the flawless-bodied Prowler. "You think you, a *one-year-old Prowler,* can boss me around? It was one Darkness wolf's fault, and it started this whole fight. Leave it alone, punk." He spat the last words and glared at Prowler Fathomer.

"Oh, that's fine. Deal with Father then," Fathomer returned with a flick of his long tail. Terror opened and closed his jaw. Who was Fathomer's father, and how had he raised his son so well to where there wasn't even a lick of a battle scar? "That's what I thought." He smiled and Terror hated it immediately.

"Where are you going to get your father? He's not here, is he?" Terror snarled at last, lashing his tail warningly and causing a few wolves to back away. "Huh? Tell me."

Fathomer smiled again and motioned to the other wolves. The Darkness wolves—a whole Pack, Terror presumed—followed the Prowler without hesitation. Pitchfork just stood there, jaw hanging as the Darkness Pack showed their loyalty to Fathomer.

"Is he, like, the leader or something?" she whispered as Terror sidled over and the other wolves were out of sight. "How did he do that? He looks so young...like one or two. And who is his father? How does he look unharmed?"

Terror, too, had many questions. He shook himself. "Well, *that* was a lost cause," he growled. "I don't care who that wolf is. At least the fight is over and you don't have to watch me do assassin work anymore. Soon we'll be back at the tribe."

"Are you sure we'll make it? I mean me?" Pitchfork whined. "My leg isn't looking so good, especially since I've been walking and running on it." She cringed, and Terror tried not to flinch again as he saw her horrible leg looking even more horrible.

The flesh around the bone was red and inflamed, and it looked especially painful. She had to be fixed somehow, and fast. "Let's go, quickly!" Terror growled hastily, and they took off at a run, Pitchfork whining softly from behind him.

"Don't worry. I'll try to pick up the Storm tribe scents along the way. We might be close or...far. I swear if we're far I'll go mark and curse the lake with my—"

Pitchfork was laughing. "Don't say it," she cut in, still cracking up. Why was it so funny? Terror was just plain annoyed was all! He caught his breath and they began to run again.

As they crossed a green valley and the unknown, Terror turned his nose in the air to try for any scents, any at all. Pitchfork surely wouldn't make it to Stormer Territory if she kept running on that leg. While they ran and he caught the scents of the wolves they were just with, Terror was thinking.

How could the Storm tribe possibly fix Pitchfork's leg? What if it was permanently damaged and couldn't be fixed? It looked so horrible, and Terror knew Pitchfork was in such pain right now. The Storm tribe would never give up on her, though, he knew that. They'd find a way, sure. That's how he thought Stormers were the best wolves in the wild: they always had a strategy, and were of course powerful.

Especially him...a smile broke his face like lightning. He was the most feared and powerful Stormer of all time. He even overpowered his one-fanged ancestor Stormer Python, who had stalked King Aghast to kill him.

Terror had seriously considered finishing the helpless Darkness prince while he was prisoner, but he had doubted his father would have wanted him to do that. And any other heir...he could follow in Python's paw-steps, right?

It doesn't always matter what my father says. I can't always listen to Anaconda. I am an assassin, and I can make my own decisions. I'm also not young anymore, six years old! I'm not one like that Fathomer! I could spin around and maul my father if I wanted to!

The scents overloaded his nose and he stifled a sneeze. It was an explosion of wolf scents everywhere, even prey scents. Terror tried to set some aside and concentrate on any sharp scent of the Storm tribe he could possibly find.

Pitchfork sneezed instead. "So many scents!" she huffed. "Terror, can you believe it?"

"Yes. Because wolves live so close to one another and are stupid," Terror replied flatly. "Overloads any wolf's nose, I should say. Just... keep your nose low. I'll take care of these junky scents." He snorted away a few of them and Pitchfork laughed quite joyously.

For someone with a hurt leg, she's pretty high spirited. Pinscher... well, she's perfect for me. Fierce, strict, and strong:, nothing like her mother or father wolves. Maybe an ancestor gave her those ways. I like them.

And soon, he'd see the wolf he loved again.

CHAPTER 7

B Y THE time Terror and Pitchfork had gone quite a distance, most of the scents had drifted away. Pitchfork had her fangs clenched with pain, and Terror knew she was straining not to scream with agony. He should not have pressured her to come this far with an injury like this.

Lummox! Hothead! Terror thought. *Why could I do something so stupid? Pitchfork can't go much farther. She'll die if we don't get to the Storm tribe soon. We must keep going!*

He glanced at the pained wolf behind him. She looked into his eyes with her colorless and agonized ones. He had to look away, because he couldn't stand that sad look on her face. "If we keep going, we'll get there" was all he managed to whisper.

T HE NEXT morning Terror finally found the Storm scent: crisp, clear, and sharp. The landscapes were familiar and he could just see the Territory borders. The Storm tribe had the most amazing and vast Territory to live in. Now the whole tribe of wolves rested here.

The sounds and clamors from some distance away caught Terror's ears. They didn't sound like fighting. In fact, the voices were a mix of noisy, relieved, shocked, and contented. Had the Storm tribe conquered the war? Terror couldn't suppress a grin.

"Pitchfork, do you know what this means?" he said joyously. "We won."

Pitchfork looked up. "We did?" she said, eyes gleaming. "Every wolf is safe?"

"We're about to find out," replied Terror with a lightning-bolt grin. "Let's go and get you fixed." Pitchfork was chuckling with relief as she followed him past the borders.

The whole Storm tribe—pups, low-rankers, high-rankers, trainees, and all—was out there together, gathered with their tails lashing silently. Pinscher stood at the rear with a relieved look. The ground was still dusty and stained with blood and fur, but the wolves all looked happy that everything was over.

Pinscher looked up, ears erect. "Terror!" she cried when her eyes fell on him. She leaped up and ran straight to him. Terror embraced her warm, furry body and felt newfound hope in his gut. No wolf was mad at him.

The Stormer fell back. "Now," she said; her voice suddenly getting firm. "Now that we are done with the *amazing* greeting, I must ask this question: Why did you leave and then come back?!"

"It's because I found this wolf that has been lost for a year now. She is returned but injured, also former commander. You may remember Pitchfork, Pinscher," Terror informed her, stepping aside. Pinscher widened her eyes in disbelief, her tail clamping to her flank.

"Mother?" she breathed incredulously. "Y-You're alive? I thought Scarr had killed you!"

"I didn't die, Pinscher," Pitchfork said slowly, "but I probably will if we don't get *this* fixed up." She revealed her leg and many wolves groaned and turned their heads away. Some others wore looks of horror.

"All right," Pinscher stammered. "You're...back, Mother. But Father is dead." Pitchfork nodded sadly with an "I know" face. "I'm sorry, Mother. Stormer Anaconda killed him, our great leader. And..." She cut herself off and swallowed.

Then uproar followed. It was so sudden that it startled Terror. Wolves shouted and snarled at him from all directions, their words hitting him like arrow blows.

"I thought he ran away!"

"He saved a wolf's life! How is that *assassin* duty?"

"You saved Pitchfork but what about any other wolf?"

Pinscher howled a snarl for quiet. "Enough," she hissed. "Let these two explain their adventures." She looked back to them and wolves bowed their heads in submission. It was quiet.

Terror growled to himself. Then he began telling about everything: the prison, the fire, the Prowler Pack's death, the Darkness wolves, their journey, and even Prowler Fathomer, the young wolf who seemed like a mystery to him.

More uproar came. The words were angry or disappointed.

"Don't save wolves' lives, assassin!"

"You let the Darkness wolf *go*? When you had a *chance*?"

"Pinscher is better at high ranks than her mother ever was! Or her father, for that matter."

"Prowler Fathomer is strange. Why couldn't you have finished him?"

"I thought he was meant to kill…"

Terror was full of rage. He flexed his claws like back in the wilderness and snorted through his nostrils. He couldn't scream or yell—but showing them that he was terrifying was the only way to stop this nonsense.

He got in a prowling position and gave snarling barks at the wolves gathered. The pups whined and backed into their mothers, ears pinned to their heads. The trainees gulped and watched him intently. Terror gnashed his overgrown fangs together and growled, creeping toward the shouting wolves.

The noise ceased and died down. Now the wolves were all staring at him, wide-eyed. A few backed up, whining. Terror snapped the air ahead of him and one wolf turned to flee. Pinscher barked.

"Stop it, Terror. They're just overwhelmed," she growled through gritted fangs. "The war has been intense and they are still calming down from it. Enough, all of you!" she barked to them. They quieted again and the pups didn't look nearly as scared.

Terror closed his jaw and looked to Pitchfork. "I'm sorry for not being the assassin you all wanted. But I was just warming up. It takes a lot of work to become a real assassin, and you all know that. Soon I will be killing wolves all under your command and mine." He grinned at them all.

No wolf said anything. Pitchfork limped forward a little and touched noses with Pinscher. At first, Terror thought Pinscher would back away, snorting. But instead the high-ranker touched her nose to Pitchfork's. "I missed you, Mother," she whispered.

"Her leg needs to be fixed," Terror said. "But before we do that, what happened in the war? Did we win?"

"Umm…not necessarily," Pinscher said slowly. "It's a long story. But it was a truce we made with the other tribes. Your sister…she helped us all, and saved us all. She made the tribes happier by this excellent idea. Each tribe has acres and acres of land to call their own, where no tribe should cross. We have already sent messengers and created Storm Land. Cobra and her comrades have already headed back toward Prince Honor's home with the Darkness wolves, but she left me as Alpha." She stopped short after the last words.

"Wait." Terror twisted his face with suspicion. "You aren't supposed to be Alpha wolf. You're commander. That's my *father's* job." He whipped his head from side to side. He couldn't see a sign of Anaconda anywhere. "Where is he? *Where is my father?*" he snarled. "And *what happened to him*?"

Pinscher's eyes had a hint of sadness but he watched her shake it away and make her eyes flicker. Her ears swiveled as she said these words: "Terror, I'm sorry. The war, and everything, and Cobra…it just couldn't go on."

"What in wolf's sake are you *talking* about? *Where is my father?*" Terror repeated, stalking low and skulking threateningly toward her. "I swear, if you did a thing to him, Pinscher, you can forget about being my—"

"I'm sorry," said Pinscher with a sigh, "but I'm afraid your father is dead."

CHAPTER 8

"**D**EAD?" **SHOUTED** Terror. His tail dropped to his flank and his muscles tensed with disbelief. No. This couldn't be. Anaconda was the strictest, strongest, and most powerful wolf Terror knew. He had ruled the tribe for almost all his life, and he had done it well. But now…this couldn't be. "Who killed him?!" he snarled.

Tears ran down Pinscher's face as she stood there, trembling. "I'm sorry," she repeated with a broken voice. "Your father…his own daughter killed him, and I will never know why."

"She, um, actually *told you* why?" Shearer offered nervously. Stormer Rebellion snarled and bit his ear. Without flinching or whining, Shearer quieted.

Terror growled and thrashed his tail from side to side. "Wait, what?!" he shouted.

Pinscher was still crying but nodded.

Terror spun around. "Argh, *Cobraaa!*" he snarled as loud as he could, throwing himself to the ground and rolling around in anger. Pitchfork was whining and stepping back, looking like she was trying not to scream when she put down her leg.

"I will kill that wolf one day, in return for killing our father!" Terror bellowed for all to hear, getting to his feet and howling snarls to the moon-risen sky. "And you all can count on your assassin to do it!" He stopped his ordeal, panting and huffing with exertion. He turned to the wolves and gave them a look.

Pinscher kept the tears rolling, and didn't try to stop them. "Terror, she saved us, her own tribe, even though we never treated her right," she whispered. "You can't kill her after all she's done, Terror, even if she did kill Anaconda. I wouldn't say she's just unordinary, she's extraordinary. And one day you will see that."

"Oh, really?" growled Terror. "Nice speech, Pinscher, but no way am I going to *not get revenge.* Forget about being my mate, Pinscher, for all that. I am going to go where destiny calls me. Enjoy the drop-off." He turned around to head back to the forest, where he was meant to go.

"More like the rip-off!" Shearer shouted from behind him. Terror spun around to face his innocent expression.

"Shut the muzzle up," was all he said. He was about to turn around again when he felt something prick into his side. It hurt, but only for a split second before his eyes closed.

A T FIRST, he thought he'd died. But his eyes opened and the world around him was still there. It was blurry, but it was still comforting. Terror heard the shuffling of wolves' paws and the chatter within. He also heard yowling.

Curious to see what the matter was, he stretched to his feet and hobbled forward. He could see that his burns had been treated during that time he'd been asleep. Whatever that thing was that had poked him—possibly a tranquilizing plant—it had been strong and extremely fast.

"No, stay still and rest," a medicine wolf said firmly. Terror growled, and she backed up. He padded in the direction of the yowling.

Pitchfork was there, being held down by about three wolves, while another wolf tried to push the bone back within and sew up the wound. The dislocation was already fixed but the stitching was most likely the worst part.

"Stop, Mother! Stay still! We're trying to help you!" Pinscher barked over the commotion. "Don't worry. Just lie still! You'll be all right!" She threw herself onto Pitchfork as well and now the Stormer couldn't go anywhere. She thrashed and yowled with pain while the wolves tried desperately to keep her down.

Oh, spirits of wolves, Terror snorted. *I've never heard Pinscher sound so kind before. Maybe she is like her mother and father.*

"Alpha Pinscher!" said a Stormer, running like the wind into the cavern. His tail thrashed dangerously and his head hit the rock wall from his movement. He looked to be young, way younger than Terror. Then Terror realized it was Stormer Blade-Edge, who was even younger than Fathomer, and none other than the wolf with a permanent limp Cobra had once caused.

Pinscher shoved her ears forward, lifting her head high. "Yes? Tell me, Blade-Edge. What troubles you?" Her eyes flickered with pride.

Blade-Edge limped forward, catching his breath. He stared at the yowling wolf Pitchfork as he spoke. "About that strange Prowler…I found a scent that might be him coming this way. What if the tribes go at war again, even after Cobra fixed everything?"

"You say they're headed to Storm Land?" Pinscher questioned. Her eyes had a flash of worry within them. Terror decided not to speak up; if he did, Pinscher would surely turn on him. Blade-Edge nodded.

Pinscher's eyes moved to the entrance to the cavern, and she paced toward the outside. Looking up at the sky, she mouthed something Terror couldn't make out. Then she looked down and around. "We need to be ready, in case Prowler Fathomer and the wolves he may have brought really do attack us." She turned and bowed her head in thanks to Blade-Edge.

Terror staggered slightly but found he could walk around easily. The burns flashed with pain but he endured and ignored it. "If Prowler Fathomer comes back," he growled, "then I will kill him."

Pinscher looked at him with eyes he had never seen before. What she said quietly next was something Terror thought she'd never say about him. "Killing isn't the right way to go, Terror. Why is it your only life guide?" She turned and padded away, leaving Terror in a state of shock.

ERROR WAS down in the dungeon. No, he wasn't chained up. No, he hadn't been made to go down there. He had chosen, because Pinscher had deserted him.

He couldn't stop the tears leaking from his eyes. He couldn't stop the low whining rising from his throat. And there was no way he was leaving this place. He had never felt so down in his life.

His father—now dead—had told him assassin duty was his destiny, and he had believed it. And still now he believed it. But now, Pinscher no longer did.

I've never heard any wolf sound less like a Stormer. 'Killing is not the right way to go, Terror, why is it your only life guide, hah, hah, blah, blah, blah!' His mockery didn't make him feel any better. The tears ran faster. Stormers were supposed to be killers, and they were supposed to be merciless.

But most Stormers now—just pride. They were careful. They were worrisome. *Is it really the darkness falling for the Great Prowler Legend, that changes every wolf? But no…it's wolf-dung. It's nonsense. It's garbage! There is no darkness falling and Great Prowler standing tall!*

He stamped the ground with his strong paws and thrashed his tail furiously. With all his might, his first-ever howl rang through the dungeon, through the Storm Land, and through his own heart.

TEPPING INTO the light of the day, Terror kept his head low and tail drooped. He had never felt less like a wimp. But if he wanted to make a good impression and not suffer Pinscher's awful words again, he needed to stay alert and careful.

Pitchfork was obviously still healing in the caves because she was not out here lining up with the others. Terror stayed still, frozen still, waiting for a command, or something to do. Pinscher's head snapped around. "What are you waiting for, assassin?" she rasped.

Terror cracked a grin but hoped she hadn't noticed it. He forever no longer wanted to be mates with her. And what kind of father wolf would he be to Stormer pups? He shook the feeling away and shuffled around inside the formations. Wolves flinched away or murmured as he passed.

He held his tongue and teeth, for he did not want to growl at them and ruin his impression. Pinscher's voice rose.

"We will take down whatever Pack is coming our way, no matter what. Prowler Fathomer could be among them. We will find out more about the wolf and most likely break his streak of flawless. He will carry one or more battle scars if he dares fight us."

Now she's sounding more merciless, Terror thought.

Hopefully, there would not be a second war within Stormer Territory.

CHAPTER 9

A **STORM HAD** gathered within the sky. Gray clouds scattered across the deep blue, and bolts of incredible lightning flashed overhead. The rumbling of the deep thunder sounded and rang through every wolf's ears. Torrential rain poured down, soaking the Storm tribe's pelts.

Terror wasn't sure how long the wolves had been waiting for their supposed enemies. It could have been five minutes, two years, or an eternity before the smell caught his nose. He watched the other wolves' ears perk and shove forward.

Pinscher sniffed incredulously. "You were right, Blade-Edge. Not that I ever doubted you," she said to the trainee with a smile. "You'd make a good High-Ranker one day." The young wolf's tail thrashed with pride.

Terror inhaled and exhaled, and not because of fear. The scent was burning strong, and he knew Fathomer and possibly several other wolves would be coming their way. He hadn't said a word this whole time, just concentrated, waited, and sniffed.

The smell was getting closer by the second. Terror watched a few wolves' hackles bunch up and tails begin to lash. Many looked ready to spring and catch the neck of the first wolf that emerged.

Shearer barked, "Here they come!" Terror wanted to yell, *Yeah, thanks, Commander Obvious,* but he kept his jaws clamped shut and teeth ground together. But almost as soon as the High-Ranker said these words, Prowler Fathomer was already stalking out from the undergrowth.

He looked the same as he had before. His body had no scars, his ears were perfect and unscored, and his bushy tail thrashed calmly. How could he possibly be fearless in a situation like this, with Stormers surrounding him with their fangs gnashed and ready to bite? Terror wanted to crunch that calm smile off Fathomer's face.

Pinscher wore a look that said, "Humph, you were right, Terror, he is strange."

Terror grinned inwardly and watched the wolves around him. What would be their reactions to the Prowler?

His answer came fast. The wolves barked and snarled and snapped into an uproar. Fathomer continued to stand there, head high and one paw rose. "Calm down, Storm tribe," he said with not even a hint of tremor in his voice. "We aren't here to hurt you."

Yeah, right, Terror snorted.

"I brought wolves with me who need to make amends with the Storm Tribe," the young wolf continued. "Where is the supposed 'assassin' you so love?"

Shut your smart jaw up now, Terror thought with rage. Fathomer had made a point, however. What if the Storm tribe only pretended to love their assassin? What if they absolutely loathed him and didn't love him at all?

"It's me," he said, speaking at last and taking a pace out of formation. Pinscher gave a low growl but he didn't heed it. "Oh, and allow me to apologize for attacking a Darkness wolf that was basically trying to *kill me!*" Terror added sarcastically.

Fathomer did something unbelievable: narrowed his eyes.

"For your information, that Darkness wolf was doing the right thing," he said all too sternly. "And besides, you killed her, didn't you? You didn't just attack her! You did what all assassins do!" His bark was rising to sharp now.

"Yes. Yes, I did." Terror smiled and raised a paw up like Fathomer.

Pinscher gave him a hard look but he mouthed "Let them believe it."

If they thought he'd killed a fellow Darkness wolf, maybe they wouldn't dare test him again. Maybe they wouldn't underestimate and attack him again. So he kept his pose and waited for Fathomer's reaction.

"We're here for the matter of *actually apologizing* for killing a wolf of our tribe. Assassin or not, you must, or we may consider attacking your tribe and Territory," Fathomer stated, a little more calmly. "Please do, assassin."

Terror tried to control his rage. First of all, Fathomer drove him crazy. Second, why use manners against him? It was infuriating to hear such kind words from another wolf.

Darkness wolves began to sneak out from the shadows, gathering in elite formation with Fathomer just in the middle. The Prowler's gaze remained on Terror, eyes flashing with something the Stormer did not know the name of.

"If you don't apologize, assassin, then you'll know what we'll—"

Fathomer was cut off by the loud rustling of the undergrowth, even louder than the thunderclaps above. Another soaked Prowler stumbled through and opened his jaw immediately. "Fathomer, that's enough. I will handle this. Step back."

The young wolf looked surprised to see the other Prowler. Then he paced back respectfully. "Yes, sir, Father," he answered, still keeping his eyes on Stormer Terror.

This is his father he was talking about, Terror realized with a pang to his stomach and overgrown fangs. Thinking about it caused him to miss *his* father even more. But at least some wolf could pay for Anaconda's death.

"Prowler Moon, everyone," the other Prowler said with a bow of his haunches. "My comrade Prowler Sun and I have worked hard to track the Great Prowler and how the darkness is reaching this world. All of which you all care nothing about." He grinned.

Terror snorted so loudly every wolf could hear him. Pinscher shot him a glare but he didn't heed that either. "Of course," he said. "It's wolf-dung—why would we believe it?"

"Your sister believes it," said Moon. Terror hung his jaw in disbelief. How could Moon have possibly known? "Yes, I heard everything. It's been a couple moons, now hasn't it? Everyone in the wild knows about it. Yes, we have trespassed on yet *your* land, but my ignorant son here needed some matters dealt with."

"Shut him up, will you?" Terror snarled to Fathomer. The young Prowler shook his head, causing the assassin to growl and sit on his haunches, enduring this lecture.

"Assassin!" said Moon, moving his eyes upon Terror. "Stormer Terror, is it?" The eyes narrowed as quickly as they had moved. "We heard you killed the Darkness wolf that stalked you and tried to stop you?"

Fathomer must have told his father everything. That made Terror all the more annoyed.

"Yes," Terror hissed, taking menacing paces forward. His hackles showed no sign of lowering, his eyes were flashing, and his tail thrashed from side to side. However, Moon did not move from where he was, and showed no sign of fear or tremor. *Moon was just as annoying as Fathomer.*

"Sun and I tracked and interviewed many wolves about who this wolf was," Moon went on. "We finally contacted Prince Honor's Darkness Pack, who now thrives in Darkness Land together. They said a wolf of theirs had left to find you, and now she's dead."

"Who is it, now?" Terror sneered.

"You have killed an important runaway wolf of theirs, one who is believed to relate to Prince Honor," Moon replied. "They say her name was Kaiju."

Terror remembered now. The wolf had yelled back, "It's Kaiju!" as he was fighting her. Now every wolf but the Storm tribe would think she was gone. He would let them believe whatever they wanted.

"Now all you have to do, assassin," Moon said, "is make amends with the Darkness wolves, and never attack them again."

"Ha!" Terror pawed the ground and laughed. "Me, make amends? Me, leave wolves alone? Spirits, no! I'm an assassin, and it's my fate. Assassins never stop stalking. Assassins never leave other wolves alone. Assassins stalk, stalk, and kill!"

Howls and barks of anger rang out from the Darkness wolves. But Terror didn't care. Pinscher's eyes were filling quickly with worry. *Why so anxious? This is what Stormers do: they're cruel, proud, mean, and deadly. Just wipe that look off your face!*

Moon curled his lips and showed his teeth. "Make amends, now, assassin, or I kill *you*!" he snarled. "And don't you lay a single fang or claw on my son either!"

"Like I wouldn't," Terror snapped. He was pushing this way too far but there was no way he was going to be a wimp-wolf and apologize to the wolves that had attacked him. Better yet, he never apologized to any wolf. All but Pitchfork...

Moon leaped—it seemed that had been the last straw. Terror felt the breath knocked out of him as the Prowler collided with him. They twisted and snapped at each other. While he had the chance, Terror sunk his overgrown fangs into Moon's hide.

A piercing howl broke out, and Terror knew he'd bitten hard. He could feel the blood rushing into his jaws and the feeling of victory through his gut.

"Father!" screamed Fathomer.

"No," howled Moon weakly under Terror's grip. His tail lashed desperately and his eyes were anxious. "Don't move, Fathomer. I don't want you getting hurt. Not at all...you're my only pup, son. Stay back and stay safe."

"Yes, sir, Father," whined Fathomer, eyes shining with wet tears. "Just don't die..." A tear ran down his face. Terror had never thought he'd see Fathomer cry.

"Fine," Terror said at last after a moment's silence. "I'm sorry, wolves, that I'm such a wimp. I hope you're happy!" He jumped off Prowler Moon and before any wolf could stop him, he headed for the forest once more.

CHAPTER 10

HE COULD hear the barks of protest from his tribe from behind him. In one quick flash, he spun around and his overgrown fangs gleamed. He snapped them quickly and spun back around to run again.

"Wait, no, Terrorrrr!" Pinscher yelled. "Come back here! As Alpha, I order you!"

Terror didn't listen. "Ha! Good luck ordering me around. Farewell wolves, for I will never return. Goodbye, Pinscher." He felt the tears pricking his eyes and tried shaking them away as he ran like the wind.

His burns flickered with pain and he stifled yelps. Despite the burns having been treated, that didn't stop the sensation. Terror ground his teeth and fangs together. *This time, I am definitely leaving, whether they want me to or not, and maybe that Fathomer will leave me alone!*

This motivation caused him to pick up his speed, faster and faster by the second. The trees, leaves, and undergrowth blurred quickly by. Twigs and branches snapped beneath his quick, turning paws. His nose twitched at the air, trying to catch every scent coming his way.

No other sign of life was around, which was the good thing. Terror let out whooshes of breath but did not stop. As long as he kept going, no wolf would ever find him again, even if he lashed out and started assassin duty once more.

THE MOON was high in the sky and Terror was digging a den to sleep in for the night. His paws quickly scraped and moved the dirt so he could make a hole big enough for his body to lay comfortably. He hadn't had a good rest for a while, and he had run for he didn't even know how long.

Dirt flew in all directions as he worked quickly. Owls and crickets sounded from above and around him. The moon was partial, a gleaming white crescent filling the sky with beautiful light. Terror panted, tongue lolling, as he dug even deeper into the ground.

Sniffing, he thought he had caught a scent. It was a sign of life, wasn't it? He stopped digging long enough to study the smell. His ears were erect and forward while his nose sniffed nearly frantically. He stiffened.

There were wolves coming.

Even quicker than before, he returned to digging. Then he had an idea—better yet, two ideas. He rolled around in the grass, leaves, and dirt until he was sure his scent was masked. He could still be seen, though...

He finished digging his den and threw himself inside hastily. Then he scrabbled at the entrance, trying to cover himself up as soon as possible. He thought he could hear thundering wolf paws. Heart beating and thundering in his chest, he covered the entrance.

Panting with exertion, he stilled himself and listened. It was pitch black in his den, and silent. But the smells and sounds from outside were nearing fast. Who were these wolves and why were they after him?

He could smell Darkness wolves, mostly. But he caught two unmixed scents in between. One was sharp and strong to his nose, causing him to sneeze. Then his ears shot up with realization. *Cobra!*

Now that wolf could pay. If he found her, he didn't know what he'd do. Either way, he'd get revenge, no matter what. A wicked grin crossed his face and his ears listened for the sounds of Cobra's and the other wolves' voices.

They came. "Kaiju?!" called his sister. "Where did you go? Please, where are you? You can't track my brother alone! We'll come with you!" Whines escaped Cobra's throat.

"It'll be okay, Cobra," replied a kind, soft voice of a Prowler. *Prowler Night,* growled Terror. He stayed as still as he could so he could listen more.

"Kaiju, you have to come—ow!" howled Cobra. Terror heard her stumble. Night gasped and must have been holding her up. Terror grinned. *I forgot. Back at the Territory, Cobra's shoulder got fractured. I heard everything, didn't I?*

"Cobra, let's go back home," said Night grimly. "We've searched everywhere. And you need rest."

"No!" Cobra snapped at him. "Kaiju is my friend and we will look until we find her!"

Terror grinned more widely. Now was the time to show himself. He scrabbled and squirmed to get out of the covered den, although it was tight around him. The wolves outside made "Huh?" sounds and were of course curious.

When he emerged he shook the dirt off himself, panting with exertion. There was Prince Honor's Darkness Pack, with Night and Cobra staring with shock and horror. "Get him!" yelled a voice from the back. *Prince Honor,* Terror thought.

Cobra had one paw up and Night was keeping her from collapsing. Terror could see the vines wrapped carefully around Cobra's shoulder and front paw. Honor emerged from the back, rage flickering within his eyes.

"Don't make one move, Terror," he growled, lashing his tail. Something was different about the wolf with the bladed tail. He also had a string of the most beautiful leaves around his neck, and one vine bracelet around each of his paws. *He can't be,* Terror thought with shock.

"Yes, I am King Honor now," the Darkness wolf said, reading the assassin's face. "Don't move, or this kills you." He lifted his blade above his tail.

"I'm not afraid of some stupid heir like you," Terror snapped. "And I'm not afraid of the 'O Great Prowler' and my insolent sister, either!"

He snapped his jaws in Cobra's direction, eyes flashing.

Cobra whined. "Why are you so angry at me, brother?" she barked.

"You know why. You killed Father!" Terror roared in her face. "And you will pay!"

Honor's face twisted with rage. "Chain him," he ordered the Darkness wolves. Before Terror could lunge toward his sister, chains caught his neck and backside. He rasped in agony and wriggled as the chains tightened. Honor's expression was fierce and unforgiving. "Take him. Don't let him lay a single claw or fang on any wolf, especially Night and Cobra."

"Yes, King Honor," responded another Darkness wolf who looked to be *his* sister. The chains tightened more and Terror thought he'd choke to death.

"Let me go!" he gurgled in the wolves' grip as he was led one direction.

"And let you kill more wolves?" Honor growled. "No." He turned and his tail flicked from side to side as he stalked off. Terror wanted to just maul the King Wolf.

"What are you going to do about *my* destiny?" croaked Terror. "That's right. You can't do anything!"

"Shut him up. I don't want to hear him," barked Honor. His sister wolf nodded and pulled the chain. Terror could barely breathe so he just had to move along. What would happen now that he was captive?

H E WAS slung over the stone on which King Honor sat. He wriggled and thrashed, snarling his head off. Wolves positioned themselves around the stone of the beautiful, vast Territory of Darkness Land they were in. Honor, Night, Cobra, and another Darkness wolf stood together in front of him, solid glares on their faces.

"Terror, how could you possibly go around killing off wolves? I don't care what your stupid father said about it—it's *not* your destiny. You could be like Cobra." Honor nodded toward Terror's sister.

"She *killed* Father!" Terror snarled back. "Why would I *ever* be like her?"

"And also," continued Honor as if Terror had said nothing, "you killed one of our wolves. Kaiju, you said?"

"Yes," hissed Terror. Cobra cried into Night's shoulder. Honor had a grim expression.

"Kaiju set out only to try to stop you," Honor said softly. "And all you did was kill her! Just killed her! Just like that! She was a great wolf, whether you think so or not."

"She was a dimwit was what she was!" said Terror. "Thought she could take me down with *manners* and *pleading.* No way!"

Honor strained his head in anger. "Kill him!" he roared. Wolves sprang.

"No! Don't!" Cobra leaped in front, growling at each of them and wincing at the obvious pain in her shoulder. Night looked at her in concern, and Honor blinked with shock.

"I thought you hated your brother," he said to her quite kindly. "We could kill him for you right here and now. No wolf will ever have to worry about him again. Come on, Cobra. One swish of this tail..." He lifted the blade.

"No," returned Cobra sharply. "For now let's keep him captive—" she shot Terror an angered look "—and see about killing later. I need to ask him some questions anyway."

"As you say," Honor sighed. "Back off, wolves," he added to the Darkness Pack, and they did. "Alpha Pebble, what do you think of this decision?"

"It's always up to what *you* think, my son. You *are* King Wolf," the other Darkness wolf between them replied. "And it's also up to Cobra. He's her brother."

Terror couldn't suppress a grin. "Thanks, kind sister," he said in a mocking grateful tone. Cobra spun around and thwacked him in the face with her tail. "Yow!" he barked in agony.

Cobra gave him a steely glare and walked away, wincing with each step. Night stepped over to help her up and every wolf turned to walk away. Honor spun around.

"Also, I need Midnight my mate, and Loyalty to guard Terror. Understand?" he said to a pitch-black wolf and his sister wolf. They nodded and murmured "Yes, King Honor."

Honor nodded and trotted off with the rest, probably for some hunting and resting from all the exertion they'd put forth forcing Terror here.

Well, Terror would find a way to escape before they decided to kill him.

Midnight, the pitch-black wolf, and Loyalty, the sister of King Honor, positioned themselves close enough to him to guard him but far enough to where he couldn't bite them. He was frustrated, hungry, and bored, lying here chained up. And there was no escape.

As of right now, he thought, grinning. *These wimp-wolves won't win this time. I'll run off again and make sure no wolf finds me! And I will follow my destiny and kill every wolf I was meant to kill.*

And if needed, every wolf will die.

CHAPTER 11

TERROR WAS thrown a sloppy red fish the next morning. Spitting and retching, he caught it between his bound paws and licked it. He wanted to barf over the edge of his rock. He was brave enough to take a bite. At first, the texture of the fish in his mouth was too much. It all went over the side of the stone.

Midnight flinched in disgust and Terror shook himself. Then he ate and ate because he was hungry. He realized just how good the fish was now that he was eating it. Licking his chops and chewing and swallowing, he finished his well-needed meal.

"Midnight, when will Cobra be here to interrogate?" whispered Loyalty to the pitch-black wolf, taking one glance at Terror. "We don't have all year to keep him captive and guard him. He's the deadliest wolf in the wild!"

Terror grinned. *Yup, that's right, you little nimrod wolf.*

"I don't know, Loyalty. It's her decision though. He *is* her brother. I'm just not sure why Cobra doesn't want him dead. He's an assassin and every wolf will have to worry if we don't finish him. Nope, I'm not sure why."

"Because she's such a merciful, kind, and life-saving wolf!" mocked Terror. The other two wolves ignored him.

"We'll just stay here until King Honor or Stormer Cobra tell us otherwise, or wolves shift around," Midnight went on quietly.

"Isn't he your mate, Midnight?"

"Yes, but it doesn't mean I can't follow his orders!" Midnight grinned.

"Just like you're his sister and you still follow him. Right?" she said.

"Yes. Of course! I would always follow my brother, who saved my life a few moons back!" Loyalty replied.

Terror wanted to cover his ears with his paws. He didn't like this conversation, especially since some of it was about him.

He heard crunching paws behind him. He snapped his head to the side. Cobra was being led by Night toward the stone. He growled as she passed and the two wolves whirled around.

"I'm here to ask questions to Terror," Cobra told Midnight and Loyalty.

"Well, speak of the spirits," Midnight said with a grin. "Go ahead. Do your thing." She and Loyalty backed up to give Night and Cobra space.

Terror gnashed his overgrown fangs together. This was stupidity, this was. "You're all stupid," he muttered. His eyes moved to his glaring sister.

"It's all right, Night," she said, keeping her steely gaze on her brother. "You can let me go now." She flinched with pain but managed to sit on her haunches.

"But," Night protested. "You're hurt, first. And second, it'll be ten times harder than it already is to move around since you're...you're..." He gazed at her stomach and Terror laughed.

"Ha, so you *are* mates now," he sneered. "Prowlers and Stormers aren't *meant* to be together. You're just stupid rule-breaking wolves, yes, you are! And I can't believe Cobra is going to have pups! Forbidden hybrid pups!"

"Shut up now!" roared Night, looking as if he could bite Terror's neck any moment now. Cobra put a paw in front of his face.

"Calm down, Night," she said. "He's trying to get under our fur. Ignore it." She sat up straighter. "So, Terror, what makes you think you can be an assassin, and go around killing wolves for no reason whatsoever?"

"First of all, there *is* a reason," Terror snapped. "Father told me which wolves I was meant to kill. So there I was! He also told me it was my destiny, and I knew it deep down! So there!" He wasn't sure why he was telling his sister all this, but if he wanted to escape, he'd have to follow along.

Cobra narrowed her eyes. "And what reason did you have to kill Kaiju?" she asked, eyes flashing with anger and gathering tears. Night nudged her sympathetically.

"Because she was a dimwit!" growled Terror. "She was *following* me and trying to stop me like I was some evil wolf making sinister plots."

"Well, you kind of are," called Loyalty from behind Night. The Prowler gave her a hard look and she quieted.

"I killed her because she drove me crazy!" Terror went on. "All you wolves are annoying, stupid, ridiculous, destiny-stopping fools!"

Night growled deep in his throat. Cobra brushed his shoulder and he looked back at her. Tears were rolling down her face and she just shook her head. He nodded. Cobra turned back with the tears glistening within her eyes and fur. "Kaiju was our good friend, a comrade," she said, looking seriously into his eyes. "And you had to kill her. You had to kill every wolf. Why is killing on your mind, Terror? Why?"

Without another word, she walked slowly off, with Night guiding her.

TERROR OPENED his eyes. Had he fallen asleep? He blinked and looked at his surroundings. He could've jumped, assassin or not, if he hadn't had chains binding him, when he saw wolves gathered all around like before.

Cobra and Night sat with Honor and Pebble again. Terror rolled his eyes. What was going on now? *Is it another interrogation or something stupid like that?*

"Stormer Terror," Honor said, raising a paw. "We have yet to decide what your fate will be. Cobra has not chosen what to do with you either. You are the worst wolf ever. You are disgraced, disappointing, vicious, ferocious, merciless, and horrible."

Terror gnashed his fangs. "Yes, that's right. What about it?"

"With one swipe of this tail, I could easily kill you whether any wolf wanted me to," Honor growled, lifting his tail once more. "But I'm not the cruel, ferocious Darkness wolf I once was, and I would never deliberately kill another wolf. Unlike *you...*"

Terror growled loudly. "Are these insults you're trying to throw at me? Trying to make me turn on you? Or possibly escape?"

"No," snarled Honor. His tail was really lashing now, and his eyes were glinting with rage. It seemed as if Terror was making *him* turn instead. The King Wolf was about to say something when suddenly, two wolves that looked to be Grays emerged from the undergrowth.

"King Honor!" they barked, half with joy and half with fear. Honor's eyes returned to normal.

"Yes, what is it?" he asked kindly. "You're Stalker Broken's messengers, right?"

"Yes, sir," the first one panted. "I am Gray Squirrel. I know, funny name, but the next one's is cooler. Gray Magnus. I think you might remember him."

Honor moved his eyes and nodded.

Night stepped up. "Magnus?" he said with disbelief. "Yes, what's wrong?"

"Well, Great Prowler," said Magnus with a gulp, "there's a terrible storm in our Territory and we believe it is spreading around the wild as we speak. It's awful. And we think the Great Prowler Legend is finally coming alive."

Night's ears went up. "It can't be," he huffed with his tongue lolling.

"Yes," Magnus said, "the darkness is falling."

CHAPTER 12

*O*H, SPIRITS *of wolves! Why are they discussing this nonsense in front of me? Are they trying to torture me?*

But the other wolves weren't paying Terror any mind. Every one of them gave fearful looks to one another and shoved their ears back then forward. Honor looked grim. And Night stood up tall.

"How severe is the storm?" asked Night with just a hint of tremor in his voice. His tail, Terror noticed, was ready to sink between the Prowler's legs.

"It's pretty severe, Your Greatness. The thunder is louder than any wolf's howl, and the rain soaks a pelt as soon as it reaches it," Magnus reported solemnly.

"There's lightning that sometimes strikes the ground!" Squirrel cried.

Night nodded to these things. "I'm so sorry," he said sympathetically to them. "Where's Broken?" he now asked.

"Stalker Broken is fine. He's been doing great as our Alpha wolf, Night, he really has," Squirrel confirmed. "He keeps us disciplined and strong even in danger and at the same time keeps us safe and comforts us."

Night smiled and nodded his head. "That sounds like Broken," he said softly. "It's been a long time." He looked back up into the fearing eyes of the Grays.

Wow. A Stalker leading Grays! I'll never hear something like that again at least for a hundred years!

Terror had an idea at this moment of solemn. He gave a sharp, signaling bark. Every wolf's head snapped around to glare at him. This was crazy, but if he told the other wolves of the good things he'd done, maybe they'd begin to trust him and let him go. Then he'd be able to escape and finally be free to follow his path of assassin duty. He was ready to try this plan.

"There are some things I've wanted to tell you," Terror told them in an intentional soft voice. Then he explained everything, all but the part about letting Kaiju go, which would definitely ruin his reputation as an assassin. Also the prisoners, but really, the messenger wolf had let them go, not him.

He told about Pitchfork, the Storm tribe, the fire, Stinger's Pack's fate, the messenger, and Prowler Fathomer with his Darkness wolves. He was panting with exertion and lolling his tongue when he finished, along with his tail thumping the stone.

"Now do you trust me?" he huffed.

The wolves were quiet. "This 'Fathomer' seems strange, although I've heard of Prowler Moon before, from *my* father," said Night aloud. "Moon is his father, you say?"

Terror nodded. Cobra growled. "It seems extremely *unlike* my brother to save wolves from a fire, now is it? I don't believe you on any of this!"

Terror felt shame, now that he'd thought more about what he'd done. Maybe this shame would show the other wolves he was telling the truth. "I'm sorry. But you wanted me to stop being an assassin, right? So why act like this *now*, when I've done something good? I feel ashamed of doing it now because of you." He hoped this would work.

Cobra was silent. Her lips twitched as if they were debating on curling back to reveal her fangs. Her tail slowly flicked from left to right. A deep growl sounded from her throat.

"We're still not letting you go, brother," she said at last, turning her head away. The other wolves did the same, and refocused their attention on the two Grays.

"I need to see Stalker Broken," Night told them. "Could you take me to him?"

Gray Squirrel gulped. "Your Greatness, our pelts were soaked when we set out to find you. The spirits of wolves were angry with us, so the storm got stronger. It was extremely difficult to get here, and we don't want you to face that danger. Alpha Broken *does* have a message for you though."

"Yes? What is it?" Night lifted his head high.

Terror growled to himself, "Stupid dimwit wolves." Of course they wouldn't believe him. He was the kind of wolf that would tell lies. They would never forgive him even if he did stop his assassin duty. *Which I will never do!*

"He says to believe in *you*, Night." Magnus's eyes filled with happy tears. "He says to believe *you* are the Great Prowler, not anyone else. He says *he* believes in you to help the wild and stop the darkness spreading."

The moon overhead shone like a silver wolf pelt in the sky. Terror knew soon the storm would most likely spread to this Territory and many others. But this Great Prowler nonsense was really starting to get under his fur.

Night's eyes filled with tears and he shook them away, smiling. He licked each wolf across the muzzle, which was a major sign of respect from a wolf. The Grays smiled back and bowed their heads. "Tell him thank you so much," Night told them.

TERROR WAS starting to get bored here. They brought him fish for a couple more days while he lay there and tried to enjoy—but instead, endure—what every Darkness wolf was doing. Cobra and Night stayed together wherever they went, not only because of Cobra's injury but of her unborn pups.

Midnight was Honor's mate, so she had to be having a pup or two as well. Her stomach was the slightest bit round and she was always whispering in Honor's ears distinctly and smiling.

Honor grinned at her now. "He could well be an heir, the third King's Heir," he said to her. "If it's a boy… So you say there's only one pup?"

"My instinct says so," Midnight returned with a grin. "I'm excited. Are you, King Honor?" She settled on the bed of moss and lay beside him.

"Please, just Honor," her mate replied kindly. "And yes, of course I am." Honor really was forever changed, Terror realized. The King Wolf yawned with happiness, making his ears and necklace flop about.

Night was sitting in the middle of the Territory, eyes closed and nose in the air. He was obviously sniffing out something. But what was it? Terror sniffed as well to try to find the same scent the Prowler smelled, but he couldn't find anything all that interesting.

"What's wrong, Night?" Honor asked from the bed of moss, standing up and padding over. His necklace flopped and he sat on his haunches next to Night. Honor sniffed.

"I sense something," the Prowler replied softly. "And I have a feeling it isn't good."

"What could it be?" Midnight asked. "I don't know of anything but the storm, and storms don't have smells, do they?"

"No," said Night, "but I'm sniffing in case there *is* a smell, besides the storm. But I sense something big coming this way, something that will wreck things."

Honor's face turned grim. "It's coming, isn't it, Night? Your time of stopping the darkness has come, Great Prowler, whether you're ready for it or not, and you know it. I'm not sure how you're supposed to stop it, but there has to be some way."

Night nodded solemnly. "Yes. I may not know it now, but maybe later I will. I *am* the Great Prowler, no matter what any wolf says about it. I've already helped so many wolves on my journey, and the time is near."

Terror ground his fangs together. *Not this nonsense talk again,* he thought desperately.

He was about to bark at the other wolves for quiet when suddenly, a crashing sound louder than a wolf's scream sounded, shaking the earth. Wolves howled and whined from where they stood, trying to keep their footing. Terror saw a cracking flash across the sky. *Lightning!*

The rain poured down. Terror sputtered and coughed in its torrential downpour. The other wolves shook their pelts and howled. This time, Terror said and thought nothing about it.

He wriggled in his chains, just as Night said loudly but grimly during the chaos, "The storm has arrived."

CHAPTER 13

"**U**M, CAN someone unchain me?!" Terror called over the thunder. "I'm stuck here enduring this stupid rain. I'd appreciate the courtesy!" His sarcasm couldn't stop the terrible storm that had hung over their Territory.

Night stopped abruptly. His ears were perked and his eyes looked faraway and…entranced. It was a little creepy to Terror, but he watched as Night stayed motionless in the rain, pupils growing smaller and smaller. Then suddenly, the Prowler was thrown to the ground.

"Night!" cried Honor. He bent over the Prowler and nosed him with concern. "What happened?"

Night found his voice again. "It was the wind, whispering to me! The Legend did say the wind would have a perilous tone!" The wind did, indeed. It blew like a howling wolf over the Territory, most likely in other Territories too by now.

The storm was spreading over the whole wild.

Terror wriggled just as Cobra limped over, and, glaring a warning at him, unlocked his chains. He jumped to his paws, shaking himself and winking at her. She had her jaw clenched as if she was trying not to snap at his ears.

At first, the assassin didn't know where to go. He stayed atop the stone, motionless and debating. He knew one thing: he was *not* helping any more wolves than he had to.

Midnight leaped quickly, covering her mate King Honor with ease. Honor scrambled from underneath her. "I'm supposed to protect *you!*" he shouted. "I'm the King Wolf!"

Loyalty whined and swerved from one side to another. She had one leg that looked as if it was permanently damaged, probably from a wound or tear. Terror took a second to wonder what it was. Then he dodged a crashing tree from behind him.

Night was lost, standing without movement. He didn't even cover his mate Cobra. His eyes grew the faraway look again and he stared out into the distance. "Voices," he rasped. "Screaming voices, just like before…"

Terror had no idea what the Prowler was talking about. Just then, he heard a cracking noise, maybe just more thunder again. The crashing noise grew louder and it sounded in his direction. He took a split second to whirl around. A tree was crashing down.

He stood there, stunned, and suddenly a bolt of fur rushed past him, bringing wind to his ears along with the natural air. Thunder and lightning sounded and flashed, making the whole Territory go white for a second. Terror shook his head as Night dashed under the falling tree and used his muscular wolf body to hold it up. "Go," he said breathlessly.

Terror decided to obey. Although he didn't need saving, he'd give it to Night this time. He knew he was lucky Night was even saving him; after all he'd done to the wild. *Am I the cause of the darkness?* The words rang through his ears.

His ancestor, Stormer Python, had somehow passed the sense of failure down to his next generations of descendants. The Great Prowler Legend could also be talking about darkness…a *wolf* of darkness.

But why a Stormer, if so…? Well, just like that Darkness wolf wrote the Great Prowler Legend. I guess he depended on the Prowlers, the kindest wolves in the wild, (except Scarr, Stinger, and the others) to fulfill it.

Wait. Why was he thinking about the wolf-dung he refused to believe? *But it's coming true, right here and now.*

What could *he* do? He didn't want to turn away from his real destiny, the one where he worked as an assassin for the Storm tribe and killed other wolves. But if there was something he could do for the Legend, something that would make many wolves like him, he would do it.

Terror stood there again, debating. The lightning flashed in the sky continuously and the thunder rang in every wolf's ears. For the first time ever, the Stormer felt lost.

There was a choice he had to make: destiny or respect? If he chose destiny, life would go the way he wanted it. But the darkness would change the world if he didn't do something. So if he chose respect, he could help in some way and get wolves to treat him correctly. But then his assassin destiny would desert him, and he would be left with nothing.

"Cobra!" cried Night when he saw his mate. He ran and covered her, the best he could, panting with fear and exertion. Every wolf's heart was obviously beating in this storm.

Honor had scrambled out of Midnight's cover and gotten over her instead, keeping his head and body low. His hackles were up, and he began barking orders. "Wolves, hide in your dens and don't come out!" Not even Terror, let alone the others, could hear Honor's voice very well over the screaming thunder.

Night's pupils grew small and the Prowler tried shaking it away, but Terror knew he was getting whatever screaming voices he'd gotten before. "Stop, stop it!" barked Night, obviously to his mind. His ears perked and he sniffed. Trees crashed around him.

"I smell other wolves. They're obviously fleeing from their Territories and following every scent possible, so that they'll be together with other tribes instead of alone. They're headed this way. They probably caught my scent."

"You bet they did, Night," Pebble told him, sniffing the air as well, nostrils flaring. "I think the whole wild is headed this way."

Loyalty limped beside Night. "Night," she whispered. "Has the time really come?" Night looked at her with shining eyes and nodded.

The clouds parted but it continued to storm over the Territory. Terror shook his soaked fur but he hadn't moved from that spot. Wolves ran past him with howls of fear, sliding on the shaking earth. Using his curved claws, Terror kept his footing on the ground.

Night's eyes lit up when he caught sight of a pack of wolves running into Darkness Land and Territory. "Broken!" he cried when a Stalker emerged from the middle, dripping and panting.

Broken looked up; his tail began to wag in the midst of the storm. "Night," he breathed, and the two nuzzled over each other and licked each other's muzzles. Night stepped back.

"It's good to see you, Broken, even in the middle of the Great Prowler Legend coming alive," said Night, grinning a little. "Broken, don't regret sending Squirrel and Magnus here." He nodded to the two messengers in the pack. "You were right to warn us about the storm like that. Now the time has finally come."

Broken's tongue lolled, and it looked as if he was smiling or grinning. But he wasn't. His tail came to an abrupt stop and his ears went back. "Yes, it has," he said solemnly. "Night, believe the Great Prowler is you. You have to, for the wild's sake. Please, Night…"

"I-I will," stammered Night, moving his eyes to the stormy night sky. The moon had appeared from behind a black cloud and it gleamed brilliantly with the darkness looming. Blackness rose in the distance.

Terror ground his fangs together after watching the reunion with Prowler Night and the Stalker. He didn't have much time left to make his decision: destiny or respect?

Broken snapped his head around; his hackles bristled and his ears shoved forward. "Who is this?" he growled, turning his nose in the air. He stiffened. "The assassin," he hissed.

"What?" Night looked from Terror to Broken. "You know him?"

"Of course, at least a little," Broken growled back. "He was just three years old when he attacked this Gray Pack's Territory. They told me once I became Alpha wolf. They said he was a runaway, and he was muttering something about 'Cobra.' I knew right away that he was the brother of your comrade Stormer Cobra. But I know he's nothing like her."

"Of course not," Terror snapped. "We are nothing alike. I thought we were at first, but now that I've experienced just how hideous of a Stormer she is, I thought differently." He glared at his sister, who was limping over beside Night.

Broken snarled, swishing his tail back and forth now. "You're just as terrible as the Grays said you were three years ago," he barked to Terror. "And that will end!" And he sprang for Terror's throat.

CHAPTER 14

TERROR REACTED quickly. He threw himself at Broken, catching the Stalker on his shoulders. The Stormer growled low in his throat as he reeled backward, sending Broken tumbling the other direction. "Stop!" cried Night.

Broken rasped with exertion, staggering to his strong paws, his tail beginning to lash with rage. His teeth were gnashed and his head was low in a most fierce bow. The rain soaked his fur but he showed no sign of knowing or caring.

"We don't have time for this nonsense!" Night was saying. "It's storming and the darkness is coming!" There was a sound of paws hitting the ground and Terror spotted more wolves coming this way, heading into the open glade of Darkness Land and Territory.

Broken snarled from behind him; Terror whirled around to face him. What was wrong with this wolf? "Why does every wolf hate me so much?" he roared over the storm.

"Why? *Why?!*" snarled Cobra. "You know perfectly well why, brother! It's because you were, and *are,* horrible, terrifying, and ferocious! It's because you have deliberately hurt wolves, whether it's killing *them* or killing their loved ones."

"Yeah, you killed my sister!" A Stalker padded out from one of the two other Packs that had shown up. "You killed Stalker Venom! And I'm Stalker Observer, her brother!" He gnashed his teeth together.

"And you killed Kaiju, my best scout wolf!" Pebble snarled from his right. "Only because she was stalking you and being the brave wolf I knew she was from the time she was a pup!"

"Pshaw! Brave?" Terror snorted. "She was using compassion to defeat me. How was that the right way to go? How—"

"Because not every wolf is like you, Terror!" growled Cobra. She sounded furious. "Every wolf is brave in their own way, even if they don't exactly do it the way wolves expect. Kaiju was like that, and you had to kill her!"

His sister's eyes had tears in them, and the unordinary Stormer looked away as if to hide them. Terror looked at each wolf in turn, not sure what to say or do. He was lost again.

"I didn't kill her," he said at last. "She ran away from me and ran into rogues."

"No! I know you killed her! I know you did!" Cobra was hysterical now. Terror rolled his eyes inwardly; this was not like a Stormer at all.

"I may have," he said, looking around at them all, "or may not have. That's all I'll tell you."

Night tipped his head to the side. A flash of lightning lit up his pensive face. "Are you meaning to say you didn't actually kill her?"

"That's *not* what I said!" Terror snapped at him, fangs gritting together.

Pebble snarled. "What are you going to do now, assassin? Whirl around and kill all of us?" She was half growling and half sneering at him, just to get under his fur.

Night looked up to the sky. "Like I said, we don't have time for this!" he repeated finally. "It's time to save the wild!"

Cobra nodded firmly, blinking away her tears and standing up. Her tail flicked and she moved her eyes upward. The black clouds were covering the entire sky, as far beyond as they could see. The whirling mass of black in the distance became heavy and foggy.

It seemed like the whole wild was here now. Better yet, yes. Pack after pack arrived, sitting on their haunches and howling desperately to the moon. The Storm tribe had not shown up just yet, but Terror knew they possibly would—half because the storm must be looming over Storm Land as well as others, and half because they wanted to see if the Great Prowler Legend was really true.

Terror sat on his haunches. He had no time left to make a decision. Why should he anyway? His destiny called to him, and so did the rest of these wolves, despite his assassin duty. He looked around into the desperate, tear-stained, and hopeful faces of the wolves gathered there. Darkness Land and Territory was nearly covered by gray, silver, tan, white, black, and russet pelts, all the wolves howling for the Great Prowler.

Broken sat down too, tongue lolling, gazing at the sky. He had obviously cooled down enough to stop attacking Terror. And besides, Broken didn't even *know* him.

Night's eyes grew small and faraway, dull and colorless. As if he were dying... But then he blinked a few times, and his eyes returned to normal. There had to be something going on, something that would prove the kind wolf was the Great Prowler.

Cobra, Pebble, Broken, Loyalty, Midnight, King Honor, and several other wolves fixed their gazes on the Prowler, the *Great* Prowler. Their faces said that they believed in him, and knew he was there for them.

But how exactly *would* he save them? Of course, the Great Prowler had a mind that could tell them everything, or possibilities, on what they needed to do. The screaming and howling voices in Night's head had to be a sign.

The storm poured and thundered and flashed around them, and the mass of swirling darkness lingered upon the trees. The wind whistled and howled within. *"The world will be as still as stone. The wind will have a perilous tone,"* Terror whispered to himself. All of that was correct.

"But far away, on the run, we will have the Chosen One," whispered the Stormer, looking to Night, the Chosen One, as it said.

A wolf rushed to Night's side. The Prowler looked at the other wolf and smiled, tears springing to his eyes. "Father," he said softly, but loud enough to be heard. The two Prowlers touched noses.

Night spoke up over the storm. "Now, every wolf—we need to howl, to let the spirits of wolves know how much we need them, and that the wild will soon be saved!" He lifted his muzzle. An in-between-high-and-low pitched sound escaped it, up to the stormy sky.

Pebble, Loyalty, Honor, Midnight, and the other Darkness wolves raised their muzzles as well, and this time their low-pitched howls cut the air with Night and the other Prowlers'. Even Prowler Fathomer and Prowler Moon joined in.

The Grays, including Broken, unleashed their high-pitched howls to the air. The howls mingled and created a most beautiful sound. The Stalkers were next, and the night was nearly full of howls of desperation, sadness, and hope, all at once.

The Stormers came running in, drifting and panting. Pinscher shoved her ears up when she saw Terror, and tilted her head. Terror shook his. Then the Storm tribe noticed the howling, but they didn't join in. Instead, they just watched.

And this time, Terror didn't mind it.

He raised his muzzle high, and watched Cobra immediately do the same. They met eyes, and Cobra's grew slightly wide as she began to howl. The most beautiful sound of all time emerged from her throat, and Terror felt his own beautiful howl come out too.

He had never known Stormers, of all tribes, were capable of this sound. He had heard it once before, at Stormer Territory, but had never, ever paid attention to it or took it all in as he did now.

The other Stormers were shocked out of their fur. Pinscher hesitated, but then followed through with Terror and Cobra, joining with the hundreds of other howls around them. A few others copied her, and soon the whole Storm tribe, mostly reluctantly, howled with the other tribes.

The howl went on for a long time. But then it all faded away into the thundering night. All was quiet except for the rumble of thunder and patter of raindrops on the ground and on wolf pelts. Terror caught his breath, partly shocked at what he had done.

Cobra met his eyes again. She nodded, but did not smile. Terror felt his tail twitch but thought better of it. He looked to the sky, but it had not changed at all.

He didn't talk. He didn't think. He just watched and waited.

Night's eyes were closed calmly, and his tail was still as a statue. He opened his eyes, and they grew faraway looks, just as Terror had expected. Night's *father's* eyes grew wide. The pupils grew smaller. And Night began to howl, running and beginning to climb up a tall tree.

"Oh, wild, why don't you listen?" he howled. *"Why don't you heed me?"*

Cobra stared in shock at her mate. Every wolf's eyes were on Night, whose eyes were closed again and muzzle was tilted.

"Why don't you have mercy on these wolves? Wolves have done what they can to save their fur and each other, but it does nothing in the midst of this darkness! But now I the Great Prowler beg you spirits of wolves to fulfill this Legend! Wolves are heartbroken, and they need you!"

Terror cast a look at Cobra, whose happy tears were streaming down her face. Her ears were up and her tail was thumping the stone where Pebble lay, aghast. Cobra was sure lucky to have Night as a mate.

"So please, spirits of wolves, cast away the clouds. Drive away the blackness and sadness. Make the skies bright and blue and the grasses green and lush. Create new life and plants, and nourish pups as they are born and grow up. Spirits of wolves, no wolf is perfect. Some don't deserve this.

"And I of all wolves know that. I started out as an ordinary lone survivor, roaming the Forbidden Forest and feeling like I had no purpose. When I heard about the Legend, it changed everything. Together with my friends, I finally feel I'm ready.

"Spirits of wolves: end the Great Prowler Legend!"

All at once, the clouds faded to white, and then away. The moon gleamed more brightly than ever. The mass hissed and cried out before disappearing completely. The wolves' faces changed to look entirely differently. The rain gradually began to stop. And Night, the Great Prowler that had saved the wild, leaped down from the top of the tree.

Cobra ran to him and the two nuzzled noses, Night's eyes returning to the way they had been before the storm. Happy tears were in the Prowler's eyes. Pebble nodded approvingly, and the wolves rejoiced with happy howls.

Terror couldn't make a choice now. The wild was saved, which was a good thing. And the Great Prowler Legend had finally come true.

"You're not as terrible as I thought you were," growled Broken from beside him. "But I will never trust you, ever."

"Yeah, well, I'm leaving," Terror snapped back, not daring to look in Cobra's eyes. He could just imagine the angered, upset, hopeless look she was wearing right now. But destiny called him, and no wolf could stop it.

As wolves left, rejoicing, haze was kicked up into the air, just near the trees.

Terror turned, making eye contact with no wolves.

And he disappeared into the dust.

EPILOGUE

A FEW WEEKS later, Pebble was curled up with her son, King Honor, and her daughter-in-law, Midnight. Darkness Land, ironically, was full of light. Prowler Night and Stormer Cobra, mates, were laying side by side, beaming at their month-old pups.

"No one is going to care about hybrids, not now that most of the tribes are getting along," Honor was saying to Cobra, eyes gleaming as he admired the four Prowler-Stormer mixes.

"And because the Great Prowler Legend was fulfilled," Pebble added, wagging her tail. *If only we could see the baffled looks on the Stormers' faces,* she thought.

Cobra sighed. Night looked at her as if in expectance. "But Terror escaped again," she said quietly. "The wild will be tense all over again with him around. Who knows what he'll do next? He could be terrorizing wolves as we speak."

"Ha, terrorizing. Get it?" Night's face told Pebble that he was trying to cheer his mate up. The four pups staggered about around them. They didn't have anything to worry about.

"What's terrorizing?" yelped the one female out of the four, who Night and Cobra had named Hybrid. She climbed over Cobra's shoulders in her excitement.

"Nothing you need to worry about, little one," Night spoke gently into the pup's ear.

"But I want to know!"

A male, named Comet, did a play bow and tumbled head over heels. "They said nothing to worry about, you idiot!" he yipped to Hybrid.

"Hey, hey, no more," Night scolded gently, nosing the little male pup. "Your sister is not an idiot. She's just curious."

Cobra smiled but sighed again. "But *I* should be worrying about it," she whispered. "Terror is my brother. I need to know where he is and what he's doing, and if he's still carrying on as an assassin."

"Cobra, you know he is," Honor pointed out. "He's not the kind of wolf that would give up on his destiny. Especially not one your father forced on him."

Cobra growled. "Yes. I know."

There was silence. "I'm sorry about Kaiju," said Night sympathetically. "I know you two were starting to get close, very close. And then your horrible brother had to take that away, and kill her."

"And what did he mean by 'may or may not have'?" snorted Pebble, hackles and tail bristling. "He's also not the kind of wolf that would tell the truth either."

Cobra stood up, wincing slightly on her healing shoulder. It had been fractured by her father, but it was nearly recovered. However, that didn't mean it didn't hurt.

Hybrid began wrestling with her brothers, yipping and rolling and barking. Pebble smiled and Cobra announced, "We have to make sure these pups are protected, and yours too, Midnight."

Midnight nodded from next to Honor. "Of course we will. We'll make sure Terror doesn't lay a single claw or fang on them. Although I'm not sure why he would! He goes after enemies and wolves that stand in his way. But who knows, maybe he could go after pups too!"

Cobra narrowed her eyes. "We won't let him."

Comet tried copying her. "We won't let him!" he yipped. Cobra laughed and licked the top of his head affectionately.

Pistol, whom they had named after a good friend of Night's who had passed away, bounded over and licked his father's face quickly and lovingly. Night laughed and licked him back. Pistol was the psycho pup of the four.

Hybrid did not get off Cobra's back. "Don't let the things terrorize, or take the pups!" she yelped, although she knew nothing about this conversation.

Every wolf laughed. But Pebble knew, deep down, that this was not the last of Terror.

But the Legend is gone. Things will be just fine.

ABOUT THE AUTHOR

EMBERLYNN ANDERSON has always had a love for reading and began writing stories at the age of eight. She created the Wolf Warriors series at age eleven; some of them were completed during long hospital stays, which is common for Emberlynn due to having Cystic Fibrosis. Wolf Warriors was inspired by her love for fantasy books about animals. She is a homeschooler who lives in Bethpage, Tennessee with her parents, four younger siblings, and beloved dog Lola.

CPSIA information can be obtained
at www.ICGtesting.com
Printed in the USA
LVHW110245211119
638043LV00001B/2/P

9 780578 612263